PRAISE FOR
SHAHRIAR MANDANIPOUR

"Shahriar Mandanipour is one of the leading novelists of our time. . . . Mandanipour is one of Iran's most important living fiction writers, with a long track record and a formidable reputation in his own country. Since 2006 Mandanipour has been living in the USA . . . where he moved to escape the censorship that was hampering publication of his work inside Iran. . . . One of Iran's greatest novelists is living and writing in the west, and readers of English are able at last to commune with his novelistic intelligence."

DAVID MATTIN, *THE GUARDIAN*

"Mandanipour's writing is exuberant, bonhomous, clever, profuse with puns and literary-political references; the reader unversed in contemporary Iranian fiction might easily think of Kundera . . . or of the Rushdie of *Midnight's Children*. . . . Mandanipour is a charming and often witty guide."

JAMES WOOD, *THE NEW YORKER*

"[Mandanipour's] works of fiction, densely metaphorical and replete with symbolisms drawn from the Persian literary tradition, reflect the extraordinary times he and his country have witnessed without being overtly political or tediously ideological. . . . As a writer in exile he has a difficult journey ahead, not least of which is to decide on his intended audience. He has, I think, the potential to create a genre of Persian literature that could breach the gap in literary sensibilities that separates readers from vastly different traditions."

MARIA BAGHRAMIAN, *THE IRISH TIMES*

"While his fiction remained unpublished in Iran for much of the 1990s on account of censorship, he is one of that country's most celebrated and accomplished contemporary novelists. . . . Mandanipour expresses the complexity of his culture—not just of the society of the Islamic Republic, but of the underlying Persian traditions that continue to influence it."

CLAIRE MESSUD,
THE NEW YORK REVIEW OF BOOKS

"Both an essayist and a novelist, Shahriar Mandanipour has been dubbed 'one of the leading novelists of our time' by *The Guardian*. . . . Mandanipour's writing style is widely loved by readers and critics alike because of his experiments with both language and context, and the way he beautifully weaves metaphoric images and symbols."

ANDREW KINGSFORD-SMITH,
THE CULTURE TRIP, "10 MUST-READ IRANIAN AUTHORS"

MOON BROW

ALSO BY

SHAHRIAR MANDANIPOUR

BOOKS PUBLISHED IN THE UNITED STATES

Censoring an Iranian Love Story

BOOKS PUBLISHED IN IRAN

The Shadows of the Cave

The Eighth Day of the Earth

Midday Moon

Mummy and Honey

The Courage of Love

Violet Orient

The Secret

Ultramarine Blue

The Book of Shahrzad's Ghosts

One Thousand and One Years

MOON BROW

SHAHRIAR
MANDANIPOUR
TRANSLATED BY SARA KHALILI

RESTLESS BOOKS
BROOKLYN, NEW YORK

First Restless Books paperback edition April 2018
Paperback ISBN: 9781632061287
Library of Congress Control Number: 2016940786

Cover design by Nahid Kazemi
Set in Garibaldi by Tetragon, London
Printed in Canada

1 3 5 7 9 10 8 6 4 2

Restless Books, Inc.
232 3rd Street, Suite A111
Brooklyn, NY11215

www.restlessbooks.com
publisher@restlessbooks.com

For Baran, Danial,

and Sara,

who know that at times one plus one does not equal two . . .

MOONBROW

PROLOGUE

The scribe on his right shoulder writes:

He thinks . . .

«I will have no relief or escape until I find my arm and discover its secret. . . . My arm, alone for so long. My left arm, how decayed and orphaned, how long food for the rain, wind, and sun, how long has it howled and called out to me and I have not heard it until now—I must go, I must cross the field of amputated legs and the desert of burned tanks with guns that resemble penises after ejaculation, to reach the mountaintop where somewhere, I don't remember where, I was hurled to the ground and there my blood spilled on the earth. I know I must go to where God the all forgiving kissed my arm, blessed my arm, and my arm fell and my hand rotted, and worms were born from the feathers of angels' wings that had fallen to earth and they fed on my flesh and turned the color of new feathers . . . and perhaps, if there still is a perhaps in the world, the remains of my arm have remained as white, mutilated bones under the sun's blade or under the dirt where even the heavenly worms have abandoned them . . . I must deceive my fear and return to the mountain, to search from peak to peak, to gather the courage to touch the stonehearted rocks and say, O mountain rocks, you did not shelter my childhood sensation of touch with which I felt the carpet, the parrot's feathers, and my mother's face. Where is the sting of the principal's whip on the palm of my hand? Where is the snakeskin chill of the prayer beads? Where is the callus from thousands of pages of homework and the wetness from masturbation? Where is the cold touch of American grenades in my hand? O wind of winds of the mountain, where in time did you take the scent of the virgin girl's unripe breasts and the sweat of her unskilled waist that lingered on my hand? I will kiss the locoweed thorns and say, O sacred thorns, pubes of the heavenly realm, why did you not scare away the corpse-scavenging dogs so that they would not lick away the lines of destiny from the palm of my hand and leave me, now, at the end of the end, to beg, Lay the corpse of my hand in my hand. I must see it and learn its secret. So that afterward, I may sit in peace on that same mountaintop and after all these years of yearning and wandering, I can at last take a quiet breath from my share of breaths and, with my eyes dry or salty wet, I can gaze out at a foggy or sunny valley out there in the world and shout, Ahoy! I spit at all of you who have mired the world in filth.»

And the scribe on his left shoulder writes:
He thinks . . .

«O bastard angels! Write of the shrewdness that is I when I am me. I the scorpion with stingers sharpened for the testicles of Mitra's cow, I the mandrake's eternal gratification of coupling, my children the semen of adultery on sheets, I the itch along the spine of the monkey beneath the baobab tree, the birth cry of script in the moors of the Tigris and Euphrates, the jug of soured milk, I the worming Silk Road, I the belch of gunpowder in the paunch of mankind; in the alcove of your altar, I the bloated corpse of the soldier, the aborted fetus, I the cuckoo's egg in a moon crater, the chant of I am God, I the right to sob, I am God. . . .

O motherless attendant angels on my shoulders! Tell me, how far down my back have you written? Clandestine scribes! Have you written as far as the red, bulging strips of raw flesh, the scars of the Basiji's whip? Did the plowing whip not cross out your earlier words? Did the red marks of a woman's nails on my shoulders not make you hard? Did you write that I hollered, No! . . . Did you write that I saw children with their mouths foaming fall out of windows? Did you write that I saw sparrows drop from the trees and crows fall from the sky? That a dog burst in the alley? You angels who only have one hole and it is in your pen, your legs strapped around my neck, did you write that you, too, were accomplices in crime? You were with me when you saw everyone die—everyone who was running and had or had not let go of their children, everyone who was standing and looking back, everyone who had fucked or prayed the night before, everyone who was a child and was drinking, was a cat and was licking, was even a fly: everyone died. Did you write that all those who were hiding rotted in the cellars and that white smoke, like camphor and cotton, filled the seven holes of the dead?

Write that I shout, O you pieces of dung descended from the sky, You killed everything!»

The scribe on his right shoulder writes:

From the full-length window in Reyhaneh's room, he looks out at the rainy, leafless garden and it occurs to him . . .

«It is good that the second floor is always the second floor.»

He sees the fog wafting from the soil beneath the naked trees, a hesitant fog with a hint of violet.

The sound of rainwater in the gutters of the old building grows louder.

Reyhaneh asks, "How can it be that in your dreams you see nothing of the girl's face?"

"I don't know. Her face is hazy. Perhaps I see it, but it doesn't stay in my memory. Maybe she has covered her face with a chador . . . I don't know. Sometimes I remember her hair, like a shadow. I think it's very long. All the way down below her breasts. I may have seen her naked. Her hair covered her breasts."

"Hey! Watch it!"

"What?"

"You're talking to your innocent dewy-eyed sister!"

"Don't play games with me, not you. . . . What if there is a crescent moon on her forehead and it shines so bright that I can't see her face?"

"This is all a tall tale."

"My dreams are not tales. In many of them I see us putting rings on each other's fingers."

"So what!" Reyhaneh snickers. "That's nothing. I dream that a prince comes to our house to ask for my hand in marriage and we get engaged."

She stares at him warily and says, "Maybe you had a bitter or painful experience that you subconsciously wanted to forget."

"That is what the idiot doctor at the nuthouse said. But I want you to help me remember. Tell me! What happened back then that could somehow be related to these dreams?"

"How should I know? As far as I could tell, up until the day you went crazy and enlisted to go to war, you were always having fun with girls. I was wrong to say that you might have had a bad experience. In those days, you were too clueless to know the difference between a good experience and a bad one. And these are just dreams . . . nice dreams. I'm surprised they frighten you."

"I am often frightened, and then I become even more frightened because I don't know what it is that I'm frightened of."

Reyhaneh's old samovar is gently simmering. He sees the fragrance of the forty-four winter sweet bushes in the garden float toward the house like layers of dragonfly wings.

"All I know is that you have to be patient, to stay calm. And don't forget, God has not abandoned you. You went to war, fine. You faked your way into the nuthouse, fine. But we finally found you and brought you home. This means that God has not abandoned you."

He stares at the mole on Reyhaneh's face. Above the curve of her plump lips. To the left. Embarrassed, Reyhaneh looks down.

"But I have abandoned God. He is useless; he is not missing an arm. He has forgotten that he is God."

He gets up from the bentwood chair and again paces the length of the room.

"This God that you love, what joy did he bring to your miserable life? Turning you into an old spinster in this damn house."

Contrary to his expectation, Reyhaneh does not reveal the pain of his sting.

> «Rain of rains, drop by drop it glides down the windowpane. And in its streams, fragments of the garden's nakedness—almond trees, cherry trees, small, tightly packed winter sweet flowers. And two streams flowing diagonally join and become one. It means . . . one plus one is one. It is just that one glides faster. I should remember, from the window in Reyhaneh's second-floor bedroom, I can see that the top half of the old eucalyptus tree still has leaves. Its leaves, its old branches, its cuckoo's nest, grooved by streaks of rain. . . . »

He does not have the heart to look at his Alfa Romeo that has sat abandoned for years under the eucalyptus tree. It has rusted. Its tires are flat.

"How could it be that I never had a photo album? There is nothing in my room. You have left nothing of me in there."

"I had nothing to do with it. Maybe you knew you were not coming back for many years and you hid your photos somewhere before you left."

"Back then, was there a girl I was with?"

Reyhaneh snickers.

> «I don't like her when she laughs like this.»

"Tell me! I remember bits and pieces. Damn it! A lousy mortar shell explodes and plenty of people and memories that were really important fly away, as if they never existed. I lose my arm and it's as if I never had it. . . . "

"Hey! I am going to say this just so you don't take me for a fool. Half the time, I doubt you've really lost your memory. It's just a hoax."

"The minute I start trying to remember, the memories disappear. One way or another, I have to find this girl."

"She is a girl in a dream. You have to sleep to find her."

"Was there a girl who was special to me?"

"There were a few."

"Not just anyone, I mean someone I was with for a long time. Like some sort of love."

"No. You mucked up whatever love there was."

"How? What did I do?"

"Nothing! You just fell in love."

"All you do is tease me."

"No, I swear. You were having a blast. Handsome, with plenty of money in your pocket and an Alfa Romeo under your feet. Any girl you picked leaped into your arms."

"Did I tell you I was having a great time? Did you ever hear me say that?"

"I don't know. Even if you didn't say it, it was obvious. If you weren't having fun, you wouldn't have been so into it."

"Into what?"

"Playing the field, partying, hanging out, going to the seaside, to the beachfront villas of rich kids like yourself. You have no idea how much I wanted to go with you. You jerk! Do you know I have never even seen the sea? While I was a headscarf-shrouded prisoner in this house, you were all over the place. God knows how many girls you tossed away like used tissues."

> «I don't want her to talk to me like this—angry, spiteful, or sad. . . . The gurgling in the gutters sounds just like it did at the nuthouse, just as it does in a water pipe.»

"Something bothers you whenever I talk about the past. At least tell me, what the hell did I do that upsets you so much?"

"Nothing. You didn't do a damn thing."

"Don't be sarcastic. Granted, the waves from the explosions emptied my head and the nuthouse muddled it up even more, but I'm not an idiot. I was listening at your door. You were crying."

"What makes you so sure I was crying for myself? Perhaps I was crying for my brother."

Reyhaneh tries not to glance at the empty sleeve of the clumsily buttoned shirt. But Amir notices.

"There was a guy in the nuthouse who was missing his right arm. He said that after his arm was severed, he was forced to eat it out of hunger. For days, they were trapped under fire by the Germans."

"The Iraqis!"

"Whoever! He used to say that it tasted better than chicken wings. I've forgotten the guy's name. . . . Every morning, we would tie the ends of our sleeves together and walk around shoulder to shoulder. The other shell-shock victims walked around, too. Out in the yard or in the corridors. And whenever this guy and I came across one of the burly two-armed nurses, we would separate and our sleeves would catch him on the chest or neck. Then we would circle around and snare the loony-hunting nurse."

He chuckles. Reyhaneh does not.

"We were forced to pray, so we would do our ablutions together. He would wash my hand; I would wash his. He knew the rituals of praying. If the nurses untied our sleeves, we would tie them together again. This way, he would be saying the prayers for me, too. If I was daydreaming when he genuflected, my sleeve would get yanked and I would know I had to kneel and touch my forehead to the floor. . . ."

"So? What is your point?"

"I am trying to say, let me tie my sleeve to yours, too."

Sounds echo in the empty chambers of his mind.

> « . . . and I should remember that it is still now. Out there, that is still our garden. It has fallen under a spell and at night, in the lingering fog, seven cuckoo bird couples turn into stone and at dawn they fly away. Abu-Yahya is hiding behind the Khezr cherry tree. He is compassionately observing my incompetence in taking on the sane butchers. He scoffs at how I struggle now that I am alone and crippled, and he is afraid when I am afraid of people because they forget nothing.»

"Tell me! Tell me, Reyha. Even if you think I am lying, even if I am one-armed, or eight-armed, tell me again everything you know. There is not even dung in the empty holes in my head, they are just empty. I don't care if you treat me like a crippled beggar, you will be doing a good deed for your God. Tell me, even if you have to tell me ten times. Why don't you clever people understand that right now is the right time, otherwise everything will be lost?"

He thinks the samovar is simmering faster. Fog is spreading in the room.

> «It is so nice that in the gurgle of the samovar there is no shriek of shrapnel coming to sever your arm.»

Ghosts of his nightly soliloquies on the peaks of the distant mountains float past a corner of his mind.

> « . . . My sweetheart! It is good that you know nothing about the loneliness of an enlisted officer on scout duty up in the mountains. The other officers and the regular soldiers don't understand my language and I don't understand their pain. The summits are always the end of the line for the wails of wounded soldiers . . . and it can always suddenly happen, and it is always suddenly afterward. Whether you are asleep or awake, fountains of blood descend upon

the earth and like acid eat away the soil. Whether it is snowing or not, the whipping wind brings snow from the mountain's ice pits up to the peaks, and there, the days and nights pass more slowly than they do in the valley. On the mountaintop, the fog is not a friend of the scout, and night is your enemy's friend, and always, very suddenly, the sheep-like soldiers go at each other with scorpion-like Russian Kalashnikovs and horn-like German G3s. Those who, trusting my eyes, are fast asleep might not even have the chance to admonish me. The scout's eyes grow heavy, eyelids melt in the darkness of the night, and enemy soldiers prowling in the shadows swallow their coughs like mucus. Eyes deceivingly say, I will close my eyelids for only a few seconds; if the enemy moves, the ears will hear—water sloshing in a canteen, the belch of a Kalashnikov's breechblock, feet tapping against a stone or treading on shell casings scattered on the ground . . . but ears know that the sound of blood always comes too late, or does not come at all. And always, it is the instant after calamity.»

In the fog, the naked winter-stricken trees look gaunt. To him, they look like the princes who have turned to stone before the beast's rock fortress. He thinks, You lying angels, have you seen the winter sweet bushes along the garden path? Their leaves grow sparse, but they flower more. Don't you think there is something amiss in this world?

And the perfume of winter sweet flowers that has crept into the room like gas from a chemical bomb caresses his skin, patiently, butterfly-like.

Reyhaneh is picking at a blemish on her pale knee.

"Doesn't she talk to you? Think about it. Perhaps she talks to you."

"Other than you, no one really talks to me. Everyone just barks orders at me so that I don't start asking them questions."

"Now don't start. . . . You should figure out why you are so obsessed with this dream. You're tormenting yourself. I hear you pacing up and down your room in the middle of the night. But the story of this girl is just a dream."

"It is not just a dream. Somehow the damn thing comes to me even when I'm awake. I'll be sitting or standing somewhere, and I'll hear her walking behind me. Sometimes I think as she walks by she whispers, 'It's safe! Come!' And as soon as I look behind me or turn to follow her, I realize there is no one there, not her and not anyone else."

And he shouts, "Of all people, why can't you understand? Would it not torment you if you were in my place and constantly heard and felt these things?"

He wipes the foam from the corners of his mouth.

The scribe on his left shoulder writes:

"If you yell at me one more time," Reyhaneh snaps, "I will leave you to rot in your room."

"Well, when the dreams come and seem like the same as the dreams I have forgotten, they can't all be bogus."

"I don't know. All I know is that you have really messed up your mind. Something is bound to happen to a sane man who fakes it for five years in a nuthouse."

"I didn't suffer like this in the nuthouse. I didn't know much, but I knew I was at peace. You dragged me out of there. All these dreams and fantasies started when you brought me to this house."

And he relents.

"Don't get angry, Reyha. I can't help it. I am begging you."

> *«Rains are waiting beyond the window, rains that are always sad. Was there ever a time when rains were happy? When rains fall in bad places, do they ever complain that they have fallen in a bad place? . . . And now Reyhaneh's eyes are no longer beautiful and kind. They look at me with suspicion and doubt. They glare at me as if I am deliberately lying so that I can catch them at their lies, or perhaps as if I am scheming against her.*

> *But I know she is hiding something from me. I am sure there are things she is not telling me so that she can catch me in a lie.»*

"At sunset the fog grows thicker among the trees. There are so many secrets and ciphers in it. Do you see? There is secret crying in it. Abu-Yahya is crying for the one whose life he could not take. Can you see him?"

Reyhaneh glances out at the garden and then turns and stares at him with an air of authority, or concern, or suspicion.

"Why do you all look at me like that? What have I done? Why are you all afraid of me?"

> *«Her soft, white hands with the sweet, childlike dimples on her knuckles take the porcelain teapot with delicate red flowers painted on it from the top of the samovar and, as if performing a sacred ritual, she pours a cup of tea for me, so that I will heal. Why? I am healing every day. The only time I am not healing is when that motherfucking storm kicks up in my head and the sparks of an image crackle in its empty holes. The whispering voices are worse. If I don't block them out, they get louder. Some of them yell as if I were born to be yelled at.»*

"If I don't find the secret to these dreams, you'll have to put me in chains like a dangerous madman. In one of them, I see her surrounded by a thousand jewelry stores. We are in Tehran's bazaar, in the goldsmiths' arcade. We are not lost. We are strolling. The glitter of gold is everywhere. We walk past a thousand jewelry stores and find the one we were meant to find. It is a small store tucked among a thousand others . . . a pair of gold rings in the shop window are waiting for us . . . inside, there is a scrawny old man with skin as white as plaster. It seems he knew . . . he knew something. . . . "

He grows quiet.

"What did he know?"

"I can't remember."

"Well . . . then what?"

"Shhh!"

He turns and stares out at the far end of the garden. Agitated, despondent, or even desperate, he raises the cuff of his empty sleeve and clenches it between his teeth. It tastes of fog and lavender and wilted winter sweet flowers.

> *« . . . and my dear heart, let me tell you about mortar-shell shrapnel. With their creases and crinkles they sometimes look like the serrated edges of nettle leaves. Before they come for your plump, succulent flesh, the shell itself drones in. You drop to the ground because the moment it hits, everything that blossoms on the earth will blossom in the sky. Then, lying on the ground, you cover your head with your arms. If it explodes nearby, you will be minced meat or the wave will get you and you will be shell-shocked. If it lands farther away, the miracle shrapnel comes. Sliced metal, all jagged edges, coming to slash you. If you are lucky, it will pierce the ground next to you or pass over your head and hit a rock with a clang—just like the sound of a goat bell. No scientist can predict the number or shape of its creases. You should not touch it; it is fresh and hot. It just lies next to you for your divine pleasure. It is terrifying, because it makes you realize how short the distance is between life and martyrs' heaven. I have stared at some of them. Their ridges, folds, and splinters, leaning against each other at sheer angles. Sharper than any knife. Hungering for lean, succulent flesh. I have touched some of them. They bear unspeakable secrets. They have the slippery, finger-escaping mischief of a fish. Some have beautiful, symmetrical, elongated outer lips. They recline like Sleeping Beauty over shy inner lips that once opened; their tiny bubbles are both death and the elixir of life. But some of them, whether their outer lips are boastfully puffed up or not, their inner lips are rebellious. The hell with beauty and symmetry, they hunger for flesh; that is why, wrinkled and rippled, they curiously peek out from between the outer lips. They are thirstier when they are wet. Now and then, an inner fold is larger than its mate and pops out more defiantly. At times*

> *so much so that it seems it wants to cover its outer partner. You cannot predict their pleats and tucks, pink or cerulean or walnut-wood puce, just like the edges of petunia petals. Just like the barbed shards of shrapnel strewn on the ground, you cannot hear their scream. Fear these lips, they will cut you in half.»*

His frail body drained of energy, he cannot do or say anything more. He goes to his room next door and notices that unlike the early evening-hued window in Reyhaneh's room, his window is tinged with night. He lies down on the floor next to his bed. He sleeps, so that he can again dream.

And the scribe on his right shoulder writes:

He dreams . . .

They are on a mountain, behind boulders that hide them from the eyes of those below. He wonders whether he should be confident of their safety or not. They have snuck up here to hide from the Revolutionary Guards and their informers. There is a crescent moon in the sky. It has not climbed too high. It looks like smiling lips, or to him, a clown's grin. His Moon Brow is sitting with her back to the moon; he cannot see her face. He thinks it is time to show his beloved the secret of his back. He unbuttons his shirt, pulls it up around his neck, and leans forward.

"Touch it."

A reluctant hand feels between his shoulder blades.

He likes the coolness of her fingers. There is a rustle behind the thorn bushes. It sounds like the swish of army pants' legs rubbing against each other.

"Go lower."

"Why?"

"Don't be scared."

The cool hand glides lower until it reaches the first strip of flesh projecting from flesh. The hand recoils.

"Don't be afraid. It won't bite!"

The hand returns to his shoulder and again moves down until it reaches the first swelling, and it slides over it to the left. With curiosity, perhaps with repulsion, it moves back to the right and all the way to the end of the scar.

"Pretend they are the writings on my birthday cake."

There is a whiff of chamomile. The hand glides further down, to the next strip of swollen flesh.

"They are like the lines on the pages of a school notebook. Do you want me to write on them for you?"

He lies down on the slope.

"Write on my chest."

The moonlit hand starts writing on his chest with a felt-tip pen.

"Write that you love me. No, write that we are in love."

In his eyes there is wonder as weighty as the cold Milky Way stretching beyond the mountain peak. He feels the coldness of the ink and delights in the feminine touch of the side of the hand resting on his chest.

"I am writing it in cuneiform."

And the writing stops.

When Moon Brow's left hand puts the cap back on the pen, the ring on her finger shines in the moonlight. He cannot tell whether the gleam is gold or silver.

"Lie down next to me. Tonight the Milky Way is so close. For you and me. It is like a quilt."

And it starts. . . . He hears laughter coming from inside the ground under his head. It is a sarcastic peal. It grows louder. It turns into a roaring howl. He wants to lift his head off the ground, but his head has turned to stone. The buried laughter grows louder. So loud that it sends specks of dirt and tiny pebbles flying into the air. They get into his ears. Now his back and midriff have turned to stone, too. He holds out his left hand for Moon Brow to help him up. And suddenly the pleasure of the writing on his chest grows warm. It feels as if every one of those nail-like shapes is giving his chest the same gratification as that first penetration into a woman's four-folds. . . . His first groan has barely ended when the burning starts. The nails have grown hot. They become hotter yet. He cannot lift his head, but peering down, he can see their fiery glow on his chest. He hollers. The vertical nails are burning his skin and piercing his chest. He smells burning lung tissue.

On his left shoulder:

He pretends that like on previous days, he is out for a stroll in the sprawling garden. He wanders around the treed section to the right. Now he drifts over to the gravel lane in the center, between two streams of winter sweet perfume. After casting a half-glance toward the house, he meanders over to the left. And again, he goes back to the right. He thinks he has sufficiently fooled his mother's and Reyhaneh's prying eyes that have been watching him from the windows. He repeats to himself the prophetic message that it is time to leave the garden. He is certain that if he shuts off his brain, which seems to be swathed in a cocoon, has faith in the prophet of his senses, makes his way to the heart of Tehran, and searches the city street by street and alley by alley, he will finally come to a house, a door, or a window that his senses will tell him is the one. Somehow, he feels today is his lucky day. That a door and a window will lovingly, without deceptions, taunts, and reprimands, help him remember everything. He will ring the doorbell and the girl of his dreams will open the door to him.

And she will say, Why are you so late? Come in, you poor lieutenant!

On his right:

And to him, the distant din and commotion of Tehran that travels as far as the garden is like the specter of an island on the horizon of the sea. He urinates at the foot of a tree, imagining that it will purge him of his fear of a city that years ago became a stranger to him. He remembers some street names, but he doubts the accuracy of the map in his memory that connects them to each other.

> «If I end up on a decent street, it will show me the way, and I will go until I reach her house. . . . I should not trust or pin my hopes on Reyhaneh and the others. The turmoil inside me will not die down until I find the secret to that ring.»

It is the first time he has come this close to the garden gates. One of the guards walks out of the guardroom. Dressed in the green Revolutionary Guard uniform and wearing a smile buried under a bushy beard, he says hello. And receives no reply.

"I have not had the honor of meeting Agha Haji's son."

"Have you had it now?"

"Of course, Sir. You living martyrs are the light and soul of Imam Khomeini and the revolution. I smell the perfume of the battlefield on you."

"Sir! The smell of perfume is from you; I just smell of unwashed ass. I cannot perform Islamic cleansing with just one hand. I need two, to pour water with one hand and wash myself with the other."

"Forget it, Amir Khan. The likes of you are the blessings of Islam. Those of us who have not had the good fortune to become a martyr have lost out."

"Were you at the front?"

"I was not fortunate enough. I had security and intelligence duties away from the battle lines."

"How come? It was easy. All you had to do was be a dimwit like me."

"Have faith in God. He is the only healer. I will pray for your recovery. . . . Did you enjoy your walk in the garden?"

"It was like a walk in heaven. Now I want to go for a little stroll out on the street."

The guard smiles apologetically and moves closer to him.

"Any shopping you have, just let me know. I would be honored."

"Thanks, I can do it myself."

He takes a step toward the gates. The bulky guard blocks his way.

"The air in the city is too polluted these days. It's unhealthy. They said on the radio that people with heart problems should avoid going outside. Isn't it a shame not to enjoy the fresh air in the garden?"

"The warning may have been for you. Perhaps if you go out your skin will turn even darker."

Then, he barks, "And my heart is as strong as a lion's. There is nothing wrong with me. I am smarter than you. Get it?"

The guard's polite and gentle demeanor changes.

"Agha Haji has given strict orders that you are not to go out. Get it? Go back to your room!"

He thinks if the guard does not step aside, he will kick him between the legs, put him out of action, and bolt out, just like he used to do when he got into scuffles long ago. But then, a second guard walks out of the guardhouse. He is even burlier. This one's eyes are shrewder, his forehead is shorter, his lips are greasier, fleshier, and his beard is scraggly and sparse.

The second guard puts his hand on the Colt strapped to his waist.

It was a lame plan. With just one arm, he would have been no match for even the first guard.

"You are right, brother. The air outside is more polluted than it is here. Go out instead of me and take a few deep breaths."

He heads toward a section of the garden wall that cannot be seen from the house. He leaps up and grabs onto the eave with his right hand. With the tips of his shoes, one foot after the other, he moves his legs up the wall, groping for a toehold in the grooves between the bricks. But his arm is not strong enough to hoist his frail body over the wall, even without the weight of his left arm. Pain churns between his ribs. The tips of his shoes leave scratch marks on the bricks.

On his left:
He falls.
"Fucking walls!"

> *«Who was the poet who seven hundred years ago wrote about a guy who was so horny he shoved it in a hole in the wall? Now I wish there was a hole in this wall for the tips of my shoes.»*

He takes off his shoes and tosses them over the wall. He is convinced that it will be easier to climb barefoot. On his fourth try, again he falls down. Out of breath, he gives up his monkey leaps and jumps, sits on the ground, and pounds his fist on his left shoulder and growls.

> *«You good-for-nothing! Couldn't you have turned just a little so that the shrapnel would take some other part of me, any other part, even my cock?»*

Black holes whirl around in his head . . . a voice echoes, "Lieutenant, Sir! Word to the wise, you should be more afraid of an unexploded shell than of a piece of shrapnel. God the almighty has made the tip so that it suddenly penetrates and plunges in."

The scribe on his left shoulder had written:

When the kitchen unit came under attack, the soldier lay flat on the ground and wrapped his arms around his head. A 60 mm shell landed right between his shoulder blades, but it did not explode. The wings at the base of the shell are sticking out of his shredded uniform and open flesh. Those who saw it happen tell the others that the wretched man neither howled nor shouted anyone's name. Lying on his stomach, he just moved his fingers as if drumming a tune on the ground. His corpse has been lying there for more than three hours. No one dares move him. The dirt has sucked up his blood and turned black. Pearly-green flies swarm around him and disperse in waves.

A soldier notorious for being a Hezbollahi and an informer says, "We can't just leave him there like that."

"Brother," Sergeant Major Neiji quips, "you go pull out the shell and I will take care of the rest. My father used to work in a mortuary."

The hot and hazy wind rolls a clump of tumbleweed past the corpse's hand. Amir, still sitting in the shade of the communications post, looks in through the window opening and asks, "No sign of the IFA?"

"No, Sir. It hasn't left yet. But there may be an ambulance nearby."

He doubts the IFA that was supposed to take him and a few others to the nearest town to go for a bath will ever make it. Perhaps because he is a lieutenant, they will let him catch a ride to town in the ambulance.

The Hezbollahi soldier says, "His name is Ali-Yaar. He used to turn the army's foul meat and rotten vegetables into a dinner so delicious that you would want to eat your fingers, too."

Amir laughs. "So every night he cooked the Last Supper for us and we had no clue."

He gets up and walks toward the corpse.

"Where do you think you're going?" Pourpirar shouts.

"Shut your trap or I will lose my nerve."

The soldiers all move back to a safe distance. The drone of the flies grows closer.

The Hezbollahi soldier shouts, "For the health of Lieutenant Yamini say praise to the Prophet Mohammad and his descendants."

No one does. Neiji wipes the sweat off his face with his kaffiyeh, which until this summer he had denounced and refused to wear. Amir kneels next to the dead soldier.

> *«No, I should not yank it out. I must touch it gently, caress it, tell it that I am not supposed to croak here. So let's be friends! Friends?»*

The sun has kept the narrow tail of the 60 mm shell hot. With three fingers, with butterfly strokes, Amir feels its curve all the way down to the soldier's flesh.

"I think you, too, have seen bodies floating on water, dead, having died as easily as you died."

And he starts to pull out the shell.

The scribe on his right shoulder writes:

And, as is his habit, he starts recalling a fairytale.

«Once upon a time, a prince put on his steel shoes, took his bow and arrow and his sword, and set out for Sangestaan Fortress. He walked and walked, for years he walked. When he reached the stone fortress, he saw tens of other princes who, just like him, had come for the love of Forty-Braids and with the hope of rescuing her. They had all turned to stone, standing here and there, still holding their bows and arrows. The witch had told him he could only shoot three arrows, and each time he missed his target, one section of his body would turn to stone. But if he hit his target, a door would appear in the tall fortress wall. Just then, a black cat crept out of a hole and, ignoring him, started darting between the rocks as if chasing a mouse. The prince aimed and shot his first arrow. It ricocheted off a rock and landed near the cat. The prince's legs turned to stone. He put the second arrow in his bow. The cat stood still, staring at the prince with its magical eyes. Its gaze spoke many words—counsels and cautions, jests and ridicules. . . . The prince shot his second arrow. But the cat leaped to the left and evaded it. The prince's torso turned to stone up to just under his heart. The cat, which like all cats had a smirk under its whiskers, coyly made its sneer even more bristly and sauntered around as if saying, Shoot your third arrow so that you turn to stone down to your core and the dream of possessing Forty-Braids turns into stone in your stone heart. . . . »

And he dreams . . .

The dusty mirrored display case in the modest jewelry shop is littered with gleaming ghosts of emptiness. Among the few remaining pieces of jewelry, a pair of gold rings resting against each other. A scrawny old man, with skin as white as plaster and hair as sparse as that of a coconut husk, stands behind the counter. He takes the rings out of the display case, hands them to him, and tells him the price. Amir thinks, This old man is trying to rip us off. His gold is phony, that's why it's so cheap. Without him asking, the old man says he has no seed or spawn left, that all he has left is cancer, that one of these days Abu-Yahya will come to claim his life. He says he can read the fate of ill-fated lovers on their foreheads, and that is why he has sold all his gold to the likes of him for less than what grandmothers' copper pots are worth. Sweat seeps from the smallpox scars on his face. To Amir, the rings have the rustic beauty and ugliness of handcrafted gold jewelry. For years, they must have appeared ugly to everyone, waiting for those two to come and make them beautiful. . . . The scent of lavender has crept into the shop from a distant herbalist's stall . . . when he has looked at the rings long enough, he looks up. There is a young man behind the counter. Sweat seeps from the smallpox scars on his face. The young man looks at the rings with sadness and asks, "Did you buy them for the price of copper?" Amir replies, "Yes." The young man sweeps the beautiful locks of hair away from his forehead and says, "The old man doesn't want to leave anything behind. Every father somehow destroys his son." He laughs. It seems he is laughing at Amir, at his ignorance.

All at once, he finds himself alone in the shop. He rushes out.

Right:

He bursts into Reyhaneh's room. The girl is threading her legs. Startled, she quickly pulls her skirt over her knees.

"I remember! There was a jewelry shop. We bought a pair of rings. When we walked out, there was the sound of laughter all around us. Mocking us. I said to her, 'Let's leave. Let's go someplace beautiful where we can be alone. Someplace where no one will see how beautifully we can put rings on each other's fingers.' She agreed to be my fiancée, but she said she couldn't wear the ring. . . . The glitter of the gold was so intense that her face was all a shimmer, or perhaps my eyes were blinded by the glow. I said, 'Every night we will take off our rings and every morning we will put them back on each other's fingers so that our engagement will be renewed every day . . . a hundred thousand times, maybe even more. . . .' I may have said that we will put the rings on every night and take them off every morning."

"You never let on that you were such a sweet-talker."

"I think I was really good at it. Help me learn it again. I am sure she is somewhere out there, but she thinks I am dead."

He memorizes the pattern of the fern-green leaves on Reyhaneh's sleeveless shirt. He steals a peek at her beautiful, fair arms.

He does not peek, he ogles.

He is tempted to bring his face close to Reyhaneh's arm, to draw in its scent. Closer, so that he can inhale the memory of the round scar from the smallpox vaccine and its shiny skin that is of a different texture than the rest of her arm. To breathe in, so that he can absorb all that she knows.

He wants to touch it, too. He wants his flesh to feel that firm, plump arm. He knows that right now Reyhaneh's well-proportioned underarms are wet with sweat.

No, it is not so. It is the sentiment of forgotten memories, the sense of touch from their childhood years, which he feels everywhere. They are ingrained in the memories of the walls and ceilings of this house, the childhood playfulness of the sister and the mischievousness of the brother.

> «This morning, when I woke up . . . I was in the garden when I remembered that I was awake . . . the morning dew on the winter sweet flowers tasted like gunpowder. The fragrance of a single winter sweet bush is enough to make a garden languish with love. The previous owner of this garden was not mad. He planted forty-four of them so that the whisper of their scent would cast a spell on those who live here or come to visit, to remind them of the hypocrisies that wreaked havoc, of the people they crushed and destroyed. . . . It is as if it wasn't before, but now that Reyhaneh is picking at a blemish on her pale knee. . . . The soft, cool skin on the underside of knees, resting on one's shoulders. . . . Why won't she let me pick at that blemish? . . . Just this morning, I was in the garden when I remembered the dream about the goldsmiths' arcade at the bazaar . . . Reyhaneh has asked me something.»

"What did you say?"

"Earlier . . . a while ago . . . you told a different story about the rings. Are all these fabrications just another one of your games meant to torture us to death?"

"What have I done for you to say 'torture us to death'?" he says angrily. "I am the one being tortured to death, by her."

He thinks he hears soft footsteps behind the door. His eyes suddenly look wild. Reyhaneh gasps. Amir tears open the door. Out in the hallway, footprints have disturbed the soft pile of the turquoise carpet. The sleepwalking scent of a perfume wafts toward him. It smells like the same perfume he smells in his dreams. The perfume Moon Brow sprays in the air and girlishly, playfully, tiptoes through its mist.

He shouts, "Damn you, lunatic!"

And he punches the doorframe. Mindlessly, he shifts his body to throw another punch with his left fist. The stump of his arm swings in the air, his shoulder slams into the doorframe, and he stumbles out into the hallway. He enjoys groaning in pain.

His mother's anxious face dawns in the middle of the staircase. He shakes an angry fist at her and retreats to the shelter of Reyhaneh's room. He stares at the frightened girl cowering in the corner. Seeing Reyhaneh like that pleases him, or perhaps calms him.

"Why are you so afraid of me? Have I ever raised a hand to you?"

Peeved, Reyhaneh sits on the floor next to her tea set.

"Why were you standing over me, watching me sleep?" he snaps.

"Me? Never!"

"Other than you, I don't want to see anyone in this house."

"All right, Dādāshi. For the love of God, don't get all worked up. I will tell them again."

"Tell them I'm crazy and if they come near me, I'll pounce on them and strangle them."

He waits for Reyhaneh's quince flower-colored lips to curve into a scowl. They don't.

"It isn't funny. If I have to, I can choke them with one hand. . . . But, if you help me, I'll get better."

"I didn't laugh. And what can a stay-at-home spinster do?"

"I have a few ideas, a few plans."

"Don't you remember anything special about her? For example, a mole on her face, or an old scar?"

> «She cracks open a pistachio. She holds out the nut to me from across the floral design of the inlaid table . . . the bone-like sound of the shell breaking . . . the silvery sound of bone being sawed . . . what a timid shade of green the nut has, what a menacing bone hue its shell has . . . far away, someone is saying, "I smoothed out the bone, soldier!" . . . »

"Back then, I must have talked to you about a girl who, let's say, had turned my life upside down, or some such nonsense."

"You never thought me worthy enough to tell me anything about yourself."

"Then how do you know so much about me?"

"When you talked on the phone with your friends, or when they came over, I would overhear. . . . You were all so dumb. You forgot I was in the room next door. You were all shameless."

The swelter in his body and brain has turned to sweat.

"Do you have any water here?" he asks, panting.

"Do you want to go and sleep for a few hours? You are not well."

"When my brain is working like a brain that works well, why do you all try to make me believe I am sick?"

"Let me walk you to your room."

"You all just want to shove me into bed. Damn you all! I don't want the pills you stuff into my mouth, they make me as thirsty as a stray dog, they make me sleepy and sluggish. . . . "

> «I'm as thirsty as a dog. When it's raining, why should you become so thirsty that even when you lick your chapped lips, your tongue is dry? . . . Reyhaneh is holding a glass of water in front of me. Silver bubbles on the sides of the glass. . . . The window in Reyhaneh's room is nice, it has more rain and clouds and bubbles than mine. And I can't even peel a pistachio.»

Reyhaneh walks over to him and bends down to pick up the pistachio he has dropped. Sister's long hair, which in his childhood memories of going to the bathhouse with Mother smells of cedar, cascades to the floor. The part in her hair a glistening line amid black, so black that the random strands of white shine brightly. He reaches down to touch it. Reyhaneh straightens her back. Her hair brushes against his fingers. She stares at his hand.

"What were you going to do?"

> «During the years I was away, things have happened here that these damn people are keeping from me.»

Reyhaneh shouts, "What were you going to do?"

"Nothing! I just wanted to touch your hair, to make sure you are real. . . . Nothing, believe me! I just wanted to. . . . "

Are they from anger or from shame, the tiny glistening drops of sweat that have simmered above the girl's lips?

"Mother and I have never thrown it in your face that we spent years going around the country, searching for you in hundreds of hospitals," she screams. "Do you know that we talked to thousands of wounded men, asking them about you? We even searched hospitals in towns that were being bombed. I am telling you now, this house cannot take any more of your games. Do you understand?"

"I just wanted to . . . "

> «The wish to touch her is still in my hand.»

"How many hands do I have to hold onto so many wishes?"

Wounded, Reyhaneh says, "With what goes on in your head, you would come short even if you had a thousand hands."

"I used to think a lot during the years I was at the nuthouse. I came to some excellent conclusions. A nuthouse is the best place to think and come to conclusions."

"I can see what clever thoughts you've had."

> «She is mocking me. Even if they are right and I have lost my mind, I know my senses are right when they sense something. Like right now, when I sense that there is someone eavesdropping behind

the door. We must talk quietly. . . . I must wait, Reyhaneh's anger always goes away quickly.»

With two fingers, Reyhaneh tucks the strands of hair on her temples behind her ears. Like women in miniatures, two locks of hair, black, curl behind her earlobes like scorpion tails.

He grips his sleeve between his teeth and stares at the gap between the closed door and the floor.

"Reyhaneh, I'm afraid!"

Reyhaneh says nothing.

«Somehow, I have to make them talk. And whatever they say, whatever I remember, I must memorize like schoolwork. I need to memorize it all so that they won't be able to accuse me of things I have not done. This rain has become so arrogant and talkative. Whenever I tell it to rain, it rains. When I was walking in the garden, I said, Rain! Pour, rain! So that it would rain and no one would be able to tell that the drops on my face were not raindrops. . . . Was it a long time ago when I said I wanted water? Reyhaneh is pouring a glass of water. Now if I repeat in my head, Reyha! Be kind, Reyha! Then Reyha will be kind.»

After some time, Reyha says, "You deserve to be afraid. You deserve whatever happens to you. . . . You should be afraid, afraid of all the things you are not afraid of."

"Everyone is scared of me, but I am scared of only one thing."

Reyhaneh looks at the wet cuff of his sleeve. Out of a sense of obligation, or maturity, she asks, "What are you afraid of?"

"That the longing to find her will stay in my heart for the rest of my life."

It is not clear whether the veil of tears in his eyes is real or fake.

"I am afraid that she was supposed to wait for me somewhere and I have forgotten where. . . . For the love of God, think hard, do you remember ever seeing me wear an engagement ring?"

"How many times do I have to tell you? No, I don't remember seeing you wear one."

"Then why do I keep seeing it in my dreams? Right now, I can clearly remember how she held out her hand and how I playfully twirled the ring and put it on her finger. Then I remember her holding the other ring with three fingers, waiting for me to put my finger through it. . . . "

He holds out the ghost of his left hand to show Reyhaneh. . . .

He stammers, "To put my finger through it. I did. I see the shimmer of gold. . . . Did I describe this scene to you differently before?"

"Perhaps you had secretly gotten engaged and, being afraid of Agha Haji, you took the ring off when you came home at night."

"I was not afraid of anyone, and I'm not afraid of anyone now that I have nothing left to lose."

"Huh! You say this now. Back then, you nagged and complained behind his back, but the minute he frowned, you wimped out, because he was always generous with you. He kept your pockets full. The one time you stood up to him, you ruined everything and this house turned into a house of mourning."

"Everything is ruined?" he lashes back. "I don't give a damn! To my left ball!"

"Yesterday or the day before, you said you had told her that being secretly engaged was a lot more fun. Do you remember telling me this?"

"Of course I remember."

He does not remember having said this to Reyhaneh.

"Father felt better after we held a memorial service for you as a missing martyr. But you have no idea how long Mother and I searched until we found you in that mental hospital. I am sure you are putting on an act just to ridicule us, just like you used to do. But this house can't take any more of your shenanigans. Do you get it, nutcase?"

"Then why does my right hand, ten, fifteen times a day, unconsciously reach over to turn the ring around my left finger?" he quietly mumbles. "This is something people who wear a ring get in the habit of doing. I must have worn one, too."

With no hope for comfort and support, he gazes out at the early evening garden, perchance to see Abu-Yahya's shadow.

> «One plus one makes one. This one just comes down faster. It means that the heavier you are, the faster you fall.»

Reyhaneh turns and listens intently. There is the sound of Father's car on the graveled driveway.

"Go to your room. I need to change and go downstairs. Agha Haji is used to me greeting him at the door."

"Why are you so afraid of him? Instead of that ridiculous black dress, go see him in the cheerful dress you are wearing now. He won't kill you!"

"No, he won't kill me," she says. "Whatever he is, he is not a murderer."

"I don't like him. The stubble on his face, the dark scab on his forehead from the prayer stone. I am sure at night, when everyone was asleep, he would heat a prayer stone and burn his forehead to fake his piety and devoutness."

"Whatever he is, his blood is in your veins."

"You haven't seen blood, stay-at-home girl. Blood is nothing. It sinks into the ground like piss. And then it is as if there never was any blood, as if the one it belonged to never existed. . . . I hope on one of those nights when Father went to some mourning ceremony, Mother made my fetus under a man who was a real man."

Reyhaneh's eyes grow wide with horror. Amir leans against the door. Deep in his throat, the roots of plants, the roots of a swelling lump. And he cannot even tell whether this is deception in his voice or the lump is real.

"If your tears were for me, then tell me, did I ever show that there was a girl who . . . I mean . . . who I was really in love with?"

Reyhaneh's face distorts from the pain in her throat. She turns away. Her shoulders shaking, she spitefully says, "Even with a maimed arm you still want to muck up love."

On his right shoulder:

He goes back to the house not knowing how long he has been strolling around the garden.

Again, his mother has taken advantage of his absence and tidied his room. He has hurled so many plates of food with meat in it down the stairs that she has finally given up. She has left two pomegranates and a gold-rimmed china plate full of vegetarian food on the small inlaid table. And an electric shaver has appeared on his neatly made bed.

> «Damn! Even when I eat only grains and weeds, my good-for-nothing body keeps gaining flesh. . . . »

Reyhaneh knocks on the door and walks in.

"If you want, come to my room and I will show you the family photo album."

On his right:

In the yellowed photographs, Mother is often in a chador, or wearing a headscarf if she is among women. And Agha Haji always has a beard—from black to salt-and-pepper. He thinks how stupid and innocent he and Reyhaneh look in the scallop-edged school photographs.

Reyhaneh points to a photograph of Uncle Kazem.

"You do remember him, don't you? Uncle Kazem."

"Tell me."

"His stomach is now much bigger than this."

"In other words, he is deprived of the pleasure of looking at his sacred business and balls."

"Don't be crude! Uncle Kazem is now the highest-ranking officer in the Army of the Guardians of the Islamic Revolution. He still boasts about his crusade for Islam before the revolution. Every time you see him, he tells a new story about his bravery in fighting against the Shah. But everyone in the family knows that all he did when he was out of town was write obscenities about the Shah, his wife, and his sister on the doors of toilet stalls at roadside restaurants. And then he would throw the evidence, the marker, in the toilet."

Their laughter sounds like the laughter of their childhood years.

Reyhaneh turns another page in the album. There are photographs of people from a different world. He doesn't know whether he is fooling himself into not remembering that he remembers them, or fooling himself into remembering that he doesn't remember them. Meaningless photographs and photographs that have meanings beyond themselves—a photo of him at fourteen, boyish fuzz above his lips and on his chin. At a Mourning of Muharram ceremony for Imam Hossein, he is beating his yet-to-be-flogged back with chains. A photograph of Mother and Reyhaneh sitting together, their chadors draped over their shoulders, resembling each other in youth and in old age. . . .

"This is on the banks of Karaj River," Reyha explains. "We used to go there on Fridays. See this mullah sitting there, looking so timid and modest? You should see the wolf he has turned into—a Member of Parliament, three wives, and a fancy beachfront villa that he bought for a pittance from a member of the Shah's royal court who was on the run. Remember the time when we were all sitting down to eat and you decided to give him a hard time?"

"The only thing I know how to do is give people a hard time. . . . What did I do?"

Reyhaneh offers him a slice of apple.

"Eat this and I will tell you."

The sound of the apple crunching between his teeth echoes loudly in his ears. It resembles the sound of shrapnel impacting arm bone.

"The women's lunch spread. Even at picnics we sat apart from the men of the pious and revered Yamini clan. But we could hear you. You had told me you were going to ask the mullah a question about Islam that he would not be able to answer and that it would make him throw his turban on the ground and give up being a mullah. You were going through your infidel phase! 'Mr. Haji,' you said. 'Is it true that on a Muslim's first night in the grave, Nakir and Munkar come to him carrying a flaming torch and ask him questions about the tenets of Islam?' Mr. Haji said, 'Of course it is true. And each time he fails to answer, they will beat him on the head with their torch.' Then you asked, 'But, Mr. Haji, Nakir and Munkar speak in the language of the Quran. How can a miserable guy like me, who doesn't speak Arabic, understand what they are saying?'"

Reyhaneh laughs.

"Until then, none of us had ever thought about this. You were right. We had always memorized the answers to Nakir and Munkar's questions in Persian. Mom and Agha Haji were baffled, and you were holding your head up high, as if you had not only confounded the mullah, but had conquered the summit of Islam, too."

"What did the guy do?"

"You were no match for a mullah. He said, 'When a non-Arab Muslim dies, the moment they put him in his grave, they read inculcations to him and he learns Arabic.'"

"So for us Iranians, our graves come with Arabic language classes!"

"Come on! Don't talk blasphemy."

"Near dawn, I dreamt of a long room with a mirror at its far end. She was there. The more I walked toward her, the fainter her reflection in the mirror became, and the farther away I was from her. It was as if I was walking backwards. When I finally reached the mirror, there was no reflection of her and no reflection of me. And the mirror wasn't a mirror, it was my bedroom window overlooking the garden."

"Mom says seeing a mirror in your dreams is a good omen. It brings light."

"Is there anything I could dream of that she would say is a bad omen?"

Reyhaneh smiles.

"No matter what you and I see in our dreams, she will interpret it as being auspicious and a blessing. She will say, Some good news or a fine trip lies ahead and wealth will follow."

"So our mother is half prophet, too."

They reach the end of the family album, which is filled with similar photographs, the only difference between them the tedious passage of time.

"Are there any other albums?"

"This is the only one we have."

"But there are no pictures of me and my friends in it."

"If you had any photos, you would never give them to us to put in the album."

He walks over to the window. It has fogged up. He raises his hand to write something on the misty glass. He thinks sometime in the distant past, there was a name or a phrase that he used to write on windows as if it were homework. He wonders whether he even remembers how to write.

He turns and looks back. Reyhaneh is not in the room. He wonders if she was ever there, or if he imagined it.

"To my left ball," he says with a shrug.

And on the foggy window, he writes, 923945.

The same coordinates that the radio operator misheard as 923955, as a result of which a detachment of Basiji soldiers came under fire and were crushed and crippled.

Again I write, it is not certain that there was an error. He could see the Basijis through his binoculars. It reminded him of the day a Basiji flogged him. It is not clear whether he intentionally spoke in such a manner that 923945 *sounded more like* 923955.

Again I write, this error was neither in his conscious nor unconscious mind.

How about in some other part of him?

The scribe on his right shoulder writes:

From the fog hovering among the trees, he hears the pulse of the undercurrent at the bottom of the sea. And when the wind blows, he hears the waves of the Caspian rolling above him, a sound he once liked. He would dig his fingers in the sand on the seafloor so that he could remain submerged and listen to the waves.

> «Some parts of the Alfa Romeo have corroded. The damn sun in this country, all it does is rot everything. Parked under the eucalyptus tree, it has turned into a toilet for the crows and the cuckoo bird, and once in a while, blue worms fall from the branches and burst on its roof . . . there is a dent from an accident on the front right side of the car. I feel uneasy every time I decide to walk over to it and open its door. I have no idea what I might have left behind in it. Not today, I won't be fooled into opening the car door today. Perhaps tomorrow. . . . Hey, rain! Start raining! . . . Under my feet, the gravel sounds like bones shattering and rusted shell casings crushing. The fog ends near the wall. Abu-Yahya is walking in step with me. The scoundrel, what if he is mocking me, aping me. He looks younger than people accuse him of being. I can't say he has a kind face, but it is certainly very sad. Perhaps it was right here, in our garden, behind the almond fog, that he stomped his foot

and hollered, "Almighty God! I am tired of taking lives, when will you take mine?" »

He knows that only he can see Abu-Yahya. Still, he cries out, "Where is my girl with the hazy face?"

There is no answer. Now the face of the one he is addressing appears as rippling waves. He learns nothing from it.

"Is she alive?" he shouts even louder.

And then:

"If you have taken her life, say so!"

Then:

"For the love of that God you believe in, tell me!"

Then:

"So that I stop searching for her. . . . "

There is no answer.

"Fuck you!"

«Once upon a time, a long, long time ago, a man was walking in the bazaar. It was morning. He suddenly came across Azrael, the Archangel of Death, who was staring at him in a strange and perhaps angry way. He thought, Damn! Abu-Yahya has come to take my life. He was terrified. He fled to prophet Solomon's palace. He threw himself at Solomon's feet and begged and pleaded for the prophet to send him to the farthest corner of the earth. Solomon felt pity for the man and ordered the wind to carry him to India. That afternoon, as soon as the wind set him down in India, the man saw Azrael standing there, waiting to take his life. He said to Azrael, "Well, if you wanted to take my life, you should have done it this morning. Why were you looking at me with such anger?" Abu-Yahya replied, "I was looking at you with surprise. This morning, I was ordered to take your life this afternoon in India. And since there have never been any mistakes in the orders, I was bewildered at how you would manage to travel this far. . . . "»

And he shouts, "You are nothing but a pimp! You pimp human lives!"
There is no answer.
"Do you pimp animal lives, too, or does someone else take care of that?"
And he remembers the white mule.

I wrote it was a horse.

The scribe on his left shoulder had written:

He sees . . .

At first, it appears to be a cluster of white smoke from a cannon shell. White, it has risen from among the boulders. He sees it from the observation post on the peak. By chance, he has turned his binoculars toward their own camp. The soldiers are climbing out of their trenches and gathering around it. From up there, they look small, the color of parched earth. The mule has perhaps walked along one of the deserted trails of a destroyed or abandoned village until it has arrived there and found humans. It is tall; who knows where in the mountains it has grazed to have remained stout. A few soldiers run their hands over its neck and back. They cannot be city people. He thinks, How beautiful and comical it would be if they were to build a trench for the mule. Dig a hole in the earth, just as you would a grave, dig as much as they can, deep into the ground, down to where the mule is shielded from exploding shells. . . . Now, this asinine mule that doesn't even know to drop to the ground when it hears the howl of an incoming shell, is standing there, lumbering and lanky. Being that big, after the third or fourth explosion it will finally get hit by shrapnel or the blast waves will have it with its legs up in the air. . . .

A couple of soldiers climb up on the mule and ride around the mounds of dirt piled up on top of the trenches.

"Games in the monotony of war . . . when was it that I saw two Iraqi soldiers trying to screw a donkey?"

He turns his binoculars to the three mountain peaks in the distance. There is an Iraqi observation post somewhere on one of them. He has not been able to locate it. Even if the Iraqi scout does not have a direct view of the Iranian camp, perhaps he can hear them on the wavelength of the mule-riding soldiers' wireless radio. From other squads, soldiers drift over to watch. . . . Not too long into the celebration, Iraqi mortar shells arrive. Today, they are aiming more accurately. The soldiers bolt into their trenches. The squad leader orders, Open fire! Amir ignores him. The squad leader curses and demands open fire. Amir laughs and speaks into his wireless radio's mouthpiece.

"Sir, I am not going to waste our allotment of shells on a mule!"

The novice third lieutenant does not get his sarcasm. He insists.

"Lieutenant, Sir!" Amir retorts. "When the enemy is hitting on target, we should not return fire!"

"Fuck the enemy and fuck you!"

"And I and the enemy fuck you and your wife!"

The shells explode, but the mule is still standing there in the open area behind the trenches. Standing there stubbornly.

"Why won't you run off? On this godforsaken mountain, with its shitty, snowy winters, you have managed to find food, and you are lucky you don't get horny like us. . . . Make a run for it!"

Not having seen humans for so long, perhaps the mule is more excited than afraid . . . the fog of black smoke from the explosions blows at the animal. . . .

The scribe on his right shoulder writes:

He cuts across the garden toward a winter sweet bush. He runs his hand caressingly along its perimeter. A few flowers fall. He heads toward the garden wall.

"Hey, bastard! Where did you disappear to? Who are you off to wipe out?"

He sees a chalk line on the wall, leading to the far end of the garden. At the start of the line a hand has written, Follow This Line. He follows the line. He does not remember that when he was a child, whenever he and his playmates found themselves in the maze of alleys in one of Tehran's old neighborhoods where his uncles lived, he would draw one of these lines from tall wall to tall wall, and at the end of the line he would write a funny, childish curse word. The line leads him to the small courtyard behind the house. He sees the garden's water pump and remembers the waterway that splits in two and stretches to the left and right sections of the garden. Without looking, he knows there are black strands of frogs' eggs stretching far into the narrow canals. And the line continues on the adjacent wall. He wonders whether he is the one who drew it. He cannot remember.

Another feverish wave rises in his body. He feels hairline lightning bolts striking in his pores. Soon, the whispers will start rushing through his mind. They will grow louder and louder.

> «The good-for-nothing voices of good-for-nothing people get all mixed up. They all keep shouting louder to shut the others up and shove their words into my head. . . . They have me by the balls so

> tight that I don't dare say, Damn you, lower your voices so that I can at least figure out what you are yapping about, what you are trying to make me see.»

Amid the chaos, now and then, there is Reyhaneh's voice. He cannot make out her words, but he knows she is saying something important. . . .

> «I don't want her to talk harshly to me. I want to rest my head on her black skirt so that it can absorb all that has welled up in my eyes, and in return, I want her to let me smell her scent. I want her to stroke my hair and say, Don't be afraid, Dādāshi, I'm here. . . . The sound of wood breaking is like the sound of bones splintering, a sound that will forever resonate in the bone's marrow.»

The scribe on his left had written:

A fragment of sound—the dry grating of bone being sawed—separates from the rest and an image flashes in his mind.

He realizes he is moaning, "Water! Water!"

He shouts, "Hey, you filthy butchers! Give me water!"

Shrapnel holes have punctured the arched metal frame of the field hospital; hazy blades of light shine in through them.

"You won't give me water so that I'll croak," he shouts, "so that I won't blab about the evil you do to us. . . . "

"Don't be afraid, soldier. I just want to even it out for you."

He leaps off the bed and runs. He is hemorrhaging again. With shreds of flesh hanging from his severed arm, he runs.

The groans and howls of the wounded men sprawled out on beds and on the floor whirl around his head. He does not know whether his own cries are there among the pleas for Water! . . . Water! Men standing next to the beds, their clothes covered with blood, are busy shaving flesh and stitching skin . . . somewhere, there is the sound of bone being sawed. He tries to ignore the pain in his arm and just run. A soldier wails a woman's name. Near and far, the sound of explosions. He sees a bright, arched doorway. Gusts of dust and smoke billow in. He stumbles over a man stretched out on the floor. He falls. Singed, scruffy hair . . . an eyeball hanging from its socket by a bloody strand glares at him.

The scribe on his right writes:

He sits next to the waterway on the right that passes by the winter sweet bushes and stretches to the far end of the garden.

> «I went to war to kill their gods. I failed. I returned with a Davālpā perched on my shoulders. . . . Once upon a time, there was an old man with legs that looked like leather straps, long and dangling, hidden, tucked under his body. His name was Davālpā. He would sit on the riverbank and whenever someone passed by, he would cry and beg for help to cross the river. But as soon as he climbed up on someone's shoulders, he would strap his leash-like legs around their neck in a stranglehold. Davālpā will never climb down. That poor passerby must give him food and water and carry him wherever he wants to go for the rest of his life. . . . Stupid me, when I was crazy, where along the river of when was it that I let Davālpā climb up on my shoulders? He is sitting there, strangling me. . . . Where was I going when I sat down?»

In the stagnant water at the bottom of the waterway, next to a crack from which roots hang in strands, a crab stares up at him with its bulging eyes. He darts his hand under the crab and tosses it out. Without knowing why, he knows he was clever at this when he was a young boy. He leans over the escaping crab and with two fingers lifts it up by its shell. Green algae has congealed on it. He turns the crab over and looks at its white underside. He wants to run the tip of his tongue over that clever armor. The crab is frightened. Suspended in the air, its legs thrash about searching for a foothold, its claws scissor the air looking for something to amputate.

"Were you here in this dump when I was a kid?"

He traps one of the crab's claws under his shoe and yanks it off.

"We're not even yet. Run along now and have fun, you still have another nine arms and legs."

He remembers being in the dressing area of the bathroom, putting on his pants. He cannot fasten the motherfucking button. He thinks, Reyhaneh and Mother were stupid to try to buy clothes for him that fit. . . . After years of wearing pajama pants in the nuthouse, he does not know why he won't wear the elastic-waist loose house pants that Agha Haji wears. He does not recall that in the past he was determined always to look good, even when he was alone and at home. He would always imagine observing himself and his actions from above, so much so that if he caught himself picking his nose in private, he would tease himself about it. Even his bowel movements annoyed him.

Helpless, he calls out to Reyhaneh. He has not properly dried himself and his jeans are wet here and there. Patiently, he calls out to her every few minutes until the girl finally answers from downstairs. Reyhaneh walks in, but quickly turns around and hurries out. Only then does he realize that he has not put on underpants. He thinks, Perhaps it would be easier if one were to lose a leg. . . . Again he calls his sister. Although Reyha has often sponge-bathed him in his room, now even more timidly she tries to button his pants with the least contact between her fingers and his skin. At the same time, she excitedly asks, "Do you like the color? It's a quiet, pale blue. I picked it out myself."

"Living in fool's paradise! So delighted you have gone shopping for me!"

Reyhaneh ignores his comment.

"There are these pieces of Velcro that we can sew onto your pants instead of buttons. The two sides stick together easily."

She fixes the clumsily fastened buttons on his shirt and steals a peek at his chest.

"What do you see there?"

"The hair is turning gray. But it's too soon."

They have forgotten to put a mirror in his room, or perhaps the "spying whoremonger doctor" has advised it.

"How many are there?"

She gives him that rare childish giggle of her younger years.

"Where is your modesty! How would I know? The hair on your head is starting to turn salt and pepper, too. You need to eat meat to get stronger. You are as thin as a water-pipe stem."

He looks at Reyhaneh's snow-white neck. The agate pendant on her necklace draws the eye to the hollow at the base of her throat.

> *«Her neck is so beautiful. It frightens me. But it's safe up here. We are far from the first-floor bedroom where the sperm worms of our fetuses did not spit out on mother's stomach. I should not go downstairs. Davālpā is sitting there on the fourth step of the staircase. No matter what I do, I know I will end up being duped by him.»*

He follows Reyhaneh out of the bathroom. Mother is standing in the middle of the staircase, peering up.

"A cripple is nothing to gawk at!" he shouts. "If I catch you spying on me one more time, I will burn this house down to the ground."

The lingering warmth of the water that had coursed over his skin and the languor of the elaborate weekly bath lull him toward sleep. He lies down on the bed.

To him, the fragrance of the fermented leaves and winter sweet flowers in the garden is like the scent of fresh, young semen infused with the churned nectar of a woman. He dreams.

> *«There is such pleasure in dreaming. Good or bad, true or false, there is such pleasure in dreaming.»*

He dreams of a memory . . .

The waves of the bedsheet have settled. . . . Ripples from the crests of peaking are still in the woman's body, and he, genuflecting, rests his forehead on her navel, a prayer stone, to catch his breath.

The woman says, "Was that an orgasm? Oh! . . . I think I had an orgasm! What was that?"

The scribe on his left shoulder had written:

The woman, euphoric and drained, moans, "You are killing me."

> *«Most of them say this when they're close to coming or after they have had their fill.»*

There is delicate white foam on his penis. Some has seeped out from the woman's inner folds, too. He does not know if it is from a disease, or if halfway through his persistent thrusts, drops of prematurely released semen mixed in with the woman's secretion and oozed out. The woman still craves kisses and the weight of a man on her.

"Come back on top."

> *«Damn you all! Proper breathing is important from the start of fucking—just as it is necessary to delay coming, it is equally important afterward. The problem is not just that a man's desire drains out with his sap. Even a romantic good-for-nothing is out of breath after he empties out. He needs air. If he stays on top of you for your sentimental satisfaction, his own weight will block his breath from coming easily . . . so, when you have had your pleasure, give the guy time to catch his breath. He can't lean on his elbows for too long, his arms become numb. . . . Me being me, and only if I have a lot of respect for you, instead of pulling away, I go on my knees and with my elbows resting on either side of you, I stick my backside up in the air and rest my forehead on your stomach, just like genuflecting on a prayer rug. This way, the weight you want is still on you and I can catch my breath on your prayer-stone navel . . . I smell the strong scent*

> *from your pubic pasture, the nectar of my body. I hear their commotion, tadpoles, waving their tails, racing toward the egg that has or has not descended from the sky of your stomach. . . . »*

The woman says, "My husband has never given me an orgasm. He is clueless."

"You have a nice body."

He is lying. He does not like the woman's spongy breasts.

"Is that all?" she grumbles.

He runs his finger over the young flesh of a cesarean scar. He likes this distinct mark that he has not seen on other stomachs.

"I said, is that all? I just have a nice body?"

> *«When they're done, they all suddenly remember divine love and never-without-you.»*

"Some feelings become trivial and meaningless if they are verbalized. You must sense them in your partner. Don't forget, words can lie, but emotions cannot. They are pure and honest."

He cannot remember to how many women he has gargled these words. Still, they are not lies.

He rolls on his side and looks with curiosity. These breasts are different from the others he has sucked and squeezed. The tips of the nipples sink in when not lusting. He thinks perhaps his hardness, which allows him to plunge into women like a pump and satisfy them, comes from his constant preoccupation with his need to observe . . . the shape of a woman's lips when they blossom out in hunger, her eyes rolling up from the thrusts, her lustful groans that sound different each time, and finally, the scent of the tragacanth-like mixture of the potions that seep out from her four-folds. . . . He wants to commit these to memory, perhaps to write of them in one of his secret poems.

This writing should not have been written. It is not beautiful.

They are just words, phrases, expressions that these humans have not been able to compose any better. Whenever the word ugly becomes ugly, and the word empty becomes empty, then the word beautiful can create beauty. The rest are the same words they were. For instance, feces, which comes out from the depths of Amir's bowels.

First day, interim days, and judgment day are always together, from one end to the other, they are linked and united. Like the symbol of infinity, they perpetually circle one another. Their repetition is not significant. What is significant are the "moments" and the unique "instances" they create. Perhaps Amir is reaching this stage—the mysticism of observing the world intently to perceive the singular instance in every moment.

To arrive at the word for the emptiness of full things.

He wants to commit to memory the slope or the previously unnoticed quiver of new breasts. Or, even if it has been repeated thousands of times, the sensation of sweats blending, chest against chest. But this very "instance" that belongs to this one "moment" is what he wants to observe, because it is unique. Under the weight of his craving muscles, to sense the wave that courses from a woman's waist down to her thighs and then returns, and this one moment will never be repeated. . . . The instinctive coiling of calves around his thighs, or the coolness of the underside of knees on his shoulders. . . . And the sounds, the murmurs of two lower bodies, the gurgles of a succulent tropical flower's fountain inside hungry petals of flesh, or the slapping sound of the breasts of a woman he has made bend over and is penetrating, angling slightly to the right, slightly to the left.

The air conditioner in the apartment works well. The drops of sweat in his chest hair give him a chill. It is exhilarating when there is a hot, white sun outside the window, it makes the woman's cool skin more pleasing. He feels like driving to the garden estates in Shemiran to inhale the sweet-and-sour breath of the sycamore and maple trees and then join his friends. The worm of temptation to smoke opium is wriggling around in his head. The few times when Kaveh smoked in front of him, he resisted the impulse.

> *«Dimwit! Try it and see what you've been missing. Man, if you smoke before a fuck, you will have even more stamina, and you will pump her so hard that your dick and the lady's 'tween will be raw. And afterward, there is another pleasure. It's a strange place, the realm between sleep and wakefulness. . . . They flog booze peddlers, and tomorrow they may start executing opium dealers—try it while you can get it!*
>
> *What if Kaveh wants to turn me into an addict?»*

He puts his left thumb and index finger right where the woman's thick eyebrows meet and gently glides them out toward her temples. And again, above her eyebrows.

> *«It relaxes them.»*

The woman smiles.

"You shouldn't have sucked my breast so hard. It's bruised. What am I going to tell my husband?"

> *«A holy halo around the breast's grape. Many of them are the same color, but there are a hundred shades of this one color.»*

The woman runs her fingers through the hair on his chest.

"It's nice. You are not too hairy and not feminine-looking either. You have a great body. Do you work out?"

> *«It seems she is not planning to go home and cook lunch for her husband. . . . »*

"I sometimes swim."

"I know! You are a worthy swimmer!"

> *«I don't like my carcass or theirs when they think they are giving me compliments. I don't like it when after a casual tumble in bed they quickly become intimate. Daydreaming nitwit pussies! What exactly have we done? At most, think of it as having shared a meal in bed instead of at the table. And I hate the fact that just like that, they fall in love. And their just-like-that love means that they are now master and possessor and a pest and nagging nuisance. They turn into the monkey that puts her child on the metal floor of the cage when it gets too hot and sits on him.»*

"I don't know why," he says, "but ever since we became an Islamic Republic, married women fool around a lot more. They are easier to score."

"I'm not fooling around. I'm exacting my right from the good-for-nothing Iranian men."

She wastes ten or twelve tissues to wipe herself clean and tosses them all over the room.

"Keep them as a souvenir," she snaps. "And next time, if you just want a piece of ass, don't come looking for me."

She opens the door a crack, peeks out into the hallway to make sure no one is around, and quickly leaves.

He is still staring at the tissues.

The scribe on his right shoulder writes:

In his dark room, one hundred twenty-seven minutes have passed with him sitting in his only chair, staring out at the changing night and the reborn shadows in the garden. Here and there, fluorescent lamps on old wooden posts cast light on the gravel lanes. He sees the flare of a cigarette near the eucalyptus tree.

> «And suddenly, winds from a distant peak or gusts from an exploding shell blow away your memories. The void that is left behind is like the open wound of a bedsore.»

The cigarette-smoking phantom walks under the fluorescent lamps and into the faint light shining from the house.

> «Lieutenant! Want to smoke a scorpion? . . . »

Davālpā is not sitting on the fourth step of the staircase. Amir tiptoes down and quietly opens the front door. The cunning man sees him.

"Hello, Amir Khan!"

"And you are?"

"The guard. We have met before."

"I'm sorry! I thought there was a burglar. I came to tell him, don't mind me, take whatever you want, your sin is absolved."

The man chuckles.

"I like your laugh. I guess you, too, have accepted the fact that I'm a nutcase."

"The likes of you are the honor and pride of the revolution, Amir Khan. I'm from the guards, too."

"You mean you are one of the brothers from the Revolutionary Guards?"

"Well, a bit higher up. Special forces. My name is Seyyed Moussa."

"I thought you were Abu-Yahya."

The man does not react to his sarcasm. There is the bulge of a Colt under his jacket.

"No, I am Seyyed Moussa."

"You are a *seyyed*, meaning a descendant of the Prophet Mohammad, and Moussa, the prophet of the Jews?"

"It is the name my father, God rest his soul, gave me. Now I'm stuck having to guard the East and the West. Nothing escapes my eyes."

The lips, dark under that beard, take on a derisive curl.

"Lend me that Colt of yours one of these days and let me take a few shots with it."

"You have taken your shots. Now you must rest. I will do the shooting."

"Then will you at least offer me one of your Moussa-esque flames?"

The man holds out his pack of cigarettes and flicks it up.

"May your afterlife be free of flames, Amir Khan."

"And may the flames of your pleasure always burn bright."

He takes a cigarette and without saying goodbye walks back into the house. Halfway up the stairs, he realizes he doesn't have any matches. Again, like a ghost he starts his nightly prowls around the house. He has until dawn when Agha Haji, Mother, and Reyhaneh wake up for morning prayers. In the kitchen, he still cannot figure out how to work the various appliances that have been added during the years he was away. He finally finds a matchbook in one of the cabinet drawers.

On his left:

Elated, he holds the fruit of his midnight plunder between his lips and sits on his chair in front of the window.

On the gravel driveway, he sees Moussa's flame being flung at a dark winter sweet bush. He tries to light a match and a memory sparks in his mind. He thinks his pet phrase used to be, The biggest drag for a man is when his lover or his lighter let him down just when he needs them most.

Even with the matchbook wedged between his knees, he cannot light a match. Whenever he gets frustrated with having only one hand, he mockingly laughs at himself. His raspy laughter may wake up everyone in the house. They will not be alarmed. They are used to it.

He grips the match between his teeth and lights it. The smell of his singed beard makes him realize that he has not thought about shaving in a long time. Unconcerned, he crosses his legs and takes a deep puff. He didn't expect not to cough. The pleasant smoke instantly makes him lightheaded.

> *«The soldier says, "Lieutenant, will you smoke scorpion with us lowly underlings?"»*

And, of course, he does not remember catching Private Eskandar smoking in the middle of the night while on scout duty on Se-Sar Mountain, or that he punished him by adding three extra hours to his shift, and near dawn, in a state of panic, he had to drag the boy's half-frozen body to his own tent to warm him up.

He satisfies his craving for a fifth puff and starts twirling the cigarette in the dark.

> *«Two pleading fingers? Two pleading prongs! . . . »*

He twirls the cigarette faster and faster until he sees the infinity symbol. He thinks, The hell with everything, these two little red circles seem to be the only thing in the world worth crying for.

The scribe on his left shoulder had written:

Lying down on the frozen ground behind the observation post trench, he watches the sun set on the far side of the mountains in Iraq and gazes at the darkness drifting toward him. Private Eskandar has just returned from leave. In his pocket, Amir has a handful of the nuts and dried fruits that the private's mother packed in her son's duffle bag. He takes three or four of them and pops them in his mouth. He chews the roasted chickpeas first, then he pushes the soft raisins from the corner of his mouth into the pulped chickpeas and mixes their tastes. Next, he chews on a fig, a process that he prolongs for a good half hour, and he will not swallow it until the very last of its flavor has gone.

Amir returns to his tent. He thinks Master Sergeant Pourpirar, tucked in a zipped-up sleeping bag, with only his head sticking out, looks like an Egyptian mummy. He switches on his small transistor radio and turns the dial to Iraq's Persian station, which mostly plays common prerevolution songs and cheap tunes by singers who ran off to Los Angeles. The soldiers listen to them out of earshot of the army's politico-ideologue snitches. The music is often interspersed with slogans against the mullah's regime and interviews with Iranian war prisoners who seemingly regret having joined the war and now encourage Iranian soldiers to seek asylum with Saddam Hussein's army. He hates the regular Iranian radio stations. They only broadcast revolutionary anthems and religious sermons. All he is hoping for is that Radio Iraq slips up and plays one of the few songs he used to like so he can distance himself from the grime and filth of war and become deaf to the sound of explosions from near and far.

In the middle of the night, the station finally plays one of those songs. He enjoys listening to it, despite the static.

. . .

Forever faithful friend, go, may you travel safe,
Do not grieve for me, I have grown accustomed to partings,

. . .

If I am indebted to you, if I owe my life to you,
It is not as precious as the moment when you showed me to myself

. . .

He has always liked the melancholy this song stirs in him. He remembers the day when Khazar gave him the cassette tape and the times he murmured the lyrics to her as if they were written for her.

He sees . . .

They have swum very far from the beach. Far away where the Caspian Sea turns from green to blue. Khazar is lying on her back, floating on the water. The small curve of her bikini top, the white of her thighs, bob in and out of the water. Her arms wide open, her legs slightly apart, now and then she gently moves her hands and feet like a dolphin to remain afloat. And the time between these flutterings in the water grows longer and longer and she becomes more and more the same color as the. . . .

"Aah!" he groans. "What did you do, Khazar?"

The scribe on his right shoulder writes:

He dreams that he and a few happy-go-lucky friends drag a naked, half-dead woman out of the river. The color of the woman's blood-drained skin is visible through her white shirt. She has a frail beauty and there is a perplexed look in her eyes. They ask her over and over who she is and what has happened to her and she says nothing.

And in his dream, he knows that several days have passed and the now stronger woman, the sad woman, is sitting behind the beautiful villa, staring out at the fog among the tall trees in the forest, expecting horror.

He dreams that he offers her a bottle of Coca-Cola. She turns her gaze away from the depths of the forest fog and looks quizzically at the bottle. For the first time, she speaks. With trembling lips, she whispers, "He will smell the weeds, the water in the river. He will come after me."

She does not say who or what it is that can track her scent even in flowing water.

Right:

> «The fragrance of a single winter sweet bush is enough to make a garden languish with love. The previous owner of this garden was not mad. He planted forty-four of them so that the whisper of their scent would cast a spell on those who live here or come to visit, to remind them of the hypocrisies that wreaked havoc, of the people they crushed and destroyed. . . . »

After much wavering between I should and I should not, he finally musters up the courage to climb into the carcass of the Alfa Romeo. Years have passed since he last drove the car. Dust has layered over dust and the dashboard and leather seats have cracked like parched clay. Perhaps it is the sunglasses falling to pieces next to the gearshift that bring the image of a girl to his mind. He racks his withered memory. Like the faucet on the first floor that starts to drip in the middle of the night, a few names trickle onto his dry-as-dust mind. He wonders whether they were ever part of his life, and if they were, which one belongs to his Moon Brow.

The scribe on his right shoulder had written:

He is still happy that after many excuses and refusals, Khazar finally accepted his invitation. On the wide armrest between their seats in the movie theater, several times his arm has accidentally touched hers.

> «It always starts like this. It starts so that it penetrates the seven orifices of everything, so that later, like a worm sliced in two by a razor, each half goes off after its own life. Why am I suddenly so tongue-tied and clumsy around Khazar, as if she is the first girl in my life? Perhaps it is because no one, not even me, can predict whether five minutes from now she will still be like this, or will cross everything out . . . It will be a dirty dig if she pulls away from me or gets up and leaves. She has never looked directly into my eyes. But sometimes the way she acts and speaks my name, it's as if we have been a match for years. . . . »

He moves his restless forearm tangent to Khazar's on the armrest. She does not pull away. Through the hair on his arm he can feel the radiance of her skin. And in the film, a woman's long hair spreads over the river. He takes Khazar's delicate hand into his. For a moment, her hand hesitates, but it stays there, trembling like a chick that has just broken out of its egg. . . . Her skin has the coolness that Amir likes. His body is always warm—they tell him it is pleasant under the blanket, like a heater on a snowy winter night. . . . And Khazar's surrendered hand is sweating. He rubs together the perspiration on their palms. He has often thought that Khazar has the gracious yet sad and distant beauty that makes unworthy men not dare approach her or fall in love with her. Next to her, a man's inferiority floats to the surface. He moves his fingers under the girl's wrist. The sultry beat of her pulse . . . a patient stroke, a silkworm, soft, seductive . . . he remembers the two pink capillaries on her wrist, Tigris and Euphrates, and the fine golden hair on her forearm, and he doesn't know why he likes these. . . . He tells himself a fortune . . .

> «If she lays her head on my shoulder, without acting coy, then just as she looks and behaves differently from girls who get around, her heart, too, is different. In which case, she can see through my act, she can sense my emotions, my loneliness. Then perhaps she is the one, my one and only, the one I was sure I would never find. And I always thought this damn destiny would complete its joke on me by putting her in my path when I am old and grumpy. . . . »

On the screen, the dense forest is untraversed and still. There is an unfamiliar drone coming from somewhere deep inside the darkness of its green folds. A combination of the whir of a metal wire spinning in the air, the sound of wood splintering, and steam hissing. Its strangeness is frightening.

> «And Khazar gently, perhaps sadly, perhaps simply out of the misery of loneliness, lays her head on my shoulder. I wrap my arm around her. My hand on the reluctant curve of her shoulder. I squeeze it. . . . It is a pleasant feeling, and it does not feel like an overture to a screw. It is good that they have built the chairs in Vanak Cinema with high backs, so that people cannot see those seated in front of them. Perhaps now her nipples are peaking against her close-fitting shirt. I am certain her breasts are small

> enough not to spill out from under one's hand, and not so small as to leave empty space. Then, in my head and my hand comes the temptation to push down on her neck so that she bends over and her mouth reaches my groin. . . . »

He scolds himself, You good-for-nothing! You should shield this poor girl from your lechery. Her hymen is probably real, not stitched up. . . .

In the movie, a man who lives in the forest has fished out a drowning woman from the river. Uncensored, the woman's cotton shirt is clinging to her large, perhaps milk-laden breasts. The demonstrations against the Shah have not yet reached this part of the city, and this movie theater has yet to go up in flames. The woman's lips are still; a clump of her long hair has been cut off. She is frightened of everything—of time, of the depths of the forest. She has either forgotten her past or is hiding it. Near the end of the film, she allows the man to straddle her and run his lips over the fresh scar under her navel. Now she is sitting outside the cabin, at a rustic wood table the man has built. She is staring at the old nicks and notches left by a knife on its surface. She forces the handle of a butcher's knife between two planks and lodges the tip of the blade between her breasts. And suddenly, she lunges forward. The knife, boldly, perhaps wisely, plunges in. Khazar jumps like a little scaredy-cat. The woman shudders. Khazar's head has left his shoulder.

The forest-dweller calmly watches from the window. The woman, with the knife handle between her chest and the table, is motionless. Her head hangs down and her long hair spreads over the table. . . . The film ends. The lights go on. The flirting couples separate. Amir smells Khazar's mint-scented whisper.

"How horrible! Why did she do it?"

> *«I can't believe she is so disturbed that her eyes are wide with horror. She is still staring at the screen. I can see the shimmer of tears in her eyes and her nails are still digging into the back of my hand. Do objects know*

> *what role they play in people's lives? When a knife stabs a chest, does it know that this is different from a potato? But forget this nonsense, it is so pleasant to walk into a cinema in bright daylight and to be surprised by the darkness of night when you leave.»*

The scribe on his right shoulder had written:

He starts the car. He knows he should stay quiet until Khazar's mood shifts. The windshield has fogged up. He writes "Khazar" as he drives . . . he writes "Khazar" . . . again, he writes . . . and on the next line he writes "I lov—" Khazar screams. He jerks the steering wheel to avoid hitting the woman in a black chador crossing the street. The woman shouts after them. When they have recovered, Khazar sighs, "You were writing a lie and God punished you."

It starts to rain. The wipers draw arches on the windshield with the soot-laden raindrops of Tehran.

"I want to take you to Kazbah."

"I like crazy people. There is one on our street. He is usually sitting on the stairs in front of a ramshackle house. I always give him an apple, and every time he calls it by a different name. 'Thanks for the orange.' Next time he will call it a pomegranate or grapes. Once he called it an egg. I am always dying of curiosity to see what he will call the apple this time. What names can you give an apple?"

"My kind of crazy is different. Do you get it?"

"Stop constantly asking if I get it. . . . Maybe that woman was running away from her husband, or from the police, the way she just darted into the street."

He speeds the Alfa Romeo onto Shahanshahi Freeway and then drives south from Elahieh. He likes the narrow tree-lined roads and alleys of this neighborhood. The car heater has cleared the fog and erased his words.

"Girls like these streets. How many have you brought here for a drive?"

The raindrops on the upper corners of the windshield have remained out of reach and safe from the wipers. Khazar puts her finger on one.

"This one is me. Right? . . . Yes, it's me."

The raindrop darkens and brightens as they drive under the fluorescent streetlamps.

"And you are the windshield wiper?" she asks.

"No, I want to be the raindrop next to you."

"If the two drops meet, then you were not lying when you said you want to make me happy. If they don't, then you are the world's biggest scoundrel."

"So you tell yourself fortunes too?"

"I learned it from you. Reyha has told me a lot about you. . . . Don't say it, don't say it. I confess. Yes, I used to manipulate her into talking about you. Is our master's Mr. Ego pleased?"

Gibing Amir about his traditional family, she pronounces "master" with the lilt of a frumpy, old-fashioned housewife.

"Then why didn't you ever let on when we ran into each other at parties?"

"First of all, you were too busy with your Fereshteh. Second of all, you got even busier with your Katayoun. And fifth of all, I didn't like you. Even now, I sometimes don't like you. If it were up to me, I would prefer not to like you at all."

"The guys are right—you are like a fish. Just when a guy thinks he has you in his grip, you slip away. Kaveh calls you Khazar Fish."

"I know. I'm famous for not giving anyone a break. But don't go out of your way to win a medal for catching me. I'm not worth it."

She slides her fingertip down the windshield. Her raindrop is rolling down. It gets in the way of the wiper and it's gone. Amir turns off the wipers. When the raindrops crowd the glass, people will not be able to see inside the car. He pulls over and parks in a dark spot under a tree. The sound of the rain beating on the roof of the car grows louder. He turns to Khazar. The raindrops and their streaks have cast shadows on her face.

> «Her quince flower-colored lips . . . half open . . . the gleam of her straight, pearly teeth . . . if she takes my hand, I will kiss her.»

Khazar runs the back of her pale hand against his on the steering wheel. He leans toward her, his lips close to her blossoming upper lip, thinner than her lower lip . . . Khazar pulls back and playfully laughs. She opens the car door and steps out.

Carefree, she chimes, "Let's go for a walk in the rain."

"That's too romantic. We will get soaked to the bone."

"Get out of the car, you sissy!"

They stroll down the narrow autumn road. She takes his hand.

"You see how cold my hand is? I'm always cold. Our lord and master should take note of these things. We would not want him to later complain that he took a bride unawares."

Amir has never mentioned marriage to Khazar. He does not like teases and wisecracks that he cannot counter.

"I love a cool body."

"I was not talking about a crystalline body with an added layer of flesh for Mr. Haji to sink his teeth into. I was talking about hands."

Still, her girlish humor is something to enjoy. He laughs and throws his arm around her and pulls her close. Raindrops are streaming down her face.

"When a raindrop falls," she says, "it never complains about where it has fallen, nor does it scream and shout expecting the place where it has fallen to be grateful. It never makes a fuss. Raindrops just want to rain. They don't care where they rain."

"But which one do you think is happier, the one that falls in the ocean or the one that falls in the desert?"

As if he has asked a childish question, Khazar snickers.

"Hey, genius! Mr. IQ! Raindrops have no notion of happiness and sadness. All that is important to them is to rain down on earth. I am jealous of them. Think about how important they are. All those raindrops, the ones that fall on people, on desert sand, on windshields of buses, on rooftops . . . on the bones of the abandoned dead, on crazy men. . . . I have to tell you, sometimes I feel really sad. I mean . . . if we are going out together, you should know that sometimes I suddenly feel sad. I can't help it. I don't know why. All of a sudden I feel anxious—I feel as if something bad is going to happen. And then I'm sad. I don't want to be alive when something awful happens."

Her voice is more fragile and melancholy than usual. Amir hates himself for longing to kiss her.

But still, he imagines skillfully, subtly, as nimbly as a dandelion rolling on water, brushing his lips past her earlobe, down her white, long neck, over her jugular, and further down to the cleft between two lemon halves. . . . The road is flanked by expensive houses. . . .

The rainwater on the asphalt glistens under the light of the fluorescent lamps and streams down the road. Their shoes are wet.

"But you don't have any problems in your life."

"That's just it! That is what scares me and makes me even sadder. Like, right now . . . being here with you. Today was a beautiful day, and now there is this beautiful rain, and there is a safe and comfortable home and a good family waiting for me, but right now when I'm happy, I get sad because I'm happy. . . . Do you think I'm messed up in the head?"

He doesn't know what to say. She has blindsided him again. And Amir cannot come up with one of his clever, spur-of-the-moment lines. The kind that women like even though they know they are lies. He thinks he could dish out a few verses of the poems he privately writes. But he thinks even the secret of his poems is too cheap and sentimental for Khazar.

"You are thinking of dishing out a poetic line as your ace. I don't want it. Obviously, I am a little messed up. It doesn't matter. I think everyone should be a little messed up. Otherwise, the earth would be a planet of robots."

"Well, I'm messed up, too. I just don't let anyone see it."

"Why do you think I came out with you, child genius!"

A man, his face hazy, hands stuffed in pockets, walks past them and says, "These are your last nights, fancy-free kids."

> «What if just this, rubbing the rain on my hand onto Khazar's hand, what if just this is what happiness is? It seems that with her I don't have the usual anxiety about the inevitable headache and misery of breaking up. Maybe I won't have to fake a good-for-nothing sad and serious expression and tell her, too, that our relationship was a mistake from the start, that I am incapable of falling in love, that I don't deserve love, that she deserves a better man, and more excuses and more drivel . . . but screw anyone who thinks all those breakups were easy for me. . . . The pleasure of rain has nothing to do with Khazar's happy-go-lucky, romantic nonsense. It's good because when it falls, no nosy, sympathetic, flunky friend can tell whether these are tears or raindrops on my face. . . .
>
> When we go back to the car, I will put my hand under her chin and lift her face. The rain will fall on her face and trickle down her chin and onto the palm of my hand. I will lap it up with my tongue. Is this part of happiness?»

The scribe on his left shoulder had written:

Kazbah Dinner Club. The waiters know him and think highly of his wallet. Shahin gives them a cozy table. The fast dance music changes to an oldie, Windmills of Your Mind. A few couples return to their tables, a few walk onto the dance floor and into each other's arms.

> *«Whatever it is, it is a good pretext to start. Heart facing heart, groin close to groin. . . . It's a good start for loosening up a skittish first-timer.»*

Shahin brings a bottle of Châteauneuf-du-Pape and with great fanfare pours half a sip in the glass for Amir to taste. He always sneers at these antics. If he didn't want to show off in front of Khazar, he would have preferred that eighteen-toman domestic Chateau Sardasht. Khazar still won't return his prowling gaze. His empty stomach quickly absorbs the tranquility of the wine. He dips his finger in the glass and draws two wet lines along his cigarette to make its taste stronger. But even two more glasses of this weak, watery wine are no match for him. The only solution is that half-bottle of Johnnie Walker that Shahin brings over. He downs the first shot. He is tempted to drag Khazar over to the dance floor.

And she is saying, " . . . she is so simple and innocent. Every time I tricked her into talking about you, I felt like such a wicked witch. All I was missing was a talking mirror."

Amir points to Serge, the DJ. With his long, white, shoulder-length hair and his sharp, young eyes in a withered face, he stands out among the crowd.

"The old guy is Serge. He has a knack for picking songs. He is so good at it that he never repeats his mixes. He has been here for years."

> *«It seems there is something wrong with Serge tonight, the way he keeps playing old, nostalgic songs that wreck the crowd's idle happiness and bring them back down to earth. Tonight he turns up the volume during the guitar-picking segments in Yesterday when I was Young.»*

" . . . Once, I was really wicked and duped her into showing me your family photos. Reyha is so sweet that even if she figured it out, she didn't say anything. I know, it was horrible of me to pinch one of them."

"Am I more handsome in my photos?"

"I am more afraid of you when I see how sure you are of yourself."

"If you find out that . . . what if you find out that I'm not what people say I am, that I'm a different kind of good-for-nothing but I just don't show it?"

"In answer to such clichéd drivel, girls say, Mr. Prince, come down to earth and let's walk together. All guys put on the same melodrama. . . . The only credit I can give you is that you're really bad at it."

A pleasant intoxication is settling in his body, and he tells himself, The hell with it! For once, let her see me naked, just as I am. Let's see what she will do, let's see if she is the one I went sniffing around for from pussy to cunt, and pussy after cunt picked me up.

"What are you brewing in that messed up head?"

"You shouldn't be scared of me when you think I'm playing games with you. You should be scared of me at times like this, when I'm feeling down."

"Stop being a spoiled brat. A guy who is feeling down is not scary, he is scared."

Serge is playing Jose Feliciano's Gypsy.

"So if you aren't scared of me, then stop your chichi-girl prudishness and see this night through with me."

"I. . . . "

"Don't worry! I mean let's go to the end of the line of wherever our minds take us. I've ODed on women, so I'm safe. If you swiped my photo, then stop playing with your wine and drink up. Tomorrow you will either tear it up or kiss it. . . . Cheers!"

> *«Dim-witted as I am, acting all honest and true, I'm starting to realize what could happen tonight. It will happen. Somehow, we will pretend we are out of it, that it's because we are drunk, and it will happen, and in the end, at the end of the night, we will coil around each other in the nakedness of sheets. I know that in a half hour, if I ask her to dance, no matter how hard-nosed she is, she will agree, and when she is in my arms. . . .*

> *The scotch is working and the reign of Feliciano's blindness has ended. . . . Emerson, Lake & Palmer's C'est la Vie is playing for romantic dimwits.»*

"There, I drank it. Now tell me where your head is."

"Damn you all for being on the watch even while you're drinking. I swear, the girl who gets duped and roped in deserves it. She deserves to have her blossom popped, and then, farewell . . . and all her plans for getting married, washed away. . . . Don't be afraid of me. I'm nothing."

Khazar, with a look of the wise at the callow, or perhaps of strained sympathy, or perhaps of 'I would have drunk it even if you hadn't asked,' raises her glass and gulps it down. She licks away a drop of wine from the corner of her mouth. Amir pours again. Wine for her, scotch for himself.

He glances at the next table and the voluptuous girl who's been giving him the come-on.

> *«You floozy! The guy who is going to do you, your fiancé or your husband, is sitting in front of you—give him the come-on! . . . Amir, remember! Never trust a woman who has a ring on her finger. . . .*
>
> *Son of a bitch Serge knows just what songs knock me down. He is playing Forever Faithful Friend. . . . »*

"If you were with some other girl, how many times would you have danced with her already? Our lord and master should not be shy."

Getting up, Khazar glances over at the voluptuous girl and with a sly smile makes Amir understand that she knows he has been eyeing her.

And the singer, his voice steeped in opium, sings:

O my savior
In my days of self-destruction,
O light of compassion
In my nights of horror,
When the night was the night of passage
Through the alleys of fear,

When every shadow led me into darkness,
When the wound of a friend's dagger was my best dress,
With a hand of kindness you healed my wounds. . . .

Slurring his words, Amir says, "I have never had anyone to think about when I listen to this song. Someone this song would be for. . . ."

"How about your poems?"

"I don't write poetry. No, not at all. What makes you think I'm nuts enough to write poetry?"

"Just a hunch. And from your answer I know I guessed right."

> *«With eyes that I wish would blur, I see them. Six couples on the dance floor. In the green, red, and blue pillars of light, in each other's arms, gently moving their hips and tiptoeing around. Moving just that part of them that lusts. How often do they tell the truth? When they are sure they are telling the truth, how much of it is lies? Where will they be next year? With whom? Will they remember everything they say and do tonight? All their bragging and boasting? Where will that couple's eye-to-eye smile go? Where will the sensation of that longhaired boy's hand on the round of that girl's ass go? Where the pleasure of their cheeks touching, the feeling that they now want to kiss, that they can't, not here, not in public. . . .»*

On his left:

And he realizes how perfectly Khazar fits in his arms. With the suppleness of a cluster of weeping willow branches . . . not too close, not too apart. . . .

> *«Have a little trust in a woman who chooses to sit with her back to the crowd in a restaurant and the candle's flame takes on a new color in her eyes. . . .»*

And he comes to as he is saying, ". . . was it my fault or hers that she got pregnant? I told her, Katayoun, I swear it's impossible, with your hymen still intact, to get pregnant from just rubbing up the door. I was careful. She said she was. She took, or I gave her, thirty thousand tomans for an abortion . . . a pregnant virgin, Tehran's Mother Mary!"

He laughs and Khazar's stunned eyes grow even wider. With all this bluntness, it seems the girl is wondering whether to stay or to leave.

"What? I'm not saying anything bad. I'm just talking about a hymen. I told her there are doctors who can sew it back together when you decide to get married. She cried. She cried a lot and said she didn't want to hoodwink some poor guy with a phony hymen. She put her finger on my so-called male pride and said, 'You mean you are that big a louse that you will not take responsibility for your own mess. . . .'"

He laughs loudly and a few of the flops and floozies dancing nearby turn and glare at him for being drunk.

He turns to Khazar and snaps, "If you want to call it off and leave, this is a good point in the story for you to split."

"If you start acting all emotional, first I will laugh at you, then I will leave."

"I agreed to marry her. I told myself, Amir, you dope, fate is finally done playing its joke on you. There is nothing you can do. Just laugh it off. It is what it is. . . . Every time I saw her, she cried so much that I didn't dare say, Now that the doctor's scalpel is going to tear into your hymen, at least let me have a go at it first. One day she called and said she had made the appointment. I drove her and her friend over there. She walked into the doctor's office crying. An hour later, she walked out very slowly with her hand on her stomach and got into the car. I thought, Here you go, stupid Amir! Now you're a murderer, too. She claimed it was two months old."

He gently leads Khazar to their table and gulps down his drink. The girl does, too. Her face has an icy look that is impossible to read. They return to the dance floor.

"We stayed together for a few months. I was a mess, but I pretended I was happy. I've never told anyone any of this. A solid man, husband material, cuckolded! One day I saw her bankbook. There it was, thirty thousand tomans, deposited a few days after I had given her the check, still there in

her account. She had no shame. . . . She said she loved me, therefore what she had done wasn't bad—faking a pregnancy so that we would get married."

Khazar moves completely into his arms.

"If I were the Shah," he says, "I would decree a national day when all the girls in the country will be allowed to lose their virginity if they want to. So that at least one country will be free of the hassle of this good-for-nothing hymen. . . . "

> *«I know what is happening. And I no longer mind if it happens. Maybe I only want to put my head on her shoulder. In fact, not too tall, not too short, her shoulders are just where I can comfortably rest my forehead, and it is very right, she is the one . . . smoke and the smell of alcohol and sweat from dancing, the horny glow of Kazbah's lights reflecting off half-empty wine glasses, moving faces and mouths, hair getting tucked behind ears so that with sexy swings it can again cascade onto half-naked breasts, hands confident of money, beckoning waiters, the gleam of teeth that shine red or purple under the dance floor lights, cigarette smoke eerily spiraling in the diagonal blades of light. . . . It was amateurish the way I threw back those drinks. I'm afraid scotch will fill my eyes and with the slightest pressure from my eyelids her shoulder will get wet.»*

"Khazar, do you understand what I'm trying to say? I made myself. When I was fifteen or sixteen, when I began to understand what a bogus God they have created for us, I started making myself. I even built my body so that it wouldn't be ugly. I didn't waste my time. I taught myself a lot of things and I was clever enough not to let anyone find out. I wanted to be a perfect man for the woman I was creating piece by piece in my mind. That is why I'm a winner in so many areas. But sometimes I intentionally lose so that my friends don't hate me. . . . Do you know what I mean? I'm the one who should be afraid of people."

"Fine! Fine! This is me you are talking to, relax, you don't need to lay it on so thick."

He didn't expect it. The comfort of Khazar's delicate fingers running through the hair on the back of his head. Her Vivre perfume, rain-washed, the damp has deepened the scent of her skin and hair. Now, her gaze is no longer evasive. Her eyes look deep into his, for as long as he stares into them. . . .

The solid muscles in his arms, touching Khazar's slim and fragile arms. . . .

He wonders whether his open demeanor and the pouring out of his heart are just new ploys to get Khazar under him tonight, or if they're sincere.

Khazar puts her finger on his lips.

"My parents are now sitting at home with their eyes glued to the door. I have never stayed out this late without calling them. I will stay another hour, but for God's sake let's not talk about sad things. I don't mean we should be giddy airheads, but just for tonight, let's talk about other things, even childish things."

"Poetic? Sentimental?"

"No, simple things. For example, let's be jealous of the color blue and talk behind its back . . . or something even sillier. . . . I'm starting to feel anxious, and then I will get depressed. Don't let me get depressed, it will be dreadful."

He holds Khazar closer. Serge is standing at the edge of the dance floor, watching the couples. He is wearing one of his youngish outfits—a snug, pistachio-green zip-up jacket and tight jeans that cling to his skinny legs.

"This guy Serge is quick to tell apart the lovers from the lusters. He likes it when they ask for an artsy song. He loves it when two people who look beautiful together enjoy his music. I think he is playing more slow songs than usual just for us."

The Armenian is standing there holding a half-empty bottle of Arak 55. Amir has never seen the Khayyam of Disco touch alcohol while working. He slowly leads Khazar toward him. Serge startles the crowd, shouting,

"Dance as much as you can, young frolickers! The booze joints are up in flames; the smolder and smoke of the dance clubs have reached the Kingdom of Heaven. One of these days, the zealous brothers of Islam will burn down Kazbah, too."

"Talk of the revolution? Here?" Khazar snickers. "What do these people know about the revolution?"

Not liking the change in subject, Amir says, "Don't dish out slogans! I like it. The old man has lost it. I like it!"

Serge takes a sip from his bottle and wipes his mouth with the back of his hand. He snaps his fingers and a new song starts.

"Guess what this song is?" Amir asks.

"Don't test me. Imagine, John Lennon. . . . "

Serge roars, "Water does not hear its own whoosh as it flows. It makes no difference if you hear it or not. Whether you are fooled or not, there is nothing you can do. Sodom's penance is flying in the sky over Tehran."

> *«He is right. Something is flying in the sky over Tehran. For some time now, I've been feeling an uneasiness in the pit of my stomach. Out on the streets, I have seen rocks and broken glass, white dust from tear gas, burnt cars, and the stains of scorched tires on the asphalt that look like festering wounds. Thick layers of soot on the facades of torched banks and above the entrance of Cinema Diamond. There is no movie poster on its large billboard anymore. It is charred. Something serious is brewing.»*

Serge holds his arms wide open, like a prophet proclaiming his calling. "Whether you like it or not, Davālpā is sitting on your shoulders. . . . Fortunate are those bereft of soul. Muslims, Judgment Day is coming! Freedom will rain from the sky, the sun will come close, and our eyes and brains will boil. Every man will run to save himself. He will know neither kin nor lover."

With his arms still held out, he looks around for his bottle's cap. It has rolled onto the dance floor and gets crushed under someone's foot.

At the far end of the hall, someone woozily shouts, "Mr. Serge! Just this one night, don't make us remember. Play a Persian 6/8 song for the pretty ones to dance."

"Their numbers are growing by the day," Serge yells even louder. "They burn everything and advance . . . they will start killing lovers. . . . "

Kazbah's manager walks over to Serge and, with a ceremonious smile, motions to him. Serge surrenders his bottle and tries to regain his composure. The song ends. Again, Moses-like, he raises his arms for another song to rumble from between the Nile's legs.

Khazar and Amir are now close to Serge. He looks serious and sad again.

"Hey, Amir! It looks like you finally found your soul mate."

"Sage! You see only her hair, I see its curls, too."

"I don't know about her soul and spirit. . . . Let me see your eyes, sweetie! . . . come on, don't be shy . . . look into my eyes for a second!"

> *«Khazar looks into his eyes. Serge seems startled. His eyes, always bloodshot from smoking weed, look chillingly wild. Khazar is afraid, she is clinging to me. I should lead her away as we dance.»*

" . . . and her name?"

"Forget it, Mr. Serge."

They step away from him, but Serge follows them onto the dance floor.

"Ask her to request a song. Ask her, for the love of whoever she loves . . . I want her to . . . I want her to ask me to play a song."

Khazar asks for I Started a Joke. In Serge's eyes, still fixed on her, there is sadness, or fear, or torment, or perhaps even hatred. With his shoulders drooping, he walks away and plays the song. The delicate tenderness of Khazar's bones tempts Amir to squeeze her in his arms, hard, so hard that her fear and her bones might crush together. He wants and he does not want.

Khazar's expression has changed.

"It was as if he was looking at a ghost," she says. "Let's leave."

"No, we are just starting to. . . . "

"He is so miserable. I have never seen anyone look so lonely. I don't want him to suffer. Amir, please, let's go."

They walk out. They stroll a few meters down the sidewalk and reach Pahlavi Avenue. They are crossing the street when a white Paykan speeds by, almost brushing against them. In the halo of light from a streetlamp, Amir catches a glimpse of the man in the passenger seat, leaning his head against the window, his face white as chalk. . . . The car disappears in the shadows of the old sycamore trees flanking the avenue.

"Did you see him?" Khazar asks.

"What if it was Serge!"

"Stop joking. Did you see him?"

"Yes. Someone going home bushed and exhausted after a long day's work."

"No. I got a good look at him . . . from the chest down, he was soaked in blood."

"In this light, how could you tell it was blood?"

"It was. On a white shirt blood looks like blood. He was taking his last breaths. He was looking at us."

"He was just jealous of me."

"I'm sure he'd been shot."

"Then he must be a thief. The police shot him and he escaped."

"Thieves don't drive around the streets at this hour of the night. His friend was driving around so the guy won't be alone when he finishes. Then he'll dump his body somewhere and get himself to a safe house."

The wind has torn a few leftover autumn leaves from the trees and scattered them on the car. He opens the door for Khazar, but she doesn't climb in. In her misty eyes, he sees the glint of a tear that will not fall.

"He was a guerrilla fighter. I am sure. SAVAK agents shot him. His friend couldn't take him to a safe house half-dead."

"Even if he was a guerrilla, what does it have to do with you, rich kid? And what does it have to do with a good-for-nothing like me? What you paid for the clothes you are wearing is what they live on for a year."

He puts his hand on Khazar's shoulder and gently pushes her to get into the car.

He starts the engine and thinks, Sometimes life is like right now—it is cold and you have to drive until the heater warms up, like Khazar is right now.

And Khazar says, "Tonight, while we were eating, drinking, and dancing, what went on in this city? We are so out of touch. There are so many secrets in this city that we. . . . You're right, we really are good-for-nothings."

"Don't start talking about the guerrillas and the student tortures. We are good-for-nothings, but we like being good-for-nothings, and we like the good-for-nothing money in our pockets. Get it?"

"He was badly wounded. He knew he was dying. He looked at me to see if I realized he was dying."

"You saw his wound, but you and I are wounded, too. We don't know it because our wounds are still fresh."

"Once we accept that we are good-for-nothings, the rest of this good-for-nothing life should be easy and straightforward."

And he sees Khazar with a desolate look in her eyes and her shoulders no longer proud, staring straight ahead.

He's itching to find some excuse to lure the girl to the apartment he shares with Kaveh.

> *«Kaveh, you whore! From now on, we will call the apartment The Riverbank. And from now on, we will go after girls who lead a guy to the river, but send him back thirsty. Screwing them is a treat. . . . Don't come home tonight. I'm bringing one over. She won't come in if she sees you there.»*

He smells surrender on Khazar's skin. And he knows that in the state she is in, the girl will not resist. . . .

> *«Like a poker player who has so little left that he's embarrassed to say "all-in," and instead says "all that's left," and he says it knowing he is going to lose. . . . Hair, pubic hair against pubic hair . . . river . . . river-bank . . . even Khazar, with all her airs, deep in her heart she wants me to take her to the river and give her one hell of a swimming lesson . . . strand against strand . . . saffron against saffron . . . sucking her small, firm breasts that, unlike large ones, my hands can completely cover . . . I have always liked large breasts, but now I seem to crave only those like hers . . . the wetness of my lips, a feather, the warmth of my lips, a feather, silky, subtle, like a ghost, brushing over an unripe cherry and its torturous halo. She is yearning for a strong touch, but no . . . a butterfly, fluttering, the faint brush of its wings against a flower, a soft stroke on the petals, and nothing more. And then to move to the small cherry's mate, and just like this, a butterfly in the end sits on the flower it wants to consume and penetrates it . . . the rest, I will learn from her body. How she wants it, what gives her pleasure. A woman's personality reveals the shape of her inner and outer petals. I can tell that Khazar's four petals are neither plump, nor thin, they are elongated. The outer earth and fire, like two slices of apple, veil the inner water and wind, pearly and smooth. Perhaps they are protecting you. Strand against strand . . . I will drive her to such frenzy that her dew will trickle . . . pubic hair against pubic hair . . . I don't have the letter K on my list. I will add it tonight.»*

The wind and rain toss a wet leaf on the windshield. The wipers push it to the lower corner of the glass and crush it.

"You are right," Khazar whispers. "Someone has to get shot, someone else has to drink a shot. . . . Take me to where you have taken me a hundred times in your imagination."

She is biting her lower lip so hard, as if she wants to suck its blood.

Suddenly edgy and shaking, she shouts, "Well take this whore and open her, too! Slam down on the gas! Slam down on the gas, you good-for-nothing, so we get there faster, faster so you can slam down on me as much as your back can take."

He can't tell if Khazar is drunk or not. He floors the gas pedal. Wildly, with no dread of the wet asphalt, without a tap on the brake, he swerves through the late-night traffic. He drives to Khazar's house. Waiting for the girl, the virgin girl, to go in, he thinks, It's not so bad. And now, it is just him and his Alfa, his friend in solitude. He'll drive to the north of Yousef-Abad, to the road with an almost ninety-degree turn, so that right before it he can speed up, hoping he'll have the nerve to make the turn without braking, and break the madness of his sixty-mile-an-hour record. It is just like fingering death. And he likes it.

In the doorway of her house, Khazar does not turn to smile or even to wave to him. She goes in. And he beats his fist between his legs.

The scribe on his right shoulder writes:

He sees himself . . .

He is sitting high on a mountain peak; the wind blows snakeskins that have been shed and abandoned in the valleys and beats them against his face and body. He feels the chill of their decomposing scales. . . .

He recalls how he felt up on the mountaintop when his misery's sole consolation was the mule led by two soldiers that would bring rations, letters, and care packages sent to the soldiers at the front. Those plastic parcels had a different smell and color than the standard camouflage khaki. He enjoyed the indulgences they offered. He remembers there were cookies, mixed nuts that were meant as cure-alls, colorful socks and gloves that a woman somewhere had knitted for the country's fighters who readily sacrificed their lives. And once in a while, there were sloganeering letters of encouragement. He does not remember complaining that the sergeant majors at headquarters would take the best of the lot and give them as gifts to their wives and children when they went on leave, and passed down the remainder to sergeants at the depot, who in turn only gave the soldiers their leftovers.

And from high up he sees . . .

> «Which peak was it? The Devil Worshiper's Peak? Or was it somewhere in Bazi Deraz? . . . »

The wind and sun are taking the scattered shadows of moonlight-colored clouds far away, across the ridges and crests of the mountains and over the sprawling plains. And from the sunny slopes he hears the echo of his own voice crying out a name.

The scribe on his left shoulder had written:

He shouts into the mouthpiece of the wireless radio, "Open fire!"

An Iranian mortar shell whirs as it flies overhead. He presses the binoculars to his eyes. The Iraqi IFA on the dirt road has picked up speed. Behind it clouds mushroom into the air from the explosions of the three shells he has directed at it. Now, another one explodes close to the IFA and hurls it off the road. The personnel carrier flips onto its side on a dune with its legs in the air. He assumes there are soldiers riding in the back, but no one climbs out. He directs three more shells at it. The shrapnel will disable anyone who might have survived in there. . . . And no one crawls out.

Left:

More than a half hour has passed and no soldiers have emerged from the IFA. But he thinks he sees cigarette smoke intermittently blowing out of its front window. Perhaps a wounded soldier has regained consciousness and has reached into his pocket, or the pocket of the man next to him, to savor a smoke.

"Shall I send you another one to ruin your rapture? . . . Or should I wait until you crawl out?"

Right:

It is growing dark. Again he turns his binoculars toward the overturned IFA. No, no one has emerged from it, and there is no cigarette smoke blowing out.

> «It is the first time I've seen that I have killed. . . . I've always directed mortar and cannon shells behind a hill or a mountain,

far away, not knowing the result. This is the first time I see that I have killed . . . »

He feels elated. He feels a certain lightness.

The scribe on his left shoulder had written:

He relishes the lightness he feels. As is his habit, he is sleeping to the left of the woman. Through the curtains, a sliver of moonlight shines on the wall, bending on the edge of the ceiling.

He thinks, Why are the dark patches of the seas and craters on the moon not reflected in moonlight?

He looks at his neither dark nor pale arm. The closest color he can think of is bronze.

« . . . only a bronze man can say that some have the consistency of mercury—metallic and liquid and just as deceiving. Firm, fleshy protrusions for the wanderings of a hand and the indulgence of its palm. The most pleasurable and appealing convexes and concaves to embrace and to release one's weight on. But some taste like quicklime—they burn or rot. Some are pure copper; they are supple and have the blood of seaside desires in them. They soften and yield with the slightest heat. All are what they are, but none are gold, and if there is one that is gold, then gold is peace and an end to wandering and searching, and a man can quiet down at the end of wherever he is, no longer needing to sniff at this and that door like a stray dog, panting for a piece of meat, copulating wherever he can. . . . It is good to be a stray dog, but not when the male dog is so large when hard and the female dog so tight that they become wedged together. Fused. Morning comes. People leave their homes. They see them. They laugh and throw rocks at them so that they separate, and bearing the pain of the rocks, the dogs try to run and they can't, because it hurts when they struggle to pull away from each other; they cannot separate.»

The scribe on his right shoulder writes:

A wall clock has been added to his deliberately bare room. It is 6:05. He guesses that the clock is Reyhaneh's doing. He suspects that his Reyha is drop-by-drop returning him to a normal life. He looks again and it is 6:30. From the window he sees Agha Haji walking to his car. He has aged. His short hair is whiter than salt-and-pepper and his shoulders have drooped. He bends down and picks up a piece of bread from the ground. He kisses it, touches it to his forehead, and with reverence places it at the foot of the eucalyptus tree. "Bread is the blessing of a spread; one should not treat it ungratefully." He watches Agha Haji's car rolling toward the garden gates. One of the guards climbs into it.

> «The hypocrite swine still drives that dilapidated Paykan to hide the fact that he is wealthy. He will be gone until evening. I'd better go for a stroll in the garden before the fog sets in.»

And from up in his room, which he has nicknamed "the observation post," he sees Shahu, the gardener, roaming around the plot of cherry trees. He thinks, What if the old man is searching for the same thing I have been looking for in the garden and I don't even know what it is?

He gently knocks on Reyhaneh's door. The curve of her white shoulder appears in the opening. Her large, dark eyes, glazed with sleep, are not sure whether they should open wide or stay almond-shaped.

"Shall we go for a walk in the garden?"

Right:

Reyhaneh comes out wearing jeans and a headscarf. They climb down the stairs and see Mother through the glass panel in the living-room door. She is sitting cross-legged on the floor, next to the dining cloth set with breakfast. She looks like she is grieving. Amir feels his mind working like a Swiss watch. He tells himself, These mothers, these women, when they can't bully you, they force you into submission with their tears and fake frailty. But once they get their way, they will wrap your shorts around your head like a turban. Do not be fooled!

Without stopping, he says a passing hello.

There is a sad expectation in Mother's eyes. Dressed in black, with the weight of her former beauty sunk into her fifty-year-old cheeks and neck. Her well-proportioned shoulders have shrunk, too. The same shoulders that in the old days when Amir was in a good mood he would point to and say, "Mrs. Mom, instead of hiding your beautiful chest and shoulders under a chador, you should wear a *décolleté* dress and let your beautiful skin shine. The pious believers' eyes will pop out of their heads. I swear, it will do more to deepen their faith in God's power than if you were to preach to them."

Mother would bite the skin between her thumb and index finger and pretend that her son had blasphemed. And Amir would snap his fingers and say, "Naughty, Mrs. Haji! You didn't ask me what *décolleté* means. Spending all your time going to prayer ceremonies, how do you know what it means?"

And he realizes that the sadness in Mother's eyes is the longing for the exchange of just a few words with her son. Since being brought back to the house, he has avoided it. He goes back to the living room door and says, "How are you, Mom?"

The woman's dark, doe eyes take on the gleam of pure ebony. She smiles. She looks down.

"Oh, thank God. So, you actually care?"

"You thank God and make a wisecrack in the same breath? Why should I inquire about your well-being? You did what you wanted to do. The truth is, you kidnapped me, you dragged me to this miserable place while I was unconscious. I was happy in that nuthouse. . . . Well, now you should be laughing and dancing with joy. . . . Do you know how to dance?"

Mother grabs the folds of her chador spread around her on the floor and runs to the kitchen. Ordinarily, he would now hear her stifled sobs, but he does not.

Outside the house, he picks up a pebble and throws it at the Alfa Romeo. There are and there are not clouds in the sky. There is and there is not the perfume of winter sweet flowers in the air. There is and there is not the tick tock of a clock. There is the smell of dead leaves fermenting and there is no cuckoo of a cuckoo bird.

"You really have a heart of stone. Would it have killed you to say hello to her like a human being? Every morning she sets the breakfast spread, hoping that you will come downstairs and sit with her and eat. Agha Haji eats and leaves. I eat and leave. Then it is just Mom sitting there with the leftovers for you and her. I wish you had died and they had delivered your corpse to us. It would have been easier to visit your grave once a week."

He thinks, Reyhaneh must have gotten up on the wrong side of the bed this morning. No, today she is not my Reyha. If I do something to make her feel sorry for me, she will be kind again. . . . The wheel tracks of Agha Haji's car on the gravel . . . the sound of the gravel under my shoes. . . .

It seems Reyhaneh feels as sorry for the two of them as he does.

"How do I manage to put on my shoes?" he says.

"Ever since Agha Haji hired the guards, I don't feel comfortable in the garden. One of them is always up and about. Don't get into a yakkety-yak with them and drive them nuts! They are armed. Sometimes I think even Agha Haji is intimidated by them."

> «This is all they are good for, to make my miserable, saffron-grinding sister wear her hijab even in the garden.»

"Why did he hire guards?"

"I don't know. He won't say. Important people, people who run the risk of being assassinated, have guards."

Floating in the yellow hue of the winter sweet flowers and their reverberating scent, they reach the cherry trees. Reyhaneh points to the Khezr cherry tree.

"Do you remember His Holiness Khezr?"

"No."

And to complete his lie, he stares at the tree and frowns.

"It blossoms earlier than the other cherry trees, and its leaves fall later. Baba Shahu gave it its name."

"Given that I am alive, why is Mom still wearing black? Make her stop."

"Why don't you tell her yourself?"

"I will. I'm just afraid it will be too late by the time I can say it."

"Mom is very patient. She wanted me to tell you, and Agha Haji also said that I should tell you. . . . "

"Stop calling him Agha Haji! It pisses me off. Why can't we call him Dad, or Father, or just call him by his lousy name?"

"Why are you barking at me? Why do I have to answer for everything? Why don't you ask yourself the same question? You used to call him Agha Haji, too."

"I was an ass. I didn't know any better."

"That's not my problem. You are only bold and daring when you are dealing with Mom and me. . . . Ugh! Will you let me finish what I was saying or not?"

In the distance, among the trees to the right of the garden, he sees cottony clusters of fog dawning. He cannot tell his fortune with them. Abu-Yahya is not there.

"I was saying . . . they want me to tell you that these days they make very good prosthetic arms, very advanced. Would you like us to get one for you?"

"I didn't piss on my arm to replace it with a fake one."

Left:

"Now, give me an answer. Why did you get rid of all the junk I had in my room?"

In a playful or perhaps calculated tone, or maybe out of exasperation over his insistence, Reyhaneh says, "How do you know I got rid of your things? Maybe I hid them."

"Show them to me . . . in the family album there are only a handful of my grade school photos with my head shaved, my ID card photos, you in a chador at some wedding, and other junk. Don't we have a single normal photograph?"

"That's all there is. I am a devout daughter. It is unseemly for me to keep photos that have men in them who are not my kin."

"You are lying. You are not my sister if you think I don't know you're lying. Nutcases can smell a liar better than anyone."

Reyhaneh sulks. Still walking together, they have almost reached the end of the path. Silently, they turn and walk back.

His mind fixates again, as it does on an image or a sound and then the whirling whirlwind of thoughts . . .

> *«It was a mistake to let on that I can detect their lies. The more they think I am a stupid nutcase, the better. If they become certain that I understand, they will close their fists and not show their hand. . . . »*

He takes on a sympathy-seeking tone of regret.

"I'm sorry, I was out of line. Memories of war invade my head like the Mongol army and drive me crazy. They make me want to run away from myself. I had gotten it into my head that the best and the worst soldiers are

those whose corpses remain at the front forever. Me, having returned like this, with my brain and my arm crippled, it's obvious I was no big shot."

"Don't talk like that . . . tell me everything you remember. How many times do I have to tell you? I like it when you talk to me."

He's discovered that when he repeats the bits and pieces of his memories to himself or to Reyhaneh, he remembers them later in a more organized sequence.

> *«We're passing the plot of almond trees again. . . . A long time ago, Reyhaneh told me, "I like it when you talk to me. You have lived in a world that I have never even dreamed of. . . . "»*

"Rain was a nasty nuisance. . . . Once in a while, for some reason that I now can't remember, I wasn't up there . . . I remember once, our detachment was transferred to a new battle line in a mountain range . . . on the other side of a mountain they called . . . something, I can't remember the name . . . the soldiers had to . . . it was almost impossible to dig trenches in the mountain. You hit rock very quickly. The spades the army issues, their good-for-nothing handles break off easily. The most important thing to have was burlap sacks. They were scarce. For each trench they would allot ten or fifteen, which wasn't enough for even one row of sandbags. They would give each trench a few L-shaped girders to put over the ditch, and there were thin corrugated metal sheets to lay on top of them. When the Iraqis could not build concrete trenches, they would take steel beams from the houses in towns they had taken over and use them to cover their trenches. But we, if a mortar shell . . . the good-for-nothing Iraqis' constant shelling didn't even give our soldiers time to dig trenches . . . they hit us constantly. If a shell hit our trench, we would be minced meat. Let me tell you about rain—the worst was when it rained. The old hands knew how to cover the corrugated sheets with plastic so that water would not get into the trenches. They would make a slanted dirt mound on the roof . . . I remember, in the army they call this side of the mountain the counterslope . . . now, thinking of counter-slopes. . . . "

"The rain."

"Rain turns into mud and sludge at the foot of the mountain, even the latrine overflows, crap and filth stick like glue, good-for-nothing boots get heavy and sometimes when they sink into the muck you can't pull them out. Then they gave us these cheap plastic boots, but not enough for everyone. The higher-ups would swipe them. The boots did well in the mess after rain. Mud doesn't stick to black plastic. Now I remember what I wanted to remind myself—even at the front I couldn't get Agha Haji out of my head. Those plastic boots constantly reminded me of Tehran's bazaar and how Agha Haji would force me to go to his trade chamber when I was a boy. There were stores that sold those boots to the peasants. . . . That's it about the rain, but I also wanted to remind myself of that burned village so that I would remember . . . it's in the mountains . . . not Dalaho, but . . . yes, we were further ahead, there was a village on the mountainside that had been burned down. Hossein said he had seen a first-rate wood beam on the roof of one of the houses—it was intact. Thicker than our railroad crossties, which the Iraqis would take to use as trench covers. The village had been ravaged. There was still soot on the collapsed walls. We went down the mountain with Hossein's trench mates. They started breaking down the supporting wall that the beam was on. Maybe it was there that I saw a stray dog digging in the ground. The Iraqis had attacked without warning and the villagers had run away, leaving behind their dogs and sheep. The dogs had turned into corpse-eaters. As that dog dug deeper, the sound of a herd of sheep coming back from grazing rang out from the hole. You know?! When sheep return from grazing, their udders full of milk, they start bleating to their lambs as they get closer to the village. And the lambs in the pen start bleating, too . . . the world fills with bleating. The sheep know the way to their pen and just walk in through the open gate. I saw a soldier yank a door out of the wall. And there was more and more the sound of the soldiers kicking the wall, and I could hear the lambs slurping milk. At one point, I saw that a second dog had come over. The two of them were fighting. One of them dug up an arm bone that still had bits of flesh stuck to it, the dog grabbed it between

its teeth and ran off. Perhaps the dog had buried it there earlier. Dogs have a doggedly good memory. I don't know if it was then that the sounds in my head started; or was it later?"

He doesn't let on that he isn't sure whether he saw the scene with the dogs in that village or someplace else, or that the dog and the arm bone may have arisen from one of the blistering waves in his mind.

Of course, he only saw a dog digging in the ground.

But there was a mysterious piece of bone. . . . He feels another disgusting ants' nest in his head—the empty place of a memory he used to remember.

"Something has been hidden for me somewhere in this garden. If I find it, I will be well again."

He veers off the path. From between the winter sweet bushes he crosses over to the plot of apple trees, toward the fog. He carefully looks at the layers of wet leaves carpeting the ground. Reyhaneh keeps an eye on him from a distance.

> *«I should remember and not forget, the hut on the right, the one with the ramshackle gabled roof, belongs to Baba Shahu. The larger, new one on the left belongs to the guards. Its windows are smoky today. I know that at this very moment they are watching me, so that they can report my every move to Agha Haji. One day when I am better, I will bang on their window and say, You goons get paid to keep watch on the outside of the garden from the inside, not keep watch on the inside of the garden from the inside. . . .*
>
> *And this garden that has fallen under a spell, why does it seem neglected? The leaves the wind has caused to fall from the trees, the wind has piled up at their feet. The ground is covered with leaves and rotten apples and dead branches that have fused and molded. There are dried-up weeds everywhere. If anything has been hidden under this rotting carpet, who can know where? . . . I should grab Shahu by the collar and confront*

> *him, What's with you, old man? Don't you get paid to take care of the garden? Or do you expect one-armed me to do the work?»*

Under the weight of his feet, he hears something breaking.

> *«Was it a branch or a bone?»*

He bends down. Large, red, and fresh, its cluster of stamen still in its calyx.

He goes back to look for Reyhaneh.

"Do we have pomegranate trees in the garden?"

"No."

"Then what is this doing here?"

"How should I know? Legend has it that the pomegranate is a heavenly fruit. Maybe it was sent to you from heaven. Someone is keeping watch over you, because you don't eat any fruits and you are going to get sick."

"Is it Mom's doing? . . . or yours?"

Reyhaneh does not answer. He can read nothing on her face.

He nestles the pomegranate between the branches of a winter sweet bush.

"The winter sweet bush has produced a pomegranate. Well, why shouldn't, for instance, an apple tree grow an eggplant? A bitter-orange tree a grenade, a green-bean bush a condom, an onion bulb a box of tissues, a cashew tree shrapnel. . . . "

There is noise outside the garden walls. Like the muddled sounds in his head, he has trouble deciphering it. It is harder to distinguish sounds in the city than it is at the front.

> *«The trees in this garden seem ashamed of their winter nakedness. They beg us not to look at them. I want to tell them, Even naked, you are beautiful. The word naked is beautiful, too. It is enticing. But these idiots don't deserve me saying such things to them. . . . Which friend was it that traveled overseas and went to a nudist island? It was Kaveh . . . Kaveh! It*

> *is wonderful that I can remember that brother-of-a-whore! Kaveh doesn't have a sister, so it's all right to call him a brother-of-a-whore. He even used to say it himself. . . . That apartment we rented for partying and fooling around. Where was it? It was somewhere in the city. . . . I've got to trick Reyha into helping me find it. . . . Was it Kaveh? He had huddled behind a rock the entire time, he was so embarrassed, because as soon as he laid eyes on a couple of naked women he got a hard-on. No, it wasn't Kaveh. It was one of those never-seen-naked-skin guys with a hang-up. The jerking-off young men of Iran. The land of kings and harems. . . . »*

"You've never told me how you were injured," Reyhaneh says. "Why did you just take off and go to war in the first place?"

He suspects Reyhaneh is baiting him to see how much he remembers. He doesn't answer her.

"If you talk about it, you will feel better, unburdened. Sacred accounts say that Imam Ali, when weary of loneliness and people's cruelty, would lower his head into a well and pour his heart out to it."

"That was someone else. And then from the water in the well a reed grew. A shepherd made a flute with it and played it, and from the holes in the flute that guy's confidences kept ringing out for everyone to hear. They grabbed the guy and arrested him. Then someone—a sovereign, a ruler, or some other good-for-nothing—ordered that the man be beheaded."

"This is me, your Reyha. You can talk to me. Tell me how you were wounded."

"I can't remember."

Sounding bitter, he is both truthful and deceitful. He is both that and this.

He is neither that nor this. He is just what he has said, "diverging streams of piss on the ground . . . the Nimrod of destinies."

No. He has said he is "the narrow parting trails on the palm of Nimrod's hand."

Reyhaneh again asks, "Then tell me about the black boots. What happened next?"

"Which black boots?"

"The rubber boots, at the front. You said they reminded you of Tehran's bazaar and Agha Haji's trade chamber. Don't you remember?"

"No."

Puzzled, Reyhaneh looks at him. She does not believe these sudden lapses in memory.

"But I do remember that he used to force me to go to his trade chamber."

"He didn't really force you. During the summer, when you were home all day, Mom would complain about your shenanigans. She used to say you sparked fires. She used to scheme to send you off with Agha so that she would be rid of you at least until evening. Of course, she killed two birds with one stone. At night she would make you tell her who had come to see Father. There were women among them. Poor Mom, she was always afraid that Agha would take a second wife or squander all his money on temporary wives. Even to this day, she is worried."

"So, be honest. How many temporary wives has our Agha Haji had?"

"I don't know. I don't think he is into those things. But I have heard that the rich bazaar merchants take four wives and as many temporary ones as they want. . . . "

Reyhaneh giggles.

"You were so dumb that all Mom had to do was promise you a *faloodeh* ice dessert and you would dish out A to Z of what Agha Haji was up to. And you had no mercy, even though every day the poor man would buy you a sour-cherry faloodeh and a saffron one, too. I was so jealous. You were clever, you ate from both the feed bag and the trough."

He likes Reyhaneh's rare, distant smiles. He looks at her and feels sad.

> «My poor stay-at-home sister, her laughter, how rarely I remember her laughing. Going to a thousand mourning ceremonies for the thousand sons of the thousand sons of whoever, crying at mosques and burials and funerals, beating her chest under her chador, praying for forgiveness for uncommitted sins, and now, how very rarely she laughs, how very rarely she has occasion to laugh, most of the time she probably doesn't remember laughter at all. The corners of her lips have drooped, but her forehead is still young. . . . How old is Reyhaneh? As far back as I can remember, she has always been there. Always in some corner of the house.»

"Agha really liked it when you went with him to the bazaar. Unlike with me, he was so proud of having a son. When you were a young boy, he loved it when you held his hand and walked along the alleys around the bazaar or went to religious ceremonies and commemoration dinners with him. When you two walked in, everyone stood up in respect, put their hands on their chests in deference, and asked if you were the gentleman's son, and he would nod and say you were their obeisant. Later, when a little fuzz grew on your face and you no longer took his hand, he would hold his head so high, as if Prince Jamshid was walking with him. Up until you were fifteen or sixteen, you were obedient. You were at his side for evening prayers at the mosque and mourning ceremonies for Imam Hossein."

A grin brings out the natural rosy color of Reyhaneh's lips.

"Later, starting with your last year in high school, you began to change. At home, Father was always complaining because you had stopped saying your prayers. And forget about when you started university! You went to extremes. Agha tried to ignore it all, hoping that you would eventually mend your ways. . . . Do you remember any of this?"

". . . What did I do that you say I went to extremes?"

"Things that were beneath the Yamini family."

"Is that why he had me flogged?"

"No. Do you really want to claim you don't remember that either?"

"I do and I don't. Tell me."

"None of us had ever seen you like that. Mom and I sensed that occasionally you drank a little. Nights that you didn't stay at your bachelor pad, you would sneak into the house and go up to your room. But that night you were really wasted. No matter how much we begged, you would not go up to your room. Like a lunatic, you yelled and shouted until Agha walked in. You threw up in the living room. You were cursing at the earth and the sky, at God and the Prophet. Cursing all pregnant girls, vulgarly."

"Why pregnant girls?"

Reyhaneh hesitates, then speaks.

"I don't know. How would I know? Chalk it up to your craziness that night. Agha grabbed you to throw you out of the house, you shoved him, he fell. He was about to have a heart attack. He could not believe that his son had raised his hand to him. Mom and I were weeping. You broke everything you could get your hands on. Even the china vase that was part of Mom's dowry . . . then you sat in your vomit and started to cry. Agha Haji called his friends at the neighborhood Revolutionary Guard station. They came with Kalashnikovs to take you away. You got into a scuffle with them, too. You were cursing and throwing punches at them. They kept their respect for Agha Haji's son for a while, but in the end they dragged you away in handcuffs. Agha was shamed and disgraced."

"No, to the contrary, he proved his piety even more fully. Wasn't there a mullah who turned in his son to be executed and then fasted in gratitude to God? When the likes of them show their faith and devoutness like this, they get a lot of leeway for their scammings and swindlings."

"Agha Haji aged overnight. He lost the little spirit he had left. He used to take Mom and me to the riverside in Karaj, where our uncles' families would gather on Fridays, but he stopped doing even that. You were set free and Mom and I became even more imprisoned in this house."

"He was always unfair."

"Don't be so cynical. When you were under arrest, Mom was killing herself crying. Agha said he had sent word to you that if in court you denied that you had been drinking, they would not flog you. But even after you sobered up you still acted crazy."

"So I was nuts even before the shell shock. That's just great!"

"You were obstinate. You cursed at the Revolutionary Guards. You called the judge a lice-ridden mullah and told him, 'Why don't you take all the money you have pilfered and go live next to your God's home in Saudi Arabia.' You told him, 'If you're a real man then why don't you give me a sip of the booze you have in your back pocket.'"

"Did I really say all that?"

"Yes. Agha Haji got news of you every day."

"Good for me!"

"If it were not for Agha Haji pulling strings, they would have probably executed you."

"How many lashes does religious law decree as punishment for being drunk?"

"I think eighty."

"Why did I do all those things?"

Reyhaneh does not answer. She leans over a winter sweet bush and smells the flowers. Two locks of her hair spread on the leafless branches. He imagines that from her hair touching the bush, the yellowness of the winter sweet flowers will permeate her body. . . .

"I asked you, what the heck was wrong with me?"

"I don't know."

He growls, "Lying has made you turn yellow. How many times have you rehearsed this story?"

He is filled with rage. His arm feels strong. He senses the skin on Reyhaneh's arm bruising under his grip. He shakes her.

"I want to know how much Agha Haji has paid you to fabricate these lies, to take his side. You have turned yellow with lies."

A clot like eye gum congeals in the corner of his mouth.

"You are an idiot for thinking that I am lying to you. You really are an idiot. I have relived your night of drunkenness a hundred times in my sleep and wakeful hours. It seems like it was only last night. For an entire year, the doctor had me taking pills to calm my nerves."

He pulls her to him. With his face close to hers and spit flying from his mouth, he shouts, "Did he come, too?"

"Where?"

"Did you know they were going to flog me?"

Reyhaneh turns away. She struggles to free her arm from his clasp.

"Did you and Mom come, too?"

Bursting into tears, Reyhaneh screams, "You are mad! You are mad!"

Sobbing, she runs toward the house. The jelly-like bouncing of her round behind prominent in her jeans . . . he imagines a mass of winter sweet perfume being dragged along behind the girl.

Left:

> *«Even with Reyhaneh gone, I will not leave the garden alone.»*

From the corner of his eyes, he glances at the guards' large hut, and then at the half-open door of Shahu's hut, where, as in the past, he hears the sound of a water pipe being lovingly smoked.

> *«I have to find Kaveh. He was my friend through it all. He must know who I played ring games with, if in fact I did. That brother-of-a-whore will tease me when he sees me like this, one-armed. I can find that apartment if I search the city.»*

On his right:

Last night's rainwater has remained stagnant in the waterway alongside the path.

He sees a river somewhere making a wide turn and stretching into the distance. It has vomited all the rusty and shiny hooks fishermen have lost over the years and spat them out on its banks.

As in the past, his not entirely released anger has aroused him. So much so that he feels its stir and weight below his stomach.

Left:

> *«Gaping, the open beaks of cuckoo chicks, wide with hunger in the nest, the color inside their beaks. . . . I cannot do much with this left arm that has been circumcised too short. In my olden-days bed, I would loop my right arm under their neck so that I could reach their right breast, and the cobra, my left arm, free to slither wherever it wanted, my left hand discovering the folds, pleats, lines, awakening their recessed or curved timidities, the hidden petals that inside the trench of the outer lips lie in wait for pleasure. To lure them out, open them, open, and with three fingers more so. The reddish pink of two delicate petals, the color inside the beaks of a hungry cuckoo chick waiting for mother to feed it a worm. Now that my left hand is lost somewhere on whichever mountain, if my right hand wanders around a breast, I have no left hand with which to finish the woman's unfinished gratification. . . . »*

The scribe on his right shoulder had written:

The minibus stops at the MP checkpoint. The soldiers returning from leave are spiritless and glum and don't care how long they have to wait there. Through the window he watches a soldier sitting on a row of sandbags with his G3 casually leaning against them. In the summer cool of the mountains, the sun feels warm and pleasant; it tastes like pomegranate seeds in a china bowl. Bored, the soldier starts to disassemble an American grenade. Amir thinks, Being an MP at the front is safe and easy work. The bearded MP boarding the minibus eyes the passengers row after row and says, "Praise be to God for the well-being of Islam's warriors." None of the warriors repeat the praise to God. Not even the driver, who looks like an opium addict. Amir's eyes follow the MP to the back of the minibus. He sees a second lieutenant sitting in the last row. He knows him. He was one of the communists at the university. Afraid of being recognized, he is looking down.

> «Don't be afraid, friend! On some mission, you have faked your way into the army. I'm not a snitch, but if they discover you, you will be executed.»

From the bottom of the valley alongside the road, tall white poplars have reached up, their silvery leaves shimmering in the sun and the breeze.

> «The trees at the bottom of the valley. . . . »

The soldier carefully pulls the timed fuse out of the grenade and triumphantly looks up at Amir.

> «The trees at the bottom of the valley are taller than the ones higher up. »

The fuse ignites. The soldier stares in disbelief at the blood bubbling out of his finger. He puts his finger in his mouth. The redness of blood infiltrates the drab army khaki. The soldier searches the ground for the blown-off tip of his finger. He finds it. Holding it in his other hand, he looks at it and looks around, dumbfounded. His eyes meet Amir's on the other side of the minibus window. . . .

The scribe on his left shoulder writes:

Among the streaks of sounds in his ears, he hears a parrot squawking. He looks for it among the tree branches. They look opalescent. He sees no shades of green. . . .

Sometime later, he hears a whistle coming from the west side of the garden.

Someone is peeking over the garden wall. He whistles again. Amir walks toward the wall and sees a bald head glistening with beads of sweat from the effort of climbing. He knows and does not know the man. Uncle Arjang has braced his arms on the eave and his feet most likely on some stand.

"Hello!" Amir says. "What are you doing there?"

"I didn't want the dogs in the garden to see me. I hear they caught you in a nuthouse."

"I was hiding there."

"You dimwit! If you didn't want to come back to the garden of the dead, you could have come to your uncle's house. It's not like I'm dead."

"Don't put me on. Being a nutcase, how am I supposed to remember where you live?"

"Don't put on an act for me, of all people."

It seems his feet slip, he falls, and a while later his head reappears above the wall.

"I'm lucky I saw you. Your mom told me you roam around the garden in the mornings. I have been peeking in for a few days now."

"Well, come in. It's ridiculous like this. To your balls if the guards report it. Aren't you my uncle?"

"Kid! Your dad will make my sister suffer for an entire year over why she let a filthy, corrupt, boozer inside his house. But I brought you a feel-good treat."

He unties a plastic bag from around his neck.

"Can you catch it? It will break if it falls on the ground. It is the tears of Her Holiness Mary."

Out of habit, Amir holds out both arms to catch the bag. And he laughs at his drooping left sleeve.

Uncle tosses the bag to him and falls off his perch.

"Haji," he growls, "fuck your wall. . . . "

Amir catches the bag with his hand and torso. Again, Uncle's head pops up.

"It's a bottle of my own homemade arak. I figured after all this time, you must be thirsty and craving some, and I know you have no way of getting any."

"You are the best! I have always loved you."

"Stop kissing ass! It's top-notch arak. Mix it with water. It's 60-proof. Get it?"

"Get what?"

"If Haji finds out, he will send us both under the whip."

"Much obliged! Did you come to watch when I was being flogged?"

"Shame on you! If I didn't love you as much as I do, I would knot your balls into a bow."

"Are you sure you're my uncle?"

"You're a piece of work, wise guy! First you take the arak then you have your doubts? My arm is getting ripped out of its socket."

He jumps down on the ground and shouts from behind the wall, "Don't let your mom or Reyha find out. They will wrap my shorts around my head like a turban."

Amir hears a car engine start.

"If you ever feel like getting out of this dreary house, drop by your uncle's. We will have a splendid drink-fest."

He cannot remember what the outside of the garden looks like—when they brought him back, he was sluggish and sleepy from the strong sedatives.

There is an old image in his head. A narrow, paved road running through cotton fields, stretching as far as the distant houses on the outskirts of Tehran.

Holding a pot of half-dried geraniums in his arm, with the plastic bag tucked behind it, he returns to his room. He strokes the flower's green stem and the two dry stubs from cuttings.

> *«Which one of you will win?»*

He stuffs the bottle of arak in the pocket of a coat hanging in his closet.

On his right:

> «What is wrong with Reyhaneh now? She won't show herself. »

He sits on the edge of his bed. He thinks if he calls his sister in his mind, it will make her come to his room. And. . . .

> «Reyha! Reyha! You should have been there! What a day today was with that butterfly. This is why you have stayed ignorant and naive. You should have come out to see the butterfly. It was sitting right there, in a safe spot between a branch and the trunk of a cherry tree. I stood there like stone so that I would not scare it away. Or perhaps it was not afraid of me. It could see me—it was saying, "Hey, cripple, you are harmless." I hadn't seen its kind before. It was beautiful. It had seven colors, and designs like a Persian carpet. I don't know how long it was before the butterfly fluttered its wings seven times and threw them down. Now, it looked like a worm. A mean little sparrow came and sat on the branch to catch it. I scared it away. I put the butterfly's wings in my pocket. Then the wind blew away its antennae. It slithered. Not like a snake. It slithered beautifully. Then in a cleft on the branch it started weaving a cocoon around itself. It wove and wove and then I think it

started getting smaller. The butterfly wove a cocoon around itself, the butterfly turned into a little cotton ball. . . . If I call you four more times, will you come? Reyha! . . . »

Right:

Sitting in his chair, he dreams . . .

With her back to him, Moon Brow is looking out the window. He reaches into his pocket and takes out fragments of a pair of colorful wings. Standing behind her, he leans his elbows on her shoulders and holds his hand open in front her hazy face. He smells the rippling scent of her dark, cascading hair.

"It is time for us to go to the goldsmiths at the bazaar to buy rings," he says.

The girl blows on the palm of his hand. Turquoise dust, sunflower petals, and purple fern leaves fly at the window and stick to the glass. Lapis mist, saffron and honey.

Right:

He wonders about the symbols he has found carved on a few trees in the garden. The trunks' flesh has bulged and crinkled around the marks, as if from pain—they must be old.

He recognizes Reyhaneh's knock and opens the door. The girl, frowning, hesitantly holds out a half-burned leather-bound notebook toward him.

"Your address book."

"Why won't you come in?"

"I don't want to."

He sees three dark marks on Reyhaneh's snow-white arm.

"What happened? Your arm!"

"You mean you don't remember?"

"No. What are you talking about?"

I cannot tell if he is lying or telling the truth.

I cannot tell if he is telling the truth or lying.

"You really are a lowlife!" Reyhaneh says. "Even Agha Haji has never raised a hand to me."

"What did you say?"

"I said you really are a lowlife."

"Now that you have insulted me twice, you should feel two times better. Come in!"

That warranted and unwarranted sorrow returns to his eyes.

That boyish, woman-deceiving innocence is back on his face. Perhaps Reyhaneh wants to believe him, or is confused by his behavior, or is simply looking at him with sympathy. As always. As in their childhood.

Amir reaches out for the notebook. Reyhaneh pulls it back.

"Swear on your life!"

"I will sacrifice my seventh life for you, I will even swear on my sister's life, whatever my sister wishes."

"Swear that you will never again raise your hand to me."

"I swear."

He takes the notebook. He desperately wants to open it, but he is uncomfortable doing so in front of Reyhaneh.

She scrupulously looks around and leans against the closet door. He paces the room.

"Do you remember your books?"

"I remember I had some on a couple of shelves. They are gone."

He has learned how to make Reyhaneh talk.

"Not just a few, you had a lot of them."

"Did you read them, too?"

"After they flogged you in public, Agha managed to send you to the hospital. They took you out of respect for him; otherwise they would have

sent you to prison. Mom wanted to come to weep and beg them not to whip you. I didn't let her. She would have been no match for them and it would have caused even more shame and embarrassment. We were sitting by the garden gates, helpless and grieving, when Agha Haji came back. He was mad enough to be put in chains. You always locked your bedroom door. No one knew what you kept in there. Like two terrified puppies, Mom and I pleaded with him to calm down. For the first time ever, he slapped Mom in the face, blaming her for having raised you a delinquent. He kicked open the door to your room."

"Did you read them, too?"

"He broke the closet door. My God! I could not believe that you had such a treasure trove. You happy-go-lucky spoiled brat, you had them stacked up all the way to the top of the closet. They were mostly poetry. . . . Agha was beating himself on the head and kicking the books. He kept saying that these corruptors led his son astray."

Right there, next to the closet, Reyhaneh sits on the floor. Her dark hair hides the bruises on her arm.

"Did you read them, too?"

"Once in a while, when for some reason you didn't think of me as a chaste stay-at-home sister, but a human being, you would put one of them in my room."

He sits next to her and leans against the closet door.

"What did we do to deserve all this?" he asks with a lump in his throat.

"We didn't have guards back then. With Shahu's help, they took your books, stack after stack, out to the garden. Shahu threw them on top of the pile of dry branches he always gathered at the foot of the wall. The flames were so high, blazing much higher than the garden wall. We had to step back from the heat. Agha Haji threw everything you had in the fire and declared, 'I no longer have a son. I will kill whoever speaks his name in this house.' It was the first time I saw tears in his eyes. He pretended it was from the smoke, but no, it was obvious how crushed he was. Mom and I came back inside, but he stood out there like a statue for a long time, staring at the ashes. The smoke had blown out over our cotton field."

"Books burn like human beings. It takes a while for them to catch fire, but then they burn really well."

"For a long time, burned paper rained down on the garden, on the trees. . . ."

"I saw it. So, the black soot on the wall is from my books."

Reyhaneh looks at him with surprise. In a burning voice she says, "There is no soot left on the garden wall. After all these years, all the rain and snow, there is nothing on the walls. . . . I found your address book among the burned books. Some of it survived the fire. It wasn't prudent to let you revisit your past. But seeing how you are driving yourself even crazier over that girl, I thought I should give it to you."

"There were other things in my room. What happened to them?"

"They all went missing, disappeared. Just the way you did. The coddled, pampered son got a few lashes and took off, vanished. . . . Do you know how many precious young men in this country have been flogged hundreds of times during interrogations and they have not peeped a word?"

"Perhaps you saved some other things from the fire, too? Did you?"

"Your clothes that survived Agha Haji's fire stank of smoke. We donated them to the poor, because every day, Mom would sit and smell them and weep . . . the poor thing was losing her eyesight."

"Were you jealous?"

"Huh! Jealous of you?"

He rests his forehead on his knees.

> *«What happened that suddenly everything croaked and smelled foul and went to the abyss of the forgotten?»*

"If you're sorry, then come downstairs tonight and have dinner with us."

"My appetite is better in my own room."

"Don't mourn your books. If Father had not burned them, you would have had to. About two years after the revolution, many people burned their political books and newspapers. People were being hanged simply for having

a political flier. You had some writings from the Organization of Iranian People's Fedai Guerrillas. I don't know who gave them to you."

And he sees. . . .

In the back roads and alleys of the city, charred and crumpled pieces of paper floating in the air or being toyed with by the wind blowing along the asphalt.

Reyhaneh walks out.

> *«Perhaps the burned ones fly up because they are burned. Then books have souls that fly up to the sky and their smoke gets into God's eyes because he wants there to be only one book in the world.»*

The scribe on his left shoulder had written:

He does not know what it is and how and from where it has come. . . . The soldiers enforcing martial law have melted into the ground, policemen and traffic cops have vanished, too. Tehran is in the hands of the people and the revolution. He does not understand what has happened and what is about to happen. On this twenty-third day of his daily wanderings around the city, he has arrived at Shahr-e No, the brothel district. And he is stunned. He has arrived at the fortress of prostitutes too late. Its large entrance doors have been broken down the middle, but they still hang from their hinges. Bulldozers have driven through the tall walls surrounding the area, creating openings large enough for people to walk through. Some of the houses along its two streets have been burned down, some are only half-scorched and smoke is billowing from them. The turmoil of the masses lingers in the air. The slogans they shouted and the curses they yelled are still burning on their faces.

> *«Without seeing, without hearing, I hear from the old bricks in the walls and from the smell blended with smoke, the echo of the sobs and pleas of prostitutes caught or fleeing toward the city streets.*
>
> *It is frightening.»*

There are no women left. There are men everywhere. Some peer into the houses with curiosity and laugh. Some take spoils—fans, metal beds, chairs, tea sets, even boxes of tissues. Some elaborately relate to newcomers the things they have done. . . . Then, a deep and dense commotion grows near. From the smoke and shifting ashes in an alley, a crowd pours out, chanting

"Allah-o-Akbar," roaring, carrying above their heads a burned door. There is a scorched heap on top of it. Part of the woman's hands are still on the sides of the door. The rest have been torn off. Her legs are incomplete, too. The stumps of her knees have swollen up toward the sky and fused together. Around the door, slogans and fists rise higher in the air and descend. "Death to the corrupt Shah . . . Death to America! Independence . . . Freedom . . . Islamic Republic. . . . " Very soon, other raging men make their way into the crowd and join them. They elbow each other to move up and see the immolated body, a few climb up the winter-stricken skeletons of trees for a better view. The gray, welded mass heaves, the corpse may fall at any moment. Greater and greater in number, pressed more tightly together, they move down Jamshid Avenue toward the city. Shouts of "Death to the Shah, Death to the infidel, God is great, Khomeini is the leader" move away with them.

He is still there, lost and helpless, because something is happening and he does not understand it.

«. . . How many of you have jerked off thinking of her, you whore-torchers?»

The scribe on his right shoulder writes:

He flips through the half-pages of the address book. No burned pieces fall from them. The pages corresponding to some letters are missing. It looks like G, C, H, and Kh have recently been torn out. Some names seem familiar to him. He searches for Kaveh's telephone number and the address of the apartment they shared. His name is not on the page for K. In S, in front of Shemirani, he has written, Kaveh's father. . . .

> «My handwriting wasn't bad. It has been a few years, many years, since I've written anything.»

The howl of a mortar shell reverberates under the ceiling. He throws himself to the floor and shields his head with the arms he has and does not have. A flickering image of boots flashes in his mind. Their heels and soles are tattered. The laces of a few are still tied in bows, bits of red flesh and bone stuck to them. . . .

On his right:

Lying on the floor, his right arm and the stump of his left arm around his head, a thought comes to him.

> «The head goes in first. . . . »

It is fading, this thought that I am writing. It does not form. It is unclear whether it should be written on this shoulder or on the left one.

His thought is becoming writable on this shoulder.

His wartime skills have remained in his muscles. Slumped on the floor, he presses his arms against his temples. A thought leaps into his mind.

> *«The head always goes in first, the head always comes out first. Bullet . . . cock . . . kid. . . . »*

Left:

He has not gone outside today. From the window, he inspects the garden and watches Shahu's comings and goings among the trees. It seems the old man is taking some things to burn in secret somewhere. Abu-Yahya is standing some distance away, observing Shahu with what might be disdain. Amir does not remember when it was and who it was that wrapped the bandage around his forearm. It takes him half an hour to undo the knot with his teeth and to unravel the bandage and the gauze. Finally, with sweat seeping from his seven holes, his eyes fixate on the jagged cuts. He cannot remember when it was and who it was that did this. Staring at the lines, he strains his mind until in its far corners he thinks he sees that with a knife clenched between his teeth, he had tried to carve a name on his skin.

He discovers a ladybird on the geranium's stem.

Left:

The wall clock in the living room reads 3:00 in the morning . . . it is better to use the telephone in the kitchen, it's farther away from his parents' bedroom, where the heavenly devout shoved in a righteous Friday-night head and pulled out an unholy, sinful head like his. . . . He doesn't know how the new telephones work. As soon as he dials the first digit, the telephone in the living room starts to yelp. He disconnects it and comes back. He calls Kaveh's father. A sleepy man answers.

"I'm terribly sorry," he whispers, "but is Kaveh home?"

"You have dialed the wrong number. Do you have any idea what time it is?"

"I'm Amir, Kaveh's friend. I'm not doing well emotionally, that's why I called at such a late hour. Could you please call Kaveh to the phone?"

"There is no one here by that name."

The man hangs up. Amir thinks perhaps he misdialed. He sits on the kitchen floor for about fifteen minutes and then dials the number again.

This time the same voice shouts, "If you are crazy, I have already told you we do not have anyone by that name here. If you are a prankster, at this hour of the night only your whoring mother and sister are awake."

Left:

The night is coming to an end and still he has not fallen asleep. Frustrated, he paces his room. When tired, he sits down in a corner and rocks one leg—it helps him think. Tonight, having drank Uncle Arjang's arak, the empty holes in his mind do not bother him as much. They are not painful; the sounds that echo in them are not like the screeches of a grainy chalk on a blackboard.

> *«When you're drunk, you realize how drunk the people who consider themselves sober are.... I said this to someone, somewhere. Who was it?»*

Having not had a drink in years, just two sips have affected him.

Occasionally, unconsciously, he rubs his groin. It is somehow comforting. The words "always," "out," and "in a thinking way," that now and then pop into his head and spin around his mind, come from his memories of Sergeant Major Neiji. On those rare occasions when Neiji would be lost in thought, if someone inquisitively asked, "It's not like you to be sad, what are you thinking about?" Neiji would answer, "I'm in a thinking way about why I can't. Mind you, I think a lot. But I just can't. No matter how hard I think about it, I just can't figure out why, no matter what I do, two get left out."

And somehow, randomly, he remembers . . .

No, he does not randomly remember. I had written:

As is his habit, Sergeant Major Neiji holds out two fingers to bum a cigarette.

And, as usual, Amir says, "There you go again, holding out the two pleading prongs."

Neiji's bushy eyebrows curl up. When joking around, the look in his eyes becomes more mischievous. As always, he says, "If you don't like these two prongs, I have a single one I can stiffen up for you, foxy lieutenant."

"Corkscrew it up your ass."

Ever since becoming friendly with the foulest-mouthed noncommissioned officer in the detachment, his language has become more vulgar by the day. . . . But today, there seems to be something wrong with Neiji. "Just hand over a cigarette," he says bitterly. "In return, the houris in heaven will give you Marlboros."

A shell, sounding like a bird fluttering its wings, passes overhead and explodes in the distance. Neiji's hand does not move. He takes a deep drag on the cigarette and pensively blows the smoke toward the entrance of the trench. Amir had missed him. He had counted the days for the Sergeant Major of the Third Foot Detachment to return from leave, throw down his duffle bag, lean his rifle against the wall of the trench, and hold out his two pleading prongs. Even now, when Neiji comes across a senior officer or commander, unlike the bungling enlisted officers at the front, he stands at attention and formally salutes.

"Your devotee, first sergeant major Neiji, clarinet player of the Music Band, ready for martyrdom."

And when the officer, having taken him seriously, tells him to stand at ease, Neiji, in his thick Shirazi accent, starts his routine.

"Sir! Brother! I have served beloved Islam in the music band at the base. I am devoted to one and all, and as God is my witness, I know the clarinet inside and out, but I don't know the first thing about guns and rifles and such. The political ideologues who shout slogans—war, war, until I-don't-know-when—are all huddled up in their holes at the base, and the base captain sends me to the front by force. You being an officer, you have all the wisdom in the world, so, when do you think we will invade Israel and get it over with and go back to our lives?"

Because of his deliberate oafish behavior and buffoonery, the detachment commander has still not dared send him out on a mission.

Neiji glances at his cigarette butt. He takes another deep puff, picks up his rifle, and loads it.

"I have something important to do. I will take care of it and come right back."

He walks out.

The Koureh-Moush hills and the plains surrounding them are still full of spring weeds and colorful desert flowers—chamomile, wild poppy, and desert anemone . . . their colors and perfumes last only a few weeks. They dry up and leave the plains with flowerless stems, yellow thorns, and a dust-colored terrain pregnant with mines. In the shelter of the hills, the hunched mounds of the trenches covered with dirt and rocks, and around them, the khaki color of uniforms, the olive green of gunstocks and grenades, and the brassy-hay color of G3 bullets. . . .

And the days of diarrhea outbreaks on the defense lines pass in filth and dreariness. It is only the hours of Iraqi shelling that create vomitus waves in the swampland of their days . . . time drags, days crawl away for night to arrive. And when night comes, it passes sluggishly. The rats running along the trench roof, causing dirt to pour in from the joints, become a subject for swearing. The mosquito bites bring about forgetfulness, and swatting them becomes a pastime.

Three days remain until his turn to go on leave. Perhaps for the thousandth time, he spews profanities at the detachment commander who as punishment for Amir's criticisms sends him on leave to the lines of the Third Foot Detachment instead of behind the battlefront. In three days, he'll have to again take his backpack, sleeping bag, scout gear, and rifle and head down the mountain with his squad. To take the narrow mule trail that snakes from mountain to mountain. And to again see the eternal skeleton of the mule. Carcass-eating dogs from abandoned villages have devoured its skin and flesh; a rusted piece of shrapnel dangles in its ribcage, another sits in its skull. . . . And then, tired and gloomy, to again climb up to the peak to relieve the previous squad eagerly waiting with their backpacks strapped on and ready to head down.

He hears a single shot fired nearby. Followed by Sergeant Major Haji's shouts for help. Everyone rushes out. Neiji hollers, "I will kill you! . . . I will make your wife mourn for you, you motherfucker!"

Haji, with his lanky figure and wearing only his briefs, is dodging between the boulders; Neiji chases after him with his rifle, shooting and cursing.

Neiji's clumsy shots make everyone in the vicinity drop to the ground. Wiggly wobbly Haji is snaking his escape.

"Phony Haji! How dare you burn my haji?"

Haji takes cover behind a trench mound and shouts, "What is wrong, dear Neiji? I swear I haven't done anything!"

"If you have balls, stand up and let me put a bullet in them!"

Neiji circles the trench behind Haji. Gasping, Haji freezes. Neiji aims at his cock bulging in his briefs.

"Don't make a move. If you do, I will shoot you in the head by mistake. You shamed me in front of my wife. I will castrate you, you pimp!"

Haji shields his cock with his hands. He hunches over and begs. At the sound of a shot, he yelps and dives on the ground. He howls, he squirms.

"He shot me! The motherfucker shot me!"

Terrified, he looks down at his hands still covering his front. And then, he opens them and checks his briefs. They are wet, but there is no blood.

The soldiers burst into laughter. Haji runs his hand over the wetness and smells it.

"You see, Neiji? I just pissed on your father's grave."

Neiji aims again. Haji, flat on the ground, rolls over and lifts his ass—a target for Neiji's rifle. A 120 mm timed shell explodes in the air. Everyone looks up at the blue sky. Clusters of smoke and pieces of shrapnel pour down. A few of the soldiers who are near trench entrances dive in. Others stand perfectly straight and shield their heads with their arms. Haji is the only one lying down. Pieces of shrapnel pierce the ground around the soldiers or ricochet off the rocks. Haji leaps up and makes a dash for the detachment commander's trench, comically trying to zigzag his way.

Neiji sends another bullet his way. And then, there is only the dry sound of a firing pin in an empty barrel.

The detachment commander has climbed out of his trench and looks at the crowd with confusion. Amir grabs Neiji's arm and drags him to his own trench.

"Let me go!"

"You are going to get yourself hanged over nothing."

During these stale and moldy days at the defense front line, this incident has become a source of entertainment for everyone.

In the trench, Amir pours a cup of tea from the kettle and hands it to Neiji. He takes his rifle away from him and tosses it aside. Without saying a word, Neiji slurps his tea. Beads of sweat have simmered from the smallpox scars on his face.

"Now, did you really want to kill him?"

The sergeant smirks.

"What did he do to you?"

"You have no idea what this phony bastard did to me when I was on leave. . . . Too bad I have only played the clarinet in the army. If I take another shot at Haji, it will end up in the commander's ass."

His waggish smile returns to his thin lips.

"Fuck that base captain for sending me to the front."

He holds out two fingers. Amir lights a cigarette and puts it between the two pleading prongs. Neiji takes a deep puff.

"But why did you want to kill him?"

"I will kill him."

"Fine, so you'll kill him. Why?"

"In sex class the motherfucker told us. . . . "

"Haji teaches a sex class?"

"Huh! All the sergeants in the detachment attend."

"Nights when you all said you were going to Haji's trench for lessons in Islamic rituals, you were . . . "

"Yep. He talked about stuff we had never even heard of. In these wastelands, when even your cock rots, it was good fun. In one of his classes he said the medic unit has this cream for sore muscles—if you rub it on the tip of your cock you won't come too quickly. You don't have a wife, you don't understand. After a month or forty days in the middle of nowhere, there is nothing to do but get horny. Then, well, by the time you get some, the minute you shove it in, and in and out a couple of times, psssh! It squirts out. Seven or eight of the sergeants who had used the stuff when they were on leave told us it made them as hard as a rock. Some guys in the Second Detachment were using it, too."

"Did you get some?"

"Yeah. I went to the medic unit. The doctor said he couldn't figure out why everyone was suddenly falling down and getting hurt. But he did right by me."

"Did it work?"

"That's why I want to kill that phony mullah. When I got home, the kids were out. I said, God, you are the best. I told the missus I was craving her. I told her to fix herself up and put on a little perfume while I took a bath and shaved. As the Prophet said, cleanliness is part of faith. And then I rubbed on the cream. I figured I would put some a little further down, too. I think I even smeared it on my balls. When I walked out, I saw the missus had gone all the way and made herself really pretty. Before I could say something nice to her, I felt it getting warm. It got warmer, warmer, and

then it started to burn . . . I thought it was because I was too horny. But as soon as I went in and out a couple of times, the burning got so bad that it went limp. You don't know how bad it was. It was as if I were grilling it over fire. And now the woman wouldn't let me be. 'Mr. Neiji, Mr. Neiji, what is the matter?' I kept saying, 'Woman, shut up and let me see what has happened to me.' And disaster! She started burning, too. It was so bad. I was holding my cock, running around the yard, and howling like a circumcised baby. No matter how much water I splashed on it, it wouldn't cool down. The wife's was no different. She held the garden hose to it and that didn't do any good. Her hands between her legs, she was sitting on the stairs wailing. . . . Next time I go on leave, I am going to fuck this phony Haji's wife."

Amir bursts into laughter. Neiji glowers at him.

A soldier pops his head in and says, "Sergeant Neiji! In case you are interested, Haji is holed up in the captain's trench."

The sergeant major hurls a mess kit at him and the soldier runs off roaring with laughter. It seems Neiji has been paid back for all his teasing and the pranks he has played on everyone.

Again Neiji's anger boils over.

"Give me my rifle! I'm going to send that deadbeat's gonorrhea-infested little birdie flying."

Amir laughs and says, "Dimwit! You all kept running to the medic for the cream until he ran out of it and started giving you the kind that heats up. You rubbed it on a sensitive cock and got as hard as a donkey. Well, you got your kicks!"

"In your own way, you're no better than Haji."

Amir walks out and heads for the latrine that has been set up away from the cluster of trenches. When the wind changes direction, the stench blows directly at them. A ditch one-and-a-half meters deep that they all relieve themselves in. Four lopsided wooden beams have been hammered into the ground around it and a tattered piece of burlap has been draped around them. Nauseated, he squats over the ditch. Hundreds of large and small parasitic worms wriggle around in the feces. They seem to be making a droning sound.

Somewhere a shell explodes. Halfway done, he pulls up his pants and hurries back to his trench. He is terrified of being hit while in the latrine and his flesh getting mixed in with the worms. In the trench, he sits on the ground with his legs crossed, his closely cropped hair brushing against the ceiling. Neiji, now calm, is tracing lines on the gray army blanket with his finger.

"You are just back from leave and you are feeling homesick," Amir says. "You will get used to it by tomorrow."

Amir turns on his pocket transistor radio. On Iran's frequency, they are broadcasting a mullah's sermon. This time, the subject is neither Imam Hossein nor the joy of those who have ascended to heaven, but rather ablutions before praying and how in the absence of water, fighters at the front should clean their hands and feet by rubbing them with dirt. And then instructions on how they should cleanse themselves with rocks and clumps of dirt after going to the toilet, and how they should use two fingers to squeeze out any urine remaining in their business. Manners of Estebrā. . . .

"Listen carefully," he says to Neiji. "It will come in handy."

"Don't make me go after of you instead of Haji."

The scribe on his right shoulder had written:

"I'm going to do her. How much do you want to bet that in one hour I can work her up and bring her over to the apartment?"

"If you win, I will give you a hundred tomans," Kaveh says. "But if you lose, I will do you instead."

Kaveh again looks at the melancholy girl sitting in the corner of the cafeteria. Amir glances at her, too. He is still groggy from last night's lack of sleep, and the bitter morning coffee is no match for the hangover of boozing at The Riverbank.

He gets up and heads toward the girl's table. Her slanted Mongol eyes, rarely seen in Tehran, will be a good addition for his collection.

> «If she doesn't turn away from me with crude coyness, the way she did with that other guy, it will mean, come on over and sit down.»

With Hollywood-ish flair, he puts down his cup of coffee on the girl's table. He exaggerates his cinematic gesture and coffee spills on the table. He returns the girl's snicker with a smirk, at her and at himself. He sits down.

"Someone has cheated on you, that's why you're so down."

"How would you know, wise guy?"

"Because I'm the biggest cheating boyfriend in the world."

On his left:

The Mongol girl keeps saying she has very little time. And adds, "I'm not a virgin. Relax."

Amir pulls the girl's panties down her wide, horse-like thighs. The girl runs her hand over her dark pubic hair and belligerently says, "Tell your friend to come in, too."

He shouts, "Kaveh, come on in!"

Kaveh walks into the room and says, "Just so that you know, I'm not a car wash."

"Miss Mongol here wants to be sandwiched."

"I know a mullah who charges a thousand tomans for a temporary marriage permit," Kaveh says, "so that if we are caught we won't get whipped."

And he pulls down his pants.

The girl manages the situation well. As soon as one of them is close to orgasm, she pushes him away and pulls the other one to herself. In the end, with neither of the men having climaxed, she wipes her brimming spring and pulls on her panties.

"I'm late."

She puts the wet tissue in her handbag.

"You slut!" Kaveh growls. "You do a number on us and leave? . . . You slut!"

Amir appreciates the way the girl has played them.

"No, she is not," he says. "She did a number on us sluts."

The scribe on his right shoulder writes:

"I had a friend called Kaveh."

"Yes. So what?"

"We were good friends. Weren't we?"

"You used to hang out with him a lot. So what?"

"He must know who I was engaged to."

"I don't know. . . . "

"Do you know where his family lived?"

"I think it's useless to. . . . "

"I didn't ask for your opinion. Do you know where he lived?"

"I don't know. I have some vague memory."

"For the love of whoever you love, take me to his home . . . the guards won't let me go out alone . . . for the love of God, take me there! If you don't, I will just jump over the wall and go."

"But how? With what excuse?"

"Any excuse . . . tell them it is something urgent."

"No. It won't work. Get it out of your head."

"If you take me, I promise I will try to get better."

"But how?"

"Tell them the doctor said a change of environment, seeing people, will improve my mood. Come on, sister! Be a pal!"

The naughty child in Reyhaneh seems to be waking up. With a smile on her lips, she hesitantly says, "Should I tell them I'm taking you to the hospital for some x-rays?"

Overjoyed, he wraps his arm around Reyhaneh and kisses her forehead.

"I can lie to Agha Haji, but I have to tell Mom the truth."

"You mean you can lie to the pillar of Islam, but not to Mom?"

Right:

He is stunned. Outside the garden walls, ugly houses have been built or are under construction all around. There is no sign of the heavenly cotton field that as children they used to run around in and play under Shahu's careful eye. The white of cotton has been replaced with mounds of quicklime next to half-built houses.

"The cotton! . . . " he sighs.

They are waiting for the car service.

"Do you remember how much we played in the cotton field?" Reyhaneh asks. "What happened to our games?"

> «When the cotton bolls opened, hidden baby clouds would pop out of them and the field would turn into a green and white sky. The bushes were so beautiful and safe, green and white. How perfectly perfect they were as a hiding place for hide-and-seek. Under them, their breath was fresh. It was like the breath of a *qanat* in the desert. . . . Green and white.»

"Dādāshi, do you remember how much we used to tease poor Shahu? Running this way and that way, and the minute he turned his back, we would hide in the bushes and make him call out to us a hundred times and look for us all over the field. You used to hold me tight, one arm around my neck, and one hand pushing down my head to hide me even more. I always thought your hands could hide me from the eyes of the entire world."

And, embarrassed, she looks down.

"Agha Haji hadn't yet ordered you to wear a headscarf back then?"

"No, I still hadn't turned nine. I had thick long hair. I always cried when Mom combed it in the bath. I think Shahu told us there were jackals in the field so that we wouldn't wander off too far. But I felt safe when you were with me."

"We had fun, didn't we?"

"We used to quietly laugh at him. He kept calling out, 'Master's son, Master's daughter, where are you?' And just when he was about to lose his mind with worry, we would come out. He never once scolded us. He would just say, 'You precious rascals. . . .' Yes, we were two precious rascals."

"Yes. . . . A quilt dreams of cotton fields, too. Doesn't it?"

"Do you remember the bird with the broken wing?"

"No. Tell me about it."

"I saw it a few times. In the middle of the cotton bushes. It couldn't fly. It had trouble walking, too. One of its wings dragged on the ground, as if it were broken. I felt sorry for it. It looked like it was in a lot of pain. You would chase it, and I would scream for you to leave the poor thing alone. It kept going this way and that way and whenever you came close to it, it would leap. The first time I saw it, I cried. I saw it three or four times. Later, Shahu said what the bird was doing was a trick—that was how it lured you away from its nest and chicks. The cheat was healthy, it pretended to have a broken wing so you would go after it."

Amir groans, "Lucky for me that I have no nest and no brats. . . . Tell me about the cotton."

"When the bolls were fully grown, their shells would dry and crack open. We would pluck the cotton out of them and shred plenty of it in no time at all. It was fun throwing them up in the air to make snow."

"Weren't we scared?"

"When the farmers would see us making a mess of the harvest, they would run over, shouting and yelling. But as soon as they realized we were the landowner's children, they would just laugh. We were always so happy that instead of telling us off, they were laughing at us. It took years before I understood what that laughter meant."

In the car, Amir notices that the driver has the habit of clucking his tongue. They drive through a new suburban development on their way to Tehran proper. Reyhaneh is quiet. Amir looks out at the city streets and sidewalks. Many areas are new to him—they seem to be shrouded in the dust and smoke of an exploded shell. He cannot tell if he has forgotten them or if they were built during the years he was away. His memories have been abandoned on the sidewalks of the pre-revolution days—the mischief-making, miniskirt-wearing girls with wavy hair, the longhaired boys in colorful clothes. Now, the girls are dressed in dark colors, wearing headscarves, Islamic headdresses, and chadors . . . and the men have stubble on their chins and are dressed in grungy, scruffy clothes.

The driver is playing one of the banned songs by exiled singers in Los Angeles on the car stereo, clicking his tongue in time with the music.

Amir wants to see so badly that he does not see. In one of the side streets in Shemiran neighborhood, Reyhaneh tells the driver to turn onto a narrow road. . . . And they arrive at Kaveh's family house. That large, turquoise-colored metal door is still there. Amir's heart is racing just as it did when he stood face to face with an Iraqi lieutenant, their rifles aiming at each other.

"I will do the talking," he tells Reyhaneh.

A young boy opens the door. Seeing Amir and chador-clad Reyhaneh, he steps back to close it again. Amir sticks his foot in the doorway and tries to take on his military tone.

"Is your father or Kaveh at home?"

"I swear, my dad hasn't done anything wrong," the boy says pleadingly.

Reyhaneh wants to explain in her Reyhaneh-esque manner, but Amir pushes her back.

"Tell your father to come to the door. Or Kaveh."

"For the love of God, don't take him away again!"

"If he comes quickly, we won't."

The boy runs across the front yard toward the house that can be seen through the half-open door. It looks familiar to Amir.

The man who comes to the door has no recognizable features and looks just as terrified as the boy.

"I'm Amir, Kaveh's friend. Tell him I want to see him."

"Excuse me! Whom are you referring to?"

Reyhaneh interrupts them.

"Is this the Shemirani house?"

"It used to be. How can I help you?"

"Do you have any news of them, where they moved to?"

"I don't know. I swear on the life of my only son. We bought the house third-hand through an attorney. We just moved in."

A wintry sweat is percolating on Amir's and the man's foreheads.

The boy, half-hidden behind his father, is staring at Amir and his beard.

"Let's go," Reyha says. "It's in the past."

He waves a threatening finger at the man and the boy.

"Tell Kaveh I will find him even if he crawls under a rock."

Left:

The deceptive dawn has not yet arrived, but he can hear an untimely rooster crowing somewhere outside the garden. He realizes that his unconscious strokes are giving him a hard-on. His cock is again hungering for flesh. He grabs its middle and squeezes it hard until pain gurgles in his throat, and then again, more muddled, he paces his room from one wall to the bed, and from the window to the closet with its door wide open and nothing in it but a few clothes. . . .

He goes to the bathroom to wash his hands. Before picking up the soap, he instinctively reaches for his left hand to take off his ring using three fingers.

«Then the ring was not made of fine gold for me to have worried that it would tarnish. . . . What if I told Moon Brow that I used to behave like a whore and she was so disgusted with me that she disappeared?»

The scribe on his right shoulder had written:

And he sees the greasy char of the Iraqi soldier at the foot of the hill. It is not important for him to remember the attack, or that it was after the recapture of the Zahab plains. And he does not remember why his observation post has moved to a new battlefront. He has caught sight of the soldier burned to a crisp. Around him black, greasy patches, his arms and legs up in the air, scorched. He used to be proud of his precision in directing fire at enemy lines. . . .

Surviving Iranian soldiers, fearing an Iraqi counterattack, frantically dig ditches with broken spades. They ignore him, even if they know he is the lieutenant who with accurate calculations has aided their victory. Medics carry away two half-burned Iranian soldiers that they have identified from their dog tags and wrapped in Iraqi blankets. A soldier yanks the tags off the burned Iraqi's neck and puts it in his pocket, perhaps a souvenir. Then he walks backward, takes a running start, and kicks the corpse between the legs.

Someone yells at him and he shouts back, "It was this motherfucker who defiled tens of Iranian girls."

A burned leg drops to the ground.

Amir is still perplexed. Something has happened that he did not understand, and he does not understand what is happening now.

On his right shoulder, the scribe writes:

Wrapped in chadors, Reyhaneh and Mother walk to the garden gates. They probably know he is behind the trees, but they pretend otherwise. One of the guards walks out of the guardroom. Even from this distance, Amir knows the man's eyes are ogling his sister through the narrow slit in the front of her chador, and gaping at the curve of her backside as she walks away. When the garden gates close behind them, Amir hurries back to the house. He has waited a long time for just such an opportunity. The door to Reyhaneh's room is not locked, but the closet is. He has no choice. The knife that he fetches from the kitchen breaks the first time he wedges its blade in the closet door.

> «A motherfucking knife without a tip is strangely much more of a knife. . . . »

The lock breaks after his third kick. From deep inside the closet, the pleasant scent of perfume and the fragrance of femininity drift out. He quickly pushes aside three or four black chadors and two white ones draped over the rod, and shoves back a few coveralls, the lightest of which is gray. There is a second rod. Ignoring the underclothes and colorful T-shirts, he gets down on one hand and two knees and crawls in.

> «Things to be hidden are always hidden deep in the back. »

He opens the shoeboxes one by one and tosses them aside. He shoves aside other odds and ends. The legs of a few pairs of pants keep getting in his way. He yanks them off their hangers and throws them out. A velvet box full of jewelry, an envelope with school documents, and . . . he finally finds a photo album. He pulls his prey out of the closet and takes refuge in his room.

The pages of the album are not half-singed. He hungrily flips through them and then starts from the beginning again. His spinster sister has carefully arranged the photographs. Her grade school pictures, wearing a headscarf and a rare smile, standing with her scarf-less classmates. Her high school pictures, wearing a chador that she has bravely, so she foolishly thought, left slightly open, revealing her face for the camera, standing next to girls dressed in bright-colored miniskirts. There are photos of her at commemoration dinners for who-knows-which prophet and at women's gatherings with no one wearing hijab, the women bejeweled, their wrists heavy with gold bangles, their legs showing, their chadors draped over expensive armchairs . . . and then there are photos of the countless members of the Yamini family at outings on the banks of the Karaj River, which Reyha had mentioned. He is in some of the pictures—with long hair and wearing flared pants. "What a dope!" . . . Standing next to Agha Haji's nieces and nephews and others who he is not sure if he should recognize or not. . . . At last, after all his probing, he finds a photograph hidden between two others that have been flipped over. Reyha, himself, and a torn off section large enough for at least two other people.

"Reyha, you are a conniver just like the others!"

Right:

She starts screaming the moment she sets foot in her room. Weeping, she tears into Amir's room. Her photo album lies open on the floor, her photographs scattered, a few torn in half. Amir, sitting triumphantly with his back against the closet door, shakes the discovered evidence in the air.

Reyhaneh, shrieking wildly, claws at her hair.

Unperturbed, he asks, "Who were the people you tore out of this photograph?"

Reyhaneh drops to the floor. Running her hands around, she starts gathering her treasure trove. With the hem of her coverall, she wipes away her teardrop that has fallen on a photograph. She collects the torn pictures and tucks them between the pages of the album. And looking up, she cries, "God, take his other arm, too!"

"Who was in this picture?"

"You filthy thief! Shut up!"

Amir waves the photograph in front of her face. Reyhaneh snatches it away, then throws its bits and pieces at his face.

"It is none of your business. You lunatic! Psychotic! More vicious than the devil. . . . "

The sister and brother are standing nose to nose. Chin to chin, fist to fist. Amir reaches out to grab her arm. The hatred and rage in the girl's eyes drive his hand back.

> «Nothing in the world is two. Everything is one. Always one . . . always alone.»

He has the urge to hold Reyhaneh is his arm. Perhaps even to rest his eyes on her shoulder. . . . Reyha takes a step back. As though she has just remembered, she starts to scream again. Mother walks in. Puzzled, she looks at them.

"Reyha! Stop cursing!"

"You, of all people, do not say a word! Can't you see what he has done to my closet, to my photo album? Even now that he has come home a crazy cripple, you still take his side, you still favor the male child, the idiot son!"

Mother moans, "Let's go, Reyha. It will just get worse."

"What could possibly make it worse? Again, I am forced to give in!

I cannot tolerate this house any more. I will just kill myself and we will all be better off."

> «There are military guidelines not to issue Colts to enlisted officers because it is easy to self-inflict with them—to aim at the calf and pull the trigger. . . . Hey, you blood and bullet pimps! I don't want to be free of the war! But this bastard G3 is too long, it is useless to put its muzzle under your chin and fiddle with the trigger with your big toe to see whether the motherfucker, Hitler's baby, will go off or not, Russian roulette. . . . Oh, Khazar! What have you done?»

"I will kill myself," Reyhaneh shouts, pointing her finger at him and Mother. "Even if God sends me to hell, I will kill myself. At least in hell, I will be free of you."

She shoves Mother out of her way. Perhaps for the first time in her life, she slams her bedroom door shut with all her might.

Tears have finally dried. Mother's doe eyes no longer seem to manipulate others with their look of helplessness and sorrow. Now they have a different look, one he has never seen in her. Mother recites, "To boast of love and complain about the beloved, alas, false boasts . . . such lovers deserve forsaking."

He realizes the verse can be by none other than the astute Hafez. There has always been a copy of his *Divan* together with the Quran next to Mother's bed.

> «Sly Mother, she knows Hafez by heart.»

Mother leaves, too.

It is hard to put the torn pieces of a photograph together with one hand.

He spits on the windowpane.

"No torn photograph can be glued back together with spit."

He yells, "Rey—h—a . . . forgive me!"

As though with an injured larynx, he howls the way he howled for the Iraqi lieutenant.

The scribe had written on his left shoulder:

"You idiots!" he says to the soldiers around him. "Based on regulations, the colonel should have conducted a reconnaissance of these areas before sending you in. He was too scared to come, he just looked at his bullshit map and told you where to dig trenches. If the Iraqis aim their tank guns slightly to the left, your trenches will be in their direct line of fire. I will not comply, I'm going to choose the location of my observation post myself."

Right:

> «The highest peak is not always best for a full view of the surrounding area.»

He walks along a cliff, hoping to find the best and safest spot from which to monitor the enemy.

He kneels next to a locoweed bush to pop a few of its purple bubble flowers, like he used to do when he was a boy. He hears the sound of metal knocking against stone. From the top of a boulder to his left, first a Kalashnikov and a hand, and then a torso emerge.

Panicked, he leaps up. The Iraqi sees him. Their rifles aiming at each other, both stunned, they stare at each other. The Iraqi recovers faster and fires a horizontal burst of bullets at him.

> «Faced with the enemy, do not shower him with bullets waving left to right like they do in Hollywood movies. One small spurt. Small, so that you don't run out of ammo. Fire a small vertical

spurt, high to low. If he is not hit, fire again, swinging back up to slice him.»

The bullets miss him. Buzzing like bees, they ricochet off the rocks. He has practiced this before; with his thumb he releases the G3's safety lock and fires a vertical salvo at the Iraqi. He does not wait to see if the man has been hit or not. Swinging his rifle upward, another burst. The Iraqi falls.

Right:

He has been sitting motionless behind a boulder for nearly an hour, listening to the wounded man moan and peeking at him now and then. But still, no other Iraqis have shown up. He wonders what the guy was doing up there all alone. He had always been comforted by the assumption that as a scout he would never have to engage directly with the Iraqis. They have always been phantoms in his binoculars. He is certain that despite his quick-wittedness, if he were to come face to face with an enemy soldier, he would not be able to fire first. He would gape at him, wondering what the man will do, who he is, what will happen . . . and so he will be killed.

He shouts, "Throw your rifle over here!"

The Iraqi groans something in Arabic. Amir does not understand. Then he remembers what the word 'name' is in Arabic.

"Essm? . . . Essm?"

"Yasser! . . . Yasser!"

"Amir! . . . Amir!"

«Huh! Come to think of it, my own name is an Arabic one!»

"You dimwit, why did you come here?"

The Arab babbles something again.

"If you are cursing at me, I will curse back."

The Iraqi groans something in Kurdish. Amir only understands the word "Kurdistan."

The Iraqi says in English, "Escape Saddam. . . . "

And in English, Amir answers, "Your Kalashnikov! Throw it!"

And then there is silence. Occasionally a moan.

Finally, he gathers the courage to crouch down and go over to the wounded man. The Kalashnikov is not within his reach. The Iraqi lieutenant stares at him with incredulity. . . .

> «He is a deserter. His escape route was not in our direction, but. . . . »

The man was escaping toward the mountains that Iraqi Kurds had reclaimed from Saddam's forces.

He hoists the Iraqi up on his shoulder. It is harder than the movies make it look. He hasn't gone far before he feels the man's final tremor.

He cries in his heart, Forgive me! I didn't want to. . . .

He searches the man's pockets.

> «They all have a photograph of a couple of kids, a wife, or perhaps a father and mother. Whoever they are, wherever they are now, they still don't know that this father, husband, or son has been relieved of the labor of breathing.»

A wallet and an agenda with alphabetized pages in the back, filled with Arabic names and telephone numbers.

The scribe on his left shoulder writes:

« . . . and I am fearful, sister. Not of the constant, at-all-odd-hours explosions of timed shells above my head. The fear I'm talking about bears greater horror. It bears the question, Why me, why us? Why should this devastation and tyranny come down on me and us? I know many have been slaughtered. They have been simply executed and simply relieved, or simply cut in half by shrapnel and simply relieved. But the likes of me who have been slashed and sliced, what crime did we commit to have been denied an easy death in some corner? . . . Girl! What evil has come that no one grasps what evil has come? As if something came from the moonlight, laid eggs in the water we drank, and in our guts its tadpoles emerged from black strands, or perhaps the eggs blew into our ears with the gusts of air from shouts and slogans, or they crept into our mouths through the kisses we exchanged. This fear is worse than the fear of Saddam's chemical bombs, more poisonous than the whip-wielding Basiji's sweat that with every lash splatters on the previous wounds and burns like a scorpion's sting. My innocent sister, beware! Everyone has their own sting, their own poison. I know things that you wise ones are ignorant of. . . . You miserable wretches! Something has happened that you are oblivious to. . . . O you who build an Everest out of every pile of your shitty dung, be wary! . . . Have fear, so that at least when you are fearful you might do something. Damn you, when you believe yourselves to be so clever and so all-knowing, then why don't you do something so that this fear will leave the ceiling of my room, disappear from among the trees, from my sister's room, and from the street that is so terrifying

to go to, terrifying because they may be hauling away burnt remains.... Can't you see that they are growing exponentially in number, spreading everywhere, getting smarter and more capable of hiding than you, because they can breathe under water and desert sand? I have even seen the tadpoles' shadows in the flames from a 120 mm shell and in the mouth of a tank gun. And as soon as the tadpoles saw that I see that they can also breathe in fire, they made me mad and crippled so that I would not tell you. Tell you to beware that they keep breeding, in dance music, in the veins of the eucalyptus tree, in words of admonition, in the steam rising from the cooking pot, in soap, and in the telephone receiver.... Why can't you see that we've been fattened for their dinner ... you who slashed and sliced us, don't you feel the tickle of the tadpoles' tails fluttering in your stomachs, to remind you that you, too, should piss in your pants in fear?

Fine, fine, don't all of you accost me at once to shove your stock answers into my seven holes, to saw off my other arm, too. I know that my problem is that my head is working like a pump. Now I see everything so clearly that I wonder, What if things that have been forgotten were never meant to be remembered?

Reyha! For the sake of this me that is me, why won't you come and sleep in my room so that I won't be afraid. I am afraid of sleeping and afraid of dreaming of her again, and I am afraid of remembering that I have to wake up, even if it is the middle of the night, to go and find my arm.... It sounds as if ... do you hear it, too, Reyha? Listen! ... For the love of that God you believe in, look out the window and tell me if it is the sound of rain raining rain.»

And he keeps reading and rereading the names in the address book.

On his right shoulder:

He dreams of Moon Brow. The feverish swell starts in his head. Moon Brow says, "I cannot wait for you. If you are not on time, I'll have to leave." He replies, "I will be there before you. . . . " In his dream, he looks at himself in the mirror. He is neatly dressed. He goes to the door. He has forgotten something. He looks around his room, trying to remember what it is he has forgotten. Perhaps it is in the closet—but its door is locked. He remembers it was something he has hidden between the books on the shelf.

"I'm coming. I will be on time! Don't worry!"

Searching among books is the hardest thing to do. Agitated, he tosses them out one after the other. What if he put it between the pages of some volume?

It's late . . . a few minutes late, but it's still safe. In a frenzy, he shakes the books he has thrown on the floor.

Feverish, feverish . . . he wants to shout, I'm coming! Darkness weighs on his chest, he cannot breathe. He shouts, "Forgive me!" His voice is choked.

He does not know whether he is dreaming or awake. Reyhaneh is standing over his bed, shaking him. Desperate, he shouts, "Forgive me! . . . I was late. . . . "

Right:

He peeks into Reyhaneh's room through the keyhole. Today, too, he can hear dance music playing. A twirling green skirt passes in front of the door. The beat of the *daf* grows faster. Four or five other dafs join in, *setars*, too. The music grows fuller. Little by little, the beat and rhythm becomes more impassioned. The skirt dances and twirls past the peephole. The hem, fluttering up, reappears. A passing impression of pale thighs. A chorus chants, "Ho . . . ho ho . . . ho ho ho . . . ho ho . . . " It is as if ghosts of reveling Sufis have invaded the room. Then, a glimpse of a dark whirlwind that has escaped a black headscarf, spinning, spinning. . . . and again the twirling skirt. The beat grows feverish. "Ho, hey ha, ho ho." Now, at the edge of the key-hole, hair flinging back, and a partial view of white arms writhing.

He can imagine Reyhaneh bending backward to the extent her spine allows and coiling her arms above her breasts that have rolled apart. Perhaps behind her, her hair is licking at the floor.

He pushes down on the door handle. It is locked. The music stops.

"It's a friend."

Reyhaneh opens the door. She has draped her headscarf over her half-bare shoulders. She is wet with perspiration.

"What do you want?" she snaps.

"What were you doing?"

"None of your business. What the heck do you want?"

"For the love of Mother, don't talk to me like this . . . I shouted ten times from my room that I did wrong, and I shouted from the garden that I am sorry."

"If you ever do that sort of shitty thing again . . . "

"Fine, fine . . . what were you doing?"

Stubbornly, childishly, he asks three times until Reyha says, "Exercising."

She is still panting.

"To lose weight. These days all young women do it. Has Mom come back home?"

"Did she go out?"

"Huh! And look who I'm betting my money on!"

Reyha's stereo seems still to be vibrating from the beat of the music.

"You have to listen to the music and watch the video at the same time. But I'm sorry to say that VCRs are banned in this house."

"Let me watch you dance."

"Don't be so cheeky. What do you want?"

He walks into the room.

"I know you are kind again, because you feel sorry for me."

He holds out the address book.

"I want you to make a phone call."

"To whom."

"There is a name that seems very familiar. Katayoun. I think I always remembered it."

"Why don't you make the call yourself?"

He stammers imploringly and grips the cuff of his sleeve between his teeth.

"Do you think she is the one?"

"I don't know. I have to see her."

"Do you have any idea how many years have passed?"

"Yes. It's the telephone number of a travel agency. I guess she worked there. Perhaps she still does. Tell her you are my sister, make an appointment for us to go see her."

"It's great that once in a while you remember you have a sister," Reyhaneh says sarcastically. "When you joined the war you never once called or came to see me."

"I don't know. It seems you never sought me out either."

"That is rubbish. We searched high and low hoping to find you. But after you ran away from the hospital, you completely disappeared."

"Which hospital?"

"The hospital! After you were flogged."

> «No degree of amnesia can rival the strips of protruding raw flesh on a whipped back.»

He sits down on the floor in front of the full-length window and crosses his legs. The garden is empty of winds and ghosts. The trees and the eggs of their butterflies inculcate their dreams in each other. For a while, neither one of them speaks. Now and then he hears the rustle of her skirt behind him.

> «Only a rustle remains of them in one's mind. But if they did exist, then why does their place grow empty? I was swimming in

> a nighttime sea. It was stormy. Where was I trying to reach when this happened to me? Compassionate waves pulled me along to take me with them. I became frightened and returned. That is why I turned into neither water, nor fire, nor wind. I turned into dirt in my own dirt.»

"Do you remember where you ran off to from the hospital?"

Reyhaneh's voice has become sad.

" . . . Yes."

"I think you are lying."

"Then why do you ask?"

"Kaveh came by the house and picked up your ID card. We didn't know you wanted it so that you could join the army. If Mom knew, she would have never given him all that money to bring to you. We thought you would stay away for a few months and come back after you got over your embarrassment. Five months, six months. . . . We found out where Kaveh's family lived. They were hiding him."

"Why were they hiding him?"

"Some family had filed a complaint against him—it had nothing to do with us."

"I think you know something . . . but, never mind. And then what happened?"

"Father went there and threatened his parents. He forced them to call him out. Two plainclothes agents grabbed Kaveh and took him away. After a few slaps in the face, he admitted that you had joined the army. They held him for a while until they were sure he didn't know which army unit you were in."

"Did they torture him?"

"Who was thinking about such things? Mom and I were already trying to find you. Mom was like a chicken with its head cut off. She went begging from one army base to another. Sometimes they felt sorry for her and tried to help, but there was no sign of you . . . you were probably using a fake name."

With a lump in her throat, she sighs, "You were gone for good."

"And I will not be back until I find her."

"How many times do I have to say it? I think it is better if you don't dig into your past. Every time you do, you get worse. . . . "

"You mean I get crazier!"

"Yesterday you threw the doctor out of your room with a kick in the ass."

"You are dreaming!"

Reyhaneh turns on her electric samovar. He gets up and like a good schoolboy sits in a chair with his hands on his knees, surreptitiously glancing at the broken door of Reyhaneh's closet.

"How did you find out I had been wounded?"

"We didn't. . . . Once in a while, you wrote to me, but with no sender's address. We only knew from the post office stamps on the envelopes that they were coming from the western part of the country. A few came from Tehran. . . . "

"Did I ever write anything about her?"

"Nothing. All you wrote was nonsense, meant to torment us. . . . Then for a very long time you didn't write at all. For so long that based on our calculations your military service should have already ended. Mom was sure her darling son had been wounded. She felt it in her heart. We started going to different hospitals. For a few months Father came along with us. . . . "

"Then he concluded that it served him better to be the father of a martyr?"

"No. He accepted the fact that you were missing in action. I know that without telling us, he had already spent a long time searching for you. Mom and I headed west and went to many of the military bases. Clutching a few photos of you, Mom would cry and force them to look through their files to see if they had any enlisted officers who looked like you. And then we gave up, returned home, and wore black. . . . You lowlife! Do you have any idea how many mangled bodies of soldiers we looked at in morgues?"

«Ugh! Now she will start her sniveling.»

But as if reading his thoughts, Reyhaneh snaps, "I am done crying for you."

"Will you take me out again?"

"But Mom continued sneaking off to hospitals. . . . "

"You and Father didn't go with her anymore?"

With four pale fingers Reyhaneh takes a pinch of black tea leaves from a box and pours it in the teapot. The water in the samovar has not yet come to a boil.

"How did you find me in the nuthouse?"

"Mom saw it in a dream."

He is dumbfounded.

"Huh! You numbskull, you believed me? We had already searched all these places. Often, when we showed that snazzy photo of you with long hair, people would laugh and ask, 'Are you sure this guy has been to war?' The second time Mom went to the psychiatric hospital alone, she saw you. She called Agha Haji and me. But you refused to come home. You would act crazy and holler, 'They are not my family! These people want to kidnap me!' Even though no one there liked you because of the way you behaved and the things you said, still, we had to bring tens of documents and witnesses to prove that this charming young man was in fact the light of our eyes. Father dipped into his wallet and they gave you a shot of strong sedatives so we could bring home."

He looks at Reyhaneh warily.

"You told this story differently last time."

"When?"

"I don't remember."

He was trying to trick Reyhaneh—this is the first time she's told him this story. He hid the first time he saw Mother and Reyhaneh at the nuthouse.

> *«The water has started to murmur in the samovar. It always starts like this. First there is the lament of what to do. Then the sputter of boiling . . . the nuthouse was the best and the freest slum in the world. Out in the yard, how peacefully I sat, waiting for Moon Brow to come and pick the fleas off my scalp. In the nice yard, there was less stench of the crippled nutcases' piss. My shrewd mother recognized me from behind. The miserable woman didn't realize that I was missing an arm. She noticed it when she came before me. She was dumbstruck. She fell to her knees. I don't know if she cried or not. . . . Was I all cut up and bruised from my scuffle with Aboli, or was it before then? It is just as much a pleasure to be beaten up as it is to beat up, which is a true pleasure. Aboli was two-armed. He beat me much more than I beat him.»*

Reyhaneh holds the teapot under the samovar's spout and fills it with hot water. He feels blood trickling from the lesion on his amputated arm. He opens one of the buttons on the floral shirt they have bought for him and reaches in to the stump of his arm. It is wet. Wet from the sweat that has simmered in his armpits. He pulls his hand out and smells his fingertips that bear the scent of his body. It smells the same as his upper lip when he wets it with saliva and curls it up to his nose. He likes this mysterious smell. It reminds him of the smell his lips used to have when they were wet from kisses and licks.

Right:

"It's as if we're off to ask for a girl's hand in marriage," Reyhaneh says. "I have become just like the gossipy old ladies who go to public bathhouses and pick out pretty girls with fair and flawless skin as would-be wives for their sons."

The car service driver is the same one as before. Still clucking his tongue.

"Of course," Reyhaneh says, "to you, I'm just another one of those frumpy women in mosques."

As they drive away from the garden, she takes off the chador she's wearing over her headscarf, folds it, and puts it in a plastic bag. Amir wants to kiss her emancipated shoulder.

In the smoggy air, the end of the street is a hazy blue. The noise and commotion of the city and the relentless honking of car horns are like thorns pricking his mind.

"Now, are you sure this Katayoun is the one you're looking for?" Reyhaneh asks.

He does not answer.

There are slogans painted on walls everywhere. Some have been brushed over and replaced with new ones.

War, war, till victory . . .

Even if this war lasts twenty years, we will still be standing. (Imam Khomeini)

"It seems the store names have changed, too."

"The government mandated that all foreign names be changed. The street names changed several times."

"They were no match for us," the driver scoffs. "They couldn't come up with a name to replace 'taxi.' They couldn't call it a nag-less carriage, could they!"

Praise to the warriors of Islam . . .

Death to America, death to Russia, death to Israel. Death to Britain and France.

"How many years did I spend in the nuthouse?"

Hearing this, the driver shifts into the wrong gear. The fart-like groan of the gearbox makes Amir laugh.

Death to Saddam the infidel.

The road to holy heaven passes through Baghdad.

"I only call it a nuthouse when you make me angry," Reyhaneh says, "but it wasn't a nuthouse. It was a place where they kept shell-shock victims of the war. The hospitals were in total chaos. Throngs of wounded soldiers were brought in and transferred to other places. Sometimes someone would give us a description that fit you. Happy as can be, beseeching God, we would rush to that hospital. But it was complete mayhem. . . . You might have been in that hospital in Kermanshah, but we couldn't find you. Finally, someone told us to check the psychiatric hospital for shell-shock victims. You were pretending to be crazy, and every so often you would give them a different fake name. They said you'd been there for about five years. I am sure you remembered a lot of things, but were deliberately covering your tracks. Five years in those dank rooms where one could barely stand the stench of sweat and urine for more than a minute, with those wretched men whose families had given up trying to care for them. . . . How did you tolerate it? Were you that bent on revenge?"

"Sometimes you say things too big for the mouth of an over-the-hill mosque girl."

The moment the words fly out of his mouth, he regrets speaking them.

The driver bursts into laughter and says, "In other words, the gentleman was not shell-shocked, he just hung out with the crazies for the heck of it? Huh!"

He looks at Reyhaneh in the rearview mirror.

"Sir, keep your eyes on the road," Amir snarls.

"Don't take offense, Mister! What I mean is, no one needs to hide out in a nuthouse, Tehran itself is a nuthouse. Yours truly is the general of all nutcase taxi drivers."

Again, the driver glances at Reyhaneh, and says, "Sister! They sent yours truly's shell-shocked nephew back home to his parents. In the middle of the night he hollers, 'Attack!' He sees the twelfth Imam riding a white horse on top of a hill and pointing his sword at the Iraqis, meaning, Charge! I have your back! I've heard that in the battlefields they would dress one of their own guys in a white robe, give him a sword, put him on a white horse, and send him out at night to motivate the soldiers so that they would walk into the minefields by the hundreds."

Reyhaneh bites her lips. Amir chuckles.

"It seems people's faith has weakened in my great absence."

"Some people's eyes and ears have opened. Take us taxi drivers, we don't pick up mullahs anymore."

Praise to . . .

. . . the name has been painted over.

They stop in front of a travel agency. He has a vague memory of having picked up Katayoun in his car there. He sees winter maple trees in spring bloom. He feels his heart—twisted steel twisting into his guts.

Doldol Travel Agency . . . pilgrimage tours to holy sites in Syria at the lowest prices.

"I think it used to have a different name."

People believe Doldol was the name of the horse the Prophet rode up to heaven, but in fact that horse was called Boraq. Perhaps they think the name makes the airplanes safer.

They go inside. There are four girls sitting behind a long table and a few customers sitting across from them. Highlighted locks of hair have freely crossed the boundaries of the girls' headscarves. The large desk at the end of the hall must belong to the agency's director. A woman is sitting behind it. Amir stares at her. After a while, as if she senses the sharp tip of his attention, the woman looks up. He is not sure whether he recognizes her or not . . . but her large eyes are Katayoun's. And she finally gives him a familiar smile.

The brother and sister gingerly walk over to her.

"You must be Amir's sister, the lady who called."

Reyhaneh shakes hands with her. Amir holds out his hand. With a half-smile Katayoun pulls hers back. Reyhaneh jabs him in the side.

"It is forbidden for men and women to touch!"

Katayoun haughtily leans back in her chair.

"Oh dear, you have lost so much weight, Amir!"

And her gaze weighs on his drooping sleeve.

She is wearing a ring on her left hand.

"What a surprise that you've given thought to me! Do you need airline tickets? You should know there are only two or three countries you can visit without a visa."

He cannot answer. Right about now, foam will ooze from his lips. He holds a handkerchief in front of his mouth.

"Amir wanted to see you," Reyhaneh says. "And I thought it would be wonderful for me to meet someone Amir cared for."

Katayoun chuckles.

This one is different from the Katayoun he thinks he remembers. She is fat and her coverall has puffed out over her figure. He looks at the dimples on the backs of her hands.

> *«No, it is impossible for Katayoun to have had these chubby dimples.»*

"T-tell . . . h-her I . . . I don't quite remember . . . s-some things."

"I can tell you are not normal even without you saying it."

With a forced smile, Reyhaneh tries to placate their tempers.

"Amir believes there is a possibility that. . . . Well, because his memory has suffered a bit, he thinks perhaps before he went to war he may have become engaged to you."

Katayoun laughs sarcastically. Then she quickly collects herself and looks around. She holds her pen above her lips with two fingers and leans forward. Trying hard to keep her voice down, she growls, "There was a time when something like this above a man's lips was called a mustache—it was a sign of honor and dignity. A man would pledge a strand of it for his vows and promise to stand by his word even at the cost of his life. This Mister Amir of yours. . . . "

She lowers the pen and snaps it in two.

" . . . just like this, just this easily, broke his gentleman's promise to me."

> *«A smudge of lipstick is smeared on the broken pen.»*

"They say mankind's heaven and hell is right here on this earth. So you, Mister Amir, pray that God forgives your indecency. I have been married for three years and I have an adorable baby that I love very much. May jealous eyes go blind. I will not allow anyone to ruin my peaceful life."

> *«No, this cannot be Moon Brow's voice. There is not even a trace of bygone love in its spite.»*

And he looks down, pretending he has been shamed, acting as though Katayoun's words have stabbed him in the heart like a dagger. Reyhaneh and Katayoun's eyes remain on him, waiting for his reaction. And he holds his head down long enough for his eyes to fill with tears. The kind of tears that want to flow but manly pride tries to conceal.

Across from the streaked-hair girls, customers get up and new ones replace them. In Katayoun's expression there is now regret for having railed at a man wounded in war.

"I think we should not bother the lady any more than we already have," Reyhaneh says. "Let's go, Amir."

And he raises his empty sleeve to his mouth and bites the cuff until he senses a sufficiently emotional moment to speak.

"But . . . Ka . . . Katayoun . . . you . . . me, can you read it in my eyes? For the love of God, read it in my eyes! I am the same as I was before. I hold more affection for you in this one miserable hand that ten men could."

And with his voice cracking, he struggles to keep his teeth from chattering and foam from oozing out of his mouth.

Katayoun seems to have caved in. Her gaze is no longer on his maimed arm—she is looking into his eyes.

"Are you joking?" she says.

"What does someone who has become the joke of the world have to joke about? Katayoun!"

He speaks her name as if it were suffixed by "my love."

Katayoun starts to fiddle with the papers on her desk. She glances up at him and again busies herself with the papers. She tosses the broken pen in the trashcan. Again, she looks at him. Her expression is changing.

"You rascal, you never expressed your feelings to me."

"I didn't know how. No one had taught me how, Kata. Do I have to suffer because no one tau . . . taught me, because . . . I didn't kno . . . know how?"

"Life plays games. Bad games. Some people could have been together so beautifully, couldn't they?"

"Yes . . . Your child's name?"

He has finally managed to put her to shame in front of Reyhaneh.

" . . . is it Amir?"

Katayoun looks at him cautiously and mumbles, "Yes."

"I knew it."

His mouth has stopped foaming.

"Katayoun, why didn't you wait for me?"

The look in her eyes is now like that of a meek sheep.

"You left me. You have no idea how you just dumped me and left."

"You are right, I was a louse. You taught me what love means."

"I tried to. Do you remember all the letters I wrote to you? They all went unanswered."

"Yes, you tried hard. But the red pen you wrote with had no red left in it. Someone else had already shed the ink."

Katayoun looks shaken. He is stunned, too, at the words he has just blurted. Seeing her has triggered his memory. Reyhaneh, now even more confused, has one eye on Katayoun and the other on Amir.

Katayoun pretends she has not understood his implication.

"Meaning?" she asks.

He has baited her. He smirks the same way he had smirked when he found out Katayoun had not been pregnant after all.

"I am happy to see you like this," Katayoun snarls quietly. "It is better than if you had died. This way, you will pay even more dearly for what you

did, because you are not human enough to understand what it means to break someone's heart. When I saw you with that scrawny girl, the way you groveled after her, it broke my heart. I wanted to kill myself."

"Why didn't you tell me? I knew ways that would get you to Malakut-e A'la, heaven's realm, much faster than an airplane."

Even he is surprised that the words Malakut-e A'la have come from his lips.

Turning to Reyhaneh, Katayoun says, "Madam, I don't know if you are really his sister or part of his game. Take this lunatic cripple out of here or I will have you both thrown out on your rear ends."

Again she looks around to see if anyone has been watching this scene.

On his right shoulder:

Out on the street, Reyhaneh says, "You could have been kinder to her. She might have told you some things."

"There was too much hatred in her eyes. Even if she knew something, she wouldn't have said anything, out of spite."

The street looks more familiar to him. There is a crowded ice cream shop on the other side. He is sure he has memories of it. But now that shop is like a bottomless pit wedged between a furniture store and a restaurant.

"The girl you see in your dreams is not one of these floozies. . . . Who was the scrawny girl she mentioned?"

Reyhaneh takes his sedatives out of her handbag and gives one to him.

"Who was Khazar?" he asks.

"I don't know. How should I know? Let's go . . . she was probably one of your girlfriends. Don't you remember her?"

"It's vague, but her name is in my head."

"Come on, let's go home."

> « . . . and we watch the white swans and the swans do not watch us. . . . We can see them from the window. There are three adult

swans, so white that a misty halo envelops their radiance. Two of them have gone to the other side of the pool. When the other realizes it has been left alone, it frantically flaps its wings on the water and swims toward the couple. Once beside them, it calms down. Until later, when it has again been left alone and for a while does not realize it. . . . And we watch the weeping willow leaning over the water. The reflection of the beautiful shade of blue painted inside the pool has turned the water blue, too. And we watch the rippling circles where the tips of the weeping willow's leaves touch the water. And we watch the female swan coil its neck around its mate's neck. And so, she or perhaps I say, "I have always wanted to have a magical, magnificent engagement. . . . But now . . . look at us now! . . . " I see that I look at her face, but I don't see it, because I am looking at myself looking at her. And I see us put rings on each other's fingers. I kiss her finger that now possesses a ring. The cold ring is not colder than her snow-white finger. I run her fingertip over my lips. Gently . . . it smells of a distant pine. Perhaps it is even sticky, perhaps its stickiness is from the gum of a pine tree that has reached out and come here where it is safe. . . . And I see her raise her finger, and she makes me do the same, so that we coil them together like the swans' necks. And the translucent perforations in the air around us are a sign that she has spoken. Perhaps she has asked, "Promise?"

And perhaps I answer, "Yes! Promise."

And she perhaps replies, "That in our life together we will be both 'I' and 'we.'"

"In our life together we are both 'I' and 'we.'"

"In our life together, if ever we want to lie to the other one, we will first spit in the other one's face. . . . Promise?"

"Promise, to spit if ever we want to lie."

"If we ever no longer love the other one, we will leave the other one to die alone. . . . Promise?"

"No. It has to be the other way around. Whichever one of us falls out of love, they should just die instead."

And her voice is no longer there. Her feet drag the dry leaves across the floor of the room, she walks away. . . . I follow her out. The floor inside the room was carpeted with orange leaves, or were they swans' beaks? The swimming pool is half empty. The stone edge around it is caked with algae, and there are wilted leaves floating on the water. It is not safe. The weeping willow is not there. The swans are not there.»

And he sees. . . .

Traffic has come to a stop. Hundreds of Basijis, many of them teenagers, have crowded the street. With their uniforms sagging, they march in disorderly lines. Cheap duffle bags in their hands and tens of tall green and red flags flying over their heads. They are singing an Arabic anthem that the first warriors of Islam had sung in victories.

"They are taking to the Arabs what the Arabs brought to us God knows how many centuries ago."

Reyhaneh looks at him with surprise.

"Who?"

Amir points down the street.

"Those Basijis! Some of them go because of the lower cost of rice and refrigerators their families can buy from the mosques. Others go for the canned foods that are handed out at the front, or perhaps they go to steal the dead Iraqi soldiers' watches and cash."

"What are you seeing? There are only regular people over there . . . and keep your voice down! You are being unfair, that is not true of all Basijis."

Alarmed, Reyhaneh looks to their left and right.

"Those who were good and decent, the incompetent commanders sent to the mine fields by the thousands, straight in front of the Iraqis' bullets," he says. "They were slaughtered hundreds at a time.

They called themselves moat-fillers. They would go in waves, until the Iraqis either ran out of ammo or retreated."

"They knew what they were doing."

"Then why did they go?"

"Well, why did you go?"

"Because I was brave," he says mockingly. "I wanted to avenge Islam's invasion of Iran."

Reyhaneh nervously looks around, afraid that someone might be listening.

"If you go on talking like this, next time, Mom and I will have to go looking for you in prisons, or we'll have to sit at mass graves that don't even have a gravestone, hoping that you are buried there."

But Amir raises his voice.

"Where have you been, sister? I *am* a mass grave!"

And he shouts, "Ahoy, people! Ahoy, you with two arms! A hundred men are buried in me."

The passersby, as though accustomed to run-of-the-mill madmen, give him a passing glance and grin.

The Basijis have left and traffic has resumed. Reyhaneh is looking for an empty taxi. There are none. The same driver who had brought them there is standing across the street, leaning against his car, and smoking.

"Some of these drivers are informers," Reyhaneh says. "They goad you into talking and then they turn you in. Be careful."

The man says, "I knew it would be me and my steering wheel taking Mr. Yamini's kids back home. Going back to the garden?"

"No," Amir says.

He grabs Reyhaneh's hand and drags her into the car.

"Go to the university," he snaps at the driver.

"Why the university?" Reyhaneh asks puzzled.

"That's where I was studying, wasn't it?"

"Yes."

"Don't ask any questions. My head is working, running like a clock."

"Which one of the streets around the university, Sir?"

"Just go there . . . hurry, and tell me the names of the streets."

The names of some of the streets resonate in his mind . . . Enghelab Avenue strikes a chord, but it does not spark in him the feeling he is hoping for; the same with Farvardin and Ordibehesht Avenues. . . . He scours the walls and windows of the buildings, expecting to recognize one of them.

"Do you remember the old street names or the new ones they were changed to after the revolution?" Reyhaneh asks.

He is not sure. Just as he is not sure about Takht-e Jamshid Avenue.

"They renamed it Ayatollah Taleghani Avenue," Reyhaneh says.

"The poor man was different from the other mullahs," the driver adds. "They killed him."

The same with Palestine Avenue, Kaakh . . . then Ghodss. . . .

Reyhaneh points to the street they're on and says, "When you were at the university, this one was called Anatole France, wasn't it?"

After two hours and seventeen minutes of driving around in the constipated traffic, the driver stops at a gas station. As soon as he climbs out of the car, Reyhaneh whispers, "I don't trust this guy. He hasn't stuck around for no reason. He's a snitch. They're everywhere."

"He's getting paid a tidy sum. If he's a squealer, he'll get my right fuck finger, too."

With the car now reeking of gasoline, the search through the haze continues.

"This is driving me crazy," Reyhaneh complains. "Let's go home. We can come back another day."

"No. The apartment is somewhere around here."

And then. . . .

"Turn onto this street!"

His heart beats faster, then slower . . . then. . . .

"Turn right."

"Have you seen the grocery shops in Amirabad, Sir? There are long lines in front of all of them. People buying government-subsidized rice and cooking oil with coupons. If things go on like this, we'll need coupons just to breathe. You, thank God, have no clue how much things have changed, and for the worse."

Amir senses that the mood and attitude of the people on the streets have also changed. At the end of Sixteenth of Azar Street, an old woman with a basket, slowly shuffling along, catches his eye. Her face and especially her walk are familiar to him. He thinks, Perhaps I used to see her walking by every day from the window of the apartment.

"Go back!"

Yet he does not sense the ghost of his Alfa Romeo having been parked on this street.

"Turn left!"

Then. . . .

"Go back to Enghelab Circle! Go back!"

A greasy whirlpool with rainbow-colored spirals is churning in his mind. Among the crowd of pedestrians around Enghelab Circle, he sees himself standing with his back to a cinema, looking out at the center of the circle.

"Right here! Stop right here!"

He climbs out of the car, drenched in sweat in the smoggy, cold wind. . . .

He sees a chalk line in the middle of the sidewalk, stretching far away.

«It is one of those "Follow This Line" ones. . . . »

The line does not fade under the black shoes treading on it.

The scribe on his right shoulder had written:

People are reading the afternoon newspapers that report with the largest possible headlines, The Shah Left . . . many have crossed out "left" and replaced it with "ran away" . . . and the circle is becoming more and more crowded. Smoke from buildings set on fire around the city spreads through the sky. Amir stands there, looking at the bronze Shah sitting on a bronze horse in the middle of the circle. People look at it and shout, "Death to the Shah!" And then they join the jubilant masses that do not know what to do in an era without the Shah. The slogans change. People proudly show each other rial bills with the Shah's eyes gouged out. They pass around sweets and pastries. And he, still confused and bewildered, wonders what is happening. He has never in his life shouted a slogan or the ghost of a verse. Between his teeth the sensation and in his ears the sound of shattered glass from a bank window being crushed under heavy feet. . . .

«Where is Khazar now?»

The Shah is on the run riding on a mule cart.

People dance to the slogan. A man tries to climb up the statue's tall pedestal. Someone shouts, "Not now, it's too soon!" Someone else yells, "Don't worry, he's gone for good." One man cautions, "Don't get carried away, there will be a coup d'état." A group encourages the rock climber. And Amir's anxiety deepens. Little by little, the passing waves of flesh mince and mingle his vision and senses. . . . By the time he comes to, a steel cable has been tied around the rider confident of the future, and the sound of a truck engine revving comes from somewhere nearby. The horse's legs buckle, the crowd roars, the legs give way. A huge wave passes by, knocking into him and shoving him back. . . .

The scribe writes on his right shoulder:

He gets back into the car, turns to Reyhaneh, and says, "I don't remember if it was a truck or a trailer."

Reyhaneh and the driver look at him quizzically. And Reyhaneh gripes, "This is useless, there are thousands of houses and apartments here."

"I have to search around. I saw an old woman who looked familiar. All old women look alike, but this one looked different."

And he sees Abu-Yahya standing on the bus line, pointing at something to show it to the person next to him.

"Turn around!"

On the opposite side of the street, the image of the sign above the university gates becomes etched in his mind.

"Go! Go! Turn left!"

"We have already been here. It's Anatole France Avenue."

"Keep going! Slow down!"

"For the love of God, tell me who was in that photo you tore up."

Reyhaneh frowns.

"It is none of your business. Maybe it was some nutcase like you who hurt me."

It is not clear what is going on in his mind. It is unwritable.

On this side, too, it is not clear what has sparked in his memory to make him want to drive along this street again.

And he sees a peacock.

"Right here!" he shouts.

An old, narrow three-story apartment building. On its facade, shoddy tile work depicting a peacock with its tail unfurled. The peacock is the same old peacock, except that some of its tiles are missing.

"If I go inside, I'll know which door it was."

"I'd better go with you."

"What for?"

"If people see you with a girl, they won't get too suspicious."

They climb the narrow staircase up to the third floor. He's confident he could ring the right doorbell even with his eyes closed.

> «Do left-handed people ring doorbells with their left hand or their right?»

A man with thinning gray hair opens the door slightly. Warm air and the smell of fried onions waft out; the faint scent of opium follows.

The man looks at them warily through the narrow opening and asks, "What do you want?"

His gaze pauses on Amir's empty sleeve.

The man's face is more than just familiar.

"Do you remember me?" Amir asks, quickly adding, "I'm Amir. I used to come to your home with Kaveh for lunch or dinner once in a while. I stopped by your old house, you weren't there . . . Is Kaveh home?"

The man, distrustful and churlish, pretends to be searching the nooks and crannies of his mind.

"Yes, y . . . y . . . yes. I vaguely remember you."

From somewhere inside the apartment, a woman shouts, "Who is it?"

"It's nothing, they're conducting a census to allot coupons. Your fried onions are burning."

"Is Kaveh home?" Amir asks again.

"No, he is not."

"We rented this apartment together."

"Are you the friend who joined the army and went to war?"

"Yes. Kaveh. . . . There is something important I need to speak to Kaveh about. Please. . . . "

"And your arm. . . . "

"Yes. And this is my sister—she knows how close a friendship Kaveh and I had."

Without opening the door any wider, the man edges out into the hallway.

"I remember the young lady more than I remember you. My naive son paid a high price for his friendship with you. He suffered a lot of trouble from your family."

"I just want to have a quick talk with him. It may affect my entire life. When will he be home?"

"Son!" the man says with his voice cracking, "Kaveh will not be coming home. He is gone. We sold our house in Shemiran and used the money to get him out of the country. We rent this place."

Amir feels sweat seeping from the stump of his arm.

"So you sacrificed your arm for the very holy land of Islam?"

"The nation took it from me on its way to Jerusalem. Stop making fun of me, Sir! Kaveh . . . I just want to ask him one question."

"I told you," the man says bitterly, "Kaveh has left our home. He has been gone for several years."

"Do you have any photographs of him with me and our friends?"

"No."

"Any letters or notes?"

"Ask your father, Agha Haji. . . . Whatever we had, the agents he sent took away and never returned."

"Where is Kaveh now?"

"Not here."

Again the man eyes him guardedly.

"Are you really Amir?"

"If I was not Kaveh's Amir I would not come here with one arm to knock on this door."

"Fine, fine! There are a lot of one-armed and one-legged guys these days. What do you expect me to do?"

"Where is Kaveh?"

"I keep telling you, he is gone, and we have no news of him."

Looking sad, the man leans against the wall.

Amir's words seem to have disarmed him. The wrinkled, craggy mistrust on his face, his struggle to conceal . . . and suddenly something seems to weigh on his right knee. He puts his hands on it.

"I should have had this knee operated on. But I can't manage the cost."

"But you were well-off."

"We were. . . . Of course, not like your family, with your father being a heavyweight in the bazaar. Kaveh used to say you proved to him many times that you were a true friend."

"Thank God, our family has not done badly . . . and I will do anything for Kaveh's sake."

"No, thank you. I don't need any help. There was a time when it was me who always extended a helping hand to those who needed it."

Through the barely open door, Amir sees a large mirror on the wall. Whether he remembers or not, he knows he liked to screw women in different positions in front of it and watch. The wide-eyed women and girls would get so horny looking at their reflection. . . . He thinks he hears someone crying in the bedroom he and Kaveh used to toss a coin for whenever they wanted to be alone with a girl.

And the man is saying, " . . . Kaveh always said that you are very noble, that you never abandon your friends. I want to thank you in his place."

"How much will the operation cost?"

"Oh, don't even mention it."

Reyhaneh wants to say something, but Amir does not give her a chance.

"So you are saying Kaveh is not here?" he asks again, raising his voice.

"Sir, we will not trouble you anymore," Reyhaneh says. "Our reminding you of the past has upset you. Amir, it is best that we come visit the gentleman some other time, tomorrow or the day after."

The man does not look at Reyhaneh. With tears welling in his eyes, he looks at Amir and says, "You have no idea what my family has gone through because of you. My company, its five-story building, its assets, they were all confiscated during the revolution. Now some big shot's son owns it. . . . All we managed to do was to save Kaveh. I am sure your honorable sister has told you what we have endured . . . I am sure you understand."

And he says this in a tone suggesting, You know what caused it all.

"In this country, if the high-and-mighty go after someone, the watchful angels will keep account of it. Kaveh would not tell us the whole story. My son sacrificed himself to keep your secrets."

> *«He's implying that I am beholden to him. . . . Ugh, my head! I'm all messed up again because I can't understand what is happening, who is saying what. . . .»*

With his voice shaking, the man is saying, " . . . the medical examiner reported that the girl was not a virgin. I wish that was all . . . but you know better than I do!"

> *«Something happened, but he doesn't want to tell me, but why won't he? What was it that it seems I must remember? . . .»*

The man points at Reyhaneh.

"They wanted to blame it on Kaveh. Pin it on him. . . . We paid plenty in bribes, put up our house as bail so that they would release him, and we paid a middleman all the money we had left for him to get Kaveh out of the country."

"Wherever he is, he must have a telephone number," Amir says.

"Who knows? That shady middleman may have done away with my son while crossing the mountains into Turkey and stolen his money. . . . And I am left with a leg that is going lame."

> *«Right about now, the mortar shells will land and dust and smoke will turn the air dark and dim.»*

"How much will the operation cost?"

"The doctors said about forty thousand tomans."

"I will take care of it, and you will find some trace of Kaveh for me."

The man takes on an air of graciousness.

"I am grateful for your kindness."

"Don't stand on ceremony. One of Kaveh's good traits was that he was blunt and direct, and I am not a middle-of-the-road friend."

Reyhaneh puts a firm hand on his shoulder.

"Amir! It's late, we have to go!"

He feels as sapped as a mule stuck in mud.

Confused, he asks, "Where do we have to go?"

"Uncle Arjang! We're supposed to meet him. He is waiting for us on the street."

"No, don't go," the man says. "I want to pour my heart out to my son's friend."

"Tomorrow, then," Reyhaneh says. "Tomorrow, we will pay you a visit and bring what Amir has promised you."

She yanks on Amir's empty sleeve and with even more force drags him down the stairs.

It is only near the bottom of the staircase that Amir notices his sleeve is moving ahead of him. Subconsciously, he moans, "So much has changed in my absence."

The man, leaning over the railing, calls down to them, "But you didn't leave me your telephone number."

"We will contact you," Reyhaneh replies loudly. "In a couple of days."

She pushes Amir into the car and snaps at the driver, "Back to the garden!"

Surprised by her tone, the driver quickly starts the car and puts it in gear.

"Where are we supposed to meet Uncle Arjang?"

"Nowhere. You are so stupid! It was all an act. The guy was conning you."

"Who?"

"Kaveh's father! Were you going to bequeath wealth from the Caliph's trove? You don't even have enough in your pocket to pay for our ride back home!"

On his left:

He is stunned. It has been written before. Whenever he is rattled, his mind becomes sharp. Like a boozed-up man who can for a short while pull himself together and stand up straight and steady so he won't spill his drink, and he suddenly discovers a truth, but he will not remember it the next day.

"I know, I was leading him on. But there was a mirror in the apartment that kept muddling me up. There were so many reflections in it."

And he is at a loss. His neck slumps and his head hits the side window.

"Who was the girl he was talking about?" he mumbles.

"I don't know. There was no girl. He was playing on your sentiments to get some money out of you. And he will take the money and give you a bogus telephone number."

"I kept sensing that Kaveh was in the apartment. Hiding, or being hidden somewhere in the living room."

Right:

A midday moon is in Tehran's sky. With his head still leaning against the car window, Amir stares out at the soot-covered buildings.

And he thinks . . .

> «In a strange town, when you watch the people walking along the sidewalks, the sadness you feel is not a bad sadness, because

you are certain that among them there is no one you know. Like Kerend, where I went on leave, so happy to be going to the bathhouse. Happy not just because I would masturbate—everyone masturbated—but happy that I would see ordinary people, and the four or five pedestrians in Kerend were complete strangers to me. Being in a familiar town is good, its sidewalks are somehow comforting, because among the people passing by there is perhaps someone you know, someone who will tell you the truth. . . . »

On the sidewalk, the only people he sees wearing colorful clothes are four- or five-year-old children. He sees a little girl in red who gives a coin to a crippled beggar and runs back to her mother. Farther away, among the people waiting for a taxi, he sees a pair of eyes that look like a doe's.

«Could it be her? . . . Moon Brow? . . . »

"While I was gone, some things were destroyed. . . . "

Reyhaneh is silent.

"Who was the girl Kaveh's father was talking about?"

On his left:

He has been sitting on the chair in his room, facing the full-length window, for two hours and seventeen minutes. It is dawn and from mosques near and far he hears azan, the call to prayer.

«The demanding voice of the nearest azan chanter is even more grating coming through a diphtheria-stricken loudspeaker.»

He is tempted to dive headfirst through the window, but still, despite being tired, he again starts from the letter A. He reviews all the girls' names over and over—names of flowers and princesses, names of all the nice things that become girls' names. . . . He whispers each one several times, hoping that it will stir some emotion in him that the others don't. He thinks he hears a bird landing on the eucalyptus tree.

> *«If there is a bird there, then it must be the cuckoo bird.»*

And he sees fog rising from the patterns in the carpet. A thin fog, with a tinge of blue. . . .

> *«On the mountaintop, the snow was too shy to come into our tent, but the fog was not. The wind would bring it from the valley and slip it into our tent. . . .»*

The scribe on his right shoulder had written:

Nights at the observation post, he tells stories to amuse himself:

«Once upon a time, a girl's stepmother . . . let's assume the girl's name was Farangis . . . demanded that she spin yarn every day after she finished cooking and cleaning the house. Meanwhile, she pampered her own spoiled daughter and did not let her lift a finger around the house. One day when Farangis, weary and exhausted, was sitting in the corner of the yard spinning yarn, a strong wind blew and rolled away her ball of cotton. Farangis cried, "Oh, what am I to do? My stepmother will punish me harshly!" And she ran after it. Farangis ran and ran until she reached the desert. The ball of cotton rolled and rolled and fell into a well. Farangis, afraid that her mean stepmother would beat her, climbed into the well. May you never see greater horror, but inside the well, she saw a dreadful beast sleeping and snoring loudly, just like Sergeant Pourpirar. Trembling and scared, Farangis reached out to snatch her ball of cotton, but just then the beast woke up and roared, "Aha! I smell a human! Who are you and how dare you come into my well?"

"My name is Farangis," she said. "I have come to take back my ball of cotton."

"Come and pick the fleas off my scalp," the beast demanded.

Farangis obeyed. And without betraying how filthy and smelly the beast's head was, she laid his head on her lap and one by one picked the fleas and killed them. When she had finished, the beast said, "You have been a very kind and well-mannered young girl.

Go and take your ball of cotton." Farangis went to take the cotton and saw two fountains in the corner of the well. One had water as clear as the fountain on the moon, the other had water as dark as the most poisonous poison.

The beast roared, "Wash your face in the fountain with the black water." Trembling, Farangis washed her face in the fountain. When she climbed out of the well, she realized to her horror that night had fallen. But in front of her, there was light brighter than the glow of ten lanterns. A crescent moon had appeared on her forehead, so bright and so beautiful.

Now go and sleep peacefully and tomorrow night I will tell you the rest of the story, about how a scorpion appeared on the forehead of Moon Brow's mean stepsister.»

He remembers times when he had so much fun and pleasure, times that he did not cherish and thoughtlessly let fly by, and now, on this mountain, he craves a single moment of those times. He remembers the girl who taught him how to rub up the door instead of rubbing up a panty . . . and he remembers the first time, the sensation of hardened flesh brushing against the folds of wet, crimson skin, and the memory of that titillation rises below his navel. The warmth of recollections lasts only a few minutes, and again icy winds slow the passage of time.

Finally, on the far side of the southwesterly mountains, bolts of lightning from explosions strike. There is no thunder. After a minute of silence, holy heavenly blazes of counterattacks, one after the other, randomly, spasmodically, rise in the sky.

«The attack must be coming from somewhere in the Bazi Deraz mountains. If this pre-ground attack bombardment with cannons and mortars is heavy and continues long enough to raze trenches and flesh, it is Iraqi. If it is beggarly and sparse, it is Iranian.»

After a while, the bombardment becomes one-sided.

> «The Iraqis have started celebrating. They have lowered the barrels of their antiaircraft heavy machine guns while soft Iranian flesh lacerates, tears, and mangles.»

Every few minutes he has to shuffle his feet; otherwise his boots will freeze and become one with the stone and ice, and another soldier will have to come and kick them loose.

The wind does not bring the buzz of the battle's bullets. It does not bring the barks of dogs in far-flung abandoned villages. It does not bring the crackle of gravel and the rustle of dry leaves being swept in the garden. It brings the lustful cries of a girl. "Go inside me, free me from this hymen."

> «Did I do to Khazar what tens of Iraqi soldiers did to a captured Iranian woman? . . . »

The scribe on his right shoulder had written:

He is nervous. He cannot drive any further on Eisenhower Avenue. The city is in chaos and out of control. Along the avenue and its sidewalks, crowds are frantically moving east. Among them he sees no one who resembles him—longhaired, clean-shaven, and stylishly dressed. . . . From mouth to mouth news travels that armed officers from the Air Force have joined the masses. . . . On this Judgment Day, only a handful of cars are roaming the streets. Useless traffic lights senselessly turn red and green.

Tehran looks gloomy and gray on this wintry February day. Turmoil weighs heavy on the city. . . .

Khazar jokes, "What a day we picked for a romantic date!"

"It seems so," he says, worried.

"Che Guevara should have been here with us, sitting in the back seat of your Alfa Romeo."

Shots are being fired here and there. He has never seen such pandemonium. He feels uneasy and afraid—he doesn't know whether for himself or for Khazar. Some people are carrying clubs. He takes advantage of an opening in the throng of people, turns onto a side street, and parks the car. Columns of smoke rise in the sky over the eastern and southern parts of Tehran.

Khazar opens the door to climb out.

"Are you crazy?" he shouts.

He is afraid of what Khazar's elegant outfit might incite among the agitated and angry mob reeking of smoke. He knows that at that very moment in other parts of the city unarmed men and women with hatred in their raised fists are shouting for freedom and being shot.

With the door open, cold wind and the smell of smoke flood the car. Khazar ignores him. She ignores the ambiguous, perhaps hateful glares of the people whose faces seem to have changed overnight. She asks a few of them what has happened.

There are no taxis or buses in sight. Amir wonders how to travel the long distance to the girl's home north of the city. A sneeze spurts out of his mouth and nose. Illness has finally triumphed over him. He has no tissue to wipe his nose.

A man carrying a two-gallon container of gasoline is running down the street. Another man follows with a plastic bag full of empty Coca-Cola bottles. Someone shouts, "People! Do not be afraid!"

"Martial law can't even lick your balls. . . . "

The slogans grow louder.

"Cannons, tanks, guns, no longer work. . . . "

"If Khomeini calls for jihad, the world's armies cannot stop me. . . . "

Slick, stubborn ash from burning tires clots in his throat, worsening its soreness. Khazar gets back into the car. He cannot tell whether her liveliness is real or a disguise for her fear.

"They say the army has declared that anyone who is out on the streets after 4:00 pm will be shot. It seems they are planning a coup d'état."

"I have to take you back home."

"And Imam Khomeini has said that people should ignore the martial law, that they should flood the streets. Armed struggle is starting. . . . "

"How did Khomeini's message spread from Paris to the streets of Tehran so fast? . . . I wish you had a headscarf or something you could cover your hair with."

"Hey! An Islamic regime has barely been established and already you want to put a headscarf on me?"

"Stop your slogans, girl. What do you want us to do?"

They jump at the sound of a loud blow. A young man about Amir's age has pounded his fist on the hood of the car and yells, "Prissy kids! We'll deal with you, too!" Hateful looks and scornful sneers pass by the car windows. No scream or gasp has escaped Khazar's lips, but they have turned white. Slogans from left and right entwine and palpitate.

"Bread, housing, liberty!"

A larger crowd counters the communists: "Independence, freedom, Islamic Republic!"

And united shouts of "Death to . . . Death to . . . Death to . . . " reach the rising smoke from the fires.

"I have shouted along with them at demonstrations," Khazar groans. "Now, I'm afraid of them."

With the two trapped in the car, the mob spreads out and heads toward a destination only they know.

"What have we done? What is happening?"

"Be quiet and let me figure out what to do."

Someone tosses a crumpled tissue on the hood of the car. Someone else, a crumpled piece of paper. . . . A man walks by, returns, and with his foot on the front fender and his hand on his waist, he glares at Amir. He says nothing, he just glares. Amir looks down.

"I am going to die on these streets. I don't want this death," Khazar moans.

"Places like this are not where people like us die."

Khazar asks, "Is your apartment somewhere around here?"

"Yes."

"Is Kaveh there?"

"I don't know."

"Call him. If he's not, we can walk there."

"Why?"

Khazar nervously screams, "Can you for once, just once, listen to me? Just once in your life!"

He gets out of the car, now angry.

> «Lunatic girl! She says, "Just once!" And dimwit me, I have always obeyed her orders. . . . »

His head feels heavy. He is cold and feverish.

"The tanks! The tanks!"

Bits of burned paper and ash rain down from the sky.

In the public phone booth, his hand shakes as he dials.

On his right:

Khazar is staring out the bedroom window. Night has fallen. She has not let him turn on the lights. On Tehran's horizon, the red and yellow glow of fires arches up into the relentless smoke. Gunshots sound, uncertain.

Amir sits on the twin bed with dirty sheets. He has tuned the radio to BBC Persian. The newscaster is excitedly reporting on the revolution. Fire and blood in Tehran . . . tanks and the Imperial Guards have moved into the city . . . armed struggle between the people and the armed forces faithful to the Shah . . . Ayatollah Khomeini has ordered the masses to ignore the martial law and to remain on the streets until the complete collapse of the Shah's government . . . on Tehran's streets . . . people and members of the Air Force have set up barricades . . . Ayatollah Khomeini has announced the formation of The Council of the Islamic Revolution . . . one insider who did not wish to be named said . . . in his last interview in Neauphle-le-Château, Ayatollah Khomeini said. . . .

"A lot of blood will be shed tonight," Khazar says mournfully. "I think it's all over. . . . "

Amir lights a cigarette. He swirls it in the air so that its burning tip draws the symbol of eternity in the dark.

"Amir, I am really afraid."

She turns to him. There is little light in the room; still, he can see the teardrop that has rolled down her face, now paler than ever.

"Aren't you afraid?"

"Of course, it is frightening."

The girl, angry again, snaps, "For once in your life, talk frankly about *you*. Forget sweeping generalizations. Tell me, are you afraid or not?"

"Of course I am, but to my left ball."

"What have we done so unknowingly?"

There is a half-bottle of arak in the apartment. It is not enough. He takes a stingy sip, rolls it around in his mouth, and lets it sit on his tongue.

Khazar calls her parents and tells them that she won't be able to make her way back home and will stay in a friend's room at the university dormitory. She is safe. Then she grabs the bottle from Amir and takes a swig.

"I don't remember ever lying to my parents."

"The first time is tough."

She sits down on the bed next to him. Her elbows perched on a pair of delicate knees kept together.

"Tanks are not built to roll down streets, are they? Streets are meant for walking, shopping, and for going home . . . aren't they?"

"Streets are also meant for a lot of despicable things."

"I don't think people like us will make it through this revolution alive."

"If it's us, we will make it through anything."

"I . . . I know one of these days, out on the street. . . . Don't say streets are meant for despicable things . . . I will die on the street. I feel it."

After a surge of coughs, he takes Khazar's hand.

"Hold me close, I'm cold," she says.

It is hard to hold someone close sitting side by side.

"Kiss me! The way you wanted to on that rainy night."

He brushes his lips like butterfly wings against hers and flutters over them.

"You don't need to show off. I don't want it like this. Really kiss me."

And Amir, with all his fear and anger, love and hatred, kisses her plump lower lip and then her thin upper lip, drawing them in between his fevered lips. . . . And the still hesitant and timid touch of the tip of his tongue against hers . . . and he takes her mouth in his. She moans. . . . He doesn't want it like this, not on this night. He doesn't want the two of them to plunge into those dirty sheets that who knows how many girls have slept in. . . . The windows rattle from the blast of an explosion . . . and he is burning with fever, with wanting and not wanting. And his skin craves hers.

"You are so hot! I think you are running a fever."

She wipes the sweat off his forehead. He feels the coolness of her arm around his neck.

> «Her arm is so light. Like the wing of the baby sparrow that had fallen out of its nest and was trembling. Ants were crawling on it.»

Khazar's cold fingers open the second button on his shirt. They feel his chest, and he slides his right hand under her shirt, over her back, and scales her spine vertebra by vertebra. With a single practiced move of his thumb and two fingers, he unhooks her bra. . . . Khazar, her eyes open, leans forward and with abandon inhales the scent of the hair and sweat on his chest.

"It is so natural. So feral. . . . "

And she raises her head with the rhythm of a breath from deep inside her chest. Like a cobra, his left hand slithers to her breast. With a fingertip, he feels its firm girlish tip . . . until finally taking her small breast in his hand. Something he has yearned to do for months. He shivers. He doesn't know from fever or excitement. . . .

«Something is happening that I don't understand.»

Khazar's fingers open the rest of his shirt buttons so that her hand can freely flutter over his chest.

«It seems clever Khazar, too, knows how to brush one wing forward and one wing back.»

"Give me your fever."

He wants to suppress his awareness and become all instinct.

Khazar takes another sip of arak. She puts her lips over his and lets the liquid ooze into his mouth.

"Those good-time girls you have," she says sarcastically, "do they show you a good time like this? . . . Teach me, I want to learn how."

"Shut up! You are a really good . . . (he wants to say kisser, but out of obstinacy says) smoocher."

"When we were kids, my brother and I used to imitate our parents smooching. You are the first one. No one's lips or hands have ever touched me."

He stops himself from saying, You all say this.

"Caress my hair," Khazar whispers. "I need it, so much . . . I feel so alone."

He runs his fingers through her hair. He feels her scalp with his fingertips and moves them like a snail between the strands of hair. Khazar sighs. She puts her hand between his thighs and gently glides up. Her fingertips are close to the turmoil in his middle.

Her fingertips circle his half-hardened cock. . . .

No! I will write this.

Amir pulls back.

"No! Not like this, not here. . . . "

"Why not, silly man! I want to give you my virginity. I would rather a creature like you takes it than a head-over-heels, dull and devoted suitor."

"I don't want it to be like this. I don't like it. It isn't beautiful like this."

"I have never managed to see myself in a prissy wedding dress."

She lays her hand over his, cupping her breast.

"Don't put on an act of valor and profound love. If you don't take it, I will give it to one of your friends. That Kaveh always leers at me so vulgarly."

He can smell smoke. His fever is worsening. In the light from the florescent streetlights on Anatole France Avenue, he can see the tiny beads of perspiration that have percolated above Khazar's lips . . . he wants to lick them away one by one.

And only now, he remembers he has not eaten since the previous night. He takes a swig of arak and looks at the little left in the bottle.

"If you don't make me bleed, a soldier will do it with a bullet on the street."

"Crazy . . . you're crazy, Khazar!"

"I promise I won't cry . . . I will be happy."

He walks over to the window. Aside from the eastern parts of the city, there are now random explosions in the west, too. Their glow ripples and arches up in the horizon, illuminating the darker-than-night columns of smoke. The distant roar of impassioned revolt can be heard in every direction.

He hears the sound of a gulp being taken . . . the rustle of a shirt being pulled up . . . and her voice, "If you are afraid of commitment and other nonsense, don't be! I will have no expectations. And I am not like Katayoun to fake a pregnancy."

He wants to tear open the window, stand facing the city of fire and blood, and shout, You crazy Khazar! I am in love with you. . . .

Khazar's bra hits the window and falls at his feet.

Right:

. . . when he walks out of the bedroom, with Khazar's groans of pain and pleasure still ringing in his ears, in the dim light of the living room he sees a drop of thin, pink blood on a few tangled strands of his pubic hair. . . .

The scribe on his right shoulder writes:

Reyhaneh puts an envelope on the edge of his bed. Opened.

"It's for you."

"For me? . . . You're joking."

But the girl looks serious and pensive.

"I never receive any letters, but this one was addressed to me. I opened it and realized it is actually for you."

The letter is just one sentence long. 'I heard you are looking for me. Tuesday, the thirteenth, I will meet you in front of Kazbah. 3:00 pm.'

Like an egg that has fallen on the floor, his heart cracks open and spreads.

"It's her!"

"Are you nuts?" Reyha says.

"Well, yes."

"It's a prank. Didn't you pick up on the threes—Tuesday, thirteenth, at 3:00."

"You don't even know what Kazbah is, stop blabbering!"

"Whoever she is, she must have heard something from Katayoun."

"What difference does it make? I remember some things about Kazbah. Whoever she is, she knows. . . . It's her. We will go on Tuesday."

"No!" Reyhaneh says. "I will not come. I will not play any part in such stupidity."

Right:

The mountainous cold wind of northern Tehran gusts through the streets. Every half hour he has rattled the chain on Kazbah's door, as though trying to waken the ghosts trapped inside.

> «What? Where have they all gone, who were in this place night after night, hedonists of the night? The seductions and stolen kisses of this place, the promises and vows and the I love yous? The way this place has been set on fire and chained, it's as if they never were, as if they were just the dreams of the flames that scorched this place and infused it with smoke. . . . »

He goes back to Reyhaneh, who has not moved from the opposite sidewalk. To his surprise, the disgruntled girl has not nagged at all. At 5:00, she says, "Whoever this girl is, she is hiding somewhere around here, watching us, laughing at us."

"I don't understand. If it is Moon Brow herself, it's worth waiting for her."

"Let's go. I told you, it's just some prankster."

With a lump in his throat, Amir follows his sister.

"What do I have left for someone to want to trick me like this?"

He thinks he has never in his life felt as cold as he does now. He can't feel the stump of his left arm. It's as if it froze and snapped off. He thinks the cold has seeped out from deep inside his bones.

The scribe on his right shoulder had written:

The wind is relentless. Even though they have set up their low tent on a slope behind a boulder, the furious gusts still beat the canvas against his head as he huddles inside. They slither under the plastic sheet tied over the tent and inflate it, trying to tear it away. It is Amir's shift to go up to the observation post. Sergeant Pourpirar opens the tent flap and comes in. Darkness and snowflakes come with him.

"My dick up this war's ass and the ass of every top dog giving orders," he growls.

He says it again, hinting at Amir, who has ordered everyone to be up for a night shift, to check on the soldiers on scout duty. Pourpirar tosses his ice-crusted poncho on the ground next to the tent's entrance. His boots, too. And he squats down next to the decrepit kerosene heater burning mostly yellow flames. On one end of the flimsy wick there is jagged blue in the yellow, licking up and retreating again.

Amir unfolds his poncho to pull it on over his coat. Pourpirar takes the kettle off the heater and pours himself some tea. He changes the channels on the radio until he finds an Iraqi army frequency. A woman is talking in Russian, rapidly repeating codes.

"The alligator eaters!" Pourpirar snarls, and as usual spits on the blanket spread on the ground. "The Iraqis have women at the front! They have a blast of a good time with them, and look at us."

In their brutal life on the mountaintop, constantly hunched over and chilled to the bone, with days and nights crawling by, the madness of the wind, the rocks, and the snow penetrates their minds and bodies. And the sound of the woman's voice is soothing. It stirs something in their grimy, callused bodies.

"Don't worry," Amir says as he ties his bootlaces. "Another six days and we will go back down to rest. Lieutenant Colonel King Kong is there if you want him to screw you after he is done screwing his personal orderly."

"Well, so far you are the one who is screwed," Pourpirar says. "If you hadn't argued with the squadron commander, he wouldn't have come down on us so hard. You're going to get shafted!"

"Don't forget you're talking to someone who outranks you," Amir snaps back. "I could report you."

"Whose balls paid the price when you reported the lieutenant colonel to the commander?"

Amir does not let on how these words have reopened last summer's wound.

"I did what I had to do," he says. "The man sent those poor soldiers into a minefield. He did the Iraqis' job for them. What would you do if your son was one of them and all they sent back to you was his leg?"

"Stop yapping!"

"Yapping feels pretty good. Tell me, what would you do if your daughter was in prison and a Revolutionary Guard showed up at your house with a box of pastries to tell you he is your son-in-law?"

The sergeant spits on the blanket again.

"What are you carrying on about?"

"The mullahs have said that if a woman political prisoner is still a virgin when she is executed, she will go to heaven. So, the night before her execution a Revolutionary Guard will take her virginity. Then he will show up at your door and say, 'I was the groom. Get over to the prison and take enough money to pay for the bullets in her.' . . . Of course, they will not return her body to you."

They both sit staring at their rifles flung on the floor.

"A father who got a box of pastries for his daughter's virginity went dancing on the street, mad and out of his mind, he rang the neighbors' doorbells, shouting, 'Come on over, my son-in-law has come to visit!'"

Enraged, Pourpirar lashes out, "If instead of running off scared that motherfucking Shah had ordered the army to mow you all down on the streets, your sister wouldn't get fucked like this."

"My sister got fucked a long time ago. When I was fucking other people's sisters, I didn't know that my own sister was getting fucked, too."

"If your sister is as pretty as you are, she is worth fucking."

Amir thinks, Twenty bullets in my cartridge . . . twenty, sleeping, but ready. . . . I should empty them in his gut and in his mouth. . . . But, he barks back, "She is pretty. Remind me to give you our address next time you go on leave."

The sergeant changes his tone and the subject.

"Forget it, boy. Go and check on the soldiers."

Amir assumes that after he leaves the tent, Pourpirar will jerk off.

"If it comes down to it," he says, "I will face off with the lieutenant colonel again. And this time, I will include that orderly in my report."

"You are such a stubborn mule! You filed a complaint and we were all penalized. If it weren't for you, we would still be taking it easy in the kitchen instead of freezing our balls off up here."

"I started it, but why did you sign the report in support of me?"

"I lost my mind."

"Having personal orderlies has been banned in the army. And if that King Kong is shoving his dick in that poor boy, he should be executed. I am not going to let this go."

Fed up, Pourpirar whips his hand in the air as if swatting away Amir's voice.

"Go cuddle up to your mommy! Dimwits like you started the revolution and dragged us poor slobs to these mountains and valleys so that the politico-ideologues at the base can go get our wives pregnant."

Unlike other nights, tonight they don't get into a brawl to purge their heaped-up anger and frustration, all the while choking back their growls for fear that the Iraqis might hear them. Afterward, the next day or the one after, out of loneliness, they would stop ignoring each other and one or the other would take the first step to make peace.

The woman's voice is still coming from the radio. She is now speaking Arabic.

Amir pulls on his gloves. Pourpirar changes the channel. The voice of an Iranian Kurd, a supporter of Iraq . . .

"Hey, Iranian soldiers, Basijis, Khomeini handed you a plastic key to heaven's gates so that you would come and fight with Saddam Hussein's armed-to-the-teeth army. Don't be fooled by this conniving mullah of Indian descent. None of you will go home alive. We will now broadcast a few segments from speeches given by the exalted Ayatollah Khomeini."

The man mimics the boorish Arabic accent of Ayatollah Khomeini, who in his speeches makes plain and simplistic statements and the masses roar, "Allah-o Akbar, Allah-o Akbar, Khomeini our leader."

"Imam Khomeini says . . . Pepsi is black . . . cucumbers are green . . . Imam Khomeini!"

On his right:

Amir climbs out of the observation-post trench. He has no patience for the illiterate soldiers and their drivel. With the snow crunching under his boots, he walks off and sits on a boulder some distance away from the two men on scout duty. He stares at the darkness in the valley, at the spot where the mountain pass most likely is, and then, farther away, at the obscurity of the distant plain.

The sky is filled with frozen stars, but the wind whips snow and fog from the bluffs and ice pits up to the peak. Hardly five or six minutes have passed since he sat huddled against the wind and already a sheet of ice has settled on his poncho. He calculates, eight months left to the end of his military service. . . .

Pourpirar walks over to him.

"They just broadcast a red alert. I guess there's been an attack somewhere."

He wakes up the four soldiers sleeping in the relief trench, knowing that as soon as he leaves, they will go back to sleep. The two soldiers on duty have stopped quietly laughing behind the wall of piled-up rocks. Tomorrow he must check to see if the dirt and thorn bushes they have stuffed between the rocks as camouflage have held. He puts down his regular binoculars, useless in the dark. He takes the American night-vision binoculars. They're no good either—their range is short.

> «Somewhere in secret, they made a deal—one side gave, one side took, and we ended up with this decommissioned contraption, and someone in the middle laughed. You motherfuckers, this valley that stretches straight to the heart of our battle lines is at least a thousand feet deep. If at this very moment two or three detachments of Iraqis are heading for our sound-sleeping soldiers, how am I supposed to know in this bitch-cold blizzard that blood will soon flow . . . black blood, not fresh pink blood. . . . Oh, Khazar! What did you do to me? You didn't tell me you were carrying my child so that I would exact this punishment on myself and my wretched mother and sister. . . . »

His eyes are burning from the snow. He wipes away the flakes and again stares down at the valley and the winding gorges around it. It is useless, but, as always, he performs his duty. A subtle sound to wake up the Iranian soldiers before Kalashnikov bullets put them to sleep.

> «At first it seems easy. At first you say it's nothing. Just four hours. I will manage to keep myself busy, and then I will go to the tent and sleep curled up next to the kerosene heater for four hours. I

think Pourpirar sleeps while on duty. I will catch him at it. Now not even twenty minutes have passed and already. . . . »

Not even twenty minutes have passed and already. . . .

«In six days we will go back down. A one-day leave and a bath. Heaven. It would be bliss if I could instantly go from this cold mountain straight into a steaming bathhouse, knowing that I can stay there as long as I want, until the eggs of future fleas wash out of my hair. . . . »

He tries to remember making love to Khazar. This time, too, he cannot. He was not so drunk to recall only a few random scenes, which may not even be real. Then, Khazar had not let him realize his dream—to make love with the first girl he truly loved.

The scribe on his right had written:

"It is not right," the squadron commander tells the captain. "The men can't stay there like this, in view of everyone. . . . We have to do something."

The irrigation canal leading to the once-fertile land had sometime in the past been scientifically engineered, but now there are not even the remnants of a trickle of water on the cement. The lieutenant colonel is tall and his head and shoulders stand out from the edge of the canal. He has bent his knees in a comical way so that as little of him as possible can be seen. He surveys the wasteland where clumps of earth and weeds have soldered together and the wind has bowed the remaining yellowed stalks toward the Iraqis.

Neiji whispers to Amir, "Our detachment got cock-lucky to be the reinforcement. Otherwise by now I'd be in those weeds, martyred for nothing but a donkey's dick."

Farther away, the lieutenant colonel again tells the detachment commander, "We have to do something."

The commander has forgotten, or did not have the know-how, to bring a kaffiyeh to wrap around his face. Hundreds of tiny mosquitos are circling his head and getting into his mouth and nose. His eyes are already red, but it is not clear whether the tears brimming in them are from the flies or for the dead.

"He is going to get us into some new trouble," Neiji whispers again. "After seven months, he finally mustered up the balls to come to the front. Now the motherfucker is going to get us into some new mess."

"Shut up! He'll hear you!"

Neiji's legs are tired from squatting; he drops to the ground and sits with his legs crossed on the dust and dirt inside the canal whose drought has left the wheat fields desiccated and burned.

> «A few sparse resilient stalks of wheat have popped up among the weeds, around the mines, for what?»

"It was this jackass who took me out of the Music Band and sent me to the front. If I don't give him a proper treat, may a half-burned log from hell get shoved up my ass in heaven."

His eyebrows have become even more devilish.

Crouching down, Amir sets off inside the canal. When he reaches a spot out of Iraqi view, he stands up and races toward the trenches on the Koureh-Moush hills. Mounds of dirt and rocks have been piled up on their cement roofs and moles have burrowed into them. The wind whips the dirt on the sun-blistered hills into a rage; it tears it up into the air and whirls it.

He thinks:

> *«The upward funnel of a whirlwind somehow looks like the palms of two hands held together, like a beggar's hands held up to the sky.»*

The scribe on his right shoulder had written:

He sets aside respect for the higher-ranking officers of the cadre and walks over to the lieutenant colonel and the captain. The colonel, resentful of his impudence, looks at him with contempt. As if the slaughter of the Second Detachment was his fault.

"Lieutenant Colonel, Sir! The men had barely advanced seventy or eighty yards before they were trapped. I think. . . . "

"Your job is not to think," the colonel growls. "If the likes of you properly follow orders, we won't have such incidents."

"Sir! I could see those poor guys getting caught left and right between the mines and the booby traps. There was no cleared path!"

"There was a cleared path!" the colonel barks. "And it had been cleared very carefully. They went off course. It is no one's fault. It is war, war! Do you understand, Enlisted Officer?"

He says "enlisted officer" in the condescending tone of a senior member of the cadre. There are two corpses in the nearest reaches of the plain, where the weeds have burned. Their second day of lying there with the rest of their fellow soldiers is coming to an end.

> «It is still not too late for their stench to rise. . . . They are loyal; they have not abandoned each other.»

And they are in the Iraqis' range of fire.

I am the one who should be writing this.

Amir says, "I think the plan of attack had not been sufficiently strategized."

The lieutenant colonel glares at him with the air of a skilled army officer. But to Amir, he looks more like a weary clerk returning home after an eight-hour day at the bank.

The lieutenant colonel pushes back his helmet, which is too small for his head, and snaps, "You are yapping out of line, Enlisted Officer."

The stubborn image of the night attack again raids Amir's thoughts. With the explosion of each mine, the silhouettes of the Iranian soldiers become momentarily visible. There are the booby traps, too. With each foot that gets caught in the wires, fountains of light and fire shoot up into the sky and brighten the area for the Iraqis. Then, the illuminating shells burst in the sky. With a flare under their parachutes, they float down slowly so that the plain does not return to darkness.

"Lieutenant Colonel, Sir! I could see mines exploding in every direction the men went. I repeatedly shouted into the radio to headquarters to turn them back. No one listened."

"Do you hear this, Captain? The enlisted officer ordered a retreat!"

They both laugh. The fat under the colonel's skin has tried and failed to fill the smallpox scars on his face.

"Sir, I was on scout duty and I was carrying out my orders properly. Why did you send someone to replace me?"

"Because you were shooting off your mouth. The blood of those martyrs is on your hands, too."

"No, it is not! All my communications are in code and they are all logged."

"Dime-a-dozen officer! Did the Shah's regime pay for your university?"

"Yes, Sir."

"And they gave you student loans?"

"They did."

"And it paid for your beer and the beans mezza to go with it? The university dormitory was free, too. Right?"

"It was."

"And there was plenty of pussy and ass around for you."

"Yes."

"And you all kept shouting, 'Islamic revolution! The road to heaven leads through Baghdad.' Are you better off now that you're here crying, 'Mommy, Mommy,' or were you better off when Baghdad was just your belly and under-belly and you were shouting slogans?"

"Lieutenant Colonel, Sir! I played no part in the revolution; I was a nobody."

Bits of spit from the lieutenant colonel's scornful mouth fly at his face.

"You were wrong to be a nobody. You have to be a revolutionary."

"Those who are in the wrong are those who send people's children into minefields for nothing. I will send a report of this attack to the battalion commander."

"Reports are farts in water. They will just send it back to me. You have been assigned to my squadron; you go where I tell you to go. You are screwed under my command."

"Sir! The Iraqis did not even have to fire a single bullet. They just sat and watched our guys walk aimlessly into the minefield. The Iraqis were having a ball."

"I will fuck their mothers and sisters in the next attack. And you, if you keep running off at the mouth, I will have you court-martialed in the desert. Understood?"

He thinks the lieutenant colonel's large nose has mummified from smelling some awful stench and now the wax is softening, melting.

> *«No. This smell is not the initial, restrained smell of a corpse. It is similar to the smell of a newborn, a smell that is testing itself, slowly, slowly, so that it can then engulf the world.»*

The lieutenant colonel again turns his binoculars toward the weeds and corpses.

"No, we can't leave them like this. We have to do something. Their mothers, fathers. . . . "

He sharpens his sharp ears. An Iranian mortar shell flies toward the Iraqis.

"What was that?"

"Our own fire."

After that early-morning blind and aimless exchange of fire that filled the air with dust and smoke, a second day of quiet was passing . . . and the Iranian shell explodes somewhere behind the Iraqi hills. A second one follows.

Surprised, the lieutenant colonel asks the captain, "Why is our artillery firing?"

He turns to Amir and suspiciously asks, "Did you request fire?"

"I have been right here with you!"

And a third shell.

And the Iraqis, as is their routine, start returning fire abundantly, wastefully. Their shells rain down in every direction and explode. The colonel is suddenly panicked.

"They are aiming randomly."

Without concealing his sarcasm, Amir replies, "That's how they always fire."

The captain says nothing.

A large piece of shrapnel whirs over the canal.

"How long will it go on?" the lieutenant colonel asks.

"Half an hour, one hour," the captain replies. "It depends how long it will take for them to get tired of loading their mortars. In this hot weather, I think the lazy bums will be sapped in half an hour."

There seems to be a faint hint of sarcasm in his tone, too. The lieutenant colonel pushes his helmet down on his head.

"You, don't just sit there fanning your balls, get over to communications and find out who ordered fire."

Amir runs along the canal in the opposite direction of the water that once had flowed there. He hears shrapnel flying by.

> *«They are not civilized like bullets that make a clean hole on this side and a drain hole on the other. These things spin to mutilate . . . and then, looking so innocent, they sit and rust on the ground.»*

Covered with dust and soot, he ducks into the communications post. The ends of Neiji's devilish eyebrows look more scorpion-tail-ish.

"You've been up to something, Neiji! What did you do?"

"We radioed the artillery unit and told them the lieutenant colonel has graced us with his presence, but we have nothing to welcome him with, no cookies and cakes."

The other soldiers in the post smile impishly.

They have done their deed. The artillery unit understood the connotation of their transmission and poked at a section of the Iraqi lines so that they would retaliate full-force—a welcome reception for a squadron commander not accustomed to the blast of exploding mortar shells.

As soon as the Iraqi counterattack subsides, the lieutenant colonel announces that he must return to headquarters to investigate the reason for the attack. And Amir watches the frightened commander hop into his jeep with his tail between his legs, and he follows the dust raised in his wake. Near a solitary, half-dried tree on the side of the road, the shell the Iraqis have sent for him explodes, and his jeep disappears behind the tit-shaped hills.

On his right shoulder:

Squatting in the corner of the communications post, he pounds his fist on his knee.

"An entire detachment walked into a minefield for nothing! In the old days, they used to say, 'A sound mind in a sound body.' Piss on this world where you can't find a single sound mind and a single body with no legs."

The communications duty officer lights a cigarette he has rolled with dried tea pulp and stationery paper.

"Sir, talking like this is no good for you. Some of these soldiers are ideologues and stoolies. You will get into trouble."

He wonders whether these words are a threat or a friendly warning.

"Do you get how ridiculous it is?" he growls. "Right now, in some shrine somewhere, a mother is praying and pledging alms for the health of one of the soldiers that was blown to bits the night before last. It would be good if there were some sort of equipment in shrines that would announce, 'Mother, your pledge of alms cannot be accepted. Congratulations! Your son is now mingling with seventy heavenly houris.'"

The duty officer bursts into tears. His first tears since the night the black dust of mourning spread across the region. Ignoring the man's sobs, the radio continues transmitting coded messages.

Right:

They arrive at dusk. The six-member team dispatched from the brigade's Explosive Ordnance Unit. They start their work quietly and without needless explanations. With their binoculars, they inspect the area and mark their maps.

A meager dinner has been set on the dinner cloth spread on the ground outside the detachment commander's trench. The earth and sky are so silent and still that it seems no blood has ever spilled and no mine has ever exploded there.

Away from the light of the kerosene lantern, fireflies draw lines across the dark of the summer night. Even the soldiers accompanying the explosive ordnance officers are quiet and reserved. Their faraway gazes say, You have no clue! Be happy if your first mistake is not your last. . . . Their only pieces of mine-detection equipment are black metal spikes.

"Sergeant," Neiji flippantly says, "can't this prized and victorious army cough up enough to buy those gizmos that you run over the ground like a vacuum cleaner and they beep?"

A few of the officers give him a look of the wise at the idiot.

"Sergeant, my bro," one of the soldiers from the south says, "I think you're a new bride at the front."

Neiji quips, "Yeah, darkie bro. I used to play the clarinet in an army band. For thirty years. What do I know about mine-detecting contraptions?"

The despondent captain of the Second Detachment has not touched his food.

"Do you know what a clarinet is, bro? It's really long and really black. Blacker than you. And it has a wide end. I blow in the narrow end, you get it from the wide end. . . . Now, don't get me wrong, I mean during military marches."

The swarthy man laughs.

"Sergeant Clarinet! In this battlefield, where there is shrapnel scattered every few inches, a mine detector will honk like a car carrying a bride. The Iraqis will hear it and they will come to be our grooms."

"I like you, darkie. I for one have been Imam Khomeini's bride for a while now. So bring the Iraqis, too. I'm nice and wide."

The captain snaps, "Sergeant, put a lid on it!"

On his left:

Four hours and seven minutes have passed since they started, and two explosive ordnance officers, crawling on their chests, have finally dragged the seventh body out from among the black and yellow weeds and laid it on the ground in front of the detachment commander's trench. The corpses have bloated and their smell is slowly triumphing over all others. Everyone has covered their noses and mouths with kaffiyehs. Soldiers from the Second Detachment, who had retreated without orders, had brought back tens of wounded. Most of them missing a leg. Some had started convulsing and died before they made it to the ambulances. These seven corpses are the ones left behind.

Right:

And now dawn is breaking. The last officer from the Explosive Ordnance Unit has seen a few Iraqis, worn-out and crawling, putting a few legs in burlap sacks and dragging them away.

Seven one-legged or no-legged bodies here, more one-legged or no-legged bodies somewhere in a morgue behind enemy lines, waiting.

On this side, eleven legs have been collected—severed below the knee, above the knee, lined up on the good earth.

The three ambulances that arrived before dawn, apparently unknowing and therefore innocent, are parked to the side with the sun rising above them. The captain has assigned six soldiers to match the retrieved legs to the bodies. The leg of the dark-skinned soldier from the Explosive Ordnance Unit is easily found, because it is still fresh. The soldiers start to complain. It is difficult to pair mutilated legs, caked with dirt and blood or stripped of flesh and wearing tattered boots, to bloated corpses. In most cases, there are no personal clues left, such as non-army-issued socks. Strips of burned flesh tangled with shreds of army pants hang from the stumps.

Amir watches the six soldiers from a distance and mutters, "Puzzle players!"

The five members of the Explosive Ordnance Unit, tired from their night's work, are asleep in trenches that are somewhat cool. By the time the soldiers report that their duty is done, the summer sun is burning and rotting everything. By lottery, they have given legs to six of the corpses. There is no guarantee that the bodies have regained their own legs. The detachment commander orders that the corpses with legs be put in two of the ambulances, and the orphaned legs be loaded onto the third.

The ambulances cannot wait for the cover of night to avoid being seen by the Iraqis—they've got to deliver the bodies and legs to the morgue in the nearest town before they decompose any further. On the winding road, near the solitary half-dried tree, an Iraqi shell sees them off. The ambulances zigzag away.

The puzzle players ask the captain to grant them leave, out of their turn, so that they can go to a nearby town and take a bath.

> «With all my recklessness and claims that I joined the war to fight to the death, I do not have the courage of any of those humble,

slaughtered soldiers. To be that easily slaughtered without even understanding that you're walking into a minefield to be slaughtered. To be released, relieved. Khazar understood very well that I have neither the courage to be afraid, nor the courage to be afraid of having no courage. . . . »

The scribe on his left shoulder writes:

> *I saw you when you came with your sister. But I need to make sure that you really want me. Even now that you have lost an arm, I would not put it past you to be the same Amir who picked every apple, took a bite of it, and tossed it away. Wednesday at 4:00, Kazbah. Come alone.*

Every half hour, he reads the letter again to find a clue in its words. He gives no thought to Reyha, who he has left waiting for him on a side street. But the girl keeps peeking around the corner, worried that he may wander off. Inside Kazbah's chained doors, Amir hears the faint sound of music.

> *«What if people are being held prisoner in there?»*

He kicks the metal door. The chain clangs and the door doesn't budge. Reyhaneh walks over to him and snaps, "We are going home."

Amir follows her.

The scribe on his right shoulder had written:

He drives past Kazbah toward the city center.

". . . I'm not sure if she's still there after the revolution. Back then, she was always in Ferdowsi Circle, sitting in a corner next to a bank. She didn't look like she had a home, but her hair was always neatly done and she used to wear old-fashioned rouges and powders on her wrinkled face. She had only a red dress, but it was always clean. She'd been sitting in that corner for more than thirty years. People said she wore that red dress to a lovers' rendezvous and the guy never showed up. He'd gotten into an accident, or died. . . . "

"I know all this. If telling me that you like her is not another one of your lies, then let's go and see if she's still there."

"People called her Ruby. No one knew if that was her real name. . . . "

Khazar is holding her hand out the car window, guiding the pleasant spring breeze onto her face and long hair. Her mandatory headscarf has slipped back on her head.

"Sometimes I'd watch her from a distance. She wouldn't let on that she had noticed me. Most of the people who walked by only gave her a passing glance. One day she motioned to me to come over to her. Close up, you could see how wrinkled her face was. . . . She asked me, 'Do you know Siamak Deilami? You look like him, perhaps you are related to him.'"

Amir drives south, toward Ferdowsi Circle. Khazar, wearing a lime-green spring dress and her Dior perfume, looks fresh and beautiful. Each time he changes gears, she puts her hand on his and moves the stick shift with him.

"Why didn't you come to the theater last night?" she asks. "I was expecting you."

"I wasn't feeling well."

"Don't lie. You don't need to go to the trouble of coming up with tall tales for me. Obviously, you were between some woman's legs, playing a Brechtian role. I don't care. Sometimes I like it when you smell of semen. It oozes from your pores instead of sweat."

"Go on thinking that's what I'm like. I get so frustrated when you play games with me. When I miss you and you hide from me, it drives me mad, and I want to go and empty myself with someone. But since that first night we spent together, I haven't unbuckled my belt for anyone but you. Do you get it? . . . No, you don't."

He pounds his fist on the dashboard. Khazar giggles.

"Well, maybe I'm falling in love with you."

The spring breeze rains down green sequins from the maple trees. He speeds up and narrowly swerves between two cars. It's hardly been two months since the revolution started and already there are fewer couples driving around the city like Khazar and him.

"Noushin came to the theater last night with a Che Guevara. The guy was one of those pretentious fakes. He was wearing a shirt with a Mandarin collar, cargo pants, and a Che Guevara cap without the star. Halfway through the play they got up and left in a huff because there was nothing about the strife of the working class in it."

"Don't make fun of them."

"It annoys me. Leftists are getting stabbed on the street, and these wimps blow smoke in a theater!"

"Would you like it if they made fun of your Becket?"

"Sure. Mocking one thing or another is the only proper thing you can do in this world. I'm dying for someone to come and make fun of everything about me. But I keep getting stuck with pipsqueaks who take me too seriously."

"I have a lot of respect for Noushin."

"She puts on a show, too. All it takes is one slap in the face and people like her will snitch on their own aunt."

"You are acting too jealous these days."

"I told you, I guess I'm falling in love with you. . . . Push the clutch, I'm going to quickly shift into reverse and drive for a takeoff."

The scribe had continued:

Ferdowsi Circle's woman-in-red is sitting next to a pillar in front of Saderat Bank. The number of chador and headscarf wearers is growing by the day, but she has left her hair in sun's care. Under the bright sky of early May, the red of her dress resembles the color of dried poppy flowers. She ignores the school children's gibes and the curious looks of passersby. As soon as she sees him, a rare smile blossoms on her face.

"You rascal! Why didn't you tell me you are his cousin? You used to stage plays in the Donya-ye No Theater on Lalehzar Street."

He wants to bend down and kiss her dark, shriveled hand. He does not tell her that the theater she remembers was abandoned years ago and its derelict hall was set on fire in the early days of the revolution.

"If you think you know me, then tell me, what is my name?"

"Amir! And what a pretty girl you have with you. She is a bit shy. It's nice. Girls who are a little timid have more spice."

She stares at Khazar for a while. Khazar does not move her eyes away from hers.

"You are a cutie! You like to wear red. If you wear red, you will catch the eye better from a distance."

Then, turning away from her, she digs into her timeworn, red handbag, pulls out a frayed and yellowed piece of paper, and hands it to Amir. As he unfolds it, it tears in two along its fold line. It is a receipt for a Singer sewing machine. Dated thirty-one years ago.

"Have you seen the Singer store on Lalehzar Street?"

"Yes."

"I bought a Singer. You won't believe what a beauty it is. A miracle. From now on, I am going to make all my own dresses. They just started selling them. Edward sold it to me on installment. . . . Do you know him?"

"No, Mrs. Ruby."

"Then who do you know? Lots of girls and women in Tehran have a crush on him. He is so sweet and handsome, they keep going to see him, pretending they want to buy a sewing machine."

"You, too?" Khazar asks.

> «Khazar screwed up! If Ruby Red senses that someone is making fun of her, she will start acting as though they don't exist.»

"Missy, do you think my heart is a taxi that just lets men in and out all the time? I have given my heart to Siamak. I have no other heart to give to anyone else."

Amir squeezes Khazar's arm to stop her from saying anything more.

An orange BMW speeds around the circle with its wheels screeching. A boy sticks his head out of the window and blows a kiss to Ruby Red.

"Edward's business is a big success. . . . I'm not strong enough to carry my sewing machine home. It's too heavy. Could I trouble you to do it for me? I don't want Siamak to know. I want the first thing I sew for him to be a surprise. Oh, you don't know how the gold design on it shines against the glossy black. Will you go today and bring it to my home?"

"Yes, I will, Ma'am."

The woman peeks around him at the street.

"Well, you should go now. I'm meeting Siamak here at eleven. He is so suspicious that if he sees you, he will start badgering you, trying to find out what we've been talking about. He'll be jealous to see me with a handsome man like you. I worry he'll make you give away our secret. Go!"

She says "our secret" in a kittenish tone and winks at him. Amir thinks he sees a ladybird on the old woman's shoulder. Against the red of her dress, it is there and it is not there. He looks more closely. No, it is not there.

"Go now . . . go quickly!"

Ruby Red looks at her watch. A watch that must have stopped working years ago. And now, ignoring him and Khazar, she stares out at the street that her beloved has been coming down for thirty years.

Right:

He starts the car. If Khazar doesn't make a fuss and doesn't want to go home, he'll take her to a coffee shop, sit across from her, and look at her for as long as he wants without anyone bothering them. Khazar is silent and still. She seems sad.

"Shall we go for coffee someplace?"

"Don't you want to pick up the Singer?"

"I kept the receipt as a keepsake. As we walked away, I think I saw a man with his hair gelled back and wearing an old-fashioned gabardine suit walk toward her from the middle of the circle."

"I don't want any coffee. Just drive around. Go to Elahieh, where we went that first night."

The tree-lined roads and side streets of Elahieh neighborhood no longer have the flair for beauty and the temptation for romance. Khazar looks out with sad eyes. Both are silent.

In the end, they drive past Kazbah. The door is chained and padlocked, and streaks of soot have stained the wall around its seams.

"What was that DJ's name?" Khazar asks sullenly.

"You mean Serge?"

"Do you have any news of him?"

"No, he's disappeared. Perhaps he's sitting at home, making arak and selling it on the black market. The Armenians' arak is a lot more popular than what the Muslims make. They don't water it down and they don't lace it with sleeping pills."

As though talking to herself, Khazar murmurs, "Sitting and waiting in a red dress for thirty years. What does all this stubbornness in public mean? I felt she could read my mind and see my destiny. She meant something when she said a red dress catches the eye better from a distance. She meant that if I don't wear red I won't live long, and if I do, I will have the same fate as hers."

"Are you becoming superstitious? Her mind works in a different way."

"Don't say she's crazy. She moved me. I feel so down. I'm afraid, Amir."

"I'm here, with you."

"I'm afraid of you more than anyone else."

Amir knows that with the mood Khazar is in, it's best he stays quiet.

After a few minutes, Khazar asks, "You're not going to say anything?"

"I have nothing to say."

"I do. . . . I have been meaning to tell you for a few weeks."

". . ."

"I don't want to be with you anymore."

To conceal his shock, Amir jokes, "Why? Are you scared of falling in love with me? . . . If you stay with me, you will become a daredevil. A daredevil is not afraid of anything, not even of another daredevil."

He expects Khazar to laugh. But. . . .

"How many balls do you have?"

"Two."

And to put the girl in her place, he adds, "And mighty ones at that."

"Men have two balls, one for not being afraid, the other one for being afraid. They rub against each other and become neutral."

"I have a big ball in my stomach, too," he says.

"You are the opposite of what you pretend to be—you don't have the guts to be a daredevil, and you don't have the daredevil-ness to have no guts."

"A storm is kicking up in your head again—I'll just drive you home."

"This is the last time I will be with you as your girlfriend. Pull over, I want to walk home."

"Have you gone mad?"

"I said pull over!" Khazar screams.

And he watches the girl walk away along the sidewalk, under the green shadow of aged sycamores. He senses that Khazar has left for good, and he does not understand why.

The scribe on his left shoulder writes:

He sees himself on an old train, confused, wandering from wagon to wagon. With every jolt, powdered rust showers down on him, and there is not a soul around. He was once in one of these wagons, or was supposed to be, and he had something, something very important, but he lost it, and he knows he must find it. In some of the wagons, there are old, dusty suitcases strewn on the floor. The train lurches forward on the rails and without stopping passes through the old, dim, and foggy stations along the Caspian coast. There are groups of scrawny-looking soldiers on the station platforms, their uniforms drooping on their shoulders, their helmets too big or too small for their shaved heads, waiting for trains to take them vertical to the front and return them horizontal. And the empty train, in the haze of whistles of trains that have long gone by, travels through the stations without slowing down.

He cannot see how he goes from one wagon to the next, but he knows he is in another wagon. The corridor is carpeted with fish scales. In the next one, small and large seashells, white and shiny, are scattered on the floor. No boots or amputated legs have crushed them. Deep in his ears, the sound of their brittleness breaking under his feet resembles the sound of bone splintering. But he has no choice, he must continue moving forward, and he cannot remember the good-for-nothing important reason why. He opens the door to one of the cabins. A heap of broken army spades pours out into the corridor. He wants to run away from them, but the motherfuckers have blocked his way. . . . He sees the red handle of the emergency stop. He cannot decide whether to pull it or not . . . and the jolt of the sudden stop hurls him to the floor. The train skids on the rails with the screech of steel on steel. When it stops, the silence does not last long. Claws on the rails . . . a few moles scuttle toward him. They crawl by, over and around him. . . .

Right:

It is 10:37 in the morning, and there's been no sound coming from downstairs for the past hour. Mother and Reyhaneh must have gone out. He climbs down the stairs, peeks into the living room, kitchen, and his parents' bedroom to make sure no one's there, and walks over to the telephone. Under the letter M in his address book, there is only one girl's name. Now, clearheaded and free of doubt, he remembers that sometime in the past, he decided to sleep with enough women to complete the thirty-two letters of the Persian alphabet with the first letters of their first names.

His collection was never completed. Of course, finding women or girls whose first names started with the letters zaal and zaa was difficult, but he had repeated a few other letters several times.

«Maryamaneh! . . . Maryamaneh? . . . »

He starts dialing the number. After the second digit, he hears a busy signal. He redials eleven times before realizing that after so many years, some of the area codes in Tehran might have changed. He calls information and learns what he should dial. . . . He expects a girl with a voice as soft as an angel's to answer. An old man picks up.

It takes some effort for him to say, "H-how may I h-help you?" He's either drunk or a stutterer.

Somewhere in the back of his mind, Amir remembers that even before the Islamic Revolution, when he called a girl's house and her father or brother answered, he would not speak, and thinking he was a crank caller, they'd shower him with obscenities. But the old man's tone is not aggressive.

He gathers his courage and says, "Excuse me, Sir, may I please speak with Miss Maryamaneh."

"Hooold on."

And he hears the old man call out, "M-marya-yamaneh! . . . Maryamaaaneh! . . . It's for you."

He hears a radio or a television in the background.

> *«That peasant drawl embellished with a fake, heavy Arabic accent can only come from a mullah. . . . »*

" . . . it has seven doors, and behind each door there are seventy thousand mountains. On each mountain there are seventy thousand sides, on each side seventy thousand valleys, in each valley seventy thousand sections, each section has seventy thousand houses, in each house seventy thousand serpents. You cannot imagine! Each serpent is the length of three days' walk, with long stingers, as long as date trees. These serpents attack humans, bite them, tear into their flesh . . . seeing these serpents, the damned seek refuge in the lava that flows in hell, full of snakes and scorpions. They throw themselves into these rivers. And the rivers are so deep that the damned sink seventy jarifs *. . . and each jarif takes seventy years . . . and this is just the beginning, my Muslim brothers. . . . "*

Five minutes and forty-seven seconds pass; Maryamaneh has not come to the phone.

"H-hello! Wh-who is thisss?" the old man asks.

"My good man, you went to call Maryamaneh."

"Oooh, y-yes. I'm old and ai-ailing. I f-forgot, young man. Hold on."

"M-maryayamaaaneh!"

" . . . strangers, foreigners, chop up their flesh with flaming scissors. . . . Hell is alive! . . . it has seven floors, each floor has seven doors . . . the names on the doors: Abyss! Inferno! Purgatory! . . . "

"M-maryamaaaneh! . . . "

Another six minutes and twenty-seven seconds pass.

And again, the old man, "Hello? I c-can't hear you! Shpeak louder!"

Amir chuckles—he has only now realized he's being played. He could spew insults at the man, or he could play along and goad him to continue with his mockery and then take a swipe at him. But he feels too glum to do that.

"I'm terribly sorry, Sir. When I asked for Maryamaneh, I actually meant Mermaid. I've just been dialing numbers, trying to find out if there is anyone out there who has a mermaid at home. And if they did, I would tell them, Good for you, don't take your mermaid for granted, and then hang up."

For a few seconds, the man is tongue-tied.

"You sh-shaid m-mermaaaid?" he asks in a different tone.

"Yes, mermaid."

"Y-you and your f-friends got bored and deeecided to t-teeease me?"

"No, I'm the one who has been teased."

"I t-teeeased you good, didn't I?"

"Yes, you did."

After a long pause, during which he stops hearing the radio or television, the old man says in a sad voice, "I h-had one."

"Did you love her?"

"Don't get cheeky."

"You should have taken her to the seaside once in a while so she'd remember she's a mermaid."

The old man is again silent. Amir hears him cough, then the flick of a cigarette lighter.

> *«The cigarette lighter that right when you need it leaves you in the lurch.»*

"I used to take her o-once a m-month."

"Then why are you alone?"

"I like you. I I think you g-get it."

"I get it."

"Th-then don't ask me. Ask the glooorious rev-revolution."

"I don't have the number for the glorious revolution."

"D-don't worry. Th-there will come a d-day when eeeveryone will know it by h-heart."

"My name is Amir."

A pause to take a sip of arak or a puff on his cigarette.

Slurring his words even more, the man says, "I d-don't reeemember any Aaaamir. . . . th-they used to call me Serge."

The scribe on his left shoulder had written:

The soldier's eyes were bloodshot and his speech was slurred. Slurred from boozing. Slurred from being stoned.

"Sir, want a treat?"

"What do you have? American Winston or Pakistani counterfeit?"

"I have scorpion. Want to smoke a scorpion?"

"It's not good to smoke it."

"You're really cool, Sir. I wish you were our detachment commander."

Summer is scorpion season. On the Koureh-Moush hills, under every pile of rocks there are several translucent baby scorpions growing. They're no good. You've got to hunt adult scorpions, kill them, dry them, and save them in a hard-to-come-by jar. When you have fifteen or twenty, you put them on a sheet of plastic and use a rock to grind them. Then, just like hashish, you mix the powder with cigarette tobacco and smoke it. Whether there is some sort of drug in dead scorpions or not, at the front it seems to make you high. More than the memories of a girl. . . .

The scribe on his right shoulder writes:

"We have waited a long time," Reyhaneh says. "We'd better go back home. My feet hurt."

He will not take his eyes off the front door of Roya's house across the street. It is almost noon and the third hour of their vigil. Reyhaneh takes a bottle of water and a vial of pills out of her handbag and gives them to him.

> «Come out of the house, Roya! The sidewalk is cloudy and smells of soon-to-come rain. I have searched this street for three days to find your house. Walk through the turquoise door that is the same color as your dreams, and be the Roya of my nightmares when you do. . . . I saw a one-handed man on the street. I asked him, "One-handed man, did you, too, lose your hand in war?" He laughed at me. He said, "Thank God, no. They cut it off because I stole from the filthy rich." He is still laughing at me. So I am not this town's only one-handed man. Somewhere in your house, perhaps in that room where the curtains just parted, you've kept my ring, our rings. Perhaps you have hidden them. For the love of my loneliness, come out of the house. For the love of that bitter-orange tree that has grown tall in your front yard, for the love of the blossoms that will come in spring . . . I can see now. . . . »

"This house is deserted. All morning, no one has come out or gone in."

"They're home. I saw the curtain in one of the upstairs windows open."

"That curtain was open when we first came."

He ignores Reyhaneh, even though they've been standing on the sidewalk for several hours and every so often passersby jostle him if he does not move aside as quickly as they'd like him to.

> « . . . and the prince sat under the tree. Midnight came and the seven-colored talking bird did not come to sit on a branch. The prince fell asleep. When he woke up in the morning, he realized the bird had come and gone. On the second night, too, he fell asleep. On the third night, the besotted prince cut his finger and poured salt on it so that the stinging would keep him awake. Near dawn, the seven-colored bird came and sat on a branch. I cannot remember if the tree was the tree of Forty Songs and Tunes or not. The prince asked the talking bird, "Beautiful bird, O you who are unique in the world, show me the way to Sangestaan Fortress where Forty-Braids is being held captive. Which direction should I go?" The talking bird spoke. "It is very far away. You must put on a pair of steel shoes and eat the liver of a seven-colored bird while it is still warm. . . . "»

"I can't stand here anymore," Reyhaneh says.

"You're nagging too much. I'm not moving from this place until I see her. I know it in my heart, she is the one. . . . Why don't you go to a café or someplace and have something to eat?"

"You really are clueless! What café? If a girl goes to a café alone, ten men will start hitting on her."

"You are wearing a chador. No one will get the wrong idea."

"When I say you are clueless, accept the fact that you are. It is even worse with a chador. All the disreputable women wear chadors to avoid getting arrested. If a woman in a chador stands on a street corner, a hundred cars will brake for her."

"I guess you're not all that innocent."

"You're starting to talk nonsense. . . . I'm leaving. Take a taxi and come home by yourself."

Reyhaneh walks a few steps away, but seeing that he is determined to stay, she walks back.

"I wish you had died at the front—I would be free of you."

Amir sneers. . . .

Thirty-eight minutes later, the scribe continues:

Turquoise blue, rusted and peeling in spots, the door opens. A woman walks out.

"Let's go!" Amir snaps.

They cross the street and follow her. She is wearing a wrinkled gray coverall. Even in that loose frock her gauntness is obvious. Reyhaneh, carrying out her female plot, quickens her step and catches up with the woman. She asks if her name is Roya. The woman nods. Now, Reyhaneh will tell her that her brother, Amir, has seen her somewhere and he'd like to come with his parents to visit her family and ask for her hand in marriage. Standing a short distance away, staring at the woman's profile, Amir tries to remember his relationship with her. But the woman keeps restlessly turning and looking back at the end of the street. . . . His heart beats slowly, like a hammer, and it beats fast and races. An image sparks in his mind of the moment when he reached over to try and reattach his left arm, and the arm, hanging by skin and strips of flesh, fell off. He was as short of breath then as he is now. . . . He starts to walk. Like any other pedestrian, he passes the woman. Roya's eyes look familiar. But without two dark half moons under them. He is one step past her when he hears her voice.

"Lady, what are you talking about? Marriage? You pimp, can't you see the state I'm in?"

Left:

He sees that Reyhaneh, biting her lips, is so furious that she would not shed a drop of blood if she were stabbed. Drained, he leans his head, heavy as a rock, against the car window. Each time the car goes over a pothole, his head bounces against the glass. He ignores the pain. He sees a one-armed man across the street, waiting for a taxi.

"I'm sorry," he says.

Reyhaneh's anger erupts.

"How dare you make me deal with people like her! Did you hear what she called me?"

"It wasn't her."

"And what makes you so sure? I wish someone would ask me why I humiliate and disgrace myself like this. All because of some dream, fantasy, insanity."

"I am sure this was Roya. But she is not the one."

"This is the last time I do your bidding."

"I'm sorry! What else can I say for you to forgive me?"

"Your fantasy lover is a drug addict."

He watches the windshield wipers sweep away the raindrops. The image is familiar to him, but hard as he tries, he cannot recall where or when he's seen it. He sees the driver take his right hand off the steering wheel, grab his empty left sleeve, and wipe the steam off the side window.

Right:

It is 1:35 in the morning. Inside his room, there is no drone of flying shrapnel, no echo of a bird's fluttering wings. The world is quiet, as quiet as the nights at the front when mortar operators dream of the future shells they will fire, and in the dark, every bush looks like a hunchback. Like the winter sweet bushes away from the light in the garden's night. And a slithering reptilian silence creeps toward the trenches.

Still in his chair, he finally falls asleep.

And he dreams . . .

The mountain at night. Moon Brow swings her legs, which are dangling over the edge of a well. With her eyes fixed on the darkness inside it, she says, "The elders of this town believe it is a bottomless well. A long, long time ago, a ruler ordered that plenty of colored wood chips be poured into it. The following year, seafarers saw the wood floating on the sea."

There is a yellow full moon in the sky above the mountain peak overlooking the sleeping town. Headlights move along the empty streets, and somewhere, in the scant light from the houses, a yellow traffic light blinks and blinks. He tosses a stone in the well and listens, but no sound returns. Moon Brow sits with her back to him, facing the town. She recites Forough's poetry . . .

"I know a small sad fairy who gently, gently plays her heart in a wood saucer,

a small fairy that dies at night from a kiss and at dawn is born with a kiss. . . . "

From the bottom of the well a gust of air blows at him. It has the damp and pleasant smell of a breeze that rises from the opening of a qanat in the Lut Desert.

"What are you looking at?"

Moon Brow points at the few lights shining here and there on the outskirts of the town.

"There is a large, emerald-green light over there. It is a beautiful emerald. I am sure I've seen it on some street. I'm trying to remember where it was."

Moon Brow's voice has the delicate, nervous resonance that has been held captive in crystal globes for centuries. He looks at the emerald light. And at the moonlit silhouette of the girl who peacefully, as though for eternity, sits there gazing at it. With the night's moon he has put on his ring, and in the morning he'll take it off so that alone, the following night. . . . He feels light and happy. He taps his feet together. . . .

Suddenly he is anxious. What if his ring has fallen off his finger and into the well without him realizing? He's been leaning on his left arm for a long time and it has gone numb. He wants to raise his hand to make certain the ring is there. . . .

Despite his nightmarish horror, he does not want to wake up until he has wrenched his hand off the ground and looked at it. But the gravel in the garden is pulling at him. He is torn out of his chair, drenched in sweat, and the sound of car wheels furrowing the gravel moves closer . . . it is 4:03 in the morning. He looks out the window. The florescent lamps along the paths and the garden walls are lit. He quietly climbs down the stairs.

«Every house has hiding places.»

Agha Haji opens the front door. A man gets out of the car and walks up to him. One of the guards stands a short distance away.

"I thought you should know as soon as possible," the man says. "The news will spread tomorrow. They've given the go-ahead for the assassinations. They stabbed the guy forty, fifty times. Did the same to his wife."

"Why his wife?"

"I don't know. The secret service does its own investigations. They don't breathe a word to us. What do you think?"

Agha Haji is silent for a few moments. Then, "Regardless of our sentiments, we should not take sides. We will not voice disapproval; we will not approve either . . . they are in power. It is better that we remain silent."

The scribe on his left shoulder had written:

The long-winded whispers of the two soldiers piss him off. What if a few Iraqi commandos have wrapped themselves in white sheets and are creeping over the snow and up the mountain? Their wire guillotines primed for an easy-to-slash throat. Only fifty-eight minutes have passed. The cold has made him drowsy. He thinks, Nothing is going to happen if I go and sleep in a bed for one night. All the other officers do. . . .

> *«The muffled grunts of the man and woman next door, when they don't want the neighbors to hear them, sound like the gasps of a shell flying overhead, greedy and horny for flesh. . . . It is not the pleasure of gratification. Choking back your piss for an hour or two and then letting it go somehow has a similar satisfaction. Perhaps it is the greed of emptying one's greed that is real. . . . Khazar! Did you have greed, too? What was the greed you satisfied? If I'd never met you, I wouldn't be in this bitter cold hell up on this mountain like a mule hit by shrapnel.»*

The scribe on his right shoulder writes:

He takes his morning pill from his sister and obediently swallows it. Reyhaneh is wearing that same shoulder- and arm-revealing top. He smiles at the pimple on her arm and caresses the young leaf of his geranium.

> «If I caress it well, in the spring the Khezr cherry tree will bear more cherries.»

The third day has begun with the unknown girl's fourth letter lying on his bed with its legs spread open.

> Don't give up hope of me coming to our rendezvous. I will not show myself until you understand the meaning of waiting. On our last day together, when you took that beautiful velvet box out of your pocket, my heart skipped a beat. I thought, This silly guy has finally bought an engagement ring for me. You were talking such big words that it was hard for me to understand you. I just wanted you to open the box. And then when you did, it was a pair of pearl earrings. You broke my heart. You told me I was as beautiful and lustrous as those pearls and that you don't deserve me. The same drivel that every jerk says when he wants to break up with a girl without breaking her heart. You broke my heart and never called me again. Now I hear that with one arm lost and your head all messed up you're looking for me. I will accept you as you are. If you come to all the rendezvous I arrange, I will show myself at one of them. Wearing those pearl earrings. I have waited for you for years; now have some patience and forbearance to prove to me that this time you will not let me go. Thursday at 5:00, in front of Kazbah.

"Has she set up yet another meeting?" Reyha asks.

"Yes. But she wrote about a pair of earrings, not a ring. So it's not her . . . don't say I told you so."

"I wasn't going to."

"You're lying . . . and so is she. Someone who was in love with me wouldn't do something so spiteful."

"I called your Miss Yasmine."

"And?"

"The person who answered didn't know if someone by that name used to live there or not. This was the last name in your address book."

"When I fell in love, I had two arms, I was perfect. Then I must have fallen in love with someone who was unique, whole. She was the only one who could make this crazy guy crazy for her."

"As far as I know, when men want someone, they see her as pure gold. Then she suddenly turns into scrap metal for them."

"Yes. It's all so ridiculous. I'm tired. I've exhausted you, too."

"You're starting to come to your senses. Now, let go of this half-baked fantasy and get back to your life. You're recovering. Take care of yourself. And later, a nice girl will show up in your life. . . . "

"You're right. I will take care of myself."

"Tend to yourself until we figure out what to do. There are many solutions."

"Yes, many. One solution is for me to go back to that mountain."

"What?"

"If I was engaged to someone, even if I had kept it a secret from you, I would have worn my ring at the front. . . . "

"Even if you had, it's all in the past."

"I have to find my arm."

"You are a stupid nutcase!"

"Of course I am a stupid nutcase. A nutcase who claims he is not a nutcase is telling the truth."

"I can't listen to this nonsense anymore."

Reyha turns to leave. Amir grabs her arm. The coolness of the girl's skin makes him realize what a feverish wave is brewing inside him. He stops the rippling hot rush that wants to escape from the stub on his left side so that it flows back into his head.

"I wasn't alone. There was someone with me on my missions. He must have seen whether I wore a ring or not. He holds the key to everything. I have to find him. He will take me to where my arm fell. Then I will be at peace."

He starts pacing the room, agitated.

Exhausted, Reyhaneh says, "After all these years, there is nothing left of it."

"Vultures don't eat gold. I have to find the man who was with me. I have to go to the base. . . . Which base was it? . . . Which base? . . . "

He leans toward Reyhaneh and points his finger at her.

"For the love of your God! Be my sister. Be a pal. My head is working like a clock today."

Reyhaneh, holding her breath, stares at him.

"If I find that soldier who must have seen my ring . . . there was a P in his name . . . everything will be all right. I may have told him I was engaged. I may have even told him her name."

He tears the letter into pieces, swings open the window, and throws the scraps at the eucalyptus tree.

> «The crescent moon on her forehead shines so bright that it hurts my eyes; I cannot see her face. That is why I gave her gold—because gold doesn't rust, it lasts forever. She wanted me to have a trace of her. . . . »

The scribe on his right shoulder had written:

Blinding salty sweat drips from his eyebrows onto the rim of his binoculars. Tens of Iraqi flares continue to descend from the sky and light up the earth. The explosions of accurately aimed shells on the high Imamzadeh Heydar Hill sound like volcanoes vomiting.

He shouts into the wireless radio's mouthpiece, "Rapid fire! You gutless wimps! They're slaughtering us! Choke their artillery!"

In the pale dark before dusk, something is happening down there that he's afraid of understanding.

The Iraqis' second attack is well organized. Heavy fire rages before the incursion. Imamzadeh Heydar Hill and its soldiers will turn into dust and ash and return to the sky.

He imagines that right now, just like him, an Iraqi scout is lying on the ground somewhere high up, but he is looking triumphantly at the rainbow clusters in the air that Amir is watching with horror. And with satisfaction the scout orders that the shelling continue with the same coordinates he has provided.

The initial shelling is subsiding.

«The Iraqi foot soldiers must have set out by now.»

On his left:

Through his binoculars he sees the blazes flaring from the nozzles of Iranian guns and mortars weakening. The soldiers have either been killed or have copped out and are beating an escape.

With his throat sore from shouting into the wireless radio, now ignoring the communication codes, he yells requesting return fire. The Iranian artillery unit is sapped; they ignore his pleas. They must be running out of ammunition.

The Iraqi artillery deftly directs shells to the far side of the hill, turning the Iranian retreat route into an inferno. Coughing, he hollers, "It's done! The guys are done! It's a massacre!"

The only response is the static on the radio. . . . He presses the headset tight against his ear and mouth and shouts, "There is still a chance! Coordinates 176425! Coordinates 176425! . . . Is it clear?"

Static. . . .

"Dump everything you have on their artillery . . . dump all your cookies and candies!"

Silence.

There is so much haze and smoke that it has floated up to the peak. Now, even in his distraught imagination he cannot see the soldiers' shadows.

«A drop of pink blood on a few tangled strands of pubic hair. . . . »

And now there are many more Iraqi flares over the Imamzadeh Heydar Hill. As though high after a good fuck, they gently glide down with their parachutes. So, the Iraqi troops, greater in number than the defending survivors, have reached the trenches on the hill to riddle the remaining Iranian soldiers with their Kalashnikovs' sweet-sounding bullets and spears. And to demolish trench after trench by tossing plump Iraqi grenades into them.

The wireless radio brays.

"Amir! Amir! Direct fire to the flower patch!"

He roars back, "That is our own hill!"

"Orders from HQ."

"Fuck!"

"Provide coordinates. It's an order!"

The strangled Iranian artillery starts to fire whatever is left of their ammunition at a hill in friendly hands.

«So that not a moving creature remains . . . Arab or Iranian. . . . »

Bursting into laughter, Amir replies, "Fire where you're firing now. Directly at our own balls!"

He hurls the headset at the radio operator, lies down on the ground, and with eyes burning from salty sweat, stares up at the brown stars.

The scribe on his right shoulder writes:

The staircase is safe, without thunder, lightning, or explosion of shells, and without Davālpā waiting for him on the fourth step. He goes down to make peace.

Left:

> *«I am writing in my head so that I don't forget which one of you is writing. Do you write like me? Or do you write true lies, or false truths? . . . Noise, the sharp noise of silver and china clashing, stabs into the heart of my head. With the wail of my ancestors' ghosts, ill-tempered heirloom silver forks and spoons scrape against antique vitrified plates and haul rice and dead flesh into mouths. In the dining room of the revered Yamini family, the dinner cloth is spread on the floor. At the head of the spread, sitting with his legs crossed, Agha Haji has fixed his sideways glance on me. Across from him, holy Mother, with heaven beneath her feet, is joyfully watching her son who has come to his senses and appeared at the God-sanctified meal. She scurried off and brought my plate of weeds. Ignoring my grimace, she also piled up a plate of rice and eggplant stew and put it in front of me, hoping she can trick me into reaching for it. So finally, the entire happy family is sitting together, stuffing themselves in silence. . . . The cave dwellers used to tear off a piece of meat with their hands and crawl into a dark corner away from the eyes and greed of the others.*
>
> *To break the mummified silence, Reyha says, "Thank you, Mom, it is delicious."*

A gold-rimmed china bowl filled with lettuce, wheat sprouts, and beans. I have requested a massacre of plants for lunch. The sound of the lettuce crunching between my teeth echoes in my ears. . . .

"Lettuce and carrots love human teeth," I say.

They don't know that they should laugh. Mother's skin is so fair. Her lips bitterly curved downward, just like Reyhaneh's, show no sign of her usual naive smile.

"It's great that you all eat meat. If everyone was a vegetarian, the sheep would die of hunger."

I laugh at my own inane joke, dig out the unchewable lettuce string stuck between my teeth, and I put it on the side of the bowl.

"At the front they used to tell us that if we were martyred, we would go to heaven. I have heard that in heaven, the instant you crave grapes or apples, the tree branches bend down to you. But the Quran doesn't say if there are carrots in heaven or not. Our house is better than heaven. It has lettuce, it has carrots. And I crave these every day. After all, I am a martyr, too, but in installments."

Mother groans. I have not heard such a groan even from wounded men close to death.

"Being upset at a meal is ingratitude to God for his blessings," Father growls.

"How can I sit and watch someone who lost so much blood, who was passed around from hospital to hospital, eat only lettuce, and without care harm himself," Mother whimpers. "Agha, if you want to get angry and chastise me, do it! I do not have the heart to sit and watch my son melt away like a candle. . . . He is skin and bones. First he got himself all cut up and injured, and now. . . ."

She is short of breath.

She throws her spoon and fork on her plate and runs out of the dining room sobbing. I realize that she has long hair, like Reyhaneh, gray waves behind her like a flag in the wind. . . . I know with her eyes Reyhaneh is telling me, I told you, you are torturing us to death. . . . And the specter of Father's venom is like a hand raised to slap the left side of my face. . . . The sound of Mother's nervous scream and then her sobs come from somewhere in the garden. Lettuce tastes like sludge. I put my fork down in the bowl. Sensibly.

"Don't you want to make some changes in your behavior?"

This is the first time since I came back to this house that he has opened his mouth and addressed me.

His faint, guttural Arabic accent infuriates me. No, I was wrong to be afraid of looking him in the eyes. It is not fear—there is a spiteful, scummy disgust between us that makes me not want to look at him. Reyhaneh goes after Mother. Her fluttering hair, black, down to her waist.

"I. . . . If I am me, I know what my cure is. Being a vegetarian is the best medicine for me."

"Eat whatever you want, but if you show some concern for your mother who has mourned for you a hundred times, God will reward you. Do you not think she deserves it?"

There is a tremor in his voice.

"It is up to you whether you show respect to your mother or not. But expect consequences. . . . Do you understand?"

Meaning, you know that if I so choose, I can throw you out with a kick in the ass and you can go beg on the streets with one hand.

Huh! How come I didn't think of this? As a beggar with one arm, I will have a pretty decent income.

I lie. "Yes, Sir."

I have to fool him. From the corner of my eyes I see the halo of his white hair and beard walk out. I am left with plenty of food. Now, without their irritating words, looks, and silence, I can eat my beans in peace.»

Right:

«I hear the rain and the wail of winter sweet flowers in the garden. . . . There was a time when I liked meat. I liked to suck on skin and flesh, to leave the mark of my conquest on the round of a shoulder or above a right breast. . . . My miserable Reyhaneh, you have never had one of those dark marks on your pale skin.»

Half an hour later, he abandons the lunch spread and leaves the family dining room.

A rainy rain is drizzling and not drizzling.

He can hear Mother sniffling in the living room. Sitting on a sofa, a silk carpet's garden beneath her feet, knot after knot, color after color, arabesque and *toranj* motifs. . . .

«Drops of rain's rain sit on her clothes and hair. Mother is sitting and not sitting on this sofa that is not Agha Haji's style. She selected the sofas. Our mother, a chador-wearing, praying mother whose father did not allow her to continue her schooling past the sixth grade, who has spent most of her life in the kitchen and in mourning. How did she manage to convince her master to buy such a sofa set? Her back bent, her hair gray, streaming down to her knees, her moonlit wrists peeking out from under the cuff of her black sleeve. With the dignity of a royal dynasty's princess, she sits in her castle waiting for a Macedonian, Turk, Mongol, Arab, Afghan, British-Indian soldier to walk through the door reeking of alcohol and blood and spoils of war, and drag her under him.

The mad son kneels and rests his head on the lap of the suffering mother of Indian movies. . . . How well I can smell her rained-on scent. . . . »

"What did they do to you? What horrors have made you like this? I may be stupid, I may be uneducated, but I am your mother. My heart has a way into your heart. For the love of Fatimah, the Prophet's daughter, tell me. Perhaps I will understand the pain that is eating away at you."

"..."

"May God obliterate all wars!"

"Did I go willingly or did your husband do something to make me go?"

He presses his head on the soft of Mother's thigh. He senses her hesitant hand close to his hair.

"He is angry, isn't he? His martyred son has suddenly returned with a living ass's head! Shall I tell you the truth? Agha Haji is angry with you and Reyha, too, because you found me. Otherwise, he would still be a martyr's father."

"Don't talk this way about your father."

"Are you afraid he will hear us? Divorce you? You came to his house with snow-white teeth, do you have to leave it in a snow-white shroud? Be honest! How many plots of land worth God knows how much did he put in your name?"

"My dear, I don't understand what you're trying to say. I want to understand. . . . My son! I have heard there is a man who writes prayers. God grants his prayers. He charges a lot, but whatever he makes he spends on orphans. They say he has cured many people."

"My cure is in someone else's hands."

"Who, my son? Tell me."

"Back when I was at home, did I ever tell you that I had become engaged to someone?"

"No. . . . Tell me. Tell me if your heart is with someone, and I will go and ask for her hand in marriage. Any family would be proud to have my son as their son-in-law."

"Especially since he gave an arm so that the Iraqi soldiers would not storm into Tehran and make their daughters pregnant."

"Who is she? Tell me."

"If you are not playing me, then tell Reyha to help me some more to find her."

«Her fingers lightly run through my hair. Or am I imagining it? If Agha Haji walks into the living room and sees his full-grown son in this mama's-boy state, he will be furious."»

And he sees:

In the February cold of the schoolyard, the children hurry to wash their hands with the icy water from a row of bronze faucets and rub their knuckles against the cement sink to scrub off calluses. The school bell chimes. The children run, each class standing in line, holding out their hands, palms down. Knees trembling, but standing rigid. The school supervisor quickly inspects the reddened hands. Suddenly, his whip appears from behind him and beats a pair of callused hands. A boy's puppyish yelp.

And the supervisor hunts Amir out of the fourth-grade line and shoves him forward with a slap on the head. He pushes and pushes him up the stairs and onto the stand in front of the school office. He grabs his thick, beautiful hair that he is so proud of. With a hair clipper the supervisor shaves a stripe from his forehead to the back of his neck, another stripe from ear to ear. He puts his lips on the silver miracle of the standing microphone and his voice booms in the seven bowels of the school.

"I made an intersection for him to traipse around on like a dandy."

All the children standing in line, all the steam wafting from their mouths, burst into laughter. He bursts into tears.

All the way home, he carries his schoolbag on his head, hoping that people will not see the white intersection in his dark hair. Everyone who sees, chuckles.

"Do you remember? The school supervisor shaved an intersection on my head, and you griped and grumbled until you finally gave me money to run to the barbershop and shave the rest. Even after I came home, looking like a kid with lice, you scolded me for not having gone to the barber the day before. Remember I begged you not to tell Agha Haji. . . . But he found out and gave me an earful."

"I don't remember and I don't know why you are telling me all this. I have dedicated my life and my soul to you and your sister. And this is what I get. Both of you act as though I owe you something."

> «I don't want to lose the scent of her skirt and the softness of her lap. I want to go to sleep with the moonlight of her fingers in my hair. No, this one is not a raindrop dripping from her hair. A wayward tear has fallen on my cheek. As if my own, it rolls down. At least there is one good thing—it rains for me, too.»

He wants to say. . . .

Tell me a. . . .

The apocalyptic flash of a lightning for an instant changes the colors of the living room walls and furnishings. He jumps. Thunder explodes across the garden like a timed shell, the windows shake, the chandelier's crystal drops and sconces rattle. Rolling in the sky, it moves away.

He wanted to say, Tell me a story! . . . So that Mother would ask, Which story? And he would say, About the Raining-Rocks Fortress. . . .

He starts to convulse.

The scribe on his left shoulder had written:

He dives into the tent. Pirar, huddled in a corner, shouts, "What's going on? Where are they firing?"

The tremors of the ground have followed him from far away. The shells are landing closer.

Pirar hollers, "Where were you? Where are they hitting?"

Burning swelter simmers from his pores . . . drenched in sweat from his mad dash. . . .

"They are all dead . . . give me some water!"

"You have some, your canteen. . . ."

"Oh, no-o! . . . oh, everyone . . . everyone . . . dead."

Pirar grabs him by the collar and shakes him.

"Talk! Did the Iraqis see you?"

He cannot tell whether it is Pirar pouring water in his mouth or if he is doing it himself.

"You didn't give away our location, did you?"

"Give me water!"

"Where are they hitting? Who is dead?"

He is having another convulsion. The water in his mouth gurgles in his throat. . . .

Running, panting, trying to reach the tent, he felt the air being sucked out of everywhere. He ran, moaning, "They are all dead!" He ran, and the air kept getting thinner. The more everyone died, the more he said, "They are all dead!" He just wanted to get away, to not see, and he ran to reach water. The mountain rocks kept throwing him to the ground, his mouth bloody on dirt and thorns. He wanted someone, he wanted to reach him, to fall at his feet, to let him know that everyone, fathers, mothers, aunts, cousins, classmates, they all died, dogs, cats, horses perished. . . . Tremors cramp his muscles. He vomits the water bubbling in his throat. . . . Pirar's voice crumples somewhere far away. He cannot see.

> *« . . . the air in my lungs, the shit is all salt in my lungs . . . perhaps I can't see because night has come. Perhaps everyone died because I didn't know night's name . . . the sky's rage, the violent, icy wind lifts dogs and trees into the air and hurls them to the ground, people scream, the white wind takes away the air to breathe. It blows away the hair of the people hiding in holes, it takes away their flaking skin. The sky's roaring laughter strikes, people vomit salt, they turn into salt. And God's godly fury rains fire and sulfur from the sky. Fleeing crowds burn, burned to a crisp they run, turn into ash, scatter on the earth. . . . Who said this? Someone did. "O, earth! I piss on you! Whatever evils they did to you, you said nothing . . . they planted mines in you . . . you said nothing. . . . "»*

"Calm down!"

> *«O earth, I piss on you because they pissed on you and you said nothing! They fired mortar shells at you and you said nothing. I piss on you, earth! They poured poison on you from your own sky and you said nothing. They buried hundreds and hundreds of corpses piled on top of each other inside you and you said nothing, earth. . . . »*

" . . . can you think straight? Did the Iraqis see you or not?"
"I piss on this earth."
"Stop blabbering!"

> *«Pirar's hands, strong. . . . »*

On his hands and knees, Pirar pokes his head out of the tent.

"Salman! Salman!"

A shell flies overhead. Pirar leaps back in.

"Some place is under heavy fire. Where?"

"Everyone is dead! They hit them with chemical bombs."

"Where were you?"

Dazed, he stares at Pirar.

"How many times have I told you not to go wandering off? Who is dead?"

He likes being curled up like a fetus. It feels safe . . . Pirar tries to sit him up.

A shell explodes nearby. Pieces of shrapnel rip into the tent and exit the other side.

Pirar drops down to the ground next to him.

"Motherfuckers!"

Dust and smoke billow in through the holes.

Another shell.

The wave of the explosion blows against the tent and tears one side out of the ground.

"We've been found!" Pirar shouts. "You motherfucker, you gave away our location!"

Three rounds of shells fly overhead and explode in the valley behind them. The sergeant, still shielding his head with his arms, starts reciting prayers. The soldiers, outside or inside their tent, are shouting.

A shell lands close by. The tent collapses on top of them.

The wails of private Salman.

"Sergeant! . . . Aid! . . . Aid! . . . "

The vibration of a MIG flying high above the mountains.

Mayhem swells among the soldiers. The good-for-nothings are bursting the boils of chaos in his head with a razor. . . . He half rises.

"Get down on the ground, you lunatic!" Pirar shouts.

The sergeant grabs his shoulder and pulls him down. Under the caved-in canvas, Amir runs his hand over the ground. He finds the radio headset. Frantically, he yells into it.

"Simorgh! Simorgh! Chickpeas! Chickpeas!"

He flips the radio's switch. Again he half sits up.

Both start coughing from the smoke and dust.

"Simorgh! Simorgh!"

The groans and cries of the soldiers grow louder. They appeal to the Imam and their mothers. He crawls to where the opening of the tent ought to be.

"Where are you going, you lunatic?"

"The soldiers! . . . The soldiers! . . . "

Outside, the sun and the sky have turned brown. Shells are exploding near and far. Blasted boulders scattered everywhere, hacked thorn bushes flying in the air. The soldiers' tent is no longer there. Its tattered pieces caught on jagged rocks, its singed shreds floating in the wind. Two black, gaping craters near where the tent used to be.

By the time he makes his way to the soldiers, the pleas and howls of three of them have stopped. Like a snake, an intestine has slithered under a rock. A lacerated red mask on a face. . . . One man, sitting on his knees, his forehead on the ground, silently trembles. His uniform is soaked with blood. Is it his blood or another soldier's?

"Get down, Salman!"

The soldier just trembles. Amir grabs his shoulders and shakes him. Salman falls.

> *«Is the ground shaking from his shudders or is he shuddering from the earth's tremors?»*

There should be three other soldiers! . . . Turned to dust? Deserted? An Iraqi scout must have seen Amir through his binoculars and tracked him here. Watched him as he ran all the way. . . .

The mountain is collapsing into itself. Pirar's shouts are coming from far away.

"We have to climb down!"

The earth explodes again. The blast throws him, fragments of stone pellet him, and he is heaved against a boulder. A branding stone branded on stone. Shrapnel . . . shrapnel. . . .

He feels his ears swelling deep inside, ready to burst. A storm of grasshoppers . . . and the wind and that bitter salty wave pass over him again.

A burst of convulsing wind rolls him on the ground. A burst of heat. . . . Hundreds of thorns cut into his face and body. Air whistles out of the fissures inside his skull. He cannot hear the explosions.

> *«It is empty around me . . . which asshole pissed at the sky, yellow clouds, brown clouds, pieces of floating flesh in their folds . . . little by little, I am . . . I am . . . I am feeling well . . . like the high of good weed . . . I am well that I can hear someone moaning, his voice is familiar, moaning familiarly, right here, near my face, his voice in my throat . . . blood and dirt in my mouth, clouds in my mouth, the barks of a dog in my mouth . . . the fingers on my left hand burn so badly . . . I piss on you, earth, because they stuff you with hordes of dead bodies and you say nothing. God's cheerful whistles in my ears . . . it seems the shelling has stopped . . . it is time for me to get up. I am well. What if Pirar is dead? I have to lift myself. The palms of my hands on the dirt. . . . »*

Lying on his stomach, he struggles to push down on his forearms and use his hands to lift his weight off the ground. He feels the dirt under his left hand give way and sink in like a swamp . . . he falls on his left side. Burning arches up from his shoulder to his neck. . . . He has been hit.

> «I've been hit.»

Lying on his side, he thinks perhaps he has fallen on a pile of scorching shrapnel. He rolls onto his back. He sees the shadow of gushing blood on his left side.

> «Ejaculating blood . . . when did the desert stick to the sky? Its sand is raining down . . . how thirsty I am, because I pissed all my water on you, earth. . . . »

The fingers on his left hand feel as though they are immersed in burning coal.

> «And we watched the white swans and they did not watch us. They are so white that halos have formed around their luster . . . and through the window that was of the same texture as dragonfly wings, we watched the weeping willow leaning over the water . . . and we watched the male swan's neck coil around its mate's neck and we watched the flight of turquoise-saffron-emerald-colored dragonflies. Now and then, they brushed against the glass. Went back and brushed on the surface of the water . . . and then we saw all three swans raise their heads up to the sky and sing. Don't swans sing only at the moment of their death? . . . The only things that happen in this world without permission are bad things. . . .
>
> It is good that I am dying more easily inside the darkness that is in the darkness that I am dying in, to be free of want of water, want of air, and everyone is dead. . . . Hanna! My Hanna! What if you, too, were in the chemical fog down there in that village. . . .
>
> Was the room carpeted with orange leaves or swans' beaks? We watched the wind, the wind that blew wall to wall, and the shimmer of the water that rippled on the ceiling. And I watched myself hold her from behind. Kind flames licked from our nipples . . . and we linked our left hands together, our rings rubbed against each other, and we watched our beautiful hands.»

Like a useless appendage, his left arm hangs from his body by a bloody filament. White jagged bone juts from sliced flesh and blood. The arm looks like it can be stuck back where it belongs, like a puzzle piece. Lying on his back, he reaches over to grab it. His arm tears off. It is only now that like lightning pain strikes in his eyes and chest. It is not like the sting of a whip. It is intimate. Before losing consciousness, through a haze he sees Pirar bandaging his arm and shouting, "Lunatic! You lunatic!"

> «Where are you now, Hanna? Bloody sand of pain rains from the sky. . . . I am dying in a fountain of blood . . . did you see that we could do nothing and they have filled the world with Everests of their shit and our blood? . . . The whoosh of blood echoes in my ears. . . . I flap my right arm to keep myself underwater and with my left hand I claw at the sand on the seafloor that now has no color. . . . »

The scribe had written on his left shoulder:

« What happens to colors when night falls?

The rain has kept us all indoors. The sea is muddy. Its horizon has moved closer and is littered with clusters of heavy, low-lying clouds. This sea is a bummer. Yesterday, when it was sunny and the wind was just a breeze, the sea was a thrill. Swimming and fondling Soheila's pale thighs in the water was fun. If she wasn't itching for it she wouldn't keep pushing me under so that I would grope her shapely legs while supposedly trying to resurface. Even underwater I could hear her lusty laugh. . . . Now, the foaming waves leap out of the murky water, trying to reach our beach house, and there, twenty or thirty yards away, they run out of steam and cave in. We all look like a bunch of fly-sprayed mosquitos . . . but sitting next to this window, surrounded by happy-go-lucky dimwit friends . . . in the flower patch, the sunflowers with their heads bent down are so . . . the only thing spoiling the view is that odd-looking Meysam, sitting in the rain at the water's edge like a miserable orphan. . . . Now, me, here at this window, what am I in this very now? Now, in the world out there, in its big cities, so much is happening, and I wonder, Do I mean something to someone? Right now in Tehran, even with the revolution over and the war crushing hordes and hordes of ants, people have again poured into the streets to holler and shout death to America, to Israel, to Russia, to France, to England, and to whatever other hellhole. You, standing in line for subsidy coupons or for martyrdom, you deserve whatever happens to you. Charge forward, ants! You Iraqi ants, you charge forward, too. Cut each other in half . . . and now, overseas, in beautiful cities full of beauties who will not be punished for being beautiful, there are great pleasures that I don't even know about. Suit-and-tie-wearing Goofys are dreaming of being promoted, dancers are strutting and swaying, screwers are screwing in places where I have never screwed, cocaine is being snorted up politicians' cavernous nostrils, and a diarrhea of guns and bombs and shells is being shipped to the ants. . . .

"Are you feeling gloomy again, pretty boy?" Kaveh asks.

"No. I was thinking of my grandmother. The old woman used to come and stay with us for a week every month. And every morning she would tell me, 'Amir, when I go to sit on the sofa, the thorns of these red roses you put in the vase scratch my arms.' She couldn't see well. The flowers were artificial. One day I put real roses in the vase. She didn't say anything."

"Old women's greatest contribution to mankind is their death. We are going to have a couple of drinks. Are you in?"

"Where did you get the booze?"

"My uncle. I keep telling you, don't underestimate your Kaveh. I poured it in the car's windshield washer container. I added some green food coloring. When the patrol at the Chalous Road checkpoint stopped me, he barked at me to open the hood. He poked around everywhere. The peasant twerp didn't find it. Don't you love this genius?"

"Why didn't you let on yesterday?"

"Yesterday was weed day."

"Any news about your military service?"

Kaveh looks surprised.

"My dad is getting a medical exemption for me. Screw the rest. The more the brothers kill each other, the better. And Islam's troops that are supposed to conquer Baghdad will go on to take Istanbul, too, and then the gates of Europe will spread wide for their circumcised swords! This time, they won't give up halfway. They will charge straight into the heart of Europe and take their chubby, white kids as slave boys and their round-assed, fair wives as slave girls. And they will ram Islam's nail into

the Land of Sin. And what a shafting that will be! The same way they shafted us and are shoving it in all the way."

"Medical exemption based on what? Blue balls caused by rubbing up the door?"

"Forget it . . . it's a secret. . . . Listen, I have a new joke. . . . "

He says this out loud to attract everyone's attention.

"The guy comes out of the bridal chamber, dripping sweat and panting. His friends ask, 'So you finally conquered the peak?' He says, 'The damn thing was more like burlap than hymen. But I finally tore through it.' Then the bride walks out and says, 'This mule didn't even give me a chance to take off my panties!'"

Everyone laughs. . . . I look at Khazar. She's acting like I'm not here again. At the edge of the water, a white ribbon of seashells on the sand. Meysam is tossing them in the sea. It wasn't right for me to pick on him the way I did and put him down in front of the others. Even Khaza, who stuck up for him, was no match for me.

Everyone is shouting. I hear glasses being filled. I can tell the difference between the sounds of beer, vodka, and Chateau Sardasht being poured. But what if Meysam is right to be angry with me because I didn't bring Reyhaneh? First of all, I don't want my sister around these sleazy guys. And second, I don't want a deadweight with me. What's more, he should know that Agha Haji won't allow Reyhaneh to come on these trips. . . . Yes! Just as I said, anyone who's not having fun should go back to Tehran instead of being a killjoy.

Khazar pours drinks for everyone and sips from the bottle, perhaps as tax. I heard she's been drinking a lot these days. She's wearing a red, sleeveless, open-neck shirt. Her nipples are peaking against it.

Kaveh clears his throat and raises his glass. Everyone knows what to do. They all hold up their glasses for Kaveh to repeat the parable he learned at a tried-and-true Turk's drinking ceremony.

"One day, people were chopping down a weeping willow tree. They were the same people who used to sit in the tree's shadow. But you guys

are different. Before we sit in memory of each other, let's sit with each other. . . ."

Khazar likes these clever sayings popular among the roughnecks of Tehran. She adds the rest, "To the health of three people—the prisoner, the soldier, and the mateless thug. To the health of the chain, it sits under rain and snow for a hundred years, it rusts, it rots, but it neeeeever breaks."

Noushin chimes in, "To the health of those who have no gold, no power, no inside track, no kin and kindred, those with dirty collars, cartons for homes, and parks for beds, those who wash their shirt at night and put it on in the morning."

Bahram cuts her off, "Love in drunkenness, in drunkenness truth."

Kaveh resumes, "The eagle that soars to Seventh Heaven flaunts its wings, the beautiful flaunt their beauty, the crooners flaunt their David-esque voices, soccer players flaunt their kicks, boxers flaunt their jabs, chess players flaunt their tactics, but. . . ."

We all raise our glasses higher and say in one voice, "But we flaunt our cherry-picked friends. To each and every one of us. . . . Cheers!"

And we take a swig.

Saiid wants to start a card game, hoping that Soheila will be his partner and sit across from him. He drove me nuts last night. I could hear him whining behind the house. In the middle of the night he had dragged the curvy girl outside and was messing with her head. Whispering, begging her to let him do her. That, and the thought of Khazar in the next room, would not let me sleep. I imagined I was free of her. But it's all back. The sensation of the butterfly flicks of the tip of her tongue on my body, discovering places that I didn't even know were sensitive. She took pleasure in her discoveries, and she gave pleasure.»

On his right shoulder:

Dawn has barely broken when, frustrated, he goes outside.

> «Have I frustrated the sea or has the sea frustrated me?»

He is still tempted to open the door to Khazar's room, go over to her, and even if she starts screaming and yelling, grab her by the arm, and ignoring his friends who will have woken up from the noise and are greedy for drama, drag her outside and over to the sea to tell her that he is still in love with her.

At the water's edge, he takes off his swimming trunks; the sense of his manhood becoming heavy bothers him. He wades into the foamy water.

> «Calm me down so that I don't do what I think that good-for-nothing Khazar is scheming for me to do. Help me not to beg her, not to ask her to be my bride . . . make me cold so that I don't go down on my knees for a girl.»

But the sea is not compassionate this dawn. A wave hits him on the chest. As it ebbs, he senses his body being dragged further in. He enjoys the water playfully fondling him. He stands facing the waves. He feels the pull behind his knees. The shallow space between an ebbing wave and one that is rising resembles the space between a pair of breasts whose weight has spread them apart; it frightens him. He moves further into the sea and thinks of squirting his semen at the waves, but the lashing waves do not give him the chance. The sky is and is not cloudy. The white clouds are moving and scattering faster than he has ever seen; black ones replace them. As he relaxes his body, a returning wave pounds against his chest. He falls back. By the time he raises his head above the water, his nostrils are burning from the salty seawater. He stands up. He moves forward. He remembers the day in fourth grade when Agha Haji dropped him off at school. Before walking in, an old man pushing a bicycle called him and said he was his father's friend. "I called out to him several times to say hello, but he didn't hear me. What a shame. . . . " Amir does not remember what the man said to gain his trust and lure him into a dead-end alley, nor what the message was that he wanted him to relay to his father, which he murmured as he smelled and sniffed his face and neck, inhaling, deeply, breathlessly. His eyes rolled back. And Amir realized the man was not his father's friend, but he was too afraid to run, too afraid to stay.

He comes to himself just as a more powerful wave throws him back and rolls toward the shore. He thrashes about trying to raise his head above the surface. And the pull of the ebbing wave spins him under.

The sea is more of a sea. This old friend is showing him what it means to be a friend and what it means to be. How ignorant he's been in understanding friendship and being.

The waves are not high, but they are powerful. One pushes him toward the shore. He tries to walk backward with it. Then, more powerful, it returns and drags him out again. His steps forward and backward on the seafloor are not under his control. And there is a hole on the seafloor. Like a well.

> *«I am drowning, and in the morning when my friends wake up, the ghost of my thoughts will play tricks on them.»*

And the stronger yet silent waves drive him further into the belly of the sea. He cannot understand that his friend the sea is teaching him how easy it is for the strong arms and muscles he has built at Vanak Hotel's swimming pool to drown. He does not pull back. As soon as a wave rises and before it hurls him backward, he punches it with his right fist. . . . Like a wrestler, a wave tears his feet off the sand, knots his arms and legs together, and pounds him against the seafloor. He doesn't know which side is up, which side is down.

> *«You are not my sea, you good-for-nothing! If you have a sister I will drag her under me. If you are not a liar like the others, then you're tricking me into wading further in so that you can drown me.»*

And he flails his hands around hoping to touch sand and determine which side is down.

Right:

The sun has risen by the time he drags his exhausted body out of the water. The sea seems calmer now that it has humiliated him. He pulls on his swimming trunks. Nausea churns inside him. He heads toward the beach house. He wants to vomit at the foot of the sunflowers. And he wonders whether Saiid finally managed to get on top of Soheila or not. Khazar is sitting on the stairs in front of the house.

"It seems you couldn't sleep either, girl?"

The gray of a dawn cloud is in Khazar's eyes and the humor of having seen him naked on the beach is on her lips. He sits down on the same step, as far from her as possible. He thinks he can smell that strange scent of her blood. He had smelled it when Khazar pushed him off of her. He saw streaks of that pink blood on the inside of her thigh. She ran her fingertip over the narrow trickle and said, "Lick it." He had, and its scent stayed with him. A blend of mildewed papyrus paper and the breast milk of a mountain dweller. The aroma of fertile ovules inside a flower that, when crushed and rubbed between two fingers, yielded hundreds of fertile cells, slaughtered.

Khazar had licked his finger, too.

And the gentle breeze from the sea drives away the scent.

"Are you all right, girl?"

"Did you see the color of the fog over the sea, boy? There was a hint of pink in it. Wasn't there?"

He is surprised that there is no sadness in Khazar's voice.

"Yesterday, around this time, when I went to the water . . . right there . . . look . . . exactly parallel to the white poplars on the grounds of the house next door, there was a puddle with three baby fish trapped in it. If I hadn't gone there, they would have died! . . . When the tide moves back, the water in the puddle slowly drains. . . . I guess a few more have gotten stuck there today . . . don't you think so?"

"The poplars look like they're lacking something. Their leaves aren't firm, they're drooping and blotched with white spots. They're dying, just like their owner. . . . "

"Have you paid attention to the old guy? Every time I see him I promise myself that when I am old and sick, I will do away with myself."

Then she whispers, "It looks like he's searching for something among the seashells!"

The old man inches along near the water's edge, between the property lines of the two beach houses. It takes him some thirty minutes to go twenty or thirty yards and walk back.

Yesterday morning, too, at exactly ten o'clock, ignoring their games and laughter, he had strolled along the high tide line until noon.

Sounding strange, Khazar says, "Perhaps he's waiting for the waves to bring him something."

Amir is itching to make fun of her and say, You are in la-la land, girl! . . .

The sun is high on the far side of the clouds and the horizon has turned red.

"Do you think there are baby fish caught in the puddle again?" Khazar says.

"Florence Nightingale! With a heart this tender, how could you dump me the way you did?"

"If you go and check, I will brew some tea for you. As a prize for myself, I am going to fry three eggs. I will make some for you, too, if you want. . . . Will you go?"

He guesses Khazar is afraid the fish will wriggle in her hands and she'll drop them on the sand.

"If you do this one good deed, you will be happy all day long and you will make me happy, too. And stop acting like a jilted lover. We came here to have fun. Be like me. I'm having a great time."

As he sets off toward the sea, Khazar calls out, "The baby fish will bless you!"

«Is she making fun of me or. . . . »

On his left:

«There was nothing in that puddle, not even a piece of driftwood that the sea brings, perhaps all the way from the coast of Russia. The ones that the waves have sanded and polished into strange shapes, like wood carved by pirates.»

"We'd better hide the arak," Bahram says. "And put the glasses out of sight. My dad said the Revolutionary Guards come and peek in through the windows. Just as we're couples here, we may end up couples under their whips. It would be a shame if they took our booze, too."

"Amir, want to play poker?"

«So, if Khazar is not making wisecracks and not showing any sign of how beautiful we were together, then it really ended the way it ended. . . . But this crazy girl! I want to slap her in the face! Why won't she at least tell me what I did that made her throw me away. . . .

Sitting on either side of the cold fireplace, Bahram and Noushin start playing the guitar and singing.

"If one day you go away . . . leave my side without a word . . . I will fall captive to my dreams. . . . "

For a moment I catch Khazar looking at me. There is worry in her eyes.

She looks stupid. . . . I give the cigarette back to Soheila. The filter is wet with her spit. I am sure her spit is not as bitter as it tastes on the filter.

Kaveh and Noushin sing louder.

"If one day your name . . . echoes in my ears . . . again your sorrow will come. . . . "

Soheila dips her finger in her glass and runs it over the cigarette.

Khazar cheerfully says, "Bahram, play something happy! On this rainy day, sad songs will make our buddies mope and sulk."

She may be taunting me. Her nipples . . . the halo around them that is not brown, that has a tinge of pink, that unlike other nipples I have nibbled are neither goose-pimply nor perfectly smooth. From the milky skin of her breasts they gently taper toward their tips and make them pointy. As though constantly aroused and lusting.

Khazar thinks Kaveh and his boorishness are cheap, but that dreamy Bahram and his guitar . . . what if Bahram has tasted those nipples?

Bahram starts to strum a corny upbeat song. Saiid starts rocking in his chair. Khazar gets up and pulls Soheila along with her to the middle of the room. I have never seen her dance these bawdy dances. She coils her slim, bare arms like a pair of snakes. It doesn't suit her to flirtingly run her fingers through her hair, fling it back, and again swing her head and whip her hair over her face and chest like floozy dancers in raunchy cafes.

" . . . I adore you, you beauty . . . I adore you, you flower from the garden of desire. . . . "

Saiid starts to sing along and dance. Each time they repeat the words "you beauty," he holds his arms out to Soheila and moves his hands suggestively, as though he is holding her ass. Noushin watches me from the corner of her eyes. As much as she dislikes me, I dislike being caught off guard. If she didn't have that eagle nose and ashy, blotchy skin, N would have been a good letter to add to my collection. Saiid offers Khazar the bottle. She plays coy.

"Take a swig, dear! You won't get drunk enough for us to come on to you."

Bahram, glaring at Khazar, takes his anger out on the guitar strings. Khazar grabs the bottle and takes a few gulps. Soheila and Saiid cheer her on. Noushin takes a sip from the small narrow-waisted glass that is always at her side. Perhaps she would not dislike me as much if she knew how much I appreciate the way she drinks—like disciplined drinkers in two-bit joints on Lalehzar Street who value their arak and know how to pace themselves. And it's not just her drinking style that I like. Every time I remember that she dropped out of her three fields of study at the university despite top grades, I admire her. Perhaps I'm even jealous of her courage. . . .

She takes a sip and says, "Did you read that article in the newspaper? Another one about girls being seduced. It was in the Incidents section. Two guys took two girls to the Caspian coast without the girls' families knowing, and they deceived them three times."

Saiid bursts into laughter and says, "Girls like to be deceived. . . . Am I not right, Miss Khazar?"

"Why are you asking me? Ask your dear Soheila!"

Bahram's eyes are fixed on Khazar's bare chest and arms. A drop of sweat on her pale skin that dancing has turned the color of quince flowers has rolled down her cleavage. Still swaying, she holds out the half-empty bottle toward me. Kaveh stops playing. Khazar dances over to him.

"Play Night in the Desert!"

And she starts dancing in front of him, for him.

It is still raining. Meysam is no longer in view of the window. Does Reyhaneh know that Meysam really likes her? Soheila looks at me and lets loose her loose laugh.

Saiid says, "A girl who wants to be deceived has to make sure her father and brother are not the zealous, fanatical type. Then, she can let herself be deceived as many times as she wants. But if they are, she must first get married, then find someone to deceive her. We had two cases in our neighborhood. A girl on our street got pregnant. In the middle of the night her father cut off her head and laid it on her chest. What happened two streets away was interesting. A girl had a sex-change operation and became a lovely guy like Amir. Not one, but both of his hot-blooded, devout brothers knifed him, because he had ruined their honor and integrity!"

Khazar and Soheila have stopped dancing.

"I didn't say these things to upset you," Saiid says. "I meant them as words of caution, gentlemen, little ladies! You should thank God that you don't have fanatical fathers and brothers."

Meysam walks in looking like a drenched mouse.»

The scribe had continued:

«"You don't have to toss a coin. I'm bored, I will go buy the meat for kebab. I will get some liver, too. . . . Meysam, will you come with me?"

Without looking at me, he snaps, "No."

But Soheila says she will come, because she needs to buy some women's things. Saiid is waiting for me to ask him, too.

"Saiid, you start a first-rate, hot and glowing charcoal in the grill."

Confident in my Alfa Romeo's wide custom tires, I push down on the gas pedal. . . . 90 miles per hour on a wet road, mud flying at the windshield.

Soheila presses both hands to the dashboard.

"They are going to make up stories about us."

"Saiid was fuming."

"Good! . . . He's being a real ninny. No matter how many times I tell him it's over between us, he just doesn't get it."

Every time I end up behind a truck and the wipers can't rival the splashing mud, I get a thrill from turning the nose of the car into the opposite lane. Half blind, it takes a few seconds to see if the shadow of a car or a truck is nose-to-nose with us or not.

"You are mad, Amir!"

"You don't like it?"

"In a way I do."

"You get wet?"

"Shut up!"

A dilapidated pickup truck could crumple my blood in its crumpled metal.

"You are mad! If we get stopped at one of the checkpoints, we will be done for. Both of us drunk, and I have come to the shore for you to seduce me . . . what will we do then?"

"That woman's thing you said you need to buy, did you mean sanitary pads?"

She again grabs hold of the dashboard with terrified hands.

"Yes. It started this morning. . . . Amir, watch out! You are driving way too fast."

"Damn! What rotten luck. I was going to take you out on the beach tonight, and until dawn. . . . "

Soheila lets loose her loose laugh. I push a cassette tape into the car stereo.

. . . Who cares about the weather? Listen to the falling rain, listen to it fall. . . .

I think of turning onto one of the dirt roads and driving into the woods, someplace out of the way, and wrapping Soheila's fleshy lips around my cock.»

Left:

When they walk into the beach house, everyone turns and looks at them with suspicion.

"You're late!" Saiid says angrily.

But Khazar, her face still the color of quince flower, walks over to him, and with an unfamiliar smile on her lips takes the bag with the meat and liver from him.

"Soheila, my dear, didn't his driving drive you mad?"

"Yes! He is a lunatic."

Whispering together, they walk over to the open kitchen.

Amir throws back a half shot of arak as his bonus for having done the shopping. Bahram's guitar, silent, leans against the fireplace. . . . Noushin sits at the table, fortune-telling with a deck of cards.

"Will you tell my fortune?" he asks.

She looks at him with piercing eyes.

Between the clusters of clouds moving away, patches of the late-afternoon sky have emerged. Noushin raises her empty glass to her lips and says, "To the health of all the clever scoundrels."

Meysam and Saiid chuckle.

"Make a wish."

"Damn! We're out of arak," Saiid says irately. "I spit on this country where you can't even get a bottle of liquor on the up and up. I will go find some."

He walks out and a car engine revs.

Kaveh comes in and sits next to Amir and throws a heavy arm around his shoulders. . . . He seems drunk.

"Do you know what I want to say to you, Amir?"

"Yes, I know what you want to say."

"If you know what I want to say then say what I want to say."

"You want to say I don't know what you want to say."

"Bravo! . . . I don't want to say anything to you. I want to ask you a question. Do you know what I want to ask?"

He notices that Noushin is observing their conversation with her penetrating eyes.

"No, I don't know what you want to ask."

"I just want to know how you get girls with the first shot, like ducks in the sky."

Looking into Noushin's eyes, Amir says, "You have to use chicken-catching tactics."

Noushin turns away.

"Their weak spot is when you ignore them. They want attention. Just ignore them, especially when they think they're so beautiful that everyone is dying to have them. And always remember that they have eyes in the back of their heads."

"Exactly! Girls are sharp. They know if you so much as steal a peek at their backside, which they deliberately flaunt."

"You have to eye them without them noticing. Take a quick, sharp look to see if they're worth it or not. If they are, you must be as quick as a chicken-catcher. . . . Ignore them. It will infuriate them. . . . Have you ever tried to catch a chicken?"

"A couple of times."

"So you know that as soon as you jump to grab it, it darts off in a direction you never expected. You think it's pecking at the ground unaware you're moving closer, but the second you leap for it, it dashes off so fast that you end up with empty hands between your legs. . . . If you're naive, you think it's scared, but far from being scared, it is. . . . can you guess?"

"It is making fun of us."

"Exactly! We idiots should not head straight toward it. The technique is not to look at it at all. Look far away, at the sky and the clouds, so that it thinks it's not such a great catch after all. With your hands in your pockets, whistle at the stars and some long-ago love, roam around nearby so that the chicken will sneak peeks at you. Then slowly inch closer to it, pretending you're going after another chicken, pretending that your belly is full of chicken. Then, pounce on it and grab its legs. That's it. After you catch it, it will be grateful. It will be proud of itself for having been caught by you."

"Did you learn this stuff at Quran readings in your daddy's mosque?"

"Maybe."

Chirping, Khazar and Soheila go outside with Kaveh, Bahram, and Meysam. He watches them from the window. Soheila grabs a handful of sand and chases after Kaveh, probably because of some wisecrack he made.

She throws it at him. . . . Meysam wanders away from them. Bahram walks alongside Khazar with his head down. Perhaps he's trying to think of something to say, or he may be whispering to her.

> *« It is time for the planet Venus to appear. I will tell the clouds to drift away out of respect. So Khazar is a floozy, too, just like Soheila, Katayoun, and all the others. In my dim-witted mind, I had made her out to be who I wanted her to be.»*

Noushin carefully turns over the cards and arranges them on the table. Amir wishes he had another glass of arak. He remembers yesterday—the Caspian coast's sun and golden sand.

On his right shoulder:

Everyone is in the water; he is lying down on the sand. With his eyes closed, he turns his face to the gentle sun. The darkness in his eyes turns red. The blood flowing in his eyelids frightens him.

Right:

"Why don't you come in the water?"

He opens his eyes. With her hands on her knees, Khazar is leaning over him. He looks at her smooth, shapely legs.

"I was thinking that if you stumble over a rock, you should not throw it to the side of the road."

"You should throw it down the road, so that when you reach it again, you will know you have gained ground. Then you should throw it farther down the road."

A drop of water drips from her chest onto his face.

> «Khazar's dew dripped on my face. How many times have I licked her dew?»

He glances at Khazar's not plump, not skinny thighs that have broadened as she sits on her heels. There is a soft dip between her muscles. He wants to wrap his arms around her knees and brush his lips over the seawater that has wet them. To draw in the taste of her salted skin. In the water, Saiid and Kaveh hold Soheila's hands and feet and swing her, and she lightheartedly screams. They fling her in the water. Water drips from Khazar's body onto the sand and creates small, dark circles.

"It looks like you're in a good mood, Khazar."

"Why shouldn't I be? I'm alive, there is the sun, the sea, the beauty, and no watchdog. They're all in a good mood, too. Aren't you?"

"To be honest, no, I'm not. I still don't understand why you broke up with me."

"So, Mecca of the Universe's ego has been hurt because a scrawny girl turned her back on His Grace before he did so to her. . . . You will be fine. Just now, in the water, Bahram asked me to marry him. He is so much your opposite that it took everything he had to finally say it, he is so simple and shy. He said something beautiful. He said, 'No one has proposed to Khazar in the blue of Khazar's sea.'"

"Did you accept?"

"I told him, 'You have stayed a virgin all these years, you deserve a virgin.' He didn't care. I told him I would give him my answer tomorrow."

She gets up and fixes her bathing suit, which has slid between her buttocks. She looks up at the clouds on the horizon.

"I know these clouds. It's going to rain tomorrow."

She runs to the sea, runs in the water, and jumps over a foaming wave. And she descends in sequins of light. And Amir knows that this will be an immortal image in his mind—Khazar, the glow of her pale skin surrounded by silver sparks, the side of one calf above the water, the other now submerging.

Right:

Noushin again asks, "Was the wish you made an important one?"

"My fortune didn't work out?"

"I'm not done yet, but there is little chance that it will turn out well."

"You sound so serious, as if you really believe in these things."

"Stop baiting me. I want to talk to you about Khazar. Why did you break up with her?"

"She's a really great girl. She loves everyone. She once said something beautiful about you. She said long ago the desert was a sea, it dried up, but the sea fairies remained—Noushin is a sea fairy. Every time you went to Kerman to visit your family, she said you'd gone to the desert to taste the sea's salt."

She takes a bottle from her handbag.

"Now that the booze-wasters are not around . . . want some?"

He looks out the window at his friends who are trying to start a bonfire on the beach. Noushin recites, "My hand and my heart's desire was for love to be a shelter, not a flight, but a refuge. Love, O love, I cannot see your blue face."

He adds, "And a cooling balm on the flame of a wound, not a blistering blaze on the cold within. Love, O love, I cannot see your rosy face."

Noushin looks surprised that he knows this poem.

"We are so young, emotional, flaky . . . Noushin, do you really not like me at all?"

"How did you know?"

"Those whom the communists want to hang have brains, too."

"What was wrong with Khazar that you let her go?"

"Nothing. I didn't deserve her."

"Then you are a big, fat, self-sacrificing creep. After you have done a girl, as you guys like to say, and had your fill of her, you come up with the excuse that she is too good for you, that she should go find a man who deserves her."

"Something like that."

"That is really vile. Tell me, when you're having a blast with them, do you know that sooner or later you will ever so gallantly dump them?"

"Most of the time, yes. The girl always knows that I will dump her, but she still wants to be with me. And they all think they're different from the others, that they can snare you into marriage. . . . "

"You're right. Wretched Iranian girls have these delusions. Your market is hot this year."

"Come on! Don't you all demand equality between men and women? Then why is it that when a man dumps a girl he's a creep, but when a woman does it, it is her right. . . . Are you a virgin?"

"No."

"Who did you give it to?"

"None of your business."

"You are laying me bare; therefore, it is my business."

"It was one of the guys at the university."

"Was he handsome?"

"He was joining the People's Fedai Guerrillas, and he knew their average life expectancy was six months. I gave it to him because I wanted him to experience the pleasure of living before they riddle him with bullets on the street or kill him under torture."

"Did he understand?"

"Three months later, their safe house was surrounded and he bit into a cyanide capsule. The likes of you don't understand these things."

The scribe on his right shoulder had written:

Like always when the politically active students plan to hold demonstrations, there is an air of angst and gloom in the university building, an air of suspense. It is again December 7, the anniversary of the killing of three university students. Classes have been canceled. Students who are not involved in politics have seen the handful of anti-Shah fliers pasted on columns around the campus and saved themselves the trouble and left. Only the political students remain in the building. The reflection of the clouds on the windows hides them from view. They are waiting. Hulky university guards, batons strapped to their waists, sit in American REO military trucks parked along the two main streets of the campus. They are waiting. The last of the aged sycamore trees' autumn leaves fall into the narrow gutters flanking the soccer field. The sound of the flowing water takes no notice of what is about to happen.

Kaveh tries not to show that he is sad.

"Amir," he says, "let's go. This is no place for us."

He and Kaveh, together with a group of other students who despite not being politically active do not have the heart to leave, are standing outside the building, waiting. Crows' nests sit in the nervous and naked branches of the trees. The guards jump out of the REOs, walk in formation to the front of the Faculty of Economics, and stand in line. A thickset second lieutenant is their commandant.

"The kids from the Faculty of Law came to help our guys," Amir says.

"How do you know?"

"I saw their fliers. . . . They shout slogans to get beaten up, the guards beat them up, and others win."

Kaveh looks around, worried that a snoop may have overheard them.

"You are no less of a dimwit than they are," he says. "Let's leave!"

Behind them, the yellowed turf of the soccer field, empty of a rolling ball, empty of young athletic legs, is waiting. The stifled clamor of the city sidewalks and distant car horns is not waiting.

Then it starts. The sound of a window shattering rips through the still air as far as the crows' nests. Amir sees an elbow breaking off the remaining glass. And then, other windows, one by one, yielding to the shouts of a crowd of students.

"Unity! Resistance! Victory!"

They repeat it over and over again. Pieces of glass from second-floor windows, with reflections of torn clusters of clouds, rain down on the stone pavement.

The commandant of the guards shouts, "Strike these bastard traitors!"

The guards take out their batons and storm the building. . . . Their shouts of vulgar insults, the shrieks of girls being yanked by the hair, and the howls of guys being beaten by batons rise from the heart of the shattered glass, louder and harsher than the last hollered slogan.

"Teach these pimps a lesson, too," the commandant orders the squad that has remained with him.

His finger of command points at Amir and the others standing nearby.

The guards tear toward them.

Kaveh shouts, "Run, Amir!"

Everyone beats an escape, running together toward the main university gates. Amir thinks, You haven't done anything, why would they hit you? He shifts his books to his left hand and starts walking away like a regular pedestrian passing by.

Running, Kaveh shouts, "Come on, you lunatic!"

From the corner of his eyes, Amir sees the shadow of a raised baton aiming for his head. He breaks into a sprint. The baton rips through the air with a whoosh. Amir runs with the stubborn guard's boots pounding the ground behind him. He picks up speed, running faster than the group of escaping students, among them a few soccer players. He draws close to them. Kaveh is still motioning for him to catch up. They are all running toward the university gates. Without thinking, Amir turns and heads for the soccer field. He leaps up onto the third bleacher, jumps down on the running track, and dashes onto the turf.

Behind him, the guard yells, "Where do you think you're going?"

He has always chased slogan-shouting students running toward the main gates. He did not expect one of them to separate from the crowd. . . . Amir stops at the sideline, takes a breath, and holds out his hands, and shrugs, I don't know. The others have reached the gates; the guards do not pursue them beyond that point. The guard separated from the pack stares at Amir, his disappointed baton pointing at him. Amir dashes off.

> «I didn't know I was this good at making a good-for-nothing getaway.»

And he knows he has left behind the broken arms and cracked skulls of those who could have escaped and did not. Splattered blood on the university pavement, strands of girls' hair in the claws of the guards.

The scribe on his left shoulder had written:

Noushin turns over another card.

"Khazar was too good for you. She is not the type of girl for you to mess around with and toss away."

"I'm good at making a getaway. I run faster than the soccer players at the university. It's all I know how to do. I cut and run, I catch my breath, I cut and run. I am what I am. I don't have the hypocrisy of people who call the bristle under their stomach 'love.'"

He grabs the bottle from Noushin. He enjoys the loathing in the girl's eyes.

"Your fortune didn't turn out."

She throws the cards down on the table with disgust. It is night. The crescent moon shows itself from behind the passing clouds and hides again. Flames from the bonfire on the beach lick up into the air.

"The guys have started a fire. I'm going to join them. It's fun."

"So you can torture Khazar by flirting with Soheila right in front of her?"

"I am free, so is she. Why would it torture her? One of these days she'll find someone else and fall in love with him."

He gets up and takes a card from Noushin's stack. He shows her the queen of hearts. He is tempted to tell her the truth, but he thinks, in this good-for-nothing world where everyone professes honesty, why should he, a hundred times more good-for-nothing than others, join the crowd? Before he takes a sip from the bottle, Noushin snatches it away from him.

"Were you raped when you were a boy, that now you take it out on girls?"

"Yes."

He is waiting for her to spit in his face. He thinks it will calm him if her spit sticks to his skin. Perhaps it will wash Khazar's love out of his head.

"I'm going to leave this shit-filled house in the morning and go back to Tehran. You all make me sick," Noushin growls.

"That's because on the one hand you eat out of the same feed bag as us good-for-nothing bourgeois kids, and on the other, you eat out of the trough of the communist kids."

"I want to get to know you filthy lot."

"You don't know us? Really? On every bench at the university you have written, 'The difference between a bedbug and a bourgeois is that after sucking blood the bourgeois falls on the bed, the bedbug falls under the bed.' And me being a bat, where is my place?"

He reaches out for the bottle. Noushin holds it away.

"A bat has wings to fly. You are a leech."

He walks away. In the doorway, the banter continues.

"The blood of pure, innocent girls is far more delectable."

Infuriated, Noushin hurls the bottle at him. He grabs it in the air and leaves it by the door.

On his right:

> «Who will write this night? The beauty of the color of fire reflecting on the sea. . . . I won't move from my place. Meysam is grilling the kebab instead of me. It is almost midnight. Teeth chomp on skewered liver. The sound of firewood breaking is similar to the sound of bone cracking. But these airheads don't seem to realize that the Revolutionary Guards can ambush us in the dark, beat us with the butts of their rifles, handcuff us, and drag us away. . . . Bahram is playing the guitar and singing.
>
> "La la, la la, la lai . . . rain, drizzle . . . quench the thirsty earth! Sing the anthem of life! I am feeling blue, I am feeling blue. . . . "
>
> The sea has become worthy of being written. Away from the fire, moonlight's reflection on the water, wide silver ribbons, some hesitant, stretching far away into the darkness. . . .

> Everyone is singing.
>
> "Sleep, my little bird, the world is a fairytale . . . every groan of this sad guitar bears the tears of thousands of nest-less little birds. . . . "
>
> Hugging her knees, Khazar sways to the music. The surges and swells of the flames turn her the color of fire, then darken her, and again turn her the color of fire . . . perhaps they were waiting for me, so that in the sad melody of a lullaby I would see the gleam of tears in her eyes. But she is just staring at the fire.
>
> Each time the clouds move away from the moon, the seashell-strewn edge of the sea takes on a snowy luster.
>
> My stomach is sick with all the heartache I feel. . . . I don't want Khazar to see that tears, silently, have rolled down my face. The best tears are those without sobs and sniffles.»

He gets up. It's hard for him to control his stagger and choke back his vomit. He hears the sea's vanished waves roll inside his stomach. As he walks away from the fire, he sees the silhouette of the old man next door, sitting on the edge of his yard, watching them.

Drunkenness is spinning around in his head. He has pulled himself out of the swamp several times. Now, all he understands is that he understands he is drowning in the swamp.

> «It has snared me. It will kill me with its dark nausea. It is good, it will rid me of constantly desiring desire . . . and nothing will make me understand better that I am falling. . . . Khazar! What are you doing? . . . What a bed the sand makes . . . I should pull its blanket over me, too. . . . »

On his right shoulder:

Soheila's scream grows distant . . . Meysam's shouts, too. . . . Dawn and the pink fog have vanished from above the sea. The water, clear of foaming swells, its embryonic waves gently, gently, edge onto the shore and with the rustle of seashells withdraw. And again, they push the body sleeping on water toward the shore, and again they pull it to themselves. Her white skirt has blossomed around her legs. Diaphanous. Floating, her arms open and close, sink and surface. Her eyes open, staring, grains of sand streaking their corners . . . on her wrists, two deep cuts . . . and with the heave of languid waves, tiny fish surround the body that is slowly turning translucent, swaying to and fro and drinking the halo of blood surrounding Khazar. . . .

Left:

All he remembers is Kaveh driving the Alfa Romeo. He has no recollection of traveling the Haraz–Tehran route. Khazar, Khazar constantly reverberates in his mind. He hears himself having cried out her name. He hears Soheila's wails, Bahram's sobs, and Meysam's shouts as he tore into the water.

> *« . . . there was a ladybird there . . . on a piece of driftwood sculpted by the sea . . . it stayed and stayed. . . . »*

He sees himself huddled in a corner of the apartment, trembling. He sees Kaveh picking up two empty bottles of arak and putting another gallon in front of him. He pours two glasses.

"All I see is the look on her parents' faces at the Medical Examiner's office. How that man wailed," Kaveh says.

"Why didn't you let me show myself?"

"Are you crazy? I'm your friend. You were involved with her. I didn't want you to get caught up in it all. Being interrogated and, I don't know, they might have even thrown you in the slammer."

A pause of hesitancy, to say or not to say, in Kaveh's voice.

"Tell me! It can't get any worse than it is."

"It seems Khazar was pregnant."

Homemade arak has a stinging, medicinal taste.

He slams the empty glass down on the floor and throws a punch at Kaveh's face. He runs off to the other end of the apartment.

"If you start acting nuts, I will leave you here and go."

"Where is Khazar's letter?"

"The police confiscated it. If she hadn't written it, they would not have let us out of the detention center. . . . "

> *«Crying and laughing are both ridiculous. Other than these, is there no other good-for nothing thing to do?»*

"Was it your child?"

"My child?"

Confused, he stares at he knows not where.

"I guess it was . . . " he moans. "Definitely . . . yes."

Out on the street, people are shouting. Kaveh walks over to the window.

"There's been an accident. They're beating each other up. . . . Piss on this country!"

"Was there a ladybird there, on the beach?"

> *«I will drink until I puke out my guts. . . . My child! What does 'my child' mean? . . . Am I really devastated and grieving or am I just pretending?»*

On his left:

Dizzy and nauseous from drinking, he crashes the right side of the Alfa Romeo's fender into the eucalyptus tree as he tries to park. He staggers over to the house.

The scribe had continued:

Everyone is asleep. He imagines it must be three or four in the morning. But he cannot remember if Khazar's death was yesterday, the day before, or the day before that. Stumbling, he knocks into the inlaid table that the hundred-year-old crystal tulip candelabrum sits on. The sound of glass shattering rips through the slumber of the house. He kicks a piece of the colorful crystal shade and shouts obscenities. He needs something to lean on. His vision is blurring.

Later, he remembers laying his head on Reyhaneh's shoulder. Mother's frightened and worried eyes staring at him. Reyhaneh's feminine scent makes him queasier. He shoves her away.

> *«Wicked Khazar, she knew what to do to make me suffer.»*

"Piss on everything that breaks!" he shouts.

Hiccupping, he kneels on the floor next to the pieces of the candelabrum.

"I'm s-sorry! It just . . . it just bumped into my leg and b-broke. I . . . I'll . . . fix it . . . I'll . . . glue it . . . b-back together."

He grabs at the rounded pieces of crystal. Mother screams. She tries to pull his hand away. The scuffle makes his fingers bleed even more. Then Mother tumbles back on the floor and Reyhaneh is crying. The living-room chandelier's reflection on the piece of broken crystal in his hand is distorted, its gold-leaf trim shimmers. He looks at his left wrist. There is a suitably enlarged vein there. He curses again and kicks the coffee table in front of the sofa. A crystal bowl, the strawberries in it, a stack of china dessert plates, all crash down on the silk Kashan carpet. Frightened, Reyhaneh steps back. His ears are ringing so loudly with the protracted noise of everything breaking that he cannot hear the words coming out of Reyhaneh's and Mother's mouths.

> *« . . . we waited until the smell of the previous night's drinking was no longer on our breaths, we ate a lot of cucumbers, and then we called the police. We were chewing gum when the ambulance took Khazar away.»*

"They were good cops," he shouts at Reyhaneh. "They didn't give us too much of a hard time. The filthy rich fathers called the Commissioner of Police, they fixed everything. But between you and me, they were kind cops. They only took a small bribe."

He staggers over to the cabinet that holds Mother's treasures. The antique ancestral dishes have caught his eye. His hands are so bloodied that he no longer cares. He puts his fist through the cabinet's glass door. He pulls them out, he hurls them down. Plates with gold rims, turquoise rims, tea glasses with silver holders, an enameled crystal rosewater carafe . . . they break more easily than he expected. It is delightful . . . he hears them shattering even after he has turned his back to the cabinet. It is delightful. . . .

And then Agha's shouts come from the other side of the living room.

"What is going on in this house?"

His mind clears. He feels lighter. As though with every punch that he has thrown, painful thoughts and memories have shattered as well. He turns to Agha Haji. He locks eyes with him. Agha's bushy eyebrows are puckered in rage. Amir feels his legs weaken. He doesn't try to resist. He lets himself fall to his knees. He likes the expression of regret and forgiveness-seeking that is settling on his face. Tears have spontaneously welled in his eyes, too.

He stammers, "I. . . . "

He hangs down his head.

"I . . . did something . . . bad. Really bad."

Agha Haji is not loosening up.

"What the heck happened to you? Spit it out!"

Mother's and Reyhaneh's sobs come to his aid. He wipes his nose with his sleeve. His speech is heavy with drink.

"Today, I, I mean, just tonight . . . it's hard for me to believe it, but I . . . I realized tonight that I have no one in the world but you. I have no place in the world but with all of you. I know a man shouldn't let anyone see his tears. But I swear on your life, dear Father, I am broken and beaten to a pulp. . . . Look at me! You must have enough fatherly compassion in you to see. Get a-angry later. Right now, I just want you to look through a father's eyes. There is nothing left of your Amir."

Agha has one eye on him and one eye on the broken crystal and china all over the room. Mother takes a step toward him in pity.

"Don't, Mother! I . . . I want to talk. At least have the p-patience and tolerance to watch your son cry."

And sobbing, he says, "Agha Haji! For the love of God! Bring your prayer rug and spread it open. . . . I . . . I want to stand behind you and pray. I haven't prayed in a long time. I want to repent . . . to beg forgiveness from you and from God, and . . . I have sinned . . . even worse than mortal sins, much worse than the sins of God-cursed Satan. . . . Be a good Muslim and fix me up tonight!"

He realizes he is starting to sound like an addict beggar.

"Tonight, I'm really heartbroken. . . . God accepts the pleas and sobs of the brokenhearted. Bring your prayer rug. . . . God is g-great, he is f-forgiving."

Even though Agha Haji is still glaring at him with fury and suspicion, he quietly says, "It is obvious you have been guzzling ungodly filth. Go wash your mouth and then come and tell me what has happened."

"Yes, Sir. I will wash my mouth a hundred times. J-just promise you will let me stand behind you and pray."

"Fine, fine. Get up. Don't frighten your mother and sister any more than you already have."

He struggles to stand up. It's hard for him to shake off the way he feels and the role he has been playing. But it's time. His drunkenness is turning into a pleasant wooziness.

«The worm is coming out of its egg.»

Standing, he looks at them one by one. The veil of tears is still in his eyes, but it is not a gimmick. Swaying, he sneers, "Islam's mercy and compassion has been bestowed upon this booze-drinking, miscreant servant of God. Recite a praise to God out loud! Mr. Khomeini should bear witness to how his subject, Agha Haji, has steered his wayward son down the righteous path!"

He cannot carry on with the elaborate talk. He staggers and scoffs, "Now that I'm a good Muslim again, you probably want to circumcise me. . . . Come on! How many times? Just cut the whole thing off and be done with it."

Agha Haji grabs him by the shoulders and shakes him.

"You are drunk! . . . Drunk! . . . Take your vile depravity out of this house!"

Amir beats his hands on Agha Haji's chest and pushes him away. The man stumbles back and falls. He gapes at his son in disbelief. Stammering, he slaps away his wife's helping hand and raises himself halfway up, but Amir shoves him back down on the floor.

"Don't you ever grab me by the collar again!" he shouts. "Get it? I'm not your tail-wagging dog anymore."

Reyhaneh's and Mother's eyes gape as if possessed after seeing, for the first time, a member of the family go up against Agha Haji. And this makes Amir even more possessed.

"You good-for-nothing louse with a prayer-stone scab on your forehead! You have taken our blood and bottled it. You want to kick me out of the house? I pissed on your house a long time ago. I will leave of my own will and I will never look back."

He digs his hand in his pocket to throw the money he has at Agha Haji's face, but his vomit spews out on the floor.

It is too late for everything. He storms out of the house and as usual heads toward the Alfa Romeo. When he realizes what he's doing, he kicks the car door and walks off on foot. There is no wind, but he imagines the summer leaves on the trees and the flowerless winter sweet bushes, branch by branch, spreading his news down to their roots so that they turn into quicklime. The smell of cherries is in the air. The smell of the chirp-chirp of the crickets. As he reaches the garden gates, he hears his mother's voice coming from the house, wailing something. She is probably begging him to come back. His resolve to leave weakens. With their weeping and pleading, Mother and Reyhaneh can clean up the mess and restore peace. . . .

But the stench of alcohol and the filth of vomit cannot be washed away from that house. He stands aimlessly in the threshold of the garden gates. . . . From the cotton field, snowflakes are flying up to the star-filled sky.

He scratches the palm of his hand and snarls, "I didn't give Mr. Good-for-nothing a good enough going-over."

His drunkenness is resurfacing. He staggers back to the house to finish the job.

The scribe on his right shoulder had written:

He does not remember what he has done. What if he hit Agha Haji? With the bones in his hands throbbing, all he remembers is punching the walls. There are probably fist prints and bloodstains on them. When he comes to, he is lying on his side in the back of a pickup truck, handcuffed. Two Revolutionary Guards armed with Kalashnikovs lean against the rail behind the truck's cab and another sits next to the driver.

"The Battle of Islam's army was mobilized to haul me away?"

One of the guards gets up, aims his rifle at him, curses, and kicks him in the stomach. Other than pain there is nothing in his stomach for him to vomit.

The guard staggers back as the truck lurches forward.

"Brother, it seems you've had a few shots, too," Amir groans.

The man steps forward to give him another kick.

"Leave the nutcase alone," the other one says. "He is Agha Haji's son."

The man sits down, his rifle still aimed at Amir.

"You devil! How do you know what a shot is?"

"Faggot! After a couple of lashes, you will be so sorry you will forget your wisecracks."

And they drive past the cotton field and the breath of its bushes. He rolls onto his back. The sky is still full of despondent or dead stars. He thinks he sees a burning cotton boll falling vertically from the sky. Inspired, he discovers. . . .

> «Not just me, but the entire world is being dragged through dung. Perhaps now something will happen for something to change.»

The scribe on his left shoulder had written:

The painkillers cannot rival the lacerated stripes on his back. His ribcage hurts, too, from sleeping on his stomach. He drinks arak and takes sedatives. It is only when he retches that the pain spills out of his body, only to again renew more intensely.

He's spread his bedding in the apartment's small living room, leaving the bedroom for Kaveh. Today, his greatest fear is that Kaveh might forget that the gallon of arak is almost empty. At last, Kaveh walks in with a girl. Amir covers himself with the bloodstained sheet.

"Don't be embarrassed!" the girl says. "I was whipped, too." And laughing loudly, she adds, "I was with a guy, up on the roof of his house, we got caught stoned and spaced out on weed. The neighbors ratted on us. Naked, under the sun, the minute we snuggled up they burst in and busted us. . . . The cuts will heal. The pain won't."

"I brought the cure to your agony."

Kaveh throws some fifteen grams of opium in front of him.

"If you act stubborn and refuse to smoke it, I don't know what else I can do for you."

> *«When they plow the earth, does its back suffer as much pain? Does it feel good?»*

"I won't smoke opium."

"Your decision! The neighbors have started complaining about you howling at all hours of the night. . . . "

"Do I sound like a wounded wolf?"

"No! Like a beaten dog."

Kaveh turns on the small Primus cooker and puts a thin metal rod on it. He sticks a needle into a small piece of opium and holds it over the flames. When it has softened, he flattens it between two fingers. Then he puts an empty pen shaft in his mouth and holds the hot rod against the opium. The ancient scent floats through the room. Kaveh blows the smoke at Amir's face and passes the pen shaft to the girl, who has taken off her Islamic coverall and is sitting there in lace underwear.

> *«She has sagging breasts. Perhaps from too much dope! . . . If her wounds from the whip were fresh, too, it would feel good sleeping with her. Lying on our sides, we would couple. I would smear my semen on our cuts like a salve.»*

Kaveh takes the girl to the bedroom. He can hear them laughing. Then moaning.

> *«Kaveh is holding up well. So, he was telling the truth when he said opium gives him more stamina.»*

The girl's lustful groans become more covetous.

"You're killing me, Kaveh . . . I'm coming again, don't stop. . . ."

On his right:

He drifts through days and nights that fold into each other. He wakes and cannot tell if it is dusk or the next day's dawn.

He remembers that last time, before leaving, Kaveh put a small piece of opium he had cut with a razor in a Winston box and hid it in the vase with artificial flowers in the corner of the living room. . . . He is really late today; the bastard hasn't come to set up the gear, the rod and the opium, next to his bedding.

> «Now that he knows I need it, he's being an asshole.»

It is difficult for him to crawl to the kitchen to bring the Primus and the makeshift pipe. In pain, he bites into the pillow wet with saliva. He slithers forward on his chest. He knocks over the dusty vase and takes out the cigarette box. He has heard that ingesting too much opium can cause death, a great death. . . . He breaks off a small piece and throws it into his mouth. Its bitterness makes him shudder. He needs some sweet tea, but there is none left in the thermos. He takes the rest of the opium and inches his way back to his bedding. Today, there are again streaks of fresh blood on the unwashed sheets. His bottle of water is empty, too.

He waits to see what the opium will do to him.

On his left shoulder:

He tries to calculate how many days and nights he has spent in that bed. He likes the fact that he cannot figure it out. He dissolves another piece of opium and a sugar cube in his tea and gulps it down. He has gotten used to the mouth-screwing bitterness of poppy. It works faster this way, and without the smell and the hassle of the paraphernalia. In the languor of delirium, napping, nodding off, the nightmares and hallucinations are more bearable. He sits up. Every now and then he touches his back and gently feels the scabs on the welts. The swellings are interesting to him.

«They have put lots of pussy lips on my back. . . . »

He drifts through the delirium and pleasant lethargy in his body and, in anger or hate, tries to push the stubborn memories of Khazar out of his mind. And he sees. . . .

They are standing at the end of a long line in front of the cinema playing Murder on the Orient Express, *stomping their feet in the cold of winter. The wind seems to deliberately blow at the people at the end of the line to drive them away.*

"Usually, you can't guess who the killer is until the end of the movie. Kaveh, do you know who Agatha Christie is?"

Khazar, thin, feels the cold more than they do.

"I am sure no matter how pretty she is, she is not as peachy as the women in Lando Buzzanca's films," Kaveh says. "I told you we should go see his film; at least we would warm up a bit."

Khazar blows into her cupped hands.

"By the time we get to the head of the line there won't be any tickets left," Amir grumbles. "The crooked ticket clerks sneak them to black marketers."

"I don't like films with people getting killed," Khazar says.

"Next time, we'll take you to see a cartoon."

A boy on a bicycle rides past the line. The little devil shouts, "Don't waste your time, the killer is all of them."

He laughs, and as he pedals away he broadcasts, "They all stabbed the guy!"

Amir's wounds chuckle with him. He tosses another lentil-sized piece of opium in his mouth. He waits for his stomach to start churning. If he can resist throwing up, then the nameless waves from the poppy farms of Afghanistan will start to swell inside him, a pleasant weightlessness, like drifting on thick, salty water in a bitter sea that keeps everything afloat and will not let you drown.

With alcohol and his dreams, the days and nights did not pass slowly. With opium, they drag by, but they are comforting. The scabs on his back itch. He wants to scratch them, scratch them until they peel off.

On his left:

"You've got to get up and get moving," Kaveh says. "You've been slumped in that corner for almost a month. If you don't want to go back home, you'd better start thinking about finding a job. Things can't go on like this. Do you know how long it's been since you took a bath? The apartment stinks."

"Why are you talking nonsense? A month?"

"I'm your friend—don't put on an act for me. Get up! Get up and go wash yourself. Your wounds are healing."

"What wounds?"

He expects Kaveh to laugh, but frustrated, he snaps, "Huh! The cuts all the way down to your ass from the flogging they gave you."

For the past half hour, ambulance sirens have blared across the city.

"Did Iran attack?"

"They're constantly bringing wounded soldiers from the front. . . . But you are my wounded warrior."

"It sounds like they're doing a good job evacuating them."

"You are such a lamebrain. There are so many of them that they're being hoarded in stadiums. Screw it. Did you hear what I said?"

"No."

"Boy! I guess opium has completely wiped out your brain . . . or are you playing me for a fool, pretending to be nuts? I said, you have to find a job. . . . I . . . I couldn't come up with the rent this month. It's too much for me."

"But your dad is loaded."

"He was *loaded. The government is confiscating everything he has."*

"There were many times when you didn't have your share of the rent and I took care of it. Why can't you make it up to me for a while?"

These penny-pinching arguments make him sick, sick of himself, sick of Kaveh.

"That is not what I meant. I meant. . . . "

"I have money in my bank account."

He no longer hears what Kaveh is saying. His body no longer reeks of pus from the lacerations and the ointment that Kaveh used to put on them. It has a different smell. He likes this stench. It is new and kind. It does not have the deception and arrogance of perfume and eau de cologne. It is familiar. Unlike Agha Haji's prayer-stone scab, it does not have the hypocrisy of the rose water at religious ceremonies. He remembers how much his mother paid to buy shroud fabric from an Iraqi refugee—a hundred times more than it was worth. No matter how hard he tried to make the woman understand that the Iraqi was lying, that he had not circumambulated Imam Hossein's shrine with it, he had failed to convince her. The shroud smelled of fake domestic rose water, shroud-ish.

"Go to my house and ask my mother for my ID card. Come up with some excuse. Tell her I really need it. I'll go to the university and get a copy of my degree. And ask her for money, too."

"What for?"

"So that you can get rid of me."

The crusty lines on his back itch and old blood flakes off. Some pieces of the scabs that he can reach and scrape off still have traces of fresh blood on them.

> *«I am sure I saw a ladybird sitting on a piece of driftwood. It didn't open its wings, polka-dotted, to fly away and leave me alone. It was not cruel and unfair like Khazar. My child was not cruel and unfair either.»*

And the peal of ambulance sirens permeates the apartment, creeping into crooks and corners, under his sheets, and he imagines that the cries of the wounded soldiers have come with it to penetrate the scabs on his back and make them bulge.

> *«I will go to war. . . . »*

The scribe on his right shoulder had written:

«To the beat of the large drum, stomp the left foot!»

Another night of sleeplessness burns his eyes. On the top bunk of a bed in the barracks at the base, he watches the snores of the enlisted university graduates swell under the ceiling. Tonight, too, he wonders if he regrets having signed up for military service. Or if he regrets having begged the intern at the clinic to give him some medication to help him cure his slight addiction to opium so that he could join the army. . . .

He hasn't yet gotten used to his bristly crew cut. He's surprised each time he runs his hand over his head, wanting to comb his fingers through the thick, beautiful mane that tens of women's hands have floated through. The sensation of those hands has been shaved off, too.

Like the others, he counts the days until the confinement of basic training ends and they get assigned to different divisions and brigades. Fifty days have passed, seventy days remain. Then, they will each have a second lieutenant's star on their shoulders. Every month, they will receive a little over a thousand tomans in pay—the cost of one or two nights at Kazbah—and no one knows which hellish war front they'll be thrown into. Every day that draws closer to the day of their assignment, when the company sergeant gives them downtime between endless drills, Amir sees greater worry and sadness in the eyes of the enlisted university graduates sprawled out on the ground in exhaustion.

The air in the barracks is heavy with the smell of breath and sweat infused in the wool army blankets. Someone, somewhere, is talking in his sleep. Someone else is groaning. Amir craves a Winston cigarette.

> «Yes, if this is someone else's hair, then how can I be sure I'm not someone else under this foul-smelling, coarse blanket? It is not without reason that they make us drill so much. They want all of us miserable souls to become identical. So be it.
>
> To the beat of the large drum, stomp the left foot! One, two, three, one, two, three. . . .
>
> Masculine legs, foaming with sweat, young, pumped up muscles, strong bones, ready, climb up vertically, thump, thump, they crash-land on the ground. . . . »

The scribe on his right shoulder writes:

The account on his left shoulder is faulty. Not that it is untrue, but it has been written from Abu-Yahya's perspective. This should not be done. The account that follows is indisputable:

Reyhaneh sits behind the wheel of the Alfa Romeo. Amir climbs in next to her.

"Why do we have to talk here, in the car?"

"The doors in the house have spies. Get it?"

Reyhaneh seems to have more patience this morning.

"I get it, Dādāshi."

These days she calls him Dādāshi more often. He likes the affection and intimacy of this word. . . . He points to the folder that Reyhaneh had photocopied at the nuthouse and is now clasping with both hands.

"You won't understand any of it," Reyha says. "It's mostly reports and prescriptions written in English in doctors' squiggles. I ended up having to go to your current doctor. He explained what your emotional state was and is now."

"Okay! Okay! And then?"

He sees the old gardener, Shahu, wandering among the trees, looking like he's lost something. The car smells of mold.

"Don't make me feel like I owe you. I know you went to a lot of trouble. But don't expect me to pray that you lose an arm, too, so that I can make it up to you. Tell me. . . . I'm going nuts."

"In short, they transferred you from the front to a hospital in Kermanshah. By the time you got there, your arm had become infected. They worked on it. . . . From the start, when you signed up to join the army, you gave them a wrong address."

> «Some tree somewhere in the garden is broadcasting the sound of a bone being sawed.»

" . . . they had to amputate another piece of it. There are several reports that you were acting crazy. They diagnosed it as shell shock."

"I know. Smoke floods the brain of a shell-shocked soldier. And?"

"Nothing. They sent you to the sanatorium for shell-shock victims. You told them you could not remember your name. For a little while, in the chaos of war and misfiled records, they tried to find your family. But with the fake name and address you gave them, they couldn't find us. Shame on you! So, you went to war without telling us, but why did you give them fake information, you nutcase?"

"Because I'm a nutcase. You just said it yourself."

"You were not nuts then."

"What else do the reports say?"

"That's it. They finally sent you to Tehran, which is where Mom found you."

Unsatisfied, he looks at Reyhaneh. Sister has a mischievous smile on her face.

"Don't worry, I have some good news, too."

"What?"

"I found the name of the army base that shipped you to the front. It was in your file. . . . Happy?"

He looks at Reyhaneh helplessly.

"Are you acting again, you rascal?" she asks. "Don't you remember why you were dying to find out the name of the base?"

"I want to see how much *you* remember."

"We can find the guy . . . the one who was with you up in the mountains . . . who was with you when you were hit."

He sees the old gardener wielding a club and chasing after Abu-Yahya, who is running off toward the garden gates. He laughs.

"I cheered you up!" Reyhaneh says. "I finally managed to make you laugh! When I call you a nutcase, don't take it to heart. I don't mean you are a nutcase, I just mean you're nutty!"

The scribe on his left shoulder had written:

As he walks past squad sergeant Helmet-y's trench, he hears a goat bleating, and then the voice of the sergeant saying, "Come in General! I have a private matter to discuss. . . . "

Amir has just returned from leave. He's got to pack his gear and head up the mountain with Pirar.

"On your dear life, please, come in."

He crawls in on all fours. Sitting on the ground, the sergeant formally salutes. Even in the trench, he is wearing his helmet. The men consider this a sign of cowardice. His helmet keeps clanging against the cement ceiling. The sergeant crawls to the entrance of the trench and warily looks around.

"Nope. No outsiders and no snoops. I am honored, General. I wanted to pay you a visit at Army Staff Headquarters, but didn't want to speak in front of those two blue-eyed spies. . . . You must be very careful, General. They pass on all the division's news. Would you like a water pipe?"

Amir nods.

"I don't have a water pipe. May I offer you a cigarette?"

"No . . . you were saying. . . . "

"I wanted to tell you that you should keep an eye on our company commander. No matter how much I beg, no matter how many formal requests I write, he won't agree. I think he's up to something. He is in contact with the enemy."

"What is your request?"

"What? You, too, General? It's obvious what my request is. I am a patriot and an officer. The army has kept me fed all these years for just such a day,

a day that I can sacrifice my life for my country. However many times I ask the commander, and request in writing, for him to give me a pistol, he just won't do it."

"What do you want a pistol for? The world is safe and sound."

Again, the tip of Helmet-y's helmet scratches the cement ceiling.

"Why, you, too, General? When the SS has invaded the country, shouldn't we go to war with them? We must organize a holy defense for the enduring sanctity of the country's borders."

He throws a sludge-green can of emergency army rations in front of him.

"Here! Open it and see what's inside. There is baby hair in it, too. The Germans canned the Jews' flesh. I, for one, have not touched food in a month. I am not a cannibal! . . . I don't want to trouble you too much, General. Just order them to give me a gun so that I can go fight the Germans."

And he stares at Amir with gaping eyes. A shell explodes somewhere. Its rumbling thunder travels from the slopes of one mountain to the foothills of another and returns.

"Give it up, Helmet-y!" Amir says jokingly. "I take offense when someone plays me for a fool. I will not tell anyone your craziness is just an act so that they will discharge you. You are such a good actor that you will win in the end. But, you idiot, they will send you to the nuthouse in the city, not back home to your wife and kids."

"The nuthouse is just great. Twice they sent me there for tests. The doctor there is German. Next time I go, I'll kill him."

He does a Nazi salute, winks, and holds out a pack of forty filterless Homa cigarettes.

"Smoke cigarettes, Sergeant?"

"Not these cigarettes."

"Do you want to smoke a water pipe?"

"What water pipe?"

"Do you want to smoke a water pipe?"

"You are driving me crazy! Yes, I will smoke it."

Helmet-y crushes a few cigarettes in his hands, clumps the tobacco, and puts the wad on top of his helmet. Then he unzips his pants with his right hand and pulls out his business.

"Please, Sir, take a puff on the water pipe!"

The scribe on his left shoulder writes:

> *«Write on my right shoulder that I like the old man. . . . Not on my left, you jerk! I like Shahu. The old man has memories of my childhood. Perhaps if I sit with him, they will come back into my head. Even if old age has made him forget some things, they've stayed safe on his shoulders. Therefore, assuming that my brain has scratched out what you wrote on my shoulders about my childhood, you should copy them from Shahu's shoulders. . . . Now, write that these days my sense of smell has become as strong as a dog's. In the smoke from the burned leaves, I smell apples and cherries and pine. When I dig the ground at the foot of the trees to find what has been hidden there for me, I smell wine on the dirt. . . . When was it that I finished Uncle's arak?»*

On his left:

Who is going to write?

Right:

> «The rain has trickled the scent of winter sweet flowers onto the soil. Among the naked purple trees, I smell layers of smoke. It has a tinge of dark blue and it waves in the wind like a bedsheet. Somewhere in the plot of apple trees, Shahu is throwing a pile of leaves into a firepit with a pitchfork. Why do they smoke so much?
>
> "Aha! You have become an early riser, Young Master!"

Steam blows from his mouth. The steam of y, b, a . . . e, r, y, m. . . .

" . . . It was very cold and windy last night. The poor trees! If you have a listening ear, you can hear them scream when the icy wind whips at them . . . the poor bare innocents."

Shahu straightens his back and groans.

"I am bone-tired and worn out, Young Master. I have been smoking the garden since last night, hoping the trees will warm up a little. . . . The blossoms, the poor things! God only knows what hole this burning cold crawled out of in the middle of spring."

"Come on, man! It's the middle of winter. What blossoms?"

"You are not feeling well. Come, let's go to my hut. I know you smoke cigarettes away from Master's eyes. I will fix you a water pipe that will fix you up."

Limping along, he leads the way. The thick layer of wet leaves sinks under my feet like a feather mattress. If there is a mine in the ground, will it explode or not? We reach the plot of almond trees. Shining drops of rain glisten on the tips of their naked branches.

"Which trees blossom sooner in the spring?"

"Almond trees, Young Master. I want to say this, just so that I have said it. If you ever have things you want to hide, give them to me for safekeeping. I saw you yesterday. If you bury something under a tree, when we water the trees the water will hide it even from you."

Write that here in his hut, I don't sense that I've forgotten it. The room is filled with fog or smoke. I will sit on one of the logs next to his fireplace . . . but I won't look at that corner that I should not look at . . . so let's look and see how beautiful the color of the wood glowing in the fireplace is. There is a layer of haze and smoke and grease on the windowpane. I smell almonds. . . . Shahu pours some tea from his patched-up teapot. How I love the sound of tea being poured. While the sound of soda being poured, the ssssssssss of its bubbles bursting, makes me think of foaming piss.

"All will we be good and well, Young Master."

The rim of the narrow-waisted tea glass has a hint of gold. . . . Oh! The sugar bowl! . . . The rascal still has his old sugar bowl. I remember it so well that if I touch it perhaps I will turn into the young boy who stole candied sugar from this sugar bowl to give to Reyhaneh. . . . The warmth of the burning wood leaves such a pleasant languor in my flesh . . . but even if I'm crazy, I should not look in any mirrors.

Shahu traps the tobacco leaves soaking in the bowl in his fist and takes them outside to squeeze them. Yellow water trickles on the ground. The tobacco comes back and goes in the bowl on top of the water pipe. A chunk of red-hot charcoal comes out of the fireplace with a pair of tongs. It gets blown on. Its ashes fly at the smoky kettle on the corner of the stove. The charcoal goes on top of the tobacco. It sizzles. Another piece of charcoal, another piece of charcoal, another piece of charcoal. . . . Shahu sucks on the water pipe's mouthpiece. The yellowed glass water vase gurgles. The little black fake sunflower starts to roll around in the water, and Shahu sucks, and finally smoke blows out of his mouth.

He puts the water pipe in front of me.

"It's burning well now. Please!"

I suck on the cracked and blackened tip of the mouthpiece. I think I remember correctly that when I was young this little sunflower was in the water vase and it was yellow, and when Shahu smoked, I would watch it, mesmerized.

"Young Master, something has been weighing on my heart that I want to tell you, but only if you don't get angry."

Dizziness from the water pipe's damp smoke bubbles and whirls in my head.

"Tell me!"

He tosses another log in the fire.

"You are breaking Agha's back . . . stop it, young man! A father is the root and trunk of every young man. Stop it, Young Master!"

"I'm not doing anything!"

"When a tiger's paw is injured by a poisonous thorn, it will look at the world with rage . . . some thorn has pricked your heart, Young Master, and it is making you angry all the time. Pluck the thorn from your heart."

"What if someone's heart *is* a thorn?"

"A poet once said, 'A heart can be thorned, but it cannot become a thorn.'"

Rasping coughs burst from his guts and with them the prickly smell of pine fills the room. And I inhale more dizziness from the water pipe.

. . . as far as the cotton field's field of cotton, ahhh. . . . That green cotton field of budding bolls that I always wanted to invite you to, to stand facing the waves of the wind, whatever fate they blew! The wind in the sail of your hair. And for you to take care not to step on the quail's nest. Three small cotton balls inside it. Let's sneak into our beautiful field so that I can watch how very beautifully, gently, gently, carefully you take each step, how your hand, your writing hand, runs white over the white-capped bushes, like a butterfly, the fingers of your right hand fluttering over the plants as if they were picking at harp strings, so that as soon as I want to want you, ayaya! To lay you down on the cotton from the bushes, to untie your headscarf, and to keep repeating that I love you. And then, for the wind to blow at the end of the field, and for me to say, If we leave the shelter of the cotton field, they will see us, we will be found out, they will turn us in. And we quickly go back. We see that night has fallen, we see that the entire cotton field has blossomed the white of white blooms, and we see moonlight moving from boll to boll, over fluffs peeking out of their pods. And then I see you among the waves of white, still slowly, slowly, carefully walking for fear of stepping on the quail's nest where three moon's eggs shine more lustrous than pearls from the Persian Gulf . . . and at midnight we will see two proud, white spheres move down the center of the cotton field, songless. . . . And we did not step on the quail's nest.»

Right:

And he sees. . . .

Years and years ago, he is a young boy, he is carving a name on the coarse and callused bark of the cherry tree with a knife. And Baba Shahu has quietly come up behind him.

"What are you up to, Champion?"

He is holding his club.

And in that early summer, the trees' branches are heavy with little green cherries, Reyhaneh's earrings, some still with dried-up blossom petals clinging to them. Caught, he shoves the knife's blade under a hardened piece of bark and breaks it off.

"Worms are hiding under there so that they can eat the cherries when they are ripe."

"If you find them, then you will have saved this tree . . . but I don't think worms have infested it . . . if they had, I would have heard the tree moan in pain at night."

"I'll find them. They are hiding under the bark . . . I'll kill them."

"If you keep breaking off the bark, the poor tree will feel cold at night, and no good will come of it. It will put a curse on us."

"What are you saying, Baba Shahu? Trees are not people."

"These trees are my children, Young Master. The same way you are Agha Haji's child. You should not cut off its skin. It will sulk and its cherries will fall."

"I am not a kid anymore for you to trick me. I have known for a long time that the stories you tell us are all made up. Reyhaneh is still stupid; she thinks they're true."

And he shouts, "Everything you say is a lie! You said there is a child snatcher outside the garden, that its arms stretch like rubber bands and it snatches children. You lied so that I wouldn't go outside."

With the blade of the sharpest knife in the house, he scratches and cuts the tree's flesh where he has peeled off the bark. The exposed paleness is soft; it has a nice, wet slipperiness to it. Shahu desperately reaches out to take the knife from him.

"Sir, don't! The tree will take offense. Don't, Champion. Have pity on it. Let's go to my hut and I will give you some candy."

Out of spite, he makes another cut. Shahu covers the tree's exposed flesh with the back of his hand.

It seems the garden's woodpecker is at work . . . tak tak tak tak. With the sharp taste of an unripe cherry in his mouth, Amir angrily squeezes the knife's handle. The palm of the old man's hand is still brownish black from peeling fresh walnuts last year. Someone seems to have already scratched lines on it. Amir puts the blade on Shahu's palm.

"I'll cut! . . . "

"Cut, Sir."

The instant he sees blood, he steps back, drops the knife, and runs. He wants to shout to stop himself from crying. He turns and looks back. Shahu is pressing his bloody palm against the cuts on the tree. He bends down, picks up the knife with his left hand, and holds it out toward Amir.

"Come and take it, Champion."

On his right shoulder:

> «I was staring at the flames licking from the logs. When did I turn to face Shahu? What has he said? On his face, wrinkles expect an answer. He is holding out his hand toward the water pipe, his hand, brownish black from having peeled fresh walnuts for our breakfast. Damn! I looked at the forbidden corner. The mirror . . . its wood frame is half burned. Here and there its mercury coating

has chipped off, most of its surface is caked with soot . . . and I have looked into the mirror's eyes and now I am afraid, because this burnt mirror must be something that has been hidden in this room, and if I clean it, who knows, perhaps an image from the past is still there under the grime.

"What is this?"

Shahu looks flustered.

"Just what you see, Young Master."

"Just what I see? I'm sure it wasn't there before. Why is it burned?"

"A couple of years ago a friend wanted to throw it away. I took it thinking I would restore it."

"You are lying, just like the other good-for-nothings . . . this mirror used to be in my room. Which motherfucker burned it?"

I feel nothing but disgust. I get up to leave. As I walk past the mirror a hazy reflection of a torso moves in the opposite direction. Parts of his mercurized body have chipped off. . . .

"Young Master! Don't leave! Where are you going? For the love of the Khezr cherry tree, don't!"

I slam the door shut. Outside, the garden has turned to night.

I shout, "You! . . . Why you? You with one foot in the grave, why do you lie, old man?"»

The scribe on his right shoulder writes:

Impatiently, he looks at his watch. Seven minutes have passed beyond the twenty the driver had said it would take to arrive at the army base. The car inches forward in the exhaust-choked traffic. Now and then, the driver clucks his tongue as if he has a piece of candy in his mouth.

"Mr. Driver!" Reyhaneh says sarcastically. "It's strange that every time we call the agency for a car, you happen to come!"

"Sister, if you have any complaints, the agency will send someone else."

"No, no complaints. By now you know our situation."

"If you're going to the base to put this officer's affairs in order, don't get your hopes up. They lie when they say the casualties of war are the life and light of this country. They give nothing. No refrigerator, no coupons, nothing. . . . "

"God be praised, we don't need assistance."

"Then why are you going there?"

Amir is now certain that Reyhaneh's suspicions that the man is an informer are correct. He looks out at the circle they've just entered. In the reflecting pool at its center a fountain jets into the air. He chuckles.

"It seems my eyes are messed up, too. The water looks bloody."

The driver laughs.

"There is nothing wrong with your eyes," Reyhaneh says. "The water is red."

As they drive around the circle, the wind sprays red drops on the car. The driver curses and turns on the windshield wipers. With her hand under her chador, Reyhaneh pats Amir on the knee.

"They made the red fountain as a memorial, so that people don't forget the blood of the martyrs of war."

"My dear sister, what martyrs? They have made a sprinkler with the blood of the country's youth! These people paint donkeys and sell them as zebras."

The old wipers fail and fail again to sweep away the drops. They draw red lines on the windshield and cannot erase them.

They leave the circle. The driver turns onto a no-entry road and pushes down on the gas.

"Whatever happens, happens! We have to take a shortcut; otherwise, we won't get there until tomorrow morning."

Turn after turn, side street after side street, water from the potholes splashes on the pedestrians along the sidewalks. Amir cannot tolerate the nervous maneuvers of the driver and the car. He looks down and shakes his knees. He's been trying to stop biting his empty sleeve. In silence, he counts eleven more minutes.

"I went to Baba Shahu's hut yesterday. He still has his tea and water pipe going."

"Baba Shahu!?" Reyhaneh says, frowning.

"The rascal has been hiding my mirror there."

"Amir, Baba Shahu died two years ago!"

"He was making smoke in the garden to warm up the trees."

They drive along a street in the outskirts of town. It looks familiar to him.

"One morning we found him under the Khezr cherry tree. God had taken him peacefully. He planted that tree himself. And gave it its name. That tree was like his child."

He gives the girl a look that makes her move her hand away from his.

Right:

One of the guards at the entrance to the base leaves them waiting until he receives instructions from the higher-ups.

Reyhaneh says, "There is this constant pain that shoots up from my right foot all the way to my waist. Good or bad, Dādāshi, I'm crazy like you. Otherwise, I wouldn't be going around knocking on this door and that door, running myself ragged for an arm that is God knows where. . . . It is past time for you to take your pills. Dear God! I forgot to bring them with me! I pray you don't go nuts in there."

"I won't. Don't worry, sister."

"I think it's all over for me. Whether my hair is black or gray, I've lost my looks. It's over. Year after year, my skin gets duller and dryer, and my eyes, with or without wrinkles, are going blind staring at a door that will never open for me to see him walk in and say, Reyha! Reyhaneh! Get up, let's go. Our time has come. . . . "

"Who?" Amir asks casually.

"Another nutcase like you. Wondering if he will ever come to ask for my hand, all winter I put winter sweet flowers in the living room vase; in the spring, almond blossoms, in the summer, branches heavy with cherries, and in the autumn . . . in the autumn I'm always waiting for the narcissus to bloom. Whether I cry any more than I already have or not, my eyes are so tired, Dādāshi. . . . I keep saying, 'God! O God! Why is there no place for me to be Reyhaneh?'"

Amir, his eyes on the guard at the gate, impatiently listens and does not listen to Reyhaneh opening her heart to him.

On his right:

He walks out of the base looking like a defeated conqueror. The two guards watch him with pity, or perhaps with relief for not having been sent to the war zone. Amir smiles bitterly.

"I found the name of the squadron I was assigned to, and the name of the sergeant who was with me . . . Pourpirar."

"I am so happy for you! So, we can go back home now. I am exhausted."

Amir hands her two photocopied pages.

"Keep this junk somewhere."

"What are they?"

"They found them while they were looking through my file. They are commendation letters from the division commander."

Right:

Pourpirar's house is poorer than anything they had imagined.

Reyhaneh explains who they are and asks for Pourpirar.

With a sad and weary tone the woman says, "My mister is not well. I doubt he will agree to see anyone. Wait here, I will go and ask him."

The rusted metal door closes.

"Are you sure you want to see him?" Reyhaneh asks again. "If he says unpleasant things about where you were . . . the doctor says it's too soon. . . ."

"The doctor?"

Reyhaneh playfully slaps his empty sleeve.

"Don't be silly! He came to see you this morning."

"That spy writes down everything I say . . . and he doesn't know how to give an injection. It really hurt. I yelled at him, 'You good-for-nothing, are you blind? You miss a hole that big and stick the needle right next to it!?"

Pourpirar's wife opens the door. Her ashen face looks more despondent than before. And she is still holding the bouquet of flowers Reyhaneh gave her.

"He didn't agree. Please forgive me. I am so embarrassed."

"God forbid! We are the ones who should be embarrassed for having troubled you. May misfortune be far away, what is your husband suffering from?"

"Oh, don't get me started, Madam! It's a long story . . . Miss Reyhaneh, you are so wonderful."

Amir cannot contain his anger.

"Tell your mister that one-armed Amir will not leave until he sees him," he snarls.

The woman goes back inside.

Left:

Pourpirar, stretched out on an army blanket spread on a frayed carpet on the floor, leaning against three pillows, remains still. He looks sapped and worn out. Every now and then he looks at them suspiciously. Reyhaneh, with nowhere else to sit but the floor, explains at great length how they found him.

" . . . Amir begged and pleaded until the officer at the base gave us your address. We went there, and they told us you'd moved away a year ago."

"After twenty years, we had to sell our house to pay for the doctors and medications," Pourpirar's wife says mournfully.

"Missus," Pourpirar snaps, "there is no need to speak about this."

" . . . as I was saying, Amir and I went to all the real-estate agencies in that neighborhood, but no one was willing to help us. After some fifteen,

twenty days it occurred to us to go back to your old house. The new owner gave us the name of the agency that sold the house for you. We thought perhaps the same agency helped you find your new home. Amir paid the agent a lot of money and he finally looked through his papers and found this address. I mean, we. . . . "

"Madam, make it short. What do you want?"

Reyhaneh looks shocked. She leans against the wall's bulging plaster. Amir interrupts.

"The moment I saw you, I realized that I had not forgotten you, Sergeant."

> *«Am I telling the truth or lying? It seems seeing me has upset him. What have I done to him? But Reyhaneh has to continue talking. If I talk, I may mess things up.*
>
> *The shouts of a scrap-metal buyer pass by the house. Reyhaneh goes on with the usual drab pleasantries and rubbish praises. It seems she has paid no attention to the ceiling, with its exposed rusted steel beams, like those the Iraqis used to scavenge from ruins to cover their trenches.»*

" . . . Amir owes you his life. My family has only recently learned this. More than anyone else, he wanted us to pay you a visit to thank you. Our parents will certainly come as well. They hope to somehow compensate you for the sacrifices you made. . . . They told us at the base that if it were not for you, Amir would not have left those mountains alive."

"I am truly beholden to the base for having my old address! It's been four years and the louses haven't come even once to say hello."

> *«On our way out, I must remember to count the number of steps we climbed down to this room that is halfway below ground. The windows are almost level with the sidewalk. No sofa, no chairs, the smell of medicine in the air, or perhaps the smell of piss that reeks of the stink of medicine. . . . Could it be that Pourpirar's hair was white and thin back then? Or has it happened recently?*

The bouquet Reyhaneh brought is still sitting on that lonely table in the middle of the room, without a vase. Next to it, an empty fruit bowl and a few mismatched plates. . . .

"Please, have some tea!"

Despite her sallow face, it's obvious that the woman once had a unique freshness and spirit about her. Her eyes look like they've shrunk from long-ago crying. Her chador carelessly thrown over her head, two locks of hair dangle in the air as she bends down to hold the tea tray toward me . . . the smell of her body is pungent. . . . Now she bends down to offer tea to Pourpirar with her back to me. Her chador clings to her body. The curves of her pear-shaped backside are and are not noticeable. . . . Tenacious as a dog, this thing hanging under my underbelly has perked up again. I don't know whether it's good or bad that shrapnel didn't chop off my business. The ugly wrinkled sack under it keeps filling up. After it empties, it looks wrung dry like a juiced pomegranate. . . . With her ashy skin, her hooked nose, and her thin but curved lips, she is neither beautiful nor ugly. But in a way she stands out. Pirar is glaring at me eyeing his wife.

. . . the clinking of a teaspoon in a tea glass . . . the rasps of a sugar cube being annihilated in tea. The sergeant is looking at me as though I'm an impostor.

" . . . when you were on top of that mountain. . . . "

"Madam, stop all this chattering. Get to the heart of the matter. These days, in this country, no one looks in on anyone without wanting something. Now, what do I have that would do you fat cats any good?"

Reyhaneh looks at me helplessly. Her eyes have filled with tears. My sensitive, weak, and miserable sister whose doe eyes . . . her doe eyes. . . .

Without meaning to, I raise my voice.

"Sergeant! All I want is the answer to one question. When we were on that mountain, do you remember the name of someone I might have talked about? . . . I have forgotten some things. My family tells me I'm

messed up in the head. I mean, they say I am so loony that . . . that . . . Reyhaneh, what is it I don't have?"

"Memory."

"That's it. Yes. Now I have come here for you to simply tell me, when we were way up there together . . . when we chatted . . . well, the days and nights must have dragged on and I must have told you things about myself. I want to know those things."

"If you're really muddled in the head, what makes you so sure you told me anything?"

A train goes by behind the house. The windows rattle as though they're about to fall.

"How could I not have? Perhaps you did, too. People talk. About friends, memories . . . things like that . . . love and being in love . . . like . . . the sergeant loves his wife . . . things like that."

"I don't want to talk about those days."

The inlaid table next to him wobbles. A rickety inlaid table that is embarrassed of being an inlaid table. Pourpirar has started picking at its leg with his fingernail.

"Did I ever talk about someone I had made certain promises to?"

Is he snickering at my question or at my nuttiness? The rotted table leg is grating, a splinter could break off at any moment. The blood under his nail is staining the wood. The lines on his face contract. They grow deeper. . . .

"It enrages me when I am forced to remember those days. Get it? I don't want to remember."

His eyes furious, he stares at his wife.

"Sergeant, I have certain dreams. I see them when I am awake, too. I can't get rid of them. . . . Do you understand, old friend? They won't leave my shitty head alone."

"I didn't say your head is shitty. Go to a doctor and get treated. Anything I can say won't help you. In fact, go chain yourself to the shrine of some Imam, that will cure you."

"Excuse me!" Reyhaneh says. "Amir has certain dreams. He thinks he was engaged to someone he cannot remember. . . . Knowing who it was will quiet his mind, God willing. Your help will have a great impact on him. I beseech you, please, help. . . . "

"Sister! Do not beg him."

Pirar is glaring at me . . . he's probably racking his brain for a juicy profanity to spit my way . . . but he has stopped picking at the table leg. His hand shakes as he raises a filter-less Homa cigarette up to his lips. His lighter shakes, too. . . . To strike the spark wheel, his thumb trembles as if it is the hardest thing in the world to do. His thumb succeeds. . . . Now, like a hyena, he gapes at the nonexistence of my left arm. His wife half-rises and steadies his hand to hold the flame under the tip of the cigarette . . . smoke spirals in the column of light shining in through the window close to the ceiling . . . like the clouds of . . . where have I seen white clouds with shadows that floated and floated over the mountainside? Pirar presses his right arm against his side from a pain he is trying hard to conceal. . . .

"All these years, I knew where you lived," he snarls. "But I didn't want to lay eyes on your cursed face. It is because of you that I am suffering like this."

A plea escapes his wife's throat.

"Please, you should leave," she says. "My husband is in a lot of pain."

"Barfeh-Banu!" Pirar snaps. "Do not talk to them!"

I shout at Barfeh-Banu, "Madam! He is not the only one in pain in this country. He is lucky he has both of his arms."

We fall silent. The train has long passed, but its clamor still resounds.

"Sergeant! Where is that kid you talked about?"

He looks stunned. His cheeks that come together in his mouth every time he takes a drag on his cigarette remain that way. His wife gapes at him.

Now, half laughing, half coughing, he says, "I never said anything about a kid to you, you louse. When did I ever tell you I had a kid? . . . We don't have children. We didn't want any. . . . Your brain has totally shut down."

"I told you, this motherfucking brain is really messed up. That's why I have come to you, to fix it."

There is so much misery and helplessness pouring from his wife's expression. I think she's hiding something.

"You louse! When did I ever say I have a kid? . . . The brother-of-a-whore asks where's your kid?"

Reyhaneh bursts into tears. Pirar's voice gets choked up.

"I keep saying, I don't want to remember, and he keeps asking! . . . What do you want from me, you creep? Why can't you leave me alone to die with my own pain?"

"My arm, Sergeant! What did you do with my arm?"

"I shoved it up your backside. . . . How would I know? . . . What kind of a question is that? It stayed up there."

"Did you bury it?"

"Yes, following full funeral ceremonies, like the public funerals for the martyrs, with a band of anthem singers, flags, elegies, chest-beating. Huh! He wants to know what I did with his arm!"

"Did you bury my arm?"

"I can't remember, not even at the cost of your life."

"Sergeant, I see your state and circumstances. It is obvious you are financially strapped. I will pay your travel expenses plus two hundred thousand tomans if you take me to where my arm fell off."

"Shove your money up your ass, you bazaar lowlife! Thanks to the government and the bazaary hajis, my finances could not be better!"

With his back aching, he gets up to come over to me. His rage is somehow familiar.

"I am four hundred percent a wounded war veteran, the pride of my country and my leaders, I am as joyous and jubilant as a donkey. . . . Madam, you are my wife, you tell this leech! Tell him they gave us a refrigerator and rugs, they gave us a car, they bring loads and loads of rice and meat and dump it at our door every week."

He is close to me. His wife, backing him up, rails at Reyhaneh.

"You should be ashamed of yourself! After all these years, to come here for the corpse of an arm? It was to save your darling brother's life that he was hit by six pieces of shrapnel. One of them is near his spinal cord, they couldn't remove it. It is moving and it will one day paralyze him."

Pirar is standing over me, fists clenched. Why do I want him to hit me? I have instinctively closed my right hand tight and raised my left arm to shield my face. I laugh.

"I swear on Imam Ali, if you say one more word about your filthy, ill-gotten money in front of me and my wife, I will tear into your jugular with my teeth. . . . Get lost!"

He leans over me, lopsided, with one hand on his back, possibly on his vertebrae. His shout, his bits of spit, land on my face. . . . I hear his wife crying. The racket of the train again comes and again passes. Perhaps it's the clatter of a freight train. . . . Reyhaneh may have said something; her mouth is still half open. Pirar grabs my empty sleeve and yanks on it.

When we walk out of that narrow alley riddled with sewage-filled potholes, we again face the train track's gravel and the sun's reflection on the murderous steel that stretches out from the heart of Tehran's smog . . . it shines like fresh shrapnel . . . and I see Sergeant Pourpirar, broad-shouldered and strong, he kneels over me, puts his arm under me to pull me up from the pool of dirt and blood. . . .

He hollers, "You gave away our location, you lunatic!"»

The scribe on his left shoulder had written:

> *«O earth! I piss on your cowardice! They pissed on you, you said nothing. They marched on your head, you said nothing. They shed blood on you, you did not do a damn thing! You just slurped it up! They dug gold out of your throat, you did not make a sound. I piss on you! They buried girls alive inside you, you did not blush with shame. They concealed mines in you, you did not breathe a word. O Earth, I piss on you! They crammed corpses by the hundreds in you, you did not rot. You returned fungus and worms. I piss on you! They stoned people buried up to their waists in you, you gave birth to more stones. The semen of those hanged dripped on you, you grew purple ferns. I piss on you, earth!»*

Today is the seventeenth day that, when bored, he says, "This is the last time." And from his observation post he heads to the trail he's discovered. This time with less caution, this time faster. It takes him less than two hours to travel across the ravines and ridges and reach the rendezvous point. He lies down on the ground behind a boulder that shields him from the eyes of the world. He turns his binoculars toward the Iraqi village of Baarin. He has arrived just in time. It's the children's recess hour. He likes their colorful Kurdish outfits. He has discovered that many of them don't know how to play the games the others play. They just watch. And then a girl or a woman who is perhaps a teacher walks out of the schoolhouse. If she doesn't go to play with the children, she will pace back and forth along the short stone wall around the schoolyard. He likes her walk, regardless of how enchanting she may be to the young men of the village, the way the damn girl saunters reminds him of Hanna . . . and when she goes back indoors, it is time for him to turn his binoculars to Buddy Whoever's house. Amir came up with the nickname Peacock for the schoolteacher, but this Kurdish man is still Buddy Whoever. . . . One, two, three . . . today there are four kids of all ages playing with mud in Buddy Whoever's yard. Therefore, just like yesterday, or two days ago, or four days ago, Buddy Whoever can now lure his woman into the room on the second floor. . . .

With or without an excuse, Buddy Whoever goes to the seemingly little-used room to do something important or something make-believe and waits until his wife goes there for something real—for Whoever to bend her over, to carefully and flirtatiously lift each layer of her skirt and drape it over her back and shoulders, and do her.

But today, Buddy Whoever's wife is out in the yard. Buddy has perhaps gone to take care of the daily tasks and errands. A man dressed in beige Kurdish clothes walks to the house and starts talking to Buddy's wife . . . and now it's time to turn the binoculars to the Flowing Stream House. Two young girls walk over to the narrow stream that flows through the front yard to wash clothes, and. . . .

> *«Given their poverty, how have they come by these clothes to wash in the stream?»*

Secretly watching the houses is his most enjoyable pastime at the front. It distances him from the day-to-day death.

The scribe on his left shoulder writes:

> *«The palm of my hand on the cold stock of the G3, the lines on the palm of my hand, placenta of the fetus of grooves in the copper-colored moors of Mesopotamia, zebra's stripes in locoweed deserts, ribs of a mule hit by shrapnel. . . .*
>
> *Without me, fingers that never passed through a torture chamber for their nails to be yanked off, but so nimbly combed through a woman's pubic hair and circled her unripe nipple to awaken it. . . . My fourth finger! In the absence of my body, when your blood dried, when your water evaporated, when the white of your bones lay bare, did you or did you not wear gold? . . .*
>
> *I need money to travel west, to go asking around, asking around the villages at the foot of the mountains, asking, until I reach the mountain I am supposed to reach. I must be clever, so that Agha Haji does not grow suspicious. I must kiss his ass so that he opens his wallet. I will pay him back later.»*

Left:

His memories are coming back from a distant abyss. He remembers the stretcher next to him. . . .

The scribe on his left had written:

"Amputate it!"

"Doctor! This leg, I think I can. . . . "

"I said amputate it above the knee! I'm going to. . . . "

The light behind his eyelids is growing brighter. The droning fog in his ears is dispersing. And smells . . . the sour smell of vomit, the rusted steel smell of blood . . . the greasy taste of marrow in a chicken bone crunching between his teeth. . . .

He is more alert. He can hear boots sloshing around. There are howls, wails, and pleas all around him. "Water, water! . . . " He is afraid to turn and watch them saw off the man's leg. Someone is groaning in pain and cursing.

"Hey! Soldier! Shut that man up."

The wails hit metal walls, they fold onto each other and blend.

"Sergeant! This leg, I think I can. . . . "

"I said amputate it above the knee! I'm going to the next bed. . . . Stitch him up! Hurry . . . then get over here. . . . "

And tin-plated heat blazes everywhere.

A cracking adolescent voice cries out a woman's name.

"Mahrokh! . . . Mahrokh! . . . I'm burning! You numbskulls, someone come do something! . . . Water! Water! . . . My blood . . . my blood. . . . Save me, Imam Zahra! . . . Someone give me water! . . . "

He looks up at the low tin roof; on it, splattered blood.

" . . . I can save this leg. . . . "

"Don't you understand? Do you want us to spend three hours on this one leg? Are you blind? Can't you see all the wounded we have on our hands?"

"Water! Water!"

"I'm going to the other stretcher. . . . Stitch him up, and come over to me. I've been on my feet for three days. . . ."

On his right shoulder:

Sprawled out on the bed, he raises his head and looks. He is in a silo, all metal. At the far end, the entrance is a blinding half-circle of bright sunlight. Shadows enter through the portal of light. Shadows run out. Far away, the earth and sky are exploding. If he does not stare at the entrance, his eyes will make out the inside of the field hospital more clearly.

All the way to the far end, there are dusty, bloody heaps the size of human beings, slumped on stretchers. There are mangled and maimed heaps in tattered clothes writhing on the floor. Their shouts, God, God, their shouts pleading for help from one Imam or another. . . . Shadows approach from the entrance, they grow clear. Carrying a stretcher, they zigzag left and right through the living dead on the floor. Their boots sloshing on the slippery floor . . . and constant, relentless explosions near and far shake the silo.

In the next row, he sees a nurse, his frock soaked red, start to saw off a leg. And a man who must be a doctor, head to toe covered in blood, walks over to the stretcher next to his.

Chapped, clay-colored hands reach out to whoever passes by . . . howls of obscenities ricochet. . . . Two men in red are bringing in another bloody heap. They look around. As soon as they find an empty spot, they unload it.

After examining the tarred and blistered body on the next stretcher, the doctor shouts, "This one is gone. Take him away and make room."

Two people take the roasted corpse by his arms and legs and drag him off the bed. His backside drags on the floor as they go.

«My lips are so thirsty! I will not let these butchers kill me from thirst like that dying wretch crying, "Water, water." There must be water somewhere nearby. These butchers' butchering doesn't give them a chance to fetch water . . . my tongue has turned into a slab of parched meat; it can't move inside my mouth.

And my howl hurls me to the floor. Pain throbs in my left arm. I must be careful with my poor arm. . . .

I get up, I stagger, I am so dizzy, what did they inject me with that has made me so woozy? . . . I must have hit my arm against something sharp and injured it. . . .

"Go back to your bed! Who told you to get up?"

"Water! . . . Water! . . . "

I walk away from him. My leg gets caught. This damned leg. . . . A hand is clutching it. The hand has reached out of a large, bloody heap and grabbed my leg; the heap is gasping, saying something to me. I pull my leg free.

"Moradi, take this nutcase and strap him down to his bed!"

Did I see wrong that an eyeball on the floor burst with a pop under my foot?

"Hell is alive! Hell is coming. Hell is coming with seventy thousand harnesses and each harness is being pulled by seventy thousand angels and in each angel's hand a steel bludgeon. And they pull Hell along by its harnesses and chains and it has hard and heavy feet, each of which has traveled the distance of a thousand years of this world. And Hell has thirty thousand heads and in each head thirty thousand mouths and in each mouth thirty thousand teeth and each tooth thirty thousand times bigger than the Ohod Mountain, and each mouth has two lips and each lip is the dimension of one story of the world and in each lip there is a chain being pulled by seventy thousand angels so that if God commands Hell to devour the earth and the sky and whatever is on them and in them it can do so easily. And then Hell will cry and wail and with dread and horror it will be towed along and all its fear is of God the merciful. And then Hell will say, 'O angels of my God! What has God willed to be done to me? What sin have I committed that is deserving of punishment?' And all the angels will say, 'O Hell, we have no knowledge.' And Hell will stand and neigh and thunder, and so much fire flies from it that if it escapes, it will burn all humankind, and all of this because of celestial fear. And then almighty God will say, 'Rest easy, O Hell! Do not fear. I did not create you to punish you, I created you for the torture and punishment of others. . . .'"

"Don't be afraid. Your arm has been severed. I want to even it out."»

The scribe on his right shoulder writes:

Reyhaneh knocks lightly on the door and opens it. When she sees him in his underwear, on the floor where he'd been sleeping, she turns away and says, "As you had ordered, I told Agha Haji that you would like to go to his trade chamber with him."

"When did I ever say I want to go to his trade chamber?"

"You told me yesterday. Agha Haji is waiting for you downstairs. . . . I guess you are becoming a good, sensible son again."

"Don't be sarcastic, Miss Reyhaneh."

Reyhaneh helps him get dressed.

"There was a photograph in your album that you had torn in half. Who were the people standing next to us that you tore out?"

"Hurry up! Go, some fresh air will do you good."

"You are all going to kill yourselves worrying about my well-being."

He walks down the stairs, acting as if he has a prosthetic leg. On the last step, he shouts, "I'm going to the bazaar with Agha Haji. . . . Any instructions you have for the healthy movement of bowels, for vigorous libido, any prescriptions from this and that doctor, pills, potions, bring whatever you have!"

> «The ground floor of the house is empty. It's as if no one has talked, or laughed, or wolfed down food between these walls for years, or . . . what else?»

He holds out his right hand to shake Agha Haji's hand. Then they are in the Paykan, in front of the garden gates. The guard who has opened the gates stares at him.

> «Amir, you good-for-nothing, get your head working. Learn the directions for when you decide to bail out . . . and remember to be kind to Agha Haji so that you can hustle some money from him. . . . »

"Do you remember this area? It was all cotton fields. God be praised, see how much has been built and is being built here. Despite the war and scarcities, with the might of heaven's powers, the needy now have homes."

"Weren't these lands yours?"

"You remember! Yes, I sold them amicably and at a fair price to people and company cooperatives. The city government of that old godless regime would not allow these lands to be built. They had zoned them as green space. Those villains! People had no roof over their heads and they wanted to build parks for them!"

"I guess you'd bought the lands cheap."

"God willing, when you are well, you will take over this work. I have decided to retire soon. I will teach you the ins and outs of the business and you will manage it. There are good brothers in the various government departments that look out for us. When a piece of land is subdivided, built, and permits for water, electricity, and services have been issued for each parcel, which of course will be sold per square foot, it reaps a healthy profit. It benefits both the seller, who, content with having pleased God, sells fairly, and the buyer. These days, office workers have the hardest time making a living. With properties being so expensive, people will be grateful to you for saving them from the clutches of godless real-estate profiteers."

"Did you have this same Paykan in the old days? Why didn't you give it away and get a good car that is more appropriate for you?"

"In this country, every quarter of a century a new government and a new regime have come to power. What do you think our dynasty's secret is that under any circumstances we have preserved our standing and financial status?"

"We have money."

"No, it is not just about money. Was our forefather, the great Yamini, rich? One hundred fifty years ago when he found a position in the Qajar court, his only capital was his intelligence and astuteness, and they protected him even after the Constitutional Revolution. Or consider your grandfather. After the fall of the Qajar dynasty, during the reign of that cursed Reza Shah, many wealthy people and great families ended up wrecked and ruined, but not the Yaminis."

Not harshly, but sarcastically, Amir says, "Perhaps those other families were not into hypocrisy. They didn't go whichever way the wind blew."

"No, allow me to finish. Your grandfather sailed this dynasty's ship safely to shore through many troubled and turbulent times. Think about it: World War II, the ousting of Reza Shah, the occupation of the country, the unrest brought about by the communist Tudeh Party, the strife over Mossadegh. . . . Were these nothing? Any one of these events alone could break a country's back. Many prominent families fell into ruin. And ever since your grandfather gave his life to God the merciful, the burden of this large family has fallen on my shoulders. There was a coup d'état in this country, there was our own Islamic Revolution, war and bombardments, scarcity . . . in all these catastrophes we have suffered, but we have kept our ground. Why? It is because of our steadfast principles and piety that we have been blessed with God's favor."

In an innocent and religious tone, Amir says, "I pray that God will bless our family and bestow upon us even greater favors because of me."

Agha Haji naively believes his performance.

"God definitely will. Every fine young man is a blessing for his family. . . . We are different from these newly rich people who by a fluke have come into a pittance and forgotten who they were and where they were. They drive around in fancy cars and show off in front of suffering, needy people. This car is still working for me. If I get into an accident, repairing it will cost so little that I won't have to demand indemnity from some God's creature. In Islam, taking indemnity is disapproved of. Always remember my advice, in this country you should never stand out among others. They will set their sights on you and every lowlife will try to find a way to swindle you, to bring you down. What's more, living modestly was the way of the Prophet and his Imams. . . . It has always been my conviction that overindulgence is ungodly. And wealth that comes from ungodly deeds will fritter away, it will go with the wind . . . God willing, when I lay down my head and die, all this wealth will be yours. By then you will be healthy and well and settled in life. And just as you will protect your mother and sister, you must protect this wealth, our name, and the standing of the Yamini dynasty. Sensibly, with wisdom, balance, and moderation . . . God willing. . . . "

"God willing."

Agha is on a roll. He carries on and weaves the earth and sky together. And Amir looks out at the people and the streets.

> « . . . I mean, is there not a single sensible wall in this city with no rubbish written on it? . . . Death to . . . Death to . . . Shitty death to shit . . . amateurish portraits of martyrs, lines from their wills . . . are they, too, advising me to be sensible? . . . I want to be friendly and kind to this old man. I want to get close to him. But crossing into his territory is so unpleasant. Every private talk or emotion becomes ridiculous and dull . . . it's easy to guess his dry

answers . . . but when he was talking about dying, I think for the first time I felt sorry for him.»

"You should say something, too. . . ."

"I think it's better for me to keep quiet . . . you talk, I will listen."

«If Reyhaneh were here she would be blown away by what I just said, and I said it in such a kind and sheeplike tone.»

"I . . . I . . . well, what can I say. We must accept reality. I am living the final years of my life. I am happy that I have raised you and seen you through thick and thin. Praise to God, your mother will lack for nothing for another hundred years. Inevitably, Reyhaneh will soon go to her husband's home, and you . . . I . . . you won't believe me . . . sometimes I feel so tired, so weary that. . . ."

«I swear, it sounds like he wants to open up to me . . . it is so strange . . . it's as if he has read my mind. There is a sadness and frailty in his voice that I've never heard before.»

"Sometimes I ask myself, What is all this running around for? . . . I wish I were a simple farmer, had a small cotton field, neat and tidy . . . just me, the might of my arms, the rain, and my God."

«This is Ferdowsi Circle. Sometime in the past, here! . . . I have been in this circle. With someone who. . . . These streets have become so dreary and dark. . . . Who was I with? . . . These jerks, constantly honking their horns . . . the memory of who I was with just flew out of my head. In this busy section of the city, the barking horns keep chomping on my nerves like a dog. What a zoo, cars trying to make way and crowds trying to cross. People just walk headlong into the traffic. Looking straight ahead, they mutter and mumble obscenities at every driver's mother and sister. . . . Agha is still carrying on about his feelings. It is the first time he has hit the dirt road of his emotions. . . . »

"People just see my appearance, they envy my circumstances. But when I sit alone, myself and my God, this me who supposedly no one has ever seen sad or weak, I wonder what I have achieved. . . . I know for a Muslim such doubts are not good, but if I don't tell you, my son, who would I tell?"

«Seeing his tight, two-handed choke hold on the steering wheel, his awkward cautions, and his struggle to make way through the cars driving wildly, I realize that Agha Haji has gotten old. Behind our Paykan, people are constantly honking, driving past us, glaring at him, and swerving in front of us.»

"That day, I remember you were sixteen years and seven months old, you confronted me, your father, and refused to come to the bazaar. The truth is, you broke my heart. But a man should never allow his pain to show in his eyes. I consoled myself thinking that you would grow up, you would become sensible and wise and realize that you made a mistake. But what could one expect from a university that the cursed Shah built for our innocent youths? . . . Year after year, you grew more distant from your father. Again, I told myself, time solves all problems. Whatever you wanted, I gave you. The best car, plenty of money for your outings and entertainments, all in the hope that you would grow tired of it all and come back to me. You didn't. Until that ominous night when you came home and. . . . "

"Don't say it. Reyhaneh has told me every detail of it."

"All these years, did it ever occur to you that you have a father? Did you ever wonder if this father who has given you everything might himself need something, even if he does not show it? That he, too, has sorrows, emotions, and affections? That he may need someone to lean on, someone to be his crutches. . . . You just wanted to take from this father."

"I tried hard to talk to you, but. . . ."

"When you stopped saying your daily prayers and no longer wanted to talk to your God, what did you expect from me, a man who is God's servant?"

«The deep, broken wrinkles on his face have sunk under his beautiful white beard. His small eyes look sleepy. On his forehead, the prayer stone callus has become thicker. . . . It seems I have never seen this face. . . .

Women pray more than men do, so why is it that this black scab doesn't pop up on their delicate foreheads?

But now that it is after after, it seems he might be right. He has suffered because of me. . . . When was it that Reyha said I made him age overnight? Perhaps if I can do something to somehow be gentle with him. The way I talk at home . . . Reyha . . . Mother . . . perhaps they're as miserable as I am. . . .

A one-armed man is holding his young son by the hand and dragging him across the street, through the traffic, ignoring the cars. We will not talk anymore until we get there.

Following him into the bazaar, I plunge into a swarm of people, we plunge into a centuries-and-centuries-old smell that seems to have once been pleasant and familiar to me. The smell of leather, the smell of the seven smells of spice shops, the smell of carpets, the smell of greasy paper money, and the breeze brings the smell of the goldsmith's arcade. . . . »

There was a time when he used to say, "The horny smell of spice shops, the smell of grinding saffron—woman's saffron grinding on woman's saffron."

He likes the counters of the spice shops, lined with trays, scent to scent, color to color, peaks of candied sugar cones. On large trays, the yellow of turmeric, the green of jujube, the off-white of ginger, the purple of violet fern, mandrake roots coupled together. . . . The chill of turquoise and agate, the acrid taste of the ink in handwritten books loaded on donkeys, the smell of sandalwood and Arab perfumes, the smell of the dust of caravans, the smell of dyed fabrics, the smell of untrodden wool carpets. . . .

Now and then, what is left of his left arm brushes against Agha Haji's arm. He does not seem repulsed by it.

"Do you remember your childhood . . . the times when I took you to Al-Reza Mosque at night? . . . Those days, your small hand was in my hand, and on the way back home, when you were sleepy, I would carry you in my arms, and over and over again I would thank God for the bliss of fatherhood."

> «Now there is a sadness in his voice that does not become him. It does not suit him or this swarming, sprawling bazaar, or the dust that rises in the air from all the comings and goings . . . I wish, I mean, why couldn't he have shown he was human like this a long time ago?
>
> "I don't know, it is not impossible that despite my gratefulness, my faith, my alms and offerings in gratitude for my family, I did some wrong and there was some reason for God the Merciful to put such sorrow in my heart. I don't mean to sound ungrateful. No, I still thank God. . . . "
>
> As we pass certain shops, I sense a faraway familiarity. Here and there, people greet him. They put their hands on their chests or they stand sideways to make way for us. And he, with such an air. . . . Is the humility with which he responds to them a pretense?
>
> I had imagined the bazaar's passages to be much wider than what I now see. The moment I catch sight of his trade chamber, I

remember. Three steps up from the ground, carpets on the floor, carpets on the walls. . . . There are three men. Two sitting behind small, rusted metal desks, the third one squatting in the corner. They all stand up as we walk in. I think those two and their desks were not here before. They immediately start kissing up to me. The poor guys don't know that showing respect to me will not make room for them in Agha Haji's heart. . . . One by one, they report on their work. I quickly realize that the unit of money here is a million tomans. Sixty tomans means sixty million tomans. Now that he is sitting behind his large wood desk, Agha Haji's expression is a million tomans different. I suppose in the past there was a framed picture of the Shah hanging on the wall. Two others—Khomeini and Khamenei—have replaced him. I think the safe next to his desk has changed, too . . . I don't remember it being so large. . . . At the far end of the chamber, the old double doors of the storage room. . . . A tea tray appears in front of me. Held by a pair of shaking hands with bulging veins. The old man is another one of the ass-kissers. Imitating him, I reach out with a shaking hand, take a sugar cube, and put it in my noble mouth, and then I take a glass of the premium, crystalline tea.

"Do you remember yours truly, Amir Khan?"

Even this scamp knows that the noble son is muddled in the head. I nod a bogus yes. I feel my mind is changing tracks again. But today, even if for the sake of Reyhaneh's joy and Agha's wallet, I have to make it stop. What's more, Agha Haji has confessed to his sadness and sorrow.

"Anything you need, just say the word. I am at your service."

The old man is just like Shahu. But Shahu was not an ass-kisser.

A sip of tea and, Amir Khan, let's forget about all this and give our heart to the old ritual of the sugar cube's grain by grain battle in our mouth. And let us watch the people swapping and switching in front of the trade chamber. The ones with stubble on their chin, those who have trimmed their mustaches right above their lips so that the holy never-get-wets do not get any spit on them. Grungy, wrinkled shirts hanging over pants, women in chadors, some make you hornier in their hijab than if they were naked. . . . I'm feeling fine. My head is working well. When Father was talking about his sadness, I even remembered that Uncle Arjang's car had a Topaz gramophone. I don't remember what our car was, but it didn't have a Topaz gramophone, I don't think it even had a radio. These ungodly Shah-y things were piously prohibited. But Uncle's sinful car had a Topaz gramophone. With God's might, you would put a record in it and Marzieh, sounding scratchy, would start singing. Uncle would snap his fingers and sing along with her. Every time we hit a pothole, the needle would skip back, and Marzieh would again chant, "The scent of Moulian stream is. . . ."

It's frightening how things change and how they are remembered. Why do the good-for-nothings change when their good-for-nothingness is supposed to be remembered? Perhaps Agha Haji's sad voice, which I would not have believed, has shaken me up a little. The scoundrel caught me off guard. Could it be that all these years it was my fault, my mistake, that I was wrong thinking that, stoic and dry as lavender, he was nothing but a praying moneymaking machine? . . . I turn and see him staring at me. The concern I see in his eyes does not seem repulsive to me. . . .

"Is this your noble son, Agha Haji?"

They are all alike—burly, dressed in black shirts and jackets, potbellied, fleshy lips that always look greasy from mutton soup, short foreheads, wide flat noses, thick round beards. The man's sharp eyes seem to be reading my mind page by page and tearing each one. Like a sensible son, Amir Khan gets up to say a polite hello. But I think I have seen this guy before.

"Agha Haji, you have finally brightened my eyes by the sight of our wounded warrior. . . . What a strapping young man!"

The man could easily crush my fingers in his large, coarse hand. And his eyes . . . in his eyes there is great confidence in himself and his clout, without a hairy strand of doubt. I should adopt a similar expression. Under his eyes, deep, dark circles. . . .

Agha Haji has stood up for him. After shaking my hand, the man touches his fingertips to his lips and then to his forehead, which boasts a prayer-stone callus. Then he pulls a chair over to Agha Haji's desk and sits down. I swear on Reyha's life, he is looking at me with distrust. He may even know the whole sum of my life better than I do.

"We owe our country to you and the likes of you, Agha Amir. May God reward you. Blessed is your good fortune. The likes of me were not granted the same chance. Even if we used to be a flowing stream, lately we have started smelling stale in this city."

"So you were at the front, too?"

"I had the honor of serving shoulder to shoulder with you for a few years."

"Were you at the western front?"

"In all its key locations."

"So you were at the Pourpirar front, too."

"Not for long."

"Well, of course. It wasn't as vital as the Neiji front."

"No, it was not."

Perhaps he has just caught on. His dubious glare is more piercing. When he digs into his pants pocket to take out his prayer beads, I see the grip of a Colt on his belt. He may have even meant for me to see it. . . . Yes, fear, fear is the feeling his eyes give me. . . . I have seen this guerrilla before. I did not see his holy face in daylight; I saw his heavenly face at night, outside the house, he came to tell Agha Haji about a stabbing.

And now the two of them are whispering. . . . I drink another tea. A drudge carrying two folded carpets on his bent back shuffles by, an Oshnu cigarette between his lips. Just now, I realize that in fact my problem is that I am not smoking. That's why I'm angry all the time. But for now, it's better that I don't go chasing after the drudge with my two pleading prongs held out for him to give a one-armed beggar a cigarette. . . . Is this my second or third tea? . . . Agha Haji takes a checkbook out of the safe and hands it to one of the desk occupants who must be the bookkeeper. With a glance from his boss, the other one gets up and leaves. And Agha again turns his ear to the brute. In the previous now, the pendulum wall clock read 9:00, and in the now now, when I turn and glance at it again, it reads 10:00. Whispering, Agha Haji asks the man something.

The man says, "The Hojatt-ol-Islam has requested seven million tomans."

I can tell Agha is irate. He can't keep his voice down.

"Of course, you should explain my constraints to the Hojatt-ol-Islam. These days, business is not as it used to be . . . I cannot manage more than three million. . . . "

"He has requested a remuneration of seven million. And you know, it will not go far."

There is a high-handedness in his tone, as if he's some big shot, and it makes Agha Haji break into a sweat. He motions to the guy at the desk. The guy writes. Agha signs. He tears off the check and hands it to the scorpion-browed bear. The bear touches the check to his forehead and tucks it in his pocket.

As he leaves, he turns to me and says, "God willing, you will honor us sometime by allowing us the pleasure of your company, Agha Amir. Our brothers are eager to meet you. You are a living martyr."

And he takes his menacing glare away with him.

I take a fourth tea and the tray goes away. It is 11:02. The minute I put the empty tea glass back on the tray it is 11:23. Agha Haji opens the door to the storage room.

"You must be tired. . . . I didn't take into account that I should not keep you waiting here for so long on your first day. That brother, may God bless him, had some urgent business."

"It's all right. I kept myself busy."

"Let's go to the storage room and smoke a water pipe . . . then we will go to Shamshiri restaurant—I am sure you have a lot of memories from there."

I follow him into the storage room. I don't know how and when a water pipe has been prepared and set on a wooden bed frame covered with a carpet at the far end of the room. Agha reclines on a purple cushion at the head of the bed and starts puffing on the water pipe.

Dimly lit, cold because of the thick, ancient walls made with dark bricks and white grout, and above them hundred-year-old crisscrossing arches, this place feels ominous. This room is unnerving me.

"The noise and the commotion of the bazaar do not come in here. This is my sanctuary, my mihrab . . . a good place to rest, to be alone with my heart and my God. . . ."

"They say God is everywhere."

"After your flogging, my reputation suffered. Everywhere I went, people made taunting and cutting remarks. I was forced to get into businesses that I did not want to get into, to put up money for deals that I will have to answer for in the afterlife. Of course, now I hold my head up high again."

And he starts babbling again. All around the storage room, there are bolts of burlap stacked on wide, three-level shelves all the way up to the ceiling. I have never liked burlap's shade of shit . . . burlap always makes me want to puke. . . . Agha Haji's voice, again sad and intimate, as though we've been buddies for years. So much so that I wonder if we actually were.

He is saying, " . . . she is the best woman in the world. Hardworking, a fine homemaker, virtuous, sacrificing . . . even though sometimes she does not understand some things, she has been a very good wife for me. Nothing I can say about her goodness will ever be enough. . . . But, well, every man, in his thoughts and dreams. . . . "

I'm starting to think that "Dad" could roll off my tongue easily.

I sit on the edge of the bed. Agha offers me the pipe.

"I have never said anything, but I know you smoke cigarettes. It is better that you smoke in front of me than behind my back. Water pipe is healthier."

I take a puff. Damp, like the breath of some creature, the smoke creeps down my throat. I feel dizzy. . . . In the bubbling bubbles in the water pipe something is moving up and down and its color keeps changing.

And Agha is saying, "For the sake of my dear children, I have never revealed my buried desire. But, if I had married that girl, my life would have been very different. . . ."

I have never heard him sigh before. He gently puts his hand on my shoulder. I think if he speaks a few more words, I will see his never-before-seen tears, too. I want to want to feel sorrier for him.

"But I am grateful . . . I beg you to keep this secret between us, father and son. I have never let Missus suspect anything, and I don't want her to find out now. For years, I have kept this sorrow deep in my heart. I told you now because I want you to understand that I, too, have had my share of sadness and loneliness. . . . What about you? I know there was a girl in your life. . . . "

So, this always-Agha Haji who is always Agha Haji, had a heart, fell in love.

But there is a strange sound coming from somewhere. Perhaps a large vent has come loose. Perhaps it is the rasps of a camel whose throat has been cut. There is so much burlap here. . . .

" . . . someone you felt a special affection for. We must find her, because it is time for you to make a family . . . we will build a modern house for you in the garden, so that every morning my grandchildren can run out the door and run over to our house. . . . "

When did I walk away from the bed? I am now running my hand over the coarse burlap.

In my ears, it seems that perhaps I am hearing the pop-pop of mushrooms popping in mushroom patches that have grown on mass graves. . . .

My left hand's ring finger is gone, but the sensation of the ring on it is still there.

Agha Haji's mouth is moving, but his voice is fading, it is fading in that strange noise that has started. It's the drone of an electrical cable spinning in the air . . . it is spinning here, too, behind me . . . it's getting louder . . . but it is in my head that it is spinning, spinning to slash . . . whir, whir, it spins. . . . Get down on the ground! . . . Incoming! . . . Its whir is closer! . . . Get down! Incoming! . . . It has been inside these old bricks . . . in the folds of the burlap . . . the sound of the fluttering wings of a hundred sparrows flying off together. A deer in the stable, a pig in the sky . . . the mushrooms pop. Clouds of spores, cerulean, purple, agate, spread in the sky as far as. . . .

I've got to pull the soldiers out from under the rocks . . . Amir, you lunatic, don't! They are dead . . . I am pounding my fist on the rubble of the collapsed trench; roundworms slither out of it.

Another canary has flown off on its own, it comes, it comes and flies into the rocks. A steal canary, blind, its edge the serrated blade of a Chinese fruit knife hits the arm. . . .

What did Agha Haji ask that he is now staring at me, waiting for an answer? . . . Get down, Amir! The trench implodes. The trench, two rows of dirt-filled burlap sacks, the rest of it rocks, the divine sacks and rocks explode. Heavenly pieces of flesh and innards among the blossoming fragments of stone. . . . Give it up, Amir! You idiot! More are coming!

A hundred sparrows flying together come to dive through the roof of the next trench.

I pound on a heap of burlap sacks, ambrosia, blessing from the gods. There is nothing you can do with a heap of shit other than to kick it and pound on it.

Sharp steel, sharp shards of stone, sharp teeth, purple, purple, they come. Divine pomegranates fall, burst, purple, purple. The wind brings snakeskins. The flight of venomous shrapnel. . . .

The chill of the storage room's cement floor beats against my forehead. . . . Get down, you moron! Trapped on the floor, my arm shielding my head . . . the left side of my head is unprotected.

And they are still calling me. . . . A hand is turning me over. The bookkeeper's face above me. Foam fills my mouth to sink down my throat. Agha Haji, proprietor of the world and the hereafter, is standing farther away, dumbstruck.

"Every time we see each other, we will get engaged again. Agreed?"

I have to get up, take my left arm off the floor, and with its fist pound against everything in sight. . . .

I throw another punch, I hit the heap of burlap sacks . . . the accountant is getting up off the floor . . . his nose bloody . . . snowless winds, winds with canaries and winds with mushroom spores and bits of brain, full of holes, holes. . . . They ricochet off my good-for-nothing skull. . . . I will punch this good-for-nothing world and say, You good-for-nothings, you have filled the world with your burlap sacks of money and burlap sacks of blood! . . . And I beat my fist against the pile of burlap.

I holler, "How much have they appreciated? A hundred million? Five hundred million? . . . Oh, I piss on your millions! I piss on your burlap sacks!"

Agha Haji is shouting at me. His spit on my face. I yell even louder so that I won't hear him.

"How long did you hoard them for their price to go up? . . . You crook! Do you know how many soldiers were maimed and mangled by the rocks from their own trenches because of the scarcity of these shitty burlap sacks?"

I throw a punch. My left hand punches the punch I threw.

"There weren't enough burlap sacks! Soldiers piled rocks around their trenches. Shrapnel and bullets hit the rocks and turn them into more shrapnel and bullets. . . . Do you get it, you burlap hoarder, you swindler? . . . I would beg that yellow-bellied commander for just a few sacks to make sandbags . . . there weren't any . . . they were all here!"

I kick. My gasps, choppy . . . the burlap tower collapses. . . .

The bookkeeper, the good-for-nothing Ba'athist, throws his arms around me to capture me. He twists my right arm. I hit him in the face with my forehead, my howls between my teeth. I spit foam at his face . . . blood is oozing from the crook of my fist . . . and the mushroom haze keeps spreading everywhere for mass graves to keep spreading everywhere. . . .

Suddenly my face swings away from the mountain of burlap, Agha's heavy hand whips by. . . . »

The scribe on his left shoulder had written:

«The snow winds spiral up from the depths of darkness and beat against the tent . . . there is a little piss-colored kerosene left in the heater, but we don't dare light it. The flicker of the lantern will die out soon. I've got to go out to take a leak.

I open our last can of food. It is frozen. With Pourpirar, fifty-fifty. . . . Bread crusts that we had not eaten have molded in the plastic bag, but they will fill the stomach. The canned fish congeals in my mouth. It makes me more ill. Pirar, dried bread crunching in his mouth, says, "I just want to cut your throat every time you defend them."

"Don't you get it? If they send out more soldiers and mules, they will be shelled too. I am sure the Iraqi scout has moved to a location with a clear view of the trail."

"That's nonsense! They won't be seen at night."

"The snow has covered the trail. They will get lost in the dark."

"I don't know whether we should stay or head down the mountain. If we go down, who knows, those lunatics may execute us for the crime of deserting our post."

"Radio them again."

"Haven't I done it enough times? . . . They had never hit the lower ridge before. We have to find their observation post."

Wearing every piece of clothing we have, we are still shivering. The kerosene heater's corpse, colder than the air, seems to be sitting between me and the sergeant to stop us from getting into a brawl.

I have noticed that the intervals between our exchanges are getting longer. It's not good. Pirar is crawling into his North Korean sleeping bag. He spits at it angrily.

"This is not a sleeping bag. It's a shroud! It's as cold as ice. What a piece of crappy shit those yellow dogs pawned off on our army!"

"You can be sure some mullah's brat or son-in-law had a hand in it. Pushing shoddy stuff and stashing the profits and commissions in some Swiss bank, the coffer of all the shits in the world. . . . Cheers to the victorious army of Islam!"

Rusted American and Iraqi grenades are piled up in the corner of the tent. The American ones look like maimers and manglers, the Iraqi-Russian ones look like balls and ball-blasters.

When the wind goes mad, it talks. It wails of its wounds. I haven't been outside for even a minute and already ice has belted me and crusted on my overcoat. It seems I can't pass my piss for its yellow to melt the snow and carve a groove in it, for its steam to blow down the mountain with the wind. . . . I shake the damned thing, it's about to freeze and it won't piss. My pubic hair brushing against a woman's plump-lipped flower, hot and wet inside, I want to. . . . Buttoning up your lousy pants with frozen fingers is so difficult!

I should check up on the two night-shift guards. The jerks will not let on how many rations they have left, they keep saying they have nothing. I want to yell at them, You idiots, I don't want your food, I want to share mine with you if you don't have any left. . . . But how would I know if they were to lie to me and like a mullah grab the little Pourpirar and I have left . . . snow rasping under my boots . . . invisible stars rasping as ice winds sand them.

The two night guards, hunched over, huddled behind a boulder and a mound of snow, are stiff with fear. It's not good that they haven't shaken the snow off themselves.

"What's up, Eskandar?"

"Nothing, Sir."

I think the other one is asleep. Eskandar nudges him with his elbow. The fog from our breaths blends together. To boost a soldier's morale, you should not reel off slogans, you should tease them.

"Eskandar, what a name your parents gave you!"

"What's wrong with it?"

"What's not wrong with it? Eskandar invaded Iran, pillaged and plundered the country."

"I wasn't around back then. Otherwise, the bum would have never set foot in Iran."

The scamp always makes me laugh.

"The guys are all sleeping?"

"With empty stomachs. They are dreaming of the mule. It's been hee-hawing and climbing up the mountain for a week now, hauling canned fish, cherry compote, rice and stew. . . ."

Second to the rice and chicken the soldiers are customarily given the night before an attack, so that they eat well before going off to be slaughtered, the canned fish and cherry compote rations are the favorite among the peasant boys. Back home, from month to month, many do not even see a plate of rice. . . . And he is still listing his favorite foods.

"Me, too; as soon as my shift is done, the minute I slip into my sleeping bag and close my eyes, I see His Holiness the Mule coming up the mountain. I fall asleep and the damned mule is still climbing up and not getting here. . . . Sir, when will the mule get here?"

"Tomorrow."

"Are they stringing us along?"

"No. They radioed and said the mule is on its way. If you listen carefully, you will hear its hee-haw in the wind."

"I know you only say this stuff to cheer us up. Sergeant Pourpirar was saying that no matter how hard he tries to convince you to let us head down so we don't die of hunger, you won't give permission."

"Eskandar, instead of your mouth, keep your eyes open! If your eyes

are open, you will stay alive, your term of service will end, you will go back home, find work, take a wife, have kids, and rest easy."

"No man is going to give his daughter to a guy with nothing but the shirt on his back. If I get out of here alive, I want to go and do a number on those wimpy rich kids. Right now, when I'm standing guard in this snow and ice, they are taking some girl to a cozy bed and climbing on top of cozy flesh. After I'm done taking care of these Iraqis, I will go back to the city and take care of those rich kids. You see this G3, I will shove it up their ass all the way to its bolt head, and then I will pull the trigger. It will feel so good."

"For now, just watch out for your own ass so the Iraqis don't pull the trigger in it."

With the tip of my boot, I kick the feet of the other soldier who is still napping. He is a new recruit—fresh, tasty flesh for the thousand teeth of war.

"Hey, zero-mileage! This time, I'm going to overlook the fact that you're sleeping on duty, but next time I will make you stand guard the entire night."

I like the way I spontaneously sound harsh. Sometimes I think I sound like the commando who occasionally came to rest in our tent early in the evening and left in the middle of the night to go to the Iraqi lines. He would return early the next morning with four or five ears on a string.

I peek into the soldiers' tent. Crammed together, one man's feet next to another man's head, they are in such deep sleep that they would not even hear someone cutting off the next guy's head and ears.

Without having taken a piss, I bend down and go back inside our low tent. After I shake the ice from my overcoat, I'll quickly slip into my sleeping bag . . . but I should not fall asleep.

"Do you remember your wedding night bridal chamber, Sergeant?"

He ignores me. Trying to restore peace, he says, "Think about it! If we had a warm, cuddly body in our arms in this purgatory, we wouldn't even notice the cold."

I don't know why we get horny more often at the front. I wake up with a hard-on and I'm too embarrassed to get out of my sleeping bag. Every time I have a brush with death, afterward there is so much pressure in my business that it wants to jet out like steam from a pressure cooker. I see myself mounting her like a rabid dog, rabidly shoving in and out, rabidly listening to the slippery slosh of her flower, sensing little bubbles popping inside her. With every thrust, her veil of fair flesh cracks like china. . . .

"Pirar! The way soft, warm houris have popped into your head makes me think you have smelled martyrdom. They say Khomeini gives every Basiji who goes to visit His Holiness a plastic key to heaven's gates. The houris there are something else. Our fathers and mothers were made of dirt and sludge; houris are made of saffron and heaven's soil. Flawlessly fair. I mean, just what a desert-dwelling Arab wants to sink his teeth into. When I was young, I spent a lot of time listening to mullahs give sermons. Houris never menstruate and they don't have a pee hole. In fact, there is no urine and feces in heaven. Whatever Muslims gobble up comes out of their body like sweat. Sweat that smells of musk and ambergris. You will appreciate this part. Muslim men don't get any when they are young; they masturbate, and many end up not having much stamina. When instead of their hand they put it somewhere soft and slippery, they come quickly. But in heaven, a pious man has so much stamina that copulating with a houri can take thirty, even seventy years. In religious accounts there is no mention of where all that semen goes, because houris' vulvas are closed and they can't bear children. Houris' bodies are clear like glass. If you end up seeing their guts and veins and such, don't blame me, that's what the mullahs say. Sir, your houri will become a virgin again after you do her. So much bloodshed in heaven! . . . In short, if you are martyred, in heaven you will have seventy houris, though there are accounts of seven hundred and even seventy thousand."

I think I've made his mouth water.

The biggest drag in this world is when a man's lighter or lover let him down just when he needs them. The warmth from my lighter's flame is so pleasant. I have one and a half cigarettes left. Pourpirar ran out this morning. I know that as much as he wants to cut off my head, he is dying for me to give him the half cigarette. I will light it and puff on it with such delight that he will know for certain that I have no intention of offering it to him. Tucked in his sleeping bag, he turns his back to me.

"Don't take offense, Sergeant. I meant nothing, I asked as a brother. I find it interesting. I have never been married. I have heard that in the old days an old woman would sit behind the door of the bridal chamber, waiting for the groom to come out with a handkerchief stained with the bride's blood of virginity, proving that she was pure. Is that right?"

". . ."

"And then the bride's father would hold up the handkerchief and the guests would ululate. Did they do that for you, too?"

". . ."

"Every time we talk about your wedding, you start brooding, Sergeant."

". . ."

What if his eyes have filled with tears, with these uneven breaths. . . . Somewhere behind the mountain, a shell has blasted out of a mortar. The way that vileness echoes against the mountains, I often can't tell which direction it's coming from. But I can tell from its roar that it is a 250. That bastard. When it explodes on the ground, it digs a crater bigger than ten graves. Perhaps right now two or three of our soldiers or theirs are howling and moaning.

"The reason I don't go on leave is because I don't want to lay eyes on my disgusting family. Even if I go, I will not visit them. I will go hoping to see the one I love. . . . Why didn't you go on leave this time? To see your wife. . . ."

Is this my good-for-nothingness, pretending to extend a hand of peace and friendship?

"Take it, Sergeant."

He sits up and takes the cigarette from me. When he sits like this in a zipped-up sleeping bag, he looks like he is wrapped in a green shroud.

One after the other, four shells, sounding like rock pigeons flapping their wings, fly over the peak and toward our lines. Why have the Iraqis started playing with fireworks at this hour of the night? And our artillery unit has probably stuck its head in the snow like a partridge or is sleeping like the dead. Or no. They will not waste their meager ammo to retaliate. This way, the Iraqis will not know that they are hitting on target.

The blast of the explosions bounces from one slope to another and returns, crushing ice.

Searching for their observation posts, I have scoured many peaks and ridges with my binoculars. Wherever they are, they have camouflaged themselves very well. Better than us. I am certain they have identified our provisions route. If midway on that trail our rations and kerosene are mingled with the blood and flesh of three soldiers and a mule . . . then in the dark of night, too, they have the trail under control. Therefore, the situation is worse than I thought. They've gone around us and closed in on our lines.

"Talk, Sergeant. Get it off your chest. You know every detail of my life, but you've never peeped a word about yours. . . . Why? You don't consider me kinfolk?"

Nothing is left of the kerosene, the lantern is flickering more desperately, and more soot is settling inside its glass globe. It's unusual that today and tonight, neither Pourpirar nor I were in the mood to clean it.

"So I am not like kin to you."

"Don't make a fuss, Lieutenant Spoof. We are like the brothers we never had. . . . You being educated, tell me, when will this war end?"

"If we fall asleep in this cold, we will never wake up."

"Why did you remind me of my wife?"

The lantern dies out. Two breaths facing each other in the dark.

Perhaps now his eyes are brimming. Perhaps a tear will roll down his cheek and freeze. Like the steam from our breaths that freezes on our nasal hair.

"What is it? She wasn't a virgin?"

As soon as I blurt it out I know that I have callously wounded him.

"Shut your trap!" he growls. "Who shafted you when you were a boy and made you so sick in the head?"

"I have lost count of how many men pulled this pretty boy into dark corners. . . . Every woman thinks of cheating. The temptation is in their mind, in their body."

"Don't compare other women with your own lewd and loose mother and sister!"

"I think the dread of a cheating wife and its shame is on every man's mind . . . that's why I pulled as many women as I could under me, so that if one day I'm cuckolded by some son of a bitch, at least I will have the upper hand."

"It's because of your filth that that poor girl killed herself."

"She killed herself because of herself. Even now that she's dead, I am still afraid that one day some goon might show up and tell me that when I was in love with Khazar, faithful to her, she spread her legs for him. I am sure she did. Just to make me a humiliated sack of shit."

"You've gone nuts."

"How much does the thought of your wife being unfaithful bother you? The suspicion that when you are away at the front for an entire month, your wife. . . . "

In the dark, the heavy stir of his muscular body slipping out of his sleeping bag. He sits on his knees. . . . In the dark, I will not see it until it hits me in the face and I slump to the ground. . . . In the dark, waiting for it is repulsive. . . . In the dark, I hear the breechblock of a G3 being pulled. If the bullet hits me in the head, will I feel the impact or the pain of my shit brain splattering?

The jerk does not shoot. I can hear his furious pants.

"Shoot so that I learn, too! So that I become like the rest of you happy cuckolds."

I can imagine the ominous flash suppressor at the tip of the barrel facing me. Cold and waiting for the cartridge that has entered the barrel extension.

"A man is someone who knows when he is not being a man."

I hear him move closer to me. I hear the safety toggle being released. Pirar's rasping breaths quicken.

In the dark you cannot accurately estimate the passage of time.

How beautifully it occurred to me. Time, no, God did not create time out of sludge, he created this bastard time out of fire . . . no, he did not create it out of fire either, he created it out of the functions of the stomach and intestines, all the way up to the bellybutton of the brain.

About three minutes pass in silence. Pirar starts to talk. There is sadness in his voice.

"I am so in love with her that I would not let her leave the house for even one minute . . . she would weep, sulk, but I wouldn't let her. She hated me. I didn't want another man to lay eyes on her. My Barfeh-Banu was offended that I did not trust her. She would stop talking to me for days. The house would become a graveyard . . . but then a time came when she understood how much I loved her. She read my hand. Not once had I ever told her."

It must be his foot kicking my knee.

"Year after year, the more I wanted her, the more I hid it from her. But in the end, she understood. She understood, and I became her sheep."

Suddenly, his fists beat me on the chest. I fall back against the tent . . . the eternal crackle of ice breaking off the canvas. . . .

"You sleazy louse! Why did you open the wound in my heart? What do you gain by seeing a man's desperation?"

As soon as I sit up, his fist on my face. . . .

My mouth tastes salty . . . a warm trickle congeals in my cold mouth.

He tears out of the tent. . . . The endless sound of falling snow and ice. . . . Outside, terrifying, radiant snowflakes, the protracted reverberation of a howl whose wolf has moved away. . . . Pourpirar has gone far-off, but the wind brings his cries.

"Barfeh-Banu!"

And his wails plunge into dead valleys.»

The scribe on his right shoulder writes:

"Go for a drive, do some shopping, and pick me up here in three hours."

"You're not going to do anything crazy, are you?"

"No, I swear on your life. For once, trust me when I swear on your life, you are the one dearest to me."

Reyhaneh stares into his eyes, wanting to read them. She hesitantly glances over at the driver, who is still clucking his tongue.

"All right. In three hours. What time is it now?"

He looks at his wrist. There is no watch on it. Chuckling, Reyhaneh takes his watch out of her coverall pocket and straps it on his wrist.

"It is 11:10. I will come back at 2:00. If you are not here, I will know you have gotten lost and we'll have to come looking for you in a nuthouse somewhere."

The car drives away. And Pourpirar's house is right there. He starts roaming around without knowing why.

He is a hundred yards away—he turns and walks back. He strolls around, trying to not look suspicious. He is four hundred yards away, again, he walks back and stares at the front door of the house. A thousand yards away, he sees a chalk line on the wall in a long alley. Follow This Line! He follows the line.

The scribes on his right and left shoulders had written:

And you two are beautiful together. And it is beautiful when at midnight Roya walks in through the garden gate that has been left open, and behind the gate your heart quiets down. And you close the gate and take her hand, you pass sleeping Shahu's dark hut and you take her to the plot of cherry trees, their branches drooping from the weight of their fruit, just like women whose shoulders droop from the weight of their breasts. Breasts full of desire or breasts laden with milk.

And although it has been done many times before, you two are beautiful when you hang two pairs of cherries on Roya's ears, covering her turquoise earrings. And you put your finger on her full lips just when she wants to ask, Are you sure they're asleep? And you lie down on the soil of the garden, your right arm under Roya's head, and you watch the Milky Way through the branches of the Khezr cherry tree.

"It is so beautiful . . . " she says. "The ugliness of beauty is that you worry it will end."

"That is the beauty of beauty."

"That is the ugliness of beauty."

And lying down on the ground, Roya takes a pack of cigarettes from her handbag. And the breeze that you had beckoned pushes the leaves and branches aside for you to see more of the Milky Way . . . and you two are beautiful when you discover that a naked body sleeping on soil has a sensation from time immemorial that cannot be felt in any bed. The girl is still timid. And you two are beautiful when without prior design, you prolong your lovemaking with the arching of the Milky Way. And you two are beautiful when close to climaxing you pull away from each other. You light a cigarette and smoke it mouth-to-mouth. And mouth-to-mouth you give the smoke in your lungs to the other. And the cherry tree is patient, letting you learn through the dialogue of your bodies what you do not know about making love to each other, letting you explore that vacuum between the stars. And you are beautiful when you wildly tear cherries off the tree and spread them on the ground, and when you lie Roya down over them and let her discover how to dance under the weight of a man, to dance on a bed of cherries so that her body takes on their scent and color. Your hand sliding over slippery crushed cherries under her waist.

"Slower," you repeat, and in the end, you press your hand over her mouth to muffle her cries.

And in the last moments of the Milky Way, she straddles you, her strong knees against your sides, and with a meteor lining or not lining the sky behind her, she rides your body. And you look at the star-filled sky of the garden, and the nectar of cherry milk spreads in the sky like a cloud. You are beautiful because you do not empty inside her, you let it flow on her stomach. She runs her hand over the wetness and runs her hand over the soil. And your caresses brush away the cherry seeds on her back.

And you are beautiful when you realize that Roya is the one. The very one. The one you have always desired since you first desired a woman.

And you two are beautiful when later, lying side by side, your nakedness facing the sky, the sky facing you, you discover that the arch of a branch heavy with cherries is beautiful, that its cherries are the twin stars of the Milky Way, that the Milky Way's branch is beautiful. And the beauty of no two cherries is greater than that of another pair.

The scribe on his left shoulder writes:

The line on the wall ends at a fork in the alley. He turns right. The line continues, and then the words, "If you don't feel up to it, go back!" He does not go back. "If you are a fake, go back!" He does not go back. "What if at the end of this line I tell you, You are an idiot to have followed it this far? Go back!" And as far as far, he goes until the end of the line, near the front door of a house that looks like all other houses. And at the end of the line, contrary to his expectation, there are no curse words or gibes. "You are a man. Only rotten scoundrels do not follow their line to the end of the line."

It seems this same sentence is what was written at the end of the chalk line on the garden wall. . . . He wants to go back to Pourpirar's house, hoping that the man will walk out and they come face to face. . . .

His sense of smell is his best guide. It leads him back to Pourpirar's neighborhood without getting lost.

Left:

The car and Reyhaneh return.

"Pirar hasn't come out of the house yet; neither has his wife."

And he thinks, Don't kid yourself, Pirar, I will be back.

On his right shoulder:

"Pourpirar is at the gates, insisting on seeing you," Reyhaneh says.

"Tell the guards to let him in. I will change and come downstairs."

"Did you say please?"

"Please!"

He takes his time. When he walks out, the guard and Pourpirar are waiting in front of the house.

"Thank you, Colonel! Please return to your post."

Irritated, the guard walks away.

"Let's go over to the eucalyptus tree—no one can hear us there."

Standing under the tree, cold and harsh, he asks, "Why did you come here?"

Still impudent, Pourpirar says, "Why are you sniffing around my house?"

"You know why."

"Know what?"

"To convince you to help me go back to our last observation post."

"Do you really expect me to put my brain and logic in the hands of a shell-shocked guy and go back there?"

"Yes, you understand correctly."

"If I ever see you snooping around my house again, I will break the only arm you have left."

"Going for a stroll is allowed in this country. And if you ever raise a hand to me, I will raise such hell that you will regret it until the day you die."

"That place is really far away, nitwit!"

"Anyplace far becomes near when you move toward it. . . . I want to find something."

"This is all a crazy prank, a madness. But . . . if you are in the market, and you pick up our travel expenses, and pay me a million tomans in cash, I will take you there."

"Five hundred thousand," Amir snaps.

"I said one million, no more, no less."

He sees the cuckoo bird's pink egg fall from the tree onto the Alfa Romeo's roof.

"My arm isn't even worth two rials. Five hundred is my final offer. . . . Did you bury it?"

"I will tell you when we are halfway there. Bring the cash to my house. Then, I will arrange the trip."

"What was the name of the mountain we were on?"

"I will tell you on the way."

And Pourpirar walks away along the path that leads to the garden gates. He stops midway. He shifts and flexes his back as if trying to drive the shrapnel and the pain up toward his shoulders.

On his right:

"Dādāshi, are you sure you want to go?" Reyhaneh asks.

Unlike the still-wintry window in his room, outside Reyhaneh's window the garden trees have given their blossoms to the wind, the brittle green skin on the almonds is hardening, and the cherries . . . there is no perfume of winter sweet flowers; in his imagination he smells the scent of the juicy apples yet to come.

"Wasn't it you who constantly prayed and gave alms so that I would be cured of madness? As a son of God, I am telling you that God will grant you your prayers if I go on this trip."

"Fine, fine. . . . But Agha Haji said he will not give you any money, because the war zones are still full of mines. He doesn't want you to come back with two missing legs, too. . . . Swear on your life that no matter what happens, you will come back."

"I swear on your life, dearer than my own bogus one, that I will come back."

"I sold my gold jewelry—you have seven hundred thousand in total."

Bundles of bills with the cliché image of the forever-glowering Ayatollah Khomeini on them are stacked on the floral design of the inlaid table.

"It looks like a lot of money!"

"On Judgment Day, you will accept responsibility for all the lies I will have to tell to cover for you. Agreed?"

"I will accept responsibility for the sins of your children and your parents, too."

"We have to wait ten or fifteen days for Agha Haji and Mom's suspicions to taper off. Then we will come up with some excuse to go out, you will get away from me, and I will come back home in tears."

"You really are an angel!"

For the first time in years, he laughs earnestly and joyfully. He holds Reyhaneh in his right arm. The girl easily glides into his embrace. He frees her hair from behind her ear and draws in its scent, the scent behind her ear, where her hairline starts thin . . . and he kisses her earlobe. Reyhaneh pulls away. She looks at him with uncertainty.

On his left shoulder:

Reyhaneh stuffs the last piece of clothing into the duffle bag she has bought for him.

"Well, do you remember that I went to see Pourpirar? Do you remember what I have given him?"

"No."

"If you don't remember, I will not walk out of the garden gates with you."

"You gave him money."

"No."

"You gave him my medications."

"Yes. If you don't take your pills, you will get all messed up and you will not get anywhere."

"I will remember."

"I will give Pourpirar his five hundred thousand. That leaves two hundred thousand for your travel expenses. Don't give it all to Pourpirar. Make sure you have money in your pocket in case he leaves you stranded. Where is the address to our house and all the telephone numbers I wrote down for you?"

"In the side pocket of my bag, in my pants pocket, in. . . . "

"In the neck wallet you are wearing, too."

He takes Reyhaneh's slightly plump hands and looks at the dimples that are there in the morning and not there in the afternoon. With all the innocence he can muster, he asks, "Who was in that torn photograph?"

Reyhaneh is unnerved.

"You really are a lowlife! I won't back you up anymore, you creep."

She beats her weak fists on his chest and walks out crying.

On his right:

One hour and five minutes have passed since he found Reyhaneh under the Khezr tree, and without speaking, without moving, just like her, he is sitting on the ground next to her. The girl, her eyes red, somberly stares at the house. Another twenty-seven minutes pass before she breaks her silence. Her voice is hoarse.

"Meysam and Khazar were standing next to us. It was the only photograph I had of them. Meysam and I were very secretly very much in love. All we looked forward to were those Fridays when the ill-omened Yamini clan would gather at the country house in Karaj. A stolen glance, a few words here and there . . . no one suspected anything. And even if you had guessed there was something between us, you didn't care. . . . Don't say a word! I don't want to hear anything from that disgusting mouth of yours. Sometimes I wonder if I came up with the money for your trip so that you'll just get the hell out of this house and go. Go in a way that we would all be certain you will never come back. . . . "

He turns his face to Shahu's hut so that Reyhaneh does not see his eyes. The cherry trees, neglected, are not bearing as much fruit as they used to. A few cherries here and there, some half-eaten by birds and worms. He sees himself in the Alfa Romeo under the eucalyptus tree. He puts the car in reverse and slams down on the gas; in front of the house he yanks the hand brake to make the car spin around and face the driveway and the gates. He shifts into drive and pushes down on the gas pedal to make gravel fly out from under the wheels and at the house. Shahu, having heard the car, has hurried over and opened the gates. . . . He is going to see Khazar.

" . . . he was going to come and ask for my hand in marriage. His father had talked to Agha Haji and had his consent. . . . All these years, I have waited for him to come with his family and propose to me. The reason Agha Haji doesn't push me to marry one of the suitors who keep showing up at the house is that he knows my heart is still with Meysam. . . ."

Abu-Yahya is sitting in the distance, watching Reyhaneh and Amir, unable to decide which one to feel sorry for. . . .

As soon as Amir opens his mouth, Reyhaneh snaps, "Not a word! I do not want to hear any more of your rubbish and lies. I do not believe that you can't remember Khazar and Meysam."

She gets up.

"Meysam was devoted to Khazar. He learned from her. He said Khazar killed herself because of you. You left her and she committed suicide. Meysam hated you. And he started hating me, too. . . . He never looked at me again."

«Khazar? Khazar! . . . I knew I know this name.»

"Has this guy, Meysam, gotten married?"

Reyhaneh walks away without answering.

Right:

Sitting in his chair, facing the garden, he repeats in his mind the story that someone who he cannot remember once told him.

> «A prince, whose father used to invite all the poor and needy to his castle once a year to offer them a pool of honey and a pool of oil, put on a pair of steel shoes to go in search of his beloved.

He walked through forests and he walked through deserts and he walked and walked and walked some more. . . . Here and there, people told him which way to go. He walked for seven years until he reached the Bitter Orange and Citron Orchard. The beast guarding the orchard was asleep and snoring loudly. He was using one of his large, drooping jug ears as his mat and the other as his blanket. The prince climbed the orchard wall and jumped down on the other side. There were bitter-orange and citron trees planted successively in the center of the orchard. Really pretty, prettier than pretty. The prince picked a citron. The citron started to scream, "Hey! He picked me off the tree!" But the clever prince ran and jumped over the wall and ran far, far, far away from the orchard. And when he was far enough, he sat down on the ground, took out his knife, and peeled the citron. All of a sudden, a beautiful girl, as beautiful as rays of sunshine, popped out of the citron. So beautiful that she would tell the moon of the fourteenth night not to show itself because she could shine brighter. Confused, the citron girl looked this way and that and said, "I am thirsty. Water! Water!" The prince said, "Water? In this wasteland?" The citron girl trembled, trembled, fell down, died, and vanished. . . .

The prince went back to the orchard. This time, he picked a bitter orange. When he was far away from the orchard, he peeled the bitter orange and a girl popped out of it. She said, "Bread! Bread! . . . "»

Left:

His mind is all scrambled from the driver's long-winded political analysis with which he wants to prove that according to what he has heard on Radio Israel and the BBC, the mullah's rule will be over in no more than four months. They arrive at the terminal for buses heading to destinations in the western region of the country. They climb out of the car.

Amir pops his head in the driver's-side window and says, "If you just get your passengers to their destinations properly, everything will work itself out."

"Let me come and hand you over to Pourpirar," Reyhaneh says.

He puts his hand on her back and pushes her back into the taxi.

"I can find him myself."

"There are a lot of buses. You will get lost."

"Let me go on my own."

He looks into her eyes for a moment and holds out his arm. Reyhaneh gets out of the taxi and slithers into his embrace.

No, Reyhaneh does not slither, she saunters into his embrace. He wants to kiss and smell her earlobes, but they are hidden under her Islamic headdress.

"Will you come back?" she says.

" . . . "

And Reyhaneh does not need to use much strength to free herself from his arm. She pushes his left shoulder back and with her right shoulder slips out from his so-called hug like a fish. But before the slippery fish gets away, with his long-ago skill of stealing kisses, he kisses her ear over her headdress. And as though nothing has happened, he again puts her in the taxi.

"For now, you for one should go back home."

On his left:

He is certain that Reyhaneh, keeping her distance, is following him in the bus terminal. He wanders around aimlessly until Pourpirar finds him. With two tickets in his hand, he leads Amir to the bus leaving for Kermanshah.

"We get off in Kermanshah. From there, we go to Kerend-e Gharb."

"And then?"

"We go to Kermanshah, from there to Kerend-e Gharb, and then to Qasr-e Shirin. From there, we will head up the mountain to Devil Worshipers' Peak. . . . This is the most absurd trip I have ever gone on."

The moment he hears the words Devil Worshipers' Peak, he knows he remembers this name.

They board the bus. Most of the passengers are Kurdish. Perhaps even the driver, who has the mien of an opium junkie.

The bus sets off. Foul-smelling Iranian cigarettes have been lit. Pourpirar lights a Winston.

"I bought it with your money. It's great."

"Give me one, too."

"You are paying my *expenses, not the other way around."*

> *«By now Reyhaneh has told Mom that while shopping for clothes with Agha Haji's money, I slipped away from her and I am lost somewhere. . . . At night, Agha Haji will interrogate her, and I don't think she will be able to bear it, she will fess up that I am heading west. Poor Reyha! They will torment her. One with tears, the other with shouts.»*

After about an hour, he asks, "What did you do with the arm?"

"I buried it. . . . Do you remember where we were?"

"You of all people, don't play psychiatrist with me."

"Do you even remember how many motherfucking peaks they sent us wandering off to?"

"No."

"They always sent us to the worst observation posts. In their opinion, the best observation posts . . . because we were really good. Do you know what that means?"

" . . . "

"Look what a lamebrain I'm telling all this to. The saying goes, Never argue with a nutcase and never go up his ass. . . . Damn you! I paid a high price for being with you, because you were a really good scout."

"Tell me."

"When the Iraqis' shelling quieted down, I went to check on our soldiers—they had all been killed. . . . When we came under fire, I kept shouting at

you to get down on the ground. You set off and went over to the men. Why? They were all dead! All you did was maim yourself. I ran over to you. You were moaning. You were trying to stick your arm back in its place."

> *«If I put it back before my blood dries, my blood will make it stick in its place. My blood will dry and it will stick in its place.»*

They drive past a garden in the middle of the desolate plain. The mud and straw walls around it are tall, but its trees, green, reveling in the summer sun, rise above them.

> *«Forty-Braids. . . . »*

"Did I call out anyone's name?"

"I wasn't your tape recorder. . . . I radioed the base. It was a miracle that I could get a wireless radio hit by shrapnel to work. They said they would send an ambulance to the foot of the mountain; from there, medics would climb up to evacuate us."

"I waited. It would take hours for them to reach the peak. You were the only one left alive."

"You, of course, were alive, too. You were smarter and more skilled than the rest of us. You survived."

"If I hadn't been, I would be sitting on this bus with your sister, going to bring back your bones. I tied your arm really tight so you wouldn't lose blood."

"And my arm?"

"You were clutching it to your chest as if it were a treasure trove. You were shell-shocked. You were talking nonsense. You dropped the arm when you passed out. I thought it was asinine that it was that dear to you. Stuck up there, there was nothing I could do until the medics came. Right next to us there was a shell crater. I wrapped your arm in a piece of plastic. I put it in the crater and covered it with dirt . . . and I stacked a few rocks from the rubble of the trench on top of it. . . . "

The scribe on his right shoulder had written:

In one of her rare mystical moods, Reyhaneh asks . . .

"Do you know who Attar was? Obviously, you are going to say no, you snake. Attar! The great poet who wrote The Conference of the Birds. *The great mystic who showed us the seven stages of love. The rulers would give anything to have him come to their court and write in their praise. He never did. He was captured during the Mongol invasion. A Mongol was taking him away when someone recognized him and offered to buy his freedom. He said he would give the Mongol a hundred sacks of gold if he set Attar free. Attar said to the Mongol, 'Don't sell me, I'm worth a lot more.' The Mongol got greedy and did not accept the gold. They came across a man with a load of hay on his donkey. The man said, 'Sell this sheikh to me in exchange for my load of hay.' Attar said to the Mongol, 'Sell me, I'm not worth more.' The Mongol got angry and cut off Attar's head with his saber. . . . They say Attar bent down, picked up his head, tucked it under his arm, and started walking. And his mouth recited poems as he went."*

The scribe on his left shoulder writes:

He remembers . . .

«So, did Reyha mean that if I really wanted the ring on my finger, out of love I should have picked up my arm and brought it back with me? . . . Does Reyhaneh understand enough to say such a thing? . . . »

Left:

They reach a sprawling sunflower field. He sees a spotted horse with skin like that of a leopard come out from among the sunflowers and watch their bus. He takes it as a good omen.

"Every time I went on leave," Pirar says, "I had to take a road that went on and on for miles. The motherfucker was even longer coming back."

"Did I go to Tehran when I went on leave?"

"The men always complained that the dimwit enlisted officer never took his leaves. But the last few months of service you did go. And each time you came back you were in a worse mood than the rest of us."

"Why?"

"You're asking me? Was I in your head? . . . You were always gloomy and you got even gloomier. When you were down, sometimes you would just sit and stare at some point. No matter how many times I would call you, you would not hear me. Then you would go nuts and start beating yourself on the head. And you hit hard! As if you wanted your brain to drop down into your mouth. Some of the men thought the crazy things you did were just an act so that you would be transferred behind the battle lines. And I would

tell them, 'Then why doesn't he go on leave so that at least for one week he can be away from the shrapnel?'"

"Why didn't you just leave me there to die in peace?"

"I knew you would be dead by the time the medics reached us. So I put you over my shoulder and headed down. . . . "

"Well, by then I weighed less."

"You have never carried a limp body to know how it robs you of your breath."

"What do you think this limp carcass is that I have been lugging around?"

"You were right. The Iraqis had a direct view of our trail. Two or three times along the way they fired shells at us."

"But you were a man and you didn't leave me behind."

"What makes a man is just a donkey stick between the legs. . . . I had almost reached the foot of the mountain when I was hit by shrapnel."

"Come on! Why are you lying? You already have your money. If I was slung over your shoulder, how did shrapnel hit your back and not me?"

"Piss on your money! When the shell came, I put you down on the ground and I lay on top of you."

"Why?"

"You were wounded, I was not."

Pirar takes a blister pack of pills out of his pocket.

"These pills they give me have opium in them. They hand them out for free. Do you want to loosen up a bit?"

"The pills they give me are better than yours. I will sell you one for a thousand tomans. Want one?"

"No."

Every time the assistant driver walks to the back of the bus, he gapes at Amir's armless arm.

They drive past wheat fields that have turned yellow.

"Where do we go from Kerend?"

"Telling you anything is a waste of time. . . . Will what I say now finally sink into your head or should I just turn around and go back? We need

to go to the last war zone we were at, Se-Sar Mountain, and from there to Devil Worshipers' Peak. Years have passed, dimwit! A lot must have changed."

"Mountains don't change."

On his left:

They open the door to their room at the inn in Kerend-e Gharb. Two metal spring beds on either side and a window facing a wall across the three-foot-wide alley.

"I will take the bed on the right," Amir says.

Right:

They have turned off the light. An orpiment-colored glow shines in on the wall facing the curtainless window and reflects into the room.

It is 12:46; every half-hour or so they have both looked at their watches and tossed and turned, making the beds' old and tired springs groan. He finally talks.

"When we were on the mountain, on scout duty . . . what were we like?"

"Confess—where did you keep running off to secretly so that you ended up giving away our location?"

He struggles to turn from his right and facing Pirar to his left to face the wall. But after a few minutes, what is left of his arm starts barking in pain under his awkwardly anchored body. And it is uncomfortable for him to sleep on his back. The weight of his ribcage, which feels heavier than that of a mule's, makes breathing difficult.

"I remember bits and pieces about the place I used to go to. Don't push me so hard and don't make me beg you so much. Why do you want me down on my knees?"

". . ."

"Pretend that I remember nothing. Tell me everything you know. I am a beggar begging for my memories, Sergeant Pourpirar. Wouldn't you give something to a beggar on the street holding out his hand to you?"

Pourpirar's breathing sounds familiar to him.

"Tomorrow, we will head out to Qasr-e Shirin," Pourpirar says. "I guess the town has come alive again. I don't know how we can go from there to the front we were at. We'll find out. Now stop yapping and let's see if we can manage to doze off."

Groaning from pain, he turns and sleeps with his back to Amir. But seven minutes later, he asks, "Do you remember the day we heard on the radio that Khorramshahr had been liberated?"

"What difference does it make if I remember one thing or not?"

"We were really happy. Hour after hour, as the radio announced the areas that had been freed, we became more ecstatic. In two or three days, they captured twenty thousand, thirty thousand Iraqi soldiers. It was no small feat. We were euphoric. We thought we had kicked out the Iraqis, the war was over. We were dimwits to be happy like that. Because everything turned to shit. . . . "

"First it was Saddam's shit . . . then the shit got shittier?"

"Just go to sleep!"

"There was shit. There was a lot of shit behind the scenes that we didn't know about. All of us, miserable, in one way or another we were torn to bits."

The scribe on his left shoulder had written:

They approach Qasr-e Shirin at three in the morning, riding in an open-top jeep at the head of a column of new IFA personnel carriers and old, expensive REOs. Captain Meena, the new commander of the Third Detachment, sits up front and Amir sits in the back. He is still wondering why this commando captain has asked him to be among the advance guards at the head of the column.

"What do you think, Lieutenant Yamini?" Captain Meena asks. "Is the war over?"

"I think so, Captain. Iraq has retreated and offered to negotiate peace."

"In other words, we'll go back to our lives and families alive."

"It seems so."

"I thought you were smarter than this, university-educated lieutenant!"

"It isn't over?"

"We keep receiving orders to advance, to engage the enemy . . . there are those who want this war to continue, scatterbrained lieutenant. Haven't you noticed that now that the Iraqis don't want to shower us with shells, our artillery units keep poking at them?"

"It doesn't make any difference to me, Captain."

"I know. I have heard a few things about you."

They enter the war-ravaged city of Qasr-e Shirin. The city, empty of people, has recently come under attack. Near and far, houses are burning along the streets. The flames turn the smoke red and transform half-collapsed walls into nightmarish shapes. A stray dog on the sidewalk runs off into an alley. The stores have been looted and heaps of bricks and plaster cover their floors. Burned cars, traffic signs riddled with holes, the corpse of a helicopter. . . .

"Don't worry, lieutenant," Captain Meena says. "We won't stay in the city. We will head out to the mountains. Just the place you like."

The scribe on his left shoulder writes:

Pirar folds his bread, uses it to spoon up the oil and pieces of egg left on the copper plate, and devours it. He seems to have his appetite back. Amir bites into one of the apples Reyha packed in his bag and stares out the teahouse window. He sees they are not there. The IFAs and jeeps that constantly drove by spewing exhaust fumes, the soldiers on leave for a bath, wandering around the small city. The Kurds have taken back their sidewalks.

Left:

They have not spoken since they boarded the minibus. Pirar has taken his sedative and is drowsy.

> «There should be a mountain pass somewhere around here. I didn't see it on the way to Kerend-e Gharb, so it must be ahead of us. . . . We will travel along the mountain's large intestine, turn after turn, winding along, and then there is the pass, and after the pass, a flat plain opens its arms wide—it has existed for two thousand years, perhaps more, a plain perfect for planting wheat and for fighting until the last drop of blood, perfect for getting off a horse or out of a car to pee. . . . I don't know if the Parsi soldiers' armor or their enemies' armor had an opening so that they could easily pull out their business and pee.
>
> The pass should be close by . . . if we pass through it, perhaps my brain will switch on again, because passes are very important for passing through.»

A distant image sparks in his mind. He sees himself on a sidewalk. The shadow of a girl walks past him and whispers, "It's safe, come!"

After a long while, they are now driving downward. The driver of the dilapidated minibus brakes constantly. They go around a turn and a sudden brake jolts the passengers forward. Their heads swing straight at the metal handrail on the back of the seat in front of them.

> «The catnappers on the thousands-of-years-old road, far from the Silk Road. . . . »

The catnappers brace themselves. Shaken, they crane their necks to look out the windshield or turn and stare out of the side windows.

Up ahead, on the road, wide, hairy patches. They are red. Cars, trucks, and buses have driven over them, making the flesh and blood and wool spread wider and wider on the asphalt. The minibus also drives over a few as if they were speed bumps.

Then, Amir sees the first cadavers on the roadside. He half stands and looks to the left. There are more on that side of the road. Slumped on the gravel shoulder or thrown farther away, looking like crumpled hairy heaps.

There are dead sheep all around, one hundred, maybe more. . . . Then, the traffic patrols on the side of the road, baffled as to what to do with this never-before-seen accident. Then, farther ahead, an eighteen-wheel trailer, scissored, lying on its side—its long end off the road, its wide steel fender, hood, windshield, and probably its wipers splattered with blood and wool. A perplexed officer standing with two traffic patrols looks at the minibus passengers with their faces pressed up against the windows, hoping for inspiration.

The minibus passes the accident scene and again picks up speed. Amir jabs Pirar with his elbow. Pirar's eyes are dazed with sleep.

"Did you see that? The trailer ran into a herd of sheep!"

"I hope you slept well! You must have had a nice dream!"

And he puts his arms on the handrail in front of him, rests his forehead on them, and again goes to the never-never-land of slumber.

I should have been the one writing this scene.

The sheep should have been the ones writing it.

Left:

They drive through the pass. On this side of the mountain, the terrain is the terrain of war. On the paved road, there are still holes and craters from mortar and cannon shells. He remembers this wasteland of burned tanks. Their corpses have not yet been cleared away. There must be a hundred or more of them. Iraqi, Iranian. . . .

«Russian, British, American. . . .»

They have faced off and blown each other up, set each other ablaze. Their guns, no longer erect, slumped and aiming at the ground. The earth is so scorched and oily that even after all these years no weeds have grown on it.

> *«Khazar! Khazar, you burned me. Like that scorched prostitute in Shahr-e No, like these tanks. Why did I not hate you then as much as I hate you now, so that you would be alive now. . . .»*

The scribe on his left shoulder had written:

As though talking to herself, Khazar murmurs, " . . . not yet. Perhaps later. . . . I still have pain."

He thought the girl had fallen asleep. He's been sitting on the chair facing the window, watching the turbulent city. It is now clear that the revolution has triumphed.

"Come sleep next to me. I need you."

The occasional gunshots and explosions have not yet died down. Some parts of the city are still burning. The smell of smoke has come all the way here. It seems his fever drained out in Khazar. . . . He picks up the bottle of arak to trickle the last drops into his mouth. He lies down naked next to her and slides his right arm under her neck. With his left hand, he caresses her hair. The girl likes this. Like a cat she lifts her shoulder and turns toward his strokes.

"It wasn't like what I had imagined at all. It wasn't like a kite tearing. Did you feel it?"

"I don't know. I doubt it."

"My entire body contracted. It was as if I turned to stone. Now I feel lost and disillusioned. It was not as big a treasure as they whispered in my ear over and over again ever since I started menstruating . . . that I shouldn't just give it away. . . . Not only was it not a treasure, it was nothing at all. It wasn't even a nothing."

"I think you'd better stop the speech."

"Thanks for being gentle. Soft. How many virgins have you opened up to have become such an expert?"

"Don't start with the sarcasm . . . you were the first and the last."

"Kiss me!"

Like a butterfly, he flutters over Khazar's lips and moves away. Again. He is easily aroused by the touch of her skin. He thinks how so very much he likes its texture. Much more than all the skins he has felt, smelled.

> «The only thing that does not get old is the sensation of skin. That is why some people can never have enough of each other.»

He has stroked with his lips and his tongue . . . and Khazar's novice lips are learning to kiss. They are moist, they've lost that afternoon's cold-stricken dryness. He presses his mouth over hers and seizes that delicious pair.

> «This girl's lips are as capricious as she is. They are no longer thin.»

Now he understands why they're so pleasing to kiss. Khazar laughs with his mouth against hers.

"Kiss me as much as you can. You know all the ways to do it. Teach me."

He gently sucks her lower lip. Khazar, imitating him, his upper lip. . . .

He likes the feel of the slim yet strong muscle in her arm, all the way down to her elbow where the skin's texture is different from the rest of her body. This skin is curiously rough, perhaps because she leans her elbows on the table, or lies on her stomach to read or think. . . .

He doesn't dare roll on top of her. Not only because she is in pain, but also because he's afraid he may not be able to stop himself from penetrating her. He runs his left hand's fingertips down her neck as far as her right breast. He circles her firm nipple. Khazar breezes a moan.

Her voice has the raspiness of lust.

"I think I will like the pain, too."

"Are you sure?"

"I think you are also in pain. I feel you against my thigh. You are about to burst . . . aren't you?"

She pulls the towel out from under her and looks at it. It is stained.

And she pulls him on top of her.

He leans on his elbows to keep his weight off her fragile body. Feeling the mysterious gratification of sliding into her, tight and silky with blood and feminine nectar, he knows that for the rest of his life he will be under the spell of this nymphic inner.

The scribe on his left shoulder writes:

Qasr-e Shirin still has many of its wartime ruins.

"This place is still a wreck," he says to Pirar. "Why haven't they rebuilt it? Where has all the oil money gone?"

"Agha Haji's son, you're asking me? . . . Sit right here!"

Pirar motions him to sit next to the ancient ruins of the Chahar Ghapi Zoroastrian temple.

"Don't move from here. If you get lost, I'll have to answer to your mother and sister. Get it?"

"I get it."

"The way I understand it, we need to hire a car and driver, if there are any, to take us to the foot of Se-Sar Mountain. This must be the world's lousiest trip. . . . So, you will not wander off, will you?"

"No. I will obey, Sergeant."

And he salutes.

"I know one day you and your pals will laugh at me and my dim-wittedness. I have to find some friends, too, so that we can laugh at you and me both."

Left:

He leans against the half-buckled stone wall. He sees Zoroastrian magi in white robes enter the temple through the four doors around it and go to its center that lies in ruins.

> *«This place fell to ruin a thousand years ago. Now it has been bombarded, too. And still, you Zoroastrian magi will not give up? Shells and bombs*

have decapitated Qasr-e Shirin's tall palm trees. If a palm tree's head is cut off, it will not grow back like other trees. It stays, it dies. Qasr-e Shirin has such beautiful pomegranate orchards, rubies weighing down the tree branches. Shells and bombs were no match for them, because they lean low. »

How does he remember all this? How can he compose these supposedly literary lines with a damaged mind?

Our job is not to question. The brains of these creatures that call themselves humans are a lot more motherfucking human.

Our job is not to judge, either. Perhaps he receives inspiration from somewhere, or receives cheat notes. I am suspicious.

Our job is not to argue with each other. Our job is not to be suspicious. You cautioned me about this on a shoulder prior to this scrawled-and-scribbled-on shoulder.

Pirar arrives in a rickety pickup truck.

"This guy was the only one who'd agree to drive us out to the mountain. He'll pick us up tomorrow. Pay him."

The driver looks like a crook. But he returns half the money Amir gives him and in a Kurdish accent says, "Give it to me when I come to pick you up."

"We have to buy some water and canned food," Pirar says. "And a blanket for you."

On his right:

Pirar throws his suitcase on the bed in the lodging house. He takes an army backpack and a sleeping bag out of it. And he stares at Amir's sad expression.

"Are you all right?"

"Couldn't be better."

"Did you take your pill?"

"Yes."

He is lying. He doesn't want to take his pill. Because he is going back to war.

On his left shoulder:

They drive across several hills and the meadows between them that are lush with weeds that have found the fertile soil of dead wheat fields.

"This whole area is full of mines," the driver says.

The dilapidated truck struggles along the army dirt roads that gradually become steeper.

"If I had a piece of these lands," Pirar says, "I would make it as clean as the palm of my hand, and I would farm it and earn my bread without being under anyone's thumb."

The driver turns the steering wheel and drives over a shell crater with the tires straddling it.

"My man!" he says, laughing. "In this world, it is impossible not to be under someone's thumb. And in the end, we are all under the earth's thumb."

Squeezed and pressed up against each other in the pickup truck's small cab, Pirar shifts and moans from his backache. The stump of Amir's arm is tight against Pirar's . . . and Amir smells lavender.

"They say the remains of a lot of Iranian soldiers are still on that mountain. No one brought them down to return them to their families."

Pirar, imitating the driver's accent, says, "We know, Champion. Just focus on your driving so you don't add us to the lot."

Holding his head half way out the window, Amir inhales the golden scent of the meadow weeds and the whispers of the ghosts of herds.

The scribe on his right shoulder had written:

«The whip introduces itself to you with the first two or three lashes. The pain of that filth is so unfamiliar that you cannot believe you are being plowed like that. You want to wake up, you want to beg to wake up, to realize that there is no one flogging you, and you cannot. Wakefulness does not waken. Then, with the seventh or eighth lash, awake, it is time to beg, Stop! And you know that even if you cry out that you are repentant, that you are remorseful, he will still strike . . . but pleading and begging for forgiveness seem to lessen the pain. . . .

I did not beg you, my whip-wielding Muslim brother. Did I! How many people had you whipped for my flesh to know that you are skilled? Brother! I did not tell you that I did wrong. I did no such wrong! I did not do so, bastard brother. In what Arabian poison had you soaked your whip the previous night for the wounds to immediately become infected, to start smelling so foul that even the attendants in the emergency room were too revolted to drain the pus? Afraid, you wear a black executioner's hood. Without seeing I can see your eyes, looking after each strike to see how deep the whip has sliced flesh. Your boss had taken a bribe not to hit hard. But you hit hard. You hit to tear through flesh. The gratification of tearing through it gratified you. Tearing through all the slits that you were dying to slit but they did not spread open for you to slit them. And the moment you saw my face, not apish like you, and the moment you realized I am a wealthy haji's son, that I had slit all the slits you craved and hungered for, you struck harder.»

«You struck with the might of your dick to make up for all the times you had jerked off thinking about the tantalizing beauties you had seen on the street. Despite you beating them over the head to observe proper hijab, despite you stabbing pushpins into their foreheads because they had let a lock of hair out from under their headscarves, year after year those shrews made their coveralls more body-hugging to make you jerk off even more and perform even more ablutions afterward. Apple- and pear-shaped asses, firm or flabby, under snug coveralls are more arousing than when bare. Year after year, those hussies made their headscarves smaller and smaller, and year after year they adorned their hijab and coveralls with more silver and gold ribbons. Their hair, which emits erection-provoking rays, cascades out from under their scarves. The seductive hussies give you a hard-on.

And you flogged my back and you jerked off perhaps two or three times a day, and then, remorseful, you begged God for forgiveness so that God would not blind your eyes. Because the seventh-grade religion teacher told us that whoever jerks off will go blind, and if any of us ever jerked off, he would know by seeing the circles under our eyes. And throughout the seventh grade, you sat in religion class with your beating hands cupped on your cheeks and your fingertips under your eyes for fear that the teacher would see that you had jerked off the night before. And a few years later, you realized that the religion teacher, who had dark sunken circles under his eyes, had tricked you. You did not go blind, you louse, because your eyes can perfectly space eighty lashes on a man's back. And your hands have become expert at gripping the hard shaft of a whip, fondling it, rubbing its middle up and down, and then the stinging cum of the electrical cable spurts out so hard that it slashes through flesh. . . . So you whip well and slit me open, you whip not just to tear my spine's hymen, but to tear my ass, too. . . . You keep whipping and I keep thinking that the best way to not let you, Muslim brother, and the greedy onlookers in the circle hear my moans is for me to think about all the times I spread them open and thrust into them. I thought about Khazar who either did not know how or was too timid to talk dirty, but had the raunchiest of raunchy groans, far more vulgar than the most vulgar words. And I kept thinking about the times when, like you, I thrust hard and repeatedly to drive her mad, and I kept asking, What do you want? . . . What am I giving you? And she never spoke its name. But as you beat me, to the beat of your music I beat into Khazar and asked her to shed her shyness. And I kept asking, What do you want, pretty girl? Don't be shy! Tell me its name. What is this thing inside you? And she would say, What do you want me to say? Say it, girl! Say what your flower is saying to me! And as I beat into her, What do you want me to say? Tell me what to say! With the last strike of your whip, brother, Khazar lustfully cries out, My cock in your cunt. . . . And I, sleeping on my stomach, shift and the sting of a few scabs cracking open makes me think that Khazar did not say this, but if she had, what could she have meant? . . . Her cock in my cunt, or my cock in her cunt? . . . »

The scribe on his right shoulder had written:

> «I like the foul stench of pus in the welts on my body, and I hate my body for not being able to make more pus.»

The scribe on his right shoulder writes:

They arrive at the wartime location of the squadron's command headquarters. The dirt-filled burlap sacks that with the slavery of soldiers had been painstakingly and meticulously stacked around the trenches have frayed and fallen. The sturdy trench roofs have collapsed, too. Here and there, the black wires of long-range field telephones have surfaced on the dirt with no message to transmit.

Pirar nudges his armless side and points to the largest sandbagged trench set apart from the rest. Sergeant Major Vessali's prayer room seems to have fallen into greater ruin because of its size.

The scribe on his right shoulder had written:

Sergeant Major Vessali, one of the political ideologues at the base, has started his first day at the front.

"Sergeant Major, so they finally let you out of the base prison," Neiji quips. "Your wish to be at the battlefront that you championed and hailed for years has come true!"

With a prayer-stone crust on his forehead, Vessali snaps, "Everywhere is a battlefront. Everywhere is Karbala."

And he starts addressing the senior officers by reciting proclamations by Imam Khomeini about jihad, martyrdom, and the blessings of war.

Left:

It is noontime. Sergeant Major Vessali is saying his prayers out loud. With an exaggerated guttural Arabic-Iraqi accent he pronounces the letter H and with his tongue between his teeth he protracts the letter Zzzzzzzzz.

The non-praying officers of the company watch him, wink at each other, and roll their eyes. The whistle of an incoming shell passes overhead. Farther away, the shell explodes on the slope of a hill. With his forehead on his prayer stone, Vessali genuflects before his God. He breaks his prayer and with a terrified look on his face asks, "What was that?"

"Nothing. Just a mortar shell."

A few more explode nearby. This front's rations.

The officers with a grudge against Sergeant Major Vessali relish the moment and contemplate the gibes and jeers they will throw at him.

"You mean they hit this close?"

"If it were close," Amir cracks, "you and I would be at heaven's gates by now."

Private Bandari, who has recently been assigned to wash the officers' dishes and clean their trench, says, "The colonel sent us to dig trenches right where the Iraqis can hit us even with a straight shot from a tank."

"Kid, big talk is not for you," Sergeant Gholami snaps. "Go brew some fresh tea."

"I won't stay here even a week," Vessali stammers.

"Where to, Sergeant Major? You showed up late to the party and want to leave early? You're our guest for a good six months."

Vessali glares at him.

Left:

Pirar, back from leave, says, "I don't see that motherfucker Vessali around. Where is he?"

Private Bandari, whose scrawny figure and gaunt face cry of hashish, says, "Right after you left, one night he came up with the excuse that he had an urgent matter to discuss with the colonel. He left with the dinner truck and never came back. We heard that he had it out with the colonel over why the squadron headquarters doesn't have a prayer room. The colonel got scared and designated him to build one. And he assigned three soldiers to him, too."

Neiji is so furious that you couldn't draw a drop of blood from him.

"Sergeant Major Flute!" Amir says. "You can be sure that building the prayer room will take the entire six months he has to serve at the front. You were happy they sent the guy here. Now, it burns your ass and your business that he's bailed out."

Neiji, clearly frustrated that the idea of building a prayer room at headquarters, out of the Iraqis' range of fire, had not occurred to him, growls, "If two dicks fall from the sky, the first one will go up my ass and the other one will wait its turn. . . . Why didn't it occur to my chalk brain that headquarters doesn't have a prayer room? I hope every donkey's dick there is will screw Vessali up and down."

"Iranian or Iraqi donkeys?" Pirar asks.

And he winks at Amir.

On his left shoulder:

At the squadron headquarters, as he lowers his pants and squats down in the clean latrine opulently built with burlap sandbags and stones from the ruins of a house in a nearby town, he sees a notice pinned to the flap that serves as the door. "Brothers, this latrine was mistakenly built facing Mecca. To avoid offending Mecca, please sit sideways."

The scribe on his right shoulder writes:

The dirt road is still climbing. There are now more craters from shells and bombs than there are gullies.

«The Iraqi scout did a good job hitting this road.»

"Do you have any news of Neiji?" he asks Pirar.

"What made you think of him?"

"I don't know. . . . Did he come back alive or horizontal?"

"Neiji wasn't one to piss against a hard surface. He went home happy and healthy. The motherfucker must be retired by now."

The driver starts humming a Kurdish song.

"What are you singing, Champion?"

"A Kurdish chant."

"My man! Sing for us, too. Sing louder."

Pirar grunts in pain and again shifts in his seat. The driver bellows out the chant.

Amir hears the howl of a wolf in the wild and unforgiving mountains of Kurdistan.

The scribe on his right shoulder had written:

Again today, at the rendezvous point, he lies down behind the boulder and looks through his binoculars at the village of Baarin.

The colorful children are not in the schoolyard. In the mechanic's shop, the first building in the village, a Toyota pickup truck is over the service pit. A man dressed in local Kurdish clothes stands outside, smoking. There is a Kalashnikov slung over his shoulder. He is probably one of the Peshmergas of the Democratic Party of Kurdistan fighting against Saddam. On the mountain trail behind the village, a man is leading three mules carrying heavy loads. Peacock has come out of the schoolhouse and is pacing her usual path. He turns his binoculars to the section of the winding village road that is within his view. There are people coming and going. He thinks he has seen some of them before. Peshmerga lights his second cigarette. Peacock is still pacing back and forth. Perhaps she is not even a native of that village. Perhaps she studied in Baghdad. Perhaps she had to escape because she is Kurdish. Or perhaps someone in her family was a member of the Democratic Party, was executed, and she came under suspicion. She herself may have even been a member of the party and had to flee to Iraqi Kurdistan. Perhaps Mina and her friends visit this village.

Regulations state that we should not write what we guess or assume.

These are Amir's guesses.

No! Not to this extent. . . . These are not Amir's imaginings.

Right:

A strange and frightening wave and rumble pass overhead. No, this is not a cannon or mortar shell. Without his binoculars, he sees two MIGs flying away. They break the sound barrier as they fly over Baarin.

The villagers, who he wishes he could be with to help, frantically run this way and that.

«You poor things, don't you have an underground shelter?»

They will huddle under a roof, a staircase, someplace. Buddy Whoever seems to have some hiding hole. His wife and children tear out of the house with Buddy following them and run toward a corner of the yard and disappear. There are shadows running along the road. The man and his three mules are still walking down the mountain trail. And Peacock is standing still, looking up at the sky. The MIGs return. He hears Kalashnikovs being fired.

"You are wasting your bullets!" he says out loud.

An explosion blossoms some distance away from the houses.

"The pilot is a decent man. He dropped his bomb far off," Amir mutters.

The scribe on his left shoulder writes:

They come across the corpse of a burned and exploded car in the middle of the road. The driver brakes.

"End of the line!"

"We haven't reached the foot of the mountain," Amir says.

The driver points to the burned car.

"The road is not safe any further. There are mines."

They climb out of the truck.

Holding his back, Pirar mumbles, "What an ass I was to agree to this lunacy."

Amir takes his blanket roll and Pirar's backpack and sleeping bag from the back of the truck. The driver turns the truck around, making sure the wheels do not cross onto the shoulder of the road.

"Tomorrow afternoon at five, right here!" the man shouts unnecessarily loudly.

Amir shouts back even louder, "The day after tomorrow!"

Pirar yelps, "Why the day after tomorrow? Are you planning to lay an egg on the mountain?"

As if addressing the distant mountains, Amir thunders, "I am paying for it. The day after tomorrow!"

And he nods to the driver to leave. The man speeds off and with his head out the window he yells, "Be careful, you dimwits!"

In the cloud of dust, Pirar desperately cries, "Don't you leave us stranded!"

And he mutters, "Fuck the mother and daughter of this world and all its lunatics."

Pirar picks up the sleeping bag and blanket roll and leaves the heavy backpack for Amir to carry. They walk past the burned car. A few steps away, he bends down to examine an old wheel track. With his fingertips he sweeps away the dirt over a bump.

"Is it a mine?"

"No."

They both stare warily at the road leading to the foot of the mountain, as if only now that they're alone they see the mistake they've made.

"If you're scared, we can go off-road and hike," Amir says.

"Who knows what went on here after we left . . . the area may have changed hands a few times. The Iraqis left or the Iranians did, one good-for-nothing left and another came, and they all left behind their mines. You sure you aren't scared?"

"To my left ball."

"You don't have a left ball anymore."

Amir starts walking along the tire tracks. Pirar, after thinking for a while, veers off the road. With his hand on his back, he starts making his way through the weeds, thorn bushes, and colorful prickly nettles.

And he shouts, "Hey, diarrhea-head! One-armed cripple! If I get back to Tehran alive, what I will do to you they will write about in books."

"Eat my dust, you old broken-backed sap!"

The wind scatters Amir's shout. He picks up his pace to make Pirar suffer more.

Here and there, he sees pieces of shrapnel on the road. He picks up one that looks like a serrated knife. It makes for a good weapon. . . . They reach the foot of the mountain where the squadron's supply base was. Buckled trenches, rusted empty cans, rotted planks of wood from armament and ammunition crates that turn to dust at the slightest pressure, and shreds of frayed canvas caught between rocks or half buried in the dirt.

He is starting to remember faces with names that he is not sure belong to them.

Some faces had stayed in his memory, but he was never sure if they were real or if his imagination had put one person's nose on another person's face, given this one's voice to that one, and another's arm to. . . .

To him, the faces resemble children's drawings on facing mirrors.

That is exactly what I wrote, but in my own words.

Left:

The burlap sandbags from trenches that have turned to rubble have decomposed under the sun and the rain; the dirt inside them has poured out and hardened into rock. Pourpirar walks among them, looking as though he is trying to remember something. He angrily kicks a pile of empty cans and, a few steps away, a tattered canvas magazine belt—a lizard dashes out from under it. Drained of strength and tolerance for pain, he sits down on the ground and digs in his pocket for his pills. Amir takes out the water container from the backpack. He takes a sip and passes it to Pourpirar.

"Where did you go all those times when you said you were out looking for a better location for the observation post? For quite a while, all you did was wander off into the mountains. Where were you when you ended up hacking and hammering all of us?"

"What do you mean by 'all of us'?"

"All our men were killed, you were crippled, and I became what you see."

He sees a pile of rusted G3 shell casings.

"So you do remember some things," Amir snickers.

"You cocky shit! I have never in my life come across a creature like you. I have a bad back, but my arms are still strong. If you start weaving tales and lies, I swear on my father's spirit, I will shove these casings down your throat until you choke to death. And back home, I will tell your family that you wandered off in the mountains and I lost you, that you are dead. . . . Be a man and tell me what you remember."

"I remember things that I don't want to remember."

He is lying.

He is not lying.

He is lying.

He is not lying. He is not telling the truth either.

"It was somewhere I went to watch people," he says. "I think I felt lonely and sad all the time."

"What mischief were you up to the day they battered us with shells?"

"Was I a good scout?"

"Yes. Why do you ask?"

"Then I didn't do anything wrong. I was not up to any mischief. . . . Did I ever go on leave?"

"How many times are you going to ask me that? You would go only once every three or four times when it was your turn. But the last few months, you went regularly, you were itching to go."

The scribe on his right shoulder had written:

He anxiously circles the garden walls. Iraqi MIGs have taken Tehran's virginity, but the walls show no signs of having been bombed.

He thinks it is unlikely that they would recognize him in army fatigues. Still, he crouches down between the cottonless bushes in the cotton field until the garden gates open and Reyhaneh and Mother walk out, probably to wait for the car service.

> «Well, they managed to survive the bombardments. And to my left ball if Agha Haji has croaked.»

The scribe on his left shoulder writes:

"We have to get going," Pirar says.

"Let's go! I remember somewhere along the way there was the skeleton of a mule."

"So you're saying that in this huge shitty world, the only important thing for us to come across is a dead mule?"

On the steep trail, he starts to feel something happening in his head because he has not been taking his pills. Following Pourpirar at a safe distance, he kneels, holds back the stump of his left arm, and pounds it on the ground hard enough for pain to churn in his shoulder.

The trail has been wiped away in certain areas. He is afraid Pirar will get them lost in the mountains.

On his left:

Exhausted, he cannot go on. Pourpirar disappears behind a turn. Drenched in sweat and not knowing what is happening to him, Amir puts his ass down on the ground and takes a sip from the water container. He knows they need to conserve enough water to last them two days. There is no snow. There is no howl of mortar shell. There is no sly Iraqi scout, either. And his hand is shaking. Pirar walks back.

"What's the matter?"

"I'm fine. Just catching my breath."

"We just started, and you were the one dying to go."

"I . . . I'm . . . fine. . . . "

"Did you take your pills?"

"How many times are you going to ask me?"

"You didn't take them!"

"I'm starting to think that you've known all along whether I had a ring on my finger or not. You didn't tell me so you could con me out of some money. Well, tell me now. Don't drag me all the way up the mountain."

Pourpirar digs into the backpack, takes out his medications, and puts one pill from each bottle in Amir's hand.

"Are you going to take them or should I shove stones down your throat?"

He puts the pills in his mouth and points to the water container. Pirar holds it away from him.

"Swallow them with your spit."

> *«My spit has dissolved in their mouths, my spit has dried on their nipples, my spit has mixed with the sap between their legs, every part of me has scattered inside them or gotten lost in their wanting . . . then, was I just wasted spit, Moon Brow?»*

On his right shoulder:

On a steep slope, he manages to get ahead of Pirar and his bad back.

As he passes him, he asks, "Did I ever tell you about Khazar?"

"The one who killed herself because you were horrible?"

"I think so."

"Once in a while, at night, you would mumble something about her. You always got teary-eyed and walked out. But I would hear you shouting her name."

As they climb higher, his image of the mountain begins to change. To him, the mountain is a harsh and stingy old hag watching him from the corner of her eye. The small, mountain almond tree has lost its blossoms and the skin on its almonds has started to harden. He passes a cone-shaped ants' nest. He thinks the nest was here back then. Therefore, its present tense is the same as his present tense.

Pirar has fallen behind and is now sitting on the ground. Amir walks back. Pirar's eyebrows glisten with sweat. He tries to hide his faintness.

"Shall we catch our breath?" Pirar says.

"We shall catch our breath."

"Did you see our buddies?"

With his thumb, Pirar points up to the right side of the mountain. On a ridge, Amir sees wolves, or perhaps dogs. There are three of them. The way they stand side by side, they look like one wolf or dog with three heads.

"Wolves?" Amir asks.

"How would I know! If I were an animal kingdom expert, I could figure out what you are."

"If they are wolves, how are we going to defend ourselves if they attack us?"

"We can't defend ourselves. We don't have G3s."

"What will happen?"

"They will eat us. Then your rich family will hire people to come and find your bones, not mine."

"They're dogs. Stray dogs from the villages abandoned during the war. They were left behind. They turned into corpse-eaters. They may have even eaten my arm."

"Be careful they don't eat the rest of you. But I think they are wolves."

> «Meysam has to go and propose to Reyhaneh. I will tell this wild oregano plant between the rocks next to Pirar that it should prick Meysam's mind and make him understand that he must go and propose to Reyhaneh. With his parents, and a magnificent bouquet of flowers as an apology. By now everyone in the family knows that I have disappeared again. And the news has reached Meysam's good-for-nothing ears, too, that I am once more paying for what

> I did. He will feel sorry for Reyha. He will go back to her. I will tell this salty rock that I have picked up to beat into that dimwit's head that he must go back to her and propose, and to beat it into Reyhaneh's head to carefully listen to everything he and his parents have to say, and then to say, No.»

Pirar picks up a rock and hurls it toward the animals. Ouch! He grabs his back. The dogs or wolves follow the direction of the poorly aimed rock.

"Sergeant Pirar, were you this good when you were a scout? I guess if you try to scratch your underarm, you will probably burst your balls."

Left:

The jagged edge of the boulder he is leaning against irritates his back. He ignores it. He still enjoys torturing his body.

"Did we pass the mule's skeleton?"

"It wasn't there."

"If a skeleton that large wasn't there, then there is nothing left of my arm bones either."

"You mean we should go back?"

"Should we or shouldn't we?"

"If you've caught your breath, let's get going."

"Pirar, I think you still haven't caught your breath."

"You didn't catch your breath yet?"

And Pirar bursts into laughter. Like a hyena. With fits and starts he says, "Two . . . cripples . . . one with no back, one with no arm . . . who used to do this in five hours . . . have taken more than half a day . . . to. . . . "

By the looks of it, neither one has caught his breath. Amir wants to take a nap. Leaning against the boulder, he closes his eyes. He is certain Pirar will not sleep, so he can wake him in case the corpse-eating dogs approach them.

Left:

He dreams there are more flies coming, glowing like phosphor, buzzing. They circle him and then sit among the other flies on his hand and stab their stingers into his skin. Looking down, he sees them carefully filling the empty spaces on his hand. He watches them as they start to turn red. Farther away, a spotted horse, taking no notice of him, wanders around.

On his right:

Sometimes visible, sometimes not, the wolves, or dogs, move along the ridge parallel to them. As was customary at the front, they do not reveal their dread for fear that the other one might lose his nerve, too.

Right:

In the fleeting afternoon, they reach a spring. Pirar struggles to fill the water container from the shallow pool.

"How much farther do we have to go?"

Pourpirar points up at a dark blue peak above all the boulders, bushes, and thorns.

"It's up there."

On the far side of the mountain, two other peaks, taller or shorter, have come into view. Pirar cups his hands and spoons water into the container.

"Were you being honest when you said you can't remember if I was wearing a ring or not?"

"I don't know. I didn't give a damn. But when you asked me, I wondered that maybe . . . I don't know. And then I figured out that you were scheming to make me say yes . . . just the way you conned me into signing that letter of complaint against the lieutenant colonel."

With his right hand he pulls the backpack's strap over his left shoulder and picks up the blanket roll and sleeping bag.

The mysterious scent of the mountain's night has started floating in the air. A blend of the perfume of short-lived medicinal herbs, purple ferns, mountain poppies. . . .

«Maybe my nose's imagination is imagining these scents.»

. . . the smell of wildflowers, locoweeds, and thorn bushes that believing they are the mountain's guards have sharpened their feeble thorns and prickles.

The wolves, or dogs, are following them in the distance. Now, darkness has risen to their midsection.

"They are not going to give up until they have eaten us," Pirar says. "Are you sure they're dogs? Look and see if you can tell whether their tails are erect or hanging between their legs."

"You go over there and check, and then come and tell me."

They look at each other and laugh. They're now talking to each other the way they did at the front.

"Let's toss a coin to see if they are dogs or wolves. Heads, wolves, tails, dogs."

Ignoring him, Pirar says, "If they're dogs, then they should still have some fear of people in their guts. Shouldn't they?"

"You're right. But if they aren't?"

"Then fear of people is not only not in their guts, it's not in their asses either."

"Meaning, there is only one way for us to find out."

"I am finally starting to like you, nutcase."

Eye to eye, they read each other's mind. They run their hands over the ground and pick up a few rocks.

With two in each fist, Pirar says, "Shall we?"

Hollering, they charge towards the wolves/dogs. Fifty yards away, they hurl their rocks. They stop, catch their breath, pick up more rocks, and again shouting, "Haaaaaaaa! Hooooooo!" they run toward them. Their war cries become synchronized. Wilder. And just when they're about to collapse, the three animals leap back and run away.

Pirar, on his hands and knees, laughs. Amir, kneeling, rests his forehead on the ground, and chortles and coughs.

"They were dogs," Pirar says.

"I told you so."

"Even if dogs pretend to be wolves, in the end they are only dogs."

Right:

At 12:11, exhausted, they drop to the ground. The moon has set and they can no longer see the trail.

"We'll camp here," Pirar says. "We're close to the peak."

He arranges Amir's blanket half under him, half over him, and unrolls his own sleeping bag. The weather is pleasant enough that he will not need to zip it up. He opens a can of tuna and a can of roasted eggplants and offers Amir his share with a slice of bread. Amir crosses his legs and nestles the can between them.

"There's no red meat in it, is there?"

"I thought the mountain air would put some sense in your head . . . no, there is no red meat, nutcase."

Then, lying down, for a while they silently stare at the sky that seems to have warped under the weight of its stars. A jackal howls in a valley.

"When we were kids," Pirar says, "we were told that if we made a wish the instant we saw a shooting star, our wish would come true. The morons! They shot all those shooting stars into the air and none of my wishes came true."

"When I was a kid, I was told that shooting stars are God's flaming arrows. The minute Satan tries to come to earth, God shoots a flaming arrow at him to stop him . . . I think God's aim is not good at all."

"Or the poor thing has gotten old and useless like us. Only God knows!"

They chuckle.

"When you said I was itching to go on leave, did I ever tell you why?"

"I think you went to see someone. Obviously a girl. Contrary to your gutsiness that was well known in the squadron, you seemed to have lost your spunk. You would take your clean clothes, and you would ask Eskandar, blessed be the dead, to tidy up your hair. You would not sleep all night. And in the morning, as soon as they radioed that the lieutenant colonel had signed your pass, you would fly down the mountain. You ran. I used to say, 'This dimwit lieutenant will finally end up falling off a cliff.'"

"I never mentioned her name?"

"Even if you did, I don't remember it. Once after you came back, you babbled some nonsense that the Kurds wanted to kidnap you."

Pirar laughs.

"You were always weaving tales," he goes on. "But that one time, you really made me laugh. Behind your back, I used to say, 'Just my luck. If two dicks fall from the sky, one will go up my ass and the other one will wait its turn. If the Kurds had taken this lunatic hostage, we would at least be rid of him for a while, and he would drive the dimwit Kurds as nuts as he is and we'd be rid of them, too.'"

The scribe on his left shoulder had written:

He's still not used to his face without a four-month-old beard. The pleasure of the bath after two months at the front lingers in his body. He decides to follow this sidewalk on a street in Kermanshah whose name he doesn't want to know, to follow it until he is lost and forced to ask someone the way back to his inn.

"That's something to do. . . ."

As he walks, he feels his business weighing between his legs.

> *«The bastard! It's full of semen. See, Khazar! I told you I don't unbuckle my belt for anyone but you. If this Islamic Republic had not burned down the whorehouses, had not turned the whores into charcoal, I would take a taxi to Kermanshah's brothel just out of spite for you. Kaveh used to say, If you feel your gun when you jump over a street gutter, you know it's loaded. . . . The bastard! At the bathhouse, no matter how long I jerked it with soap on my hands, it didn't fire a single bullet. . . .»*

Right:

He bites into his egg salad sandwich and takes a sip from the bottle of Islamic Revolution's Coca-Cola that has the fake, watered-down taste of date molasses. A girl walks into the sandwich shop. He eyes the curve of her proportionate behind (according to the scribe on his left shoulder) under her khaki coverall. Her hair is so abundant and long that even her Kurdish headscarf cannot hide it. Her large Kurdish eyes have the startling depth of the cliffs between the peaks of Kurdistan's mountains. She glances at him in his officer's uniform and turns away with disdain.

"Sir," Amir asks the shopkeeper, "does your Kermanshah have a nice place to visit for someone who has nothing to do while on leave?"

Busy preparing the girl's sandwich, the Kurd says, "The best place in Kermanshah is Bisotun. Go there and enjoy it, Tehrani lieutenant. Thousands of years ago, King Darius wrote an engraved inscription there for you. And he sent you his regards, too."

"If King Darius knew what dear Islam is doing to his country, he would not have done such a thing. In fact, he would have showered us with obscenities."

The sandwich maker points to a notice on the wall: Political debates are prohibited!

They both chuckle.

From the corner of his eyes he sees the corners of the girl's sullen lips curve into a gentle smile. She takes the paper bag with her sandwich from the man and while he is getting her change from the till, she looks straight into Amir's eyes and with a wink and a nod motions for him to follow her.

She walks out.

Amir takes another bite of his egg salad sandwich. It smells stale. He tosses it in the trashcan and spits out whatever is in his mouth.

He puts his money on the counter and says, "If King Darius knew you would one day make a sandwich like this, he would never have set foot in the champion-breeding land of Kermanshah!"

He walks out. The end-of-autumn sky, clear of the clouds that must have traveled to the mountains of war to delay an attack, is beautifully blue.

The girl is some fifty yards away. He follows her. She looks back and, seeing him, walks faster.

They continue down a street with barren land on one side and newly built and under-construction houses on the other. At the end of the street, the girl again turns to make sure that the handsome officer of the Islamic Republic's army who is on leave and has nowhere to go for some fun is still following her.

He tries to review the girl's face in his mind. Beneath a strange and somewhat masculine severity, there is beauty that does not dare flaunt itself.

They turn onto a winding alley flanked by old houses. He walks faster and stays one step behind the girl. This way, if passersby notice them, they will not think they're together. Looking away from the girl and at the wall along the alley, he asks, "Where are we going?"

"Follow me, enlisted lieutenant!"

"How did you know I'm enlisted?"

"Your looks and manner scream it."

A "Follow This Line" has started on the wall.

He falls back from the girl. The alley forks out like the agitated branches of a tree. Whenever the girl turns a corner and falls out of sight, at the next corner she stops and pretends she's looking for something in her handbag until he can see her again.

Tired of the cat-and-mouse game, again he walks up close to her.

"Where are you taking me?"

"To that nice place in Kermanshah you're looking for."

"Are you a prostitute?"

The girl continues to walk resolutely.

"If you want to follow me, don't interrogate me."

"How much do you charge? I have to see if it suits my pocket or not."

The girl stops. Amir walks past her. The girl sets off a step behind him.

"How much do you have in your pocket?"

"Seven hundred tomans."

"That's fine. You don't have a place, so follow me, we will go to my place."

The girl gets ahead of him. The line on the alley wall is still there. She walks over to a public telephone at the corner. She dials. Amir stops outside the booth, pretending he is waiting his turn.

He quietly growls, "Who the hell are you calling?"

"I want to make sure there isn't another customer at the house. Keep your distance!"

He moves away and tries to read the girl's lips, but he cannot.

He notices that there are now more Kurdish pedestrians in the alleys. He warns himself not to look back, but he feels the weight of their eyes on him.

Walking along, he again moves up to the girl and mutters, "I lied. I have more money. I don't want to hurry over to your place. I'm not like that. I will pay you more if you take me around the city. We can talk and if we get along, then. . . . "

"We will get along. We're very close to my house. Keep what you have to say until we are inside and comfortable."

Now he is certain that nowhere behind the walls and doors of these narrow alleys is there a bed waiting for him. The line on the wall ends. There is something written in Kurdish that he does not understand.

"No. I will pay you two, three times more than your other customers if you come to Bisotun with me, to walk around, to spend some time together. Then, if I see that I don't want to be with you, I will give you your money and go about my business, return to the front. But if I see that I want to, and you want to, then I will come to your house."

"It's obvious you're a beginner."

"Yes. Still a virgin."

"I don't have the patience for ham-handed clumsies and their fuss. If you are up for it, follow me. It's not far."

"I won't. I don't have the patience for ham-handed prostitutes and their fuss. If you want, you follow me. And here is your up-front pay."

He rolls three one-hundred toman bills and shoves them into a crack in the wall next to him.

"*Me* follow you, a good-for-nothing!?" the girl snickers.

Amir turns and walks away.

"Just the fact that you realize I'm a good-for-nothing means you know more than you let on."

Without looking back, he walks along the winding alleys with walls as tall as those of a fortress, hoping to find his way back to the main street.

When he reaches the street, he turns and looks back. The girl has followed him. Even from a distance, he can sense the anger in her wild eyes.

He slows down. The girl catches up with him.

"How can we get to Bisotun? Please be my guide."

"You really are an idiot! Follow me."

Left:

Sitting next to the girl on a minibus, he devours the pleasure of being close to a woman and seeing her steal peeks at him.

"I must be crazy," she says. "This is so reckless of me. We are not related. What are we going to say if they stop us? I'd better get off at the next stop."

"I'm in army uniform, the Morality Police brothers won't come near me. Even if they do, we can say we don't know each other and just coincidentally ended up sitting together on the bus . . . there's no reason to be afraid."

Sarcastically, he adds, "Unless the brothers know who you are and what you do."

"If you say any more of this rubbish, I will get off at the next stop."

"The next stop is Bisotun."

He expects the girl to pout and play coy because he has made her look sheepish. But this one does not seem to be into that sort of coquetry. Her anxiety is real.

Left:

They walk around Bisotun's reflecting pool. The girl is pensive and silent.

"Can I ask you my last good-for-nothing question?" Amir says.

"Do you ask anything but?"

"Did you come back for my money, my looks, or what?"

"None of them. I felt that you're really miserable and even more miserable because you are one of those people who understands how miserable and alone they are."

"So you're a charity organization for the miserable?"

Laughing, the girl says, "You said you wouldn't ask any more good-for-nothing questions."

"You have strange eyes. I've never seen eyes like yours."

"They are ugly."

"Don't try to make me say they are beautiful. Lots of people have probably told you how pretty they are. But your eyes must be hiding a lot of secrets to have become this dark. . . . They don't have the kind of beauty goofy poets write about."

"No one has ever said such things to me. And I don't want anyone to now."

"I've had a few pairs of eyes in my life, but none of them were the color of the gunpowder in a G3 bullet."

The girl looks stunned.

On his right shoulder:

The familiar reflection of a tree on the wide stream at the foot of the mountain and the timeless image of the mountain and its inscription and friezes on the water echo against the blue sky.

"Which front are you stationed at?"

"We've been instructed not to say. But wherever it is, we don't have anything to do with you Kurds. We're fighting the Iraqis."

"Does it make any difference to you who you kill, or who kills you?"

"I don't care who puts me out, but I choose who I kill."

"Champion!" the girl says sarcastically. "Have you chosen me to kill? My name is Mina. Why don't you have your name stitched on your uniform?"

Right:

As he rambles on, he wonders how, just like a simpleton, he has taken off his armor and is telling his life story to this fake-named Mina. He thinks perhaps it is because he knows the girl is a prostitute, or because he senses that she is neither that nor this. He has forgotten all about the heaviness below his stomach because the girl is listening to him so intently. . . . His lips are even ready to talk about Khazar.

"Let's go and look at the inscription in this Bisotun of yours."

From the foot of the tall boulder, he gazes up at the inscription of Darius the Great, King of Kings.

> «The nails have written the history of an empire that spanned half the world. The empire went with the wind, but the nails stayed.»

Tricking her, he asks, "What does it say there? I know that guy was one of our kings, but who is the poor slob under his foot?"

"Someone who wanted to rid the Persians of kings. His name was Keommana. . . . I can read cuneiform a little."

He remembers Noushin. How can a prostitute know the history of Persia from two thousand years ago? Only then does he notice that the girl is not wearing red lipstick or any other makeup. Her lips, with their bitter, secretive curve, look like they haven't seen the color of lipstick in years. As the girl gazes up at the inscription, Amir looks at her Aryan nose against the background of the boulder.

Only a vague and general image of Bisotun is being etched in his memory; the girl and her words are erasing it. But the statue of Hercules rising from rock, naked, lying on his side, a chalice in his hand, looking as though he has emerged victorious from a formidable challenge or has achieved an unachievable lovemaking, stays in his mind.

"That Hercules up there, that is me. I rose from mountain rocks to find you, to protect you."

And for the first time, Mina surrenders her eyes to his hunting gaze.

"Are you sure you can, lieutenant of the Islamic Republic army?"

For the first time, she sounds intimate, but seems to be observing him from some unknown place on high, as if assessing the ignorance of an ignoramus.

"I was just bragging."

Left:

Dusk falls as they stroll through ancient Bisotun. He likes Mina, and now he feels the weight under his stomach. The girl has been pensive and silent for a while.

"Shall we go back?"

"Go back?"

"To your place."

"So you have decided?"

"Yes."

Mina, insulted and insulting, snaps, "So you want to dump all your money at my feet."

"Yes. In the army they pay us a pittance and a little extra for being assigned to the front. I haven't had anywhere or any reason to spend it, other than giving some money to the soldiers going on leave to buy cigarettes for me. It has added up. So, I have a loaded pocket and a. . . . "

He decides not to finish his sentence.

They stand together and watch the stream. At dusk, its water reflects no mountain and no tree. It is the color of lead.

"I will finish what I was saying when we are back in Kermanshah," he says.

He speaks her name for the first time.

"Mina, don't take my good-for-nothing comments seriously. I know you are something else. . . ."

"Everyone says the same thing."

"And you say this because you have tried everyone?"

They step away from each other to avoid attracting attention, and with their backs turned, they both laugh.

Right:

Waiting for the minibus in the early evening on the sprawling plain outside Bisotun, safe from the war, he whispers, "Who are you?"

Mina turns away from him, trying to conceal the expression on her face.

Right:

I should have written the line, At dusk, its water reflects no mountain and no tree.

I am faster than you.

Right:

They get off the minibus in Kermanshah. Now, in the dark, they both feel timid. He supposes that if they were in some other country, he would invite the girl to his four-star hotel. They would have dinner, they would openly have a few drinks, and then freely and without fear they would go up to his room. And he remembers his bare-bones room at the Welcome-Guest Inn where the manager stands by the front door, watching the guests like a hawk, acting like he will alert the Morality Police the instant he sees the slightest transgression. Amir quickly concludes that it would be idiotic even to entertain the notion of bribing the man to turn a blind eye as he sneaks Mina into his room.

Walking behind her, he asks, "Are we going to your place?"

"No, silly enlisted officer!"

"Stop teasing. Let's be together."

"No."

There is a new sternness in her tone, and a hint of a plea. And he knows that persistence and honeyed words will be useless.

"Go back to the front. You are a good human being. The world has very few good human beings. Try not to get killed. And go back to Tehran and make amends with your family."

"I knew you weren't what you pretended to be. I'm sorry I gave you a hard time. You were playing a role, so was I."

"You have no idea how lucky you are!"

"What do you mean?"

"Nothing. I just blurted it out."

"I don't go on leave often—I stay at the front. This time I did and I was lucky to have run into you. I still have five days left. I have nothing to do in this town, and I don't want to go back to the front . . . may I see you again?"

"Where are you staying?"

"Welcome-Guest Inn."

A knowing smile breaks the stern lines of Mina's lips.

"I know where it is."

Amir anxiously asks, "But how will we contact each other?"

"I will find you if I want to," she says sternly. "And don't follow me any further. It's not good for me, as you Tehrani kids say."

"I am going to call you Moon Brow . . . your eyes are as dark as the night's night, which makes your forehead as bright as the moon's moon."

Mina stops. She looks at him with regret, with longing.

"Go, Amir!"

He cannot tell whether her words are a command or a supplication. Mina walks away. Mina, with the swing of her behind under her coverall. Mina, at the corner of an alley. And then, Mina, disappearing into the alley where a man in baggy Kurdish pants leans against the wall of the first house, smoking. He does not appear to be keeping an eye on him. Mina. . . .

On his left shoulder:

At 9:30 in the evening, he gets up from the humble steps in front of the inn to drift back to his room. For twelve hours, he has sat on these steps and looked around, hoping Mina would come. And she has not.

On his right:

And he is spending the second evening after the only evening with Mina on the inn's front steps. And she has still not come. He reflects with envy on the beautiful words he could have spoken to her that he did not, and the meaningless words—death's morsels—that he did speak and should not have.

He now knows that tomorrow, the fourth day of his seven-day leave, will also end with Mina not coming. Every few hours, he half-walks, half-runs to the long alley where the girl turned and disappeared, and then, regretful and agitated by the spiteful glares of the Kurds, he quickly returns to the inn, worried that Mina might have gone there.

Right:

Late at night, frustrated by sleeplessness and the dank smell of his room, he goes out. He takes the bag with the blue spray paint he's bought. This time, he walks the entire length of the road and all its alleys. He looks at the lit windows one by one, hoping to see a familiar shadow. He goes to the public telephone at the corner. He thinks it will probably end up badly for the girl if he writes her name. On the wall next to the telephone, he writes, "The waiting enlisted officer," and then he clumsily draws a few shapes that resemble cuneiform letters.

And after this wall, he continues to spray his make-believe cuneiform on several other walls as far as the main road. There, with what is left of the spray paint, he writes, "Moon Brow, shine!"

The scribe on his right shoulder writes:

At 9:04, for the eighth time, he asks, "When will we get there? What if you have taken us the wrong way?"

And Pirar, grumbling and cursing under his breath, does not answer. There is no sign of the trail that existed during the war. The rugged boulders and cliffs that continue to move closer seem like a place where he once might have lost his way in a dream.

Pirar does not let on, but the water container now seems to weigh a ton. Amir, drenched in sweat, stops for him to catch up.

"Give it to me."

"Forget it, boy. I will carry it."

"I said, give it to me!"

"You are constantly looking for an excuse to stop and rest! Why don't you just say you are about to croak, and we will stop? If you had moved faster, we would have reached the peak early last night."

"Yes, I know."

He takes the container from Pirar.

"Sometimes you would not go on leave for several months. Not even for a bath. You would melt snow in the kettle and ask Eskandar to pour it over you so you could wash yourself. I never saw you take off your undershirt. You just rubbed the soap over it. Why? We thought you had your beloved's name tattooed on your back."

"I had my father's name tattooed on my back," Amir says as he sets off.

Left:

He kneels next to a thorny cardoon bush. It offers a good pretext to rest.

"Wow! This is cardoon!"

"It is, but it's no good, it has gotten thorny."

He gives the blade-like piece of shrapnel he found along the way to Pirar.

"Dig it up and let's eat it. I think back then we used to eat them. . . . Did we?"

"No."

In their veiled rivalry, Pirar, too, now has an excuse to sit down. With the edge of the shrapnel, he digs up the thick root. And they both bite into a piece of the cardoon. As he chews, Amir thinks, It tastes lousy!

But somewhere in the back of his mind flows a thought.

> «It is beautiful, the sharp taste of thorn. Earth's water with the flavor of earth's air with the heat of earth's fire . . . earth's earth!»

"We are conserving our food supply," he says.

"Are you planning for us to wander around these mountains for the rest of our lives?"

He's starting to feel the effect of not taking his pills. Sweating profusely while hiking up the slope, heaviness in his chest, toward the left. . . .

> «It would be beautiful if up on the peak, next to my arm, I have a heart attack and am set free. This time, Pirar will carry my real corpse down the mountain. He will curse at me the entire way, but he will deliver me to the garden gates, to Reyhaneh. . . . But now it is time to kiss ass.»

"You are the boss, Sergeant. But if you stop being stubborn, you will be even more of a boss. Be nice and admit that the cardoon tastes good."

Pirar returns the shrapnel and stares at him skeptically.

On his right:

He doesn't see any remnants of mortar shells or even empty cartridges around.

"Sergeant!" he shouts. "So where was that godforsaken war?"

"It's as if it never was!"

Other than its ancient echoes, up here the mountain has no relics of the explosions, the shrapnel wounds, the shouts and curses of the living, the howls of the injured. And its ordinary sounds seem to have ghosts of stone.

Amir stands at the edge of a low cliff, unzips his pants, and says, "Come here, Sergeant!"

Pirar understands. He stands next to Amir and unzips his pants, too.

"I piss on every shell and bomb!" Amir hollers at a distant peak.

"Let it fly!"

Right:

Exhausted, their legs tread forward automatically. Now and then their knees knock into each other. The contest of prides has ended. Old and long-ignored aches and pains take their revenge. The thin mountain air lends them a hand.

"What misery did we face after you were hit?" Amir asks.

"All I remember is that I wanted to laugh. Both of us screwed, slumped on the ground . . . you, unconscious, thinking that I would be a man and save you, and I, conscious, praying that someone would be a man and rescue our half-dead bodies. I don't remember anything else. I woke up in a field hospital. I looked around and was happy that your ill-omened face was nowhere near me."

Occasionally, he sees rocks that look different from the others. And each time he thinks there must be something buried, hidden, underneath them. If it weren't for Pirar's wisecracks, he would have knelt and dug under them.

The scribe on his right shoulder had written:

Bisotun is five miles away. He sees a trail that branches away from the road. Sitting in the middle of the minibus, he shouts to the driver, "Sir, stop!"

He nudges Mina and motions for her to follow him.

The minibus drives away, and there is surprise and apprehension in Mina's eyes. Amir points to the hills the trail passes through.

"We are going to a cozy place in the middle of those hills to have a picnic with no prying eyes around. . . . "

And he triumphantly taps the bag he is carrying.

"Hey, Amir, I'm telling you now, you are not going to mess around with me!"

"No, not as long as you don't want to. On whose life would you like me to swear?"

Mina takes a switchblade from her pocket, pushes its lever, and holds the released serrated blade up to his eyes.

"No need for you to swear. . . . But these trails lead to villages. The people there are nosy. They will snitch on us."

"Leave that to me, an army officer. I'm good at camouflaging."

Right:

Behind a hill away from the trail, he spreads the bedsheet he has taken from his room at the inn. He's brought one apple, one orange, three sandwiches, two bottles of water, and a few pastries local to Kermanshah. One by one, he proudly arranges them in front of Mina. The slope of the hill is a field of cardoons whose leaves in these final days of summer have grown wide and unshapely, but they are green. Now and then, the breeze brings the scent of a wild fragrance.

"My name is Ashraf. I lied when I told you it was Mina."

"I know. What kind of work do you do?"

"I'm a teacher."

"That is a lie, too."

The trace of a faint smile appears on Ashraf's lips and fades away. She lies down on her back and with her hands tucked under her head she stares at the wide-open arms of the blue sky.

"Teaching Kurdish in schools is forbidden. The children grow up speaking Kurdish at home, then at the age of seven they start first grade and a non-Kurdish teacher starts teaching them Persian. I give private lessons to teach them to read and write in Kurdish."

"You barely have a Kurdish accent."

"I had to change it. To sound like you Tehranis!"

"I won't ask why. I want you to stay an enigma so that I fall in love with you. . . . Will you teach me cuneiform, Miss Teacher?"

"You are too dense to learn it."

And staring up at the sky, Amir blurts out the question that has been simmering in his mind.

"Are you a member of a leftist group?"

The girl does not answer, but closes her eyes. Amir sits up.

"May I have your knife?"

He takes the knife from Ashraf and puts the uncertain blade against the orange's equator.

"You must know the tale of the Bitter Orange and Citron Orchard. I've always ended up with a girl from a citron tree. And the last one died. You are my first bitter orange. When I cut this in half, you will jump out of it and ask for water. I have brought water. So, you will stay alive."

"Pampered lieutenant! Don't get romantic."

"Someone used to say the same thing to me. She died. I am still alive, which means I am not a romantic, I am a good-for-nothing."

And he cuts the orange in half.

Perhaps feeling sorry for him, Ashraf theatrically exclaims, "Water! Water!"

Amir holds the half orange over her lips. The girl opens her mouth. The juice of the orange, the color of the glistening midday sun, streams down. And Ashraf spits out a seed.

The scribe on his right shoulder writes:

At last, the mountain peak, the plateau, appear before them as they turn behind a boulder. Pirar plunks down on his backside, on the rocks and thorns. Amir stops a few steps in front of him to take a break for the hundredth time. Pirar takes a few deep breaths and takes a pack of cigarettes from his khaki raincoat pocket. He inhales the smoke with relish, and, holding his back, he stretches, arches, and groans.

In between coughs, he says, "Drop your load! We're there!"

The scribe on his right shoulder had written:

> «How very strange you are Mina, Ashraf, and Moon Brow that you are! I am becoming certain that you are impossible, that you should not be. . . . My sweet! In this world, let it not be that you were a sweetheart and were not sweet, because even if you are Ashraf and Mina and Moon Brow and a hazy face, they will find your trail in the waters of the river you waded, in the meadow where happy unknowing sheep grazed, they will trace your gun as far as the stone mountain hut in Kurdistan, as far as the drunken Persian garden whose blossoms they have converted to Islam, and they will track you down. They will smell the sweat that dripped from between your toes onto the earth, they will feel the marks the balls of your feet and the weight of the firm muscles in your beautiful calves left on the chamomile. With the tip of their tongues they will taste the drops of hatred that trickled on the heap of autumn leaves from the oyster between your thighs, they will smell your hopes of love on the breath of foxes and on the poisonous mushrooms in the woods, and they will find you. Because you are so very much too much with your so very many names, you secret full of secrets and so very much too much for this world.»

The scribe on his right shoulder writes:

He struggles to free his neck from the backpack's strap and throws the bag to Pirar. He imagines that they were both on the verge of dying, both knowing that if they had taken one more step, they would have collapsed and died. And proud Pirar, who can barely pretend that the weight of fatigue has not crushed him, carefully looks around, searching.

Amir eyes the rocky terrain that looks very different from the image he had painted in his mind, rock by rock, slope by slope, blood by blood.

But for all the mountain's long life, this place is as it should be. A flat plateau large enough for two tents set a few yards apart, and then a steep rocky slope to the tip of the peak wide enough for an observation post trench. There are more majestic and more secure summits far away, dark blue, loftier than this peak.

Here, behind the boulders, safe from the sun, there is still some snow from the previous winter. Coated with wind-blown dirt and weeds.

"Are you sure this is where we were?"

"We were right here."

"It's really crappy."

"It was even crappier."

He tries not to act like a rash idiot. He sits down because he has to sit down.

"Good."

"Very good."

He looks to his left and right.

The mountain wind's winds, the mountain rain's rains, and the mountain's snow have in the absence of desiccated thorns changed everything.

Pirar, slumped on the ground, takes a pill and a sparing sip from the half-empty water container. Amir wants to climb up to the highest height, to his observation post, to gaze out at the distant valley and the plain he had stared at for so long.

Other than some rocks heavier than the heave of exploding shells, nothing remains of the observation post. He sees no trace of the slow-passing time they spent there, no trace of his eagle eyes pinned on the Iraqis' route and the visible segment of their row of trenches, of the moments of being in control of whether they lived or died . . . but young thorn bushes are growing everywhere.

"There are no skeletons around here."

"I guess the bodies were evacuated."

Unexpectedly, Pirar continues . . .

"I knew that if I wanted to save your arm, I had to keep it fresh. I remember. It was Eskandar's poncho, or someone else's, I think it was half burned, it was caught on something, somewhere around here. I told myself, plastic will keep it fresh until they sew it back on. I wrapped it tight in the poncho, then I think I bundled it in a piece of canvas from our tent. An hour passed. Then two hours. I realized it was too late for your dead arm. I said to myself, By the time Amir makes it to the field hospital, he will be dead, too. I will put him over my shoulder and start down the mountain, and halfway we will meet up with the medics. The Iraqis had stopped firing. There was a shell crater, I don't know how deep. Burying makes your head work better. I covered it with dirt and stacked rocks on top of it . . . look around and find it."

He does not need to strain his eyes too much. It is there. The sun, the rain, and the snow seem to have wanted to preserve it. Pirar follows the direction of his gaze.

"I think your guess is right."

He had imagined that the instant he found his arm's grave, he would tear at the snow-worn, rain-worn, timeworn dirt with his fingers and nails until he reached it. Over there, rocks larger than the palm of his hand, in a cluster like they were once stacked in the shape of a pyramid.

"All right then . . . let's go back down."

Pirar gapes at him.

"Fuck you!"

On his left:

He has been sitting there, staring at his arm's grave, for one hour and thirty-four minutes. Pirar has fallen asleep. He wishes he had a pair of binoculars so that he could look all the way down there at the Iraqis' line.

"What should I do?" he asks himself out loud.

Pirar opens an eye.

"Will you dig it up?" Amir pleads.

Pirar looks at his empty sleeve.

And he is again sweating heavily; he feels his nerves straining, stretching in different directions. He does not want to take his pills. Pirar throws the rocks to the side and claws at the earth. It has hardened . . . Amir tosses the bladelike piece of shrapnel to him. Pirar digs, digs.

The scribe on his left shoulder had written:

After three wakeful nights and wait-full days, drowned in sleep, he hears someone knocking on the door. The raps started somewhere in the folds of the fallout of insomnia.

At ten in the morning, the inn manager, the sarcastic smirk on his lips warning of caution . . .

"Lieutenant, some woman is at the front door asking to see you."

You wrote this differently before.

Back from the battle of waiting, he hastily pulls on his uniform, which has wrinkled even tucked flat under the mattress.

He walks alongside Mina.

"I waited so long."

"It shows. I should not have come, but I did. This thing has made me weak. I should not let it. You are dangerous."

"Are you trying to make me feel indebted to you?"

"Precisely."

"Where are we going?"

"Bisotun again. I think it is safe there. We will blend in with the crowds."

"As long as you are with a second lieutenant of the Islamic Republic army, you are safe."

"As long as you are with me, you are not. . . . The moment I saw you, I regretted coming to the inn. I don't know why I couldn't stop myself."

«There is no place safe in this world for you and even for me—scum of Agha Haji, scum of the whip, the war, and Khazar. There is nothing in your face or manner that resembles Khazar, but you have something that makes you resemble her. Damn you all for the parts of you that resemble each other, which, no matter what I do, still end up resembling each other, and they devastate me.»

The scribe on his right shoulder writes:

Pirar pulls the bundle out of the dirt. The frayed canvas still has a hint of green.

"I'm not opening it. It's all yours!"

He tosses it to Amir and turns away, as if from a putrid stench that Amir cannot smell.

He kneels over the corpse of his arm. Strands of the canvas's warp and weft have fused with the decomposed plastic poncho. He slowly unwraps it. Muddy rainwater, snow, and fat have spread a black coat over the bones. They are scraggy and withered. They look like a bulbous root that against its will grew too long and turned into an unknown plant. With his fingers, he flicks at the wrist bone. Dirt and a strange scab fall off like pieces of old, cracked, and bulging plaster. The finger bones snap off. He snatches the fourth finger from the right, or the second one from the left, from among the dregs and death of the other fingers. He rubs it. Black powder sifts through his fingers, and then, it is there, on his black palm, an old, faint tinge of yellow.

Pirar has crept over to him. Both of them gaping and at a loss.

Amir starts to tremble. The only control he can exert over himself is to lock his fingers over the ring before his body gives in to the convulsions.

Pirar grabs his shoulders and shakes him.

"What the hell happened?"

Ice-cold, he is quivering like a flame.

"Did you take your pills?"

Like waves, the spasms roll down from his head and up from his feet, and collide in his midsection to create new waves that move up and down his body.

Frantically, Pirar splashes water on his face. Frantically, he takes the pills out of the backpack. Amir's jaws are locked. The pill Pirar is trying to force into his mouth gets lost in the foam oozing from his lips. Desperately, he splashes more water on his face. Desperately, he pins his shoulders to the ground to stop him from shaking.

Amir is in the same condition he was the day he showed up deranged and hysterically shouting, "They're all dead!" And suddenly the earth and sky were on fire and the ground shook.

Pirar wipes away the foam from Amir's mouth with the cuff of his empty sleeve and pulls him up to rest his back on his lap. He is half conscious. The seizure has drained him of energy.

"Open your mouth!"

And Pirar gives him the first pill. Then the second one.

The scribe on his right shoulder had written:

It is 12:20. Time for his rendezvous. He is on the east side of Ferdowsi Circle, waiting for Mina or Ashraf. There is no sign of the old woman in red. He sees the girl coming from a distance.

"It's safe! Come!" she whispers as she walks past him.

They meet in the first side street.

"Thank you for coming," he says.

And he nervously adds, "Ashraf, I think our garden. . . . "

The girl chuckles, "My real name is Hanna."

"I don't believe this one either."

"I came all the way from Kermanshah to this horrible city just for you, which means I now have to trust you."

"Lady! I checked the garden. It is safe. Whether I am there or not, you can hide whatever you want there. And whether I am there or not, you can jump over the wall at night and take whatever you have hidden. This Islamic garden is the safest place. No one will suspect anything."

Dressed in his officer's uniform, his second lieutenant insignias on his shoulders, his leave pass in his pocket, he feels he can protect the girl.

"I won't ask what it is you want to hide. Whatever it is, wrap it in plastic and put it in a box. Otherwise, when they water the garden it will corrode."

"Two-bit second lieutenant! Do you even understand what kind of a country you are living in? The way you openly say anything and everything makes me suspicious again that you might be an informant. Why do you want to help me so much?"

"I told Khazar that I loved her, and she died. I will not say it to you . . . I will take you to the garden tonight and you will find out for yourself whether I do or not. Somewhere safe where I can touch you . . . I mean, just sit next you without fear and anxiety. Then you will know."

"The minute you touch me in your Islamic garden, your God will turn you into stone. Where would you like to go now?"

"The goldsmith's arcade at the bazaar, shopping for engagement rings . . . if you will say yes."

"How many times must I tell you? I cannot wear a ring. My comrades should never find out I am with someone like you."

"In secret . . . like everything else we do."

On his right:

And this is how he ends unburdening himself . . .

"Like it or not, I was guilty. Wasn't I? I was a good-for-nothing. Wasn't I? I was the last person responsible for Khazar's life. I was responsible for her death, too. My friend who knew about us tried to fool me into believing that it had nothing to do with me. But how could that be? A girl who makes you go and save tiny fish trapped on the sand . . . when she kills herself, is it even possible for me to not be responsible for her death?"

"No, it is not possible. . . . What is good about being alive is that, like it or not, responsibilities keep piling up on your shoulders. The only time you are not responsible for anything is when you are dead, two-bit lieutenant!"

He looks at Hanna. Whether he agrees with her or not, he feels he has fallen in love again.

On his right:

They walk up to the window of a small jewelry shop. Although Hanna has said that the bazaar is safe for her, she is constantly biting her lips and looking around.

He thinks those two rings have been there for a long time, waiting for them.

The scribe on his right shoulder writes:

He wakes up. He is still weak. His muscles feel numb. He is lying on his blanket. Pirar is sitting to the side, eating a can of beans.

"I thought you croaked."

He does not remember the seizure.

"What happened?"

"Nothing. You didn't croak."

He opens his fist and looks at the greasy and black-streaked ring. He stares at it for four minutes and three seconds. And then . . .

"Thank you."

"You sound like a human being again."

Pirar turns away, but not before Amir sees tears welling in his eyes. A white cloud in the sky gleams blindingly. He wants it to look like a white peacock and it does not. Pirar opens a can of beans for him, too, and puts a spoon in it.

"Do you remember the girl's name?"

"I will."

He cannot sit up. He turns on his side and leans against the rock next to him. Pirar lodges the can between two of the stones that marked his arm's grave so that he can spoon out the beans.

Left:

Pirar buries the arm bones in the same hole without wrapping them in the poncho. He cleans his hands by rubbing them with dirt.

"I think you are feeling better. We should start heading down."

"Help me up."

Still sluggish, it's hard for him to keep his balance with one arm. He struggles up to the peak to look at the plain below. He doesn't know why he feels so sad. But there is a warm and gentle comfort in the sorrow. He puts his hand in his pocket to make sure the ring is there.

> *«There must have been nights when facing this plain I whispered her name. Return its echo to my mind, plain of plains!»*

A few clouds are gently floating in the sky. Their shadows hover over the greenish-yellow foothills on the far side of the plain.

> *«Return the reflection of her name to my mind, mountain of mountains!»*

Pirar packs the dirt on the grave with his foot and again stacks the stones on top of it.

"Are you still not going to tell me where the hell you went all those times you wandered off and ended up wreaking havoc on all of us?"

"Which direction would I go?"

Pirar, his back hunched in pain, points to the right and a downward slope in the mountain.

"Let's go, it can't be too far."

There is no footpath where others might have walked to guide them.

Left:

He again loses his way. They have reached a place where the mountain offers a view of distant landscapes.

"I am sure there was a village or a small town," he groans. "I would lie down on the ground and watch the people through my binoculars."

"As far as I remember, there were a couple of Iraqi villages behind this mountain. . . . To my balls! I don't care what the hell you were doing. Let's just go back."

> *«Even these good-for-nothing legs don't remember which direction they walked. Fuck you if you don't tell me which way you went!»*

"Let's go this way. Be a pal, Sergeant, come on."

"Huh! Listen to the faggot! After all this, he's telling me to be a pal! . . . You will finally get me killed on this mountain, you life-wrecking lunatic!"

Right:

After two hours and fifty-two minutes of wandering around, the instant they go around a ridge on a downward slope, he sees it. He stands there staring.

"That's it!"

The village is populated again. The survivors, the relatives of those who died, or the destitute driven from their own towns and villages have occupied the homes of the dead and are building new ones as well.

The village is far away. Without binoculars, they can see only the shadowy outlines of houses leaning against each other in clusters with narrow alleys between them. The stone schoolhouse is closer and recognizable. There are no colorful dots in it. It's the school holiday season.

With his eyes fixed on the village, he leans his hand against a boulder.

"I remember a village. Everyone suddenly died. I think they were my true family, instead of my good-for-nothing one."

The scribe on his left shoulder had written:

Two Iraqi MIGs break the sound barrier as they fly over the village.

"Filthy Ba'athists!" he growls. "Why?"

He watches people, terrified, running down the roads to their homes or underground shelters.

"Saddam is going to bomb them? His own country?"

The jets do not return. Relieved, he thinks they only wanted to frighten those poor people who want nothing but autonomy. He quietly laughs. He likes those seen and unseen people.

> *«Place to place around the world, people's flimsy happiness is different, but everywhere around the world people's fear is the same when they're being bombed—they all run and try to escape the same way.»*

The roads are empty. The schoolyard is empty. Perhaps behind the building there is a good underground shelter for the children and their teacher. And he sees the white smoke mushrooming before he hears the explosion.

"A heavy bomb?"

Another one.

"They are bombarding them! They're receiving coordinates. That's a smoke bomb."

And one after another, midget mushrooms of white clouds bulge here and there in the village. But this lazy whiteness is not the usual brown-black smoke and it is not from a smoke bomb. It is not rising. It is spreading on the ground like a heavy fog.

Now he understands. Breaking the sound barrier and then the barrage of cannon shells were a subterfuge to drive the people into basements and shelters and to shatter all the windows so that the gas can infiltrate the houses more easily. . . .

He sits up. He swallows his curses for the Saddam army like phlegm and shouts, "Go to higher elevation! Go up!"

He stands and hollers, "Get out of your basements! It's chemical gas!"

And the mustard gas patiently slithers and uncoils like a cobra. Even without seeing he can tell, sluggish and heavier than air, it creeps into every hole and through every gap it finds. He frantically looks through his binoculars, but he can't see through the smoke. He removes them from his fiery eyes and pounds his left fist on the boulder that is no longer concealing him. A pain like that of a bone fracturing restrains his rage.

Knowing there is nothing he can do exasperates him even more.

He wants to run to the village and warn those wretched people unknowingly huddled in some hole or hovel with their children in their arms, and his dazed mind knows that by the time he travels that long distance, they will all be dead.

He holds up his binoculars again. He sees Buddy Whoever's children. They are running across the yard. A shelter that is out of his view must have been large enough to suck in the curdled, milky smoke. Then he sees Buddy Whoever, carrying one of his children and running toward the shallow pool in the yard. Before he reaches water, the other children collapse. In the same place they played every day. Buddy, with his small child looking like she's been welded to him, plunges to the ground. It looks like his head hit the edge of the pool. His child under him. His wife must have not come out of the shelter. He has not seen her. . . .

And still, without seeing the new small mushrooms in the white fog, he hears more chemical bombs exploding. With every blast, a spike of horror shoots up his back. Long ago he had seen a person with epilepsy experience a seizure. He feels epileptic.

The white smoke has choked the school more than anywhere else. He does not see the colors of any colorful dots moving through the fog in the schoolyard.

He thinks of running back to his tent and to Pirar, perhaps he knows of a way to help those miserable people.

And shadows of baggy clothes, dark, khaki—Kurdish men's favorite color—appear and disappear in between the clusters of fog. Farther away, in another break in the gas, there are just khaki and green stains on the ground. Now the chemical bombs are mostly exploding in the southern section of the village, right where the wind will blow the gas toward the houses and down the roads.

Standing erect before that massacre, drenched in sweat, his hands shaking, he looks through his binoculars to perhaps find the location of the Iraqi artillery. The only thing he can do.

"I will fuck you, Saddamis! I will fuck you!"

And without seeing, he sees people coated with white, falling. Gently, with their backs or fronts facing the sky from which wrath rained.

The Kurd lies sleeping faceup or facedown beneath the Heavenly Realm that has at last bestowed upon him peace and rest away from strife and struggle in the mountains, away from war and pride. A white sheet covers him, his wife, child, sheep, the stray dog on his street, the sparrow in his tree. . . .

Should we be writing this? As a rule, these things should not be written.

At worst, our punishment will be to sleep on Amir's shoulders in his grave. It is not so bad—we won't have the hassle of writing on the shoulders of some spawn of Cain. After all the thousands of shoulders we have written on, we will at last rest, like that Kurd.

On his right shoulder:

> «I will raze their artillery unit to the ground.»

Now, he needs all his intelligence and skill as a scout to determine the coordinates of a target somewhere among the hills and mountains. He looks through his binoculars. His hands are shaking. Behind a distant hill he sees the haze from a cannon that has been fired.

He races toward his observation post, to get to his map, to his radio, to contact the artillery unit, to shout, They are killing everyone . . . to request fire. . . . He runs with all his sweat-drenched being, all the while growling, "I will stick one up your ass, Saddam . . . I will stick one up your artillery's ass and make it one with its cunt, you motherfucker! . . . I will fuck you up and down. . . . "

And somewhere in the back of his mind, there is a lament.

> «Khazar, forgive me for not having been as enraged then as I am now to stick one up your life and death's ass, to holler at you, to beat you until you dropped, because you had no right to do whatever you damn well pleased, you sweet crazy girl. . . . Forgive me for not having been as strong as I am now to fight you, to not let you take your life and take mine with it. . . . »

Like a wolf-dog, he tears across the slopes and rocks and ridges. He is out of breath; he feels seeing that white gas has burned his lungs, too. Images of Khazar, his wild drunken rant at home, the specter of the whip behind him rise with the palpitation in his stomach and the pounding in his head.

"I will pummel that artillery. . . . "

"Anyone who was alive. . . . "

Panting . . .

"Anyone who was a child. . . . "

His knees on rocks.

Gasp after gasp . . .

"Anyone who was a father, anyone who was a mother . . . was a sheep."

Panting, panting . . .

"A caterpillar under the leaf of a fig tree. . . . "

"Anyone who was a child underground . . . any . . . any . . . anyone who was someone . . . was an aunt, was a snitch . . . was a crow that stole soap from the edge of the shallow pool. . . . "

Gasping . . .

"Anyone who was a guest. . . . "

"Who was an ass. . . . "

Again he crashes to the ground. Blood from his hands stains the rocks.

«Rocks of Iran's Tower of Babel, Iraq's Tower of Babel. . . . »

The scribe on his left shoulder had written:

Write!

The scribe on his right shoulder writes:

Now, you write!

Left:

> *«The dispossessed of language, Persians of Iran's Tower of Babel, the dispossessed of language, Arabs of Iraq's Tower of Babel, kill their own and the other.»*

And now, more despairing than ever, he does not sit behind that boulder but on top of it, facing the village.

He snarls between his pursed, frozen lips, "God set them free. God the All Forgiving, God the Merciful."

Pirar looks around curiously.

Amir whispers, "And the cursed Satan says. . . . "

And he shouts toward the village, "You ignorant servants of God! What do you know of the mercy and wile of God who in his book says, I have mercy and I have wile? What do you know of Satan's cry of protest that rises from the earth to the Heavenly Realm, 'You the creator, O God! You who inscribed my fate in Seventh Heaven before creating me, I have had enough! Do not let them damn me anymore. Tell them it was you who wrote that I be Satan. . . . O God, get off my back, you taskmaster!'"

"You are ranting rubbish again."

And facing the mountains on the far side of the village he roars, "Hey, God! You who created me Satan! I was with these Kurds to teach them to be smart, your Saddam killed them with chemical bombs. They were many."

Pourpirar, staring at him, is taken aback.

"What did you say?"

He hears no response. He sits next to Amir and looks out at the village.

There is a pickup truck driving along a road. A herd of sheep is being led to the graze lands at the foot of the mountain.

> *«That teacher who always wore skirts, who wore mostly blue, perhaps she was not just a teacher, perhaps she was Moon Brow, perhaps she wanted to remind me how blue Khazar's sea was after the fog lifted that morning.»*

On his left:

Pirar is bored of watching the resurrected village.

"Come and see this. There's something carved on the side of this boulder. It may have been you who did it."

On the left side of the boulder, the amateurish etching of Hanna's name, made with the tip of his trench knife and a rock as a hammer . . . still, its rain-washed, snow-washed, sun-washed color stands out from the ancient color of the stone.

"What is it?"

"A name."

"Whose name?"

"Hanna. I think it is Hanna."

The rocky ground stings his knees. He runs his hand over the carved letters. The tips of his only five fingers burn. He inhales the air around the boulder and as his lungs fill he looks up at the sky. The sky is empty.

On his left:

They are no longer in danger of losing their way. Pirar leads him back to his arm's grave.

"Sergeant, can you sing a nice song?"

"You just reminded me of one of Neiji's jokes," Pirar says, laughing. "The guy says to the whore, 'Hey, whore, take these ten tomans and come to

Tajrish at three in the morning for me to fuck you.' The whore says, 'Should I come because of your generosity? Your convenient timing? Your pleasant tone? Or, you louse, because your place is so close by?' . . . Huh! And you want me to sing, too?"

Amir casts a farewell glance at the grave and the peak. He knows that long from now he will see them, deeper and more detailed, in his dreams and nightmares.

Tired and worn out, with the backpack empty of cans and the container empty of water, they head down the mountain.

On his right:

At the snow-water spring, Pirar cups his hands and fills their water container. The night is near.

"Are we sleeping here?"

"No, if that pickup truck guy shows up at all, he'll get tired of waiting and he'll leave us stranded. Let's just rest for a while and continue down."

He takes an apple from his pocket and tosses it to Amir.

"Eat it! You dropped it on the way yesterday. I kept it for you."

"What about you?"

"I'm not hungry."

Amir hits the apple against the jagged edge of a rock and throws half of it back to Sergeant Pourpirar.

The spring smells of pennyroyal. The same pennyroyal that lavishly grew alongside the two main waterways in the garden. No one in the house had the interest or the patience to cut them, wash them, and eat them.

Why is it necessary for us to write about pennyroyal right now?

Well, the sky is not going to fall down to earth if we write about pennyroyal.

The scribe on his right shoulder had written:

He is sitting next to the waterway, near the winter sweet bushes abundant with leaves and bare of flowers. In the dark of the night, he rubs a few pennyroyal leaves between his fingers and smells them. The windows of the house are fast asleep. Hanna, crouching low, comes back.

"Did you hide it?"

"Uh-huh."

"Did you hide it well? Are you sure water won't get into it? Will you be able to find it later?"

"All of that is none of your business."

He holds his fingers up to her nose.

"Sit closer."

Their thighs touching, he puts his left arm around Hanna. The girl collects herself. He wants to run his right hand between the buttons of her coverall, to feel the firmness or softness of her breasts.

Hanna, as though having read his mind, in a shaking voice says, "If you touch me, I will never be able to leave you. I'll have to leave the organization. If they don't kill me themselves, without their protection I will quickly end up in the hands of the secret service and they will kill me."

"You have me."

"If you stay with me, your fate will be the same as mine."

For the first time, he hears her choke back her tears.

"If I tell you that I don't give a damn, will you believe me?"

"Tonight, I believe you. But I don't want it. I want to continue down the path I am on. Perhaps one day the situation will get better. And we. . . . "

"The situation will only get worse."

"Amir, you have shown me a beauty I had never experienced. Thank you."

He reaches over and touches the ring on Hanna's finger. Neither one of them ever spoke about an engagement. They simply went and bought a pair of rings today. They lock their left hands together and kiss the ring on the other's finger.

"We will put them on at night, and take them off in the morning and hide them."

The scribe on his left shoulder writes:

Earth and time have turned to night. He thinks he hears water gurgling at the bottom of the spring. Pirar is smoking, and Amir is asking himself, Hanna? Hanna? And he keeps saying out loud, "Hanna! Hanna!"

And Pirar, sitting with his legs crossed, his back to Amir, and facing the cliff alongside which they must make their way down, quietly murmurs a song.

"Why will you not be the splendor of my spring? . . . "

His voice is wounded and tired.

"What was my sin that you will not be my beloved. . . . Perhaps my spring has passed."

And he pushes his voice, "The blossom of your beauty has bloomed in my mind."

And Amir, without remembering that he remembers, croons, "Why will you not see the paleness of my face. . . . "

And together, "Perhaps my spring has passed."

On his right shoulder:

Pirar picks up the blanket roll and the backpack.

"We have to get going!"

Night has fallen.

"Are you sure we won't get lost?"

"If we just head straight down, we'll be on the right track."

They both look back at the spring, at the scent of pennyroyal and tragacanth that surrounds it. They cannot see the bubbles that rise from the pale pebbles at its bottom and float to the surface.

"It seems it was the spring of life."

And they head down.

He notices that Pirar is discreetly keeping an eye on him as they descend the steep slope, in case Amir's knees weaken and he falls down the shallow cliff that farther away opens its deep maw.

"When we get to Tehran," Pirar says, "drop by to see me now and then. You have my address."

"I will. You have my address, too. Will you come see me?"

"Maybe."

The perfume of pennyroyal and tragacanth has overtaken them and left its trail for them to follow.

The scribe on his right shoulder writes:

The burly guard opens the garden gates. A moronic visceral thrill and sarcastic cunning unfold the harsh lines on his face.

"Hey, Amir Khan! Where did you go off to? We looked for you for a long time."

"You looked too far, brother. I was hiding in the cotton field."

"What cotton field?"

"Forget it, brother! Now, are you going to let me into my father's garden?"

"With my pleasure and Agha Haji's delight."

He makes way for him, but hauls his bulk in front of Pirar.

"Not you!"

Amir intervenes. With his shoulder he breaks away the guard's arm braced against Pirar's chest.

"The gentleman is with me."

"And who is the gentleman?"

Pirar pulls Amir back and snaps at the guard, "Your superior."

"Agha Haji has told us not to let this man in without a permit from him."

And the Revolutionary Guard sticks out his chest and pulls back the front of his overcoat to reveal the Colt 45 on his belt.

"I have a permit," Pirar barks, and he digs into his pants pocket, takes out a few small pieces of rusted shrapnel, and holds them in front of the guard.

"Do you know what these are, guard of Islam?"

". . ."

"Of course you don't, fighter who fought in a hole! They didn't fly past your ears and they didn't hit you in the back. I have a few more still lodged against my spine. Now, if you don't step aside and let me deliver this young man to his mother and sister . . . do you know where I will shove these?"

The guard does not move.

"Out of respect for this family, I am not going to rub your face in the dirt and handcuff you," he snarls. "Get lost!"

Pirar lets the shrapnel fall from his hand. The guard looks down and Pirar nimbly steps behind him, wraps his arm around the man's neck, and snatches the pistol off his belt. Then he swiftly steps back, cocks the gun, and aims it at the guard's face.

He tilts to the right because of his backache.

Right:

With the guard leading the way, they walk past the winter sweet bushes that have no flowers but are lush with leaves. They walk past the crab.

"It seems you were a Bruce Lee, too!" Amir says.

"They wouldn't issue Colts to you enlisted officers so that you wouldn't self-inflict. If you had one, I would have taught you the technique."

They pass the ditches that Shahu used to fill with dry leaves so that in the bitter cold of winter he could blow warm smoke at the trees.

Reyhaneh tears out of the house without her headscarf. Then, Mother, throwing her chador over her head. Joy blossoms on their faces. Reyha grabs Amir in her arms. Mother nods to Pirar as greetings and thanks.

"Our story came to a happy end and the black crow went back home," Amir chuckles.

Pirar, holding the Colt behind him, pushes the release button. The magazine falls on the ground. This time the guard does not look down. Pirar picks up the bullet that has ejected from the chamber. He walks over to the guard, stands tight against him, and shoves the gun in his pocket.

Furious and humiliated, the guard growls, "We will meet again."

Pirar holds the bullet in front of the man's eyes and puts it in his own pocket.

"A souvenir," he sneers.

He turns to the women.

"Sisters! I deliver to you your young man, healthy and in one piece. May the Prophet be with you."

He starts to leave.

Mother, her chador still hanging open, says, "Please, come inside, Sergeant. It is not proper like this. Some tea, fruit. . . . Reyha has told me everything. I have prayed for you . . . and I have an unworthy personal gift of myself to offer you."

Pirar does not try to hide his laugh at Mother's slip of the tongue.

"Please bring it to my home," he says, winking at Amir.

Amir lets out a laugh and cracks, "Pirar, same to your mother!"

As Amir walks into the house, Reyha runs after him.

"Did you find it?"

Mother is still staring at Pirar as he leaves.

On his left shoulder:

He jolts awake drenched in sweat. He sees that again he is not in his bed. He has folded a blanket in two and is sleeping in it on the floor. The sweat on the stump of his arm feels like blood.

Some time passes before he realizes what has woken him up. Again, it is the lone nightingale singing in the garden. He glances at the wall clock. He believes he has looked at it at other dawns with the singing of this crazy nightingale to see it is 4:47 and the stubborn bird has started chirping again. He wonders, Could it be that my brain is on the mend, since I read the time and did not think to doubt it?...

And the garden's roving nightingale, without changing branches, now and then sings and then grows quiet waiting for a reply.... No reply is sung. Tirelessly, patiently, it sings another song. The bird is sad that it has no mate, or is happy that the only song in the garden belongs to it.

It is not our job to write on the shoulders of sweet-singing nightingales.

On his left:

He follows the line on the wall. He believes this "Follow this Line" was a secret line meant for today. He remembers that he has followed it several times, aiming to go to its end, but he does not remember if he ever reached it or if somewhere along the way he forgot what he was following. He reaches the end of the line. There is nothing written there.

The line reminds him of the song Khazar liked.

I Started a Joke....

Right:

With the ring in his pocket, he goes back to the head of the garden path. He thinks, There must be a clue on one of these trees, a kind of clue that no one would suspect of being a clue.

And he starts. Not like previous times when he haphazardly, madly went from one tree to another ignoring the order and design of the garden. This time, methodically, he begins to inspect every single tree.

Right:

He finishes digging deeper into the ground under the Khezr cherry tree. He has found nothing. Twenty-nine holes, in addition to those he had dug before leaving on his trip. It seems what Hanna stashed there one night is nowhere. He has only a vague memory of that night. All he remembers is that she hid something in the garden.

He closes his eyes and spins around. Then he stops, opens his eyes, and carrying his spade walks in the direction he thinks his instinct is telling him to go.

He recalls the story Reyhaneh told him about Attar. He thinks perhaps someone should cut off his head so that he can tuck it under his arm and set off in search of the truth, reciting poetry as he goes.

A tree catches his eye.

> «Trees whisper and seduce. They seduce us into making love under them. And they whisper to us to bury our secret not on their bark, but in the ground beneath them.»

Digging in the ground for a grave or a treasure or in search of a secret is impossible to write.

The scribe on his left shoulder had written:

The smell of autumn is in the air. The third hour of waiting for Hanna is passing. He keeps a watchful eye for someone monitoring their meeting place or a suspicious-looking car driving by a second time. . . . He is starting to worry. Every time he has come on leave, Hanna has been late meeting him, but never this late. He lights his last cigarette. . . . Dressed in his uniform and standing there for such a long time is itself suspect. . . .

Finally, the girl shows up. She walks past him without saying, It is safe, come. And without showing any sign of recognition. He will follow her at a distance until Hanna finds a place that she thinks is safe. She will then turn to him and smile. But this time, there is deeper anxiety on her face than ever before. She is carrying a duffle bag. And Hanna continues walking directly to the bus depot.

Left:

He sits next to her on the bus. She is still pale.

"We have been identified. This may be the last time you and I see each other."

"What happened?"

"I can't tell you any more than this."

"What is that tucked in your cheek?"

"Cyanide capsule."

"What are you going to Tehran for?"

"For something. It is important. Worth the danger."

"Let me hold your hand."

"Don't be stupid! . . . I have to take what I hid in your garden and replace it with this. Is that all right?"

They reach a checkpoint. The driver takes his logbook and goes to the patrol station to have it stamped. A stocky Basiji boards the bus and starts eyeing the passengers one by one. Hanna puts her hands on her knees to try and stop them from shaking. The Basiji asks the man sitting one row in front of them for his ID card.

"Where is your luggage?"

"In the luggage compartment."

"Go and take it out for inspection."

His eyes on Hanna, then on Amir, he walks past them. The smell of his sweat lingers behind him.

On his right:

It is 10:03 at night. Hanna gets out of the taxi in front of the garden gates. Amir, waiting nearby, goes to greet her. Hanna's duffle bag seems emptier than when they parted ways at sunset.

"I will jump over the wall and open the gates."

"I can climb the wall. Let's go."

They walk along the wall to the left of the gates. Amir locks his hands for her. Hanna nimbly steps on them, pulls herself up, and sits on top of the wall. She reaches down to help him.

Left:

He is sitting under the Khezr cherry tree, waiting for Hanna to come back from digging up the previous duffle bag and burying the new one. Behind the trees, the first-floor windows of the house are dark. On the second floor, the lights are on in Reyhaneh's room. He sees the girl come to the window. Hanna, agile as a cat, returns from the same direction she had left, without the slightest sound of her footsteps or that of the leaves rustling. She sits next to him. Eleven minutes and thirty-four seconds pass in silence, until. . . .

"Don't you want to go and say hello to your family? After all this time, they will be happy to see you."

"They are happier without me."

Hanna's eyes are fixed on the house and its only bright window.

"At this very moment, I wish I were a bride in that house."

"You can be."

"Don't say a word! . . . Don't! Let me talk. . . . Right now, I wish I were a wife in that house. In the mornings, I would wake up before everyone else and make breakfast, knowing that my day will become night without fear or anxiety."

"It can happen, girl! Every morning, I will get up before you and bring you breakfast in your bed. Our bed."

"Crazy . . . you are being naive, Amir. In a week, I will leave you to go back to the mountains."

They take their rings from their pockets and put them on each other's fingers. Amir kisses Hanna's finger. He reaches up, pulls off her headscarf, and runs his hand over her long hair. It is silky and straight. He puts his arms around her and pulls her to him. Butterfly-like, he moves his lips over the girl's chapped lips. A gentle breeze has made the yellowing leaves of the apple and cherry trees start to whisper.

Their kisses have become longer, deeper, wetter. He has learned how to kiss her unskilled lips. The girl is breathing heavily, stifled groans escape her throat. He runs his hand over her coverall to the curve of her breast. He gently squeezes it. Hanna exhales a moan. She is trembling. Amir softly pushes her back to lie on the ground.

"No!"

"Why? Let's make. . . . "

"No."

She pulls away from him and combs her fingers through her tousled hair.

"You want it, too. I know you do."

"I want it desperately . . . I am dying for you. But if I give myself to you, I will become weak, I will not be able to fight anymore . . . not that I want to stay a guerrilla fighter. I am tired of my life. And I don't believe in the cause

any more, but there is no way out. . . . I must go on . . . the last thing I needed was to become engaged to a lieutenant in the Islamic Republic army! If the organization finds out, they will put me on trial. . . . I am probably going to go to Iraqi Kurdistan; I won't be able to see you again."

"I will come for you."

"You are still so naive. I have deep feelings for you, Amir. I have never been in love before, and I have fallen in love with you, silly man. You are always on my mind. It pains me that you are always on my mind . . . it tortures me . . . it makes me weak. If I am arrested, it will only take two or three lashes for me to give in."

Hanna turns to the house. In the light from Reyhaneh's room Amir sees the gleam of a teardrop on her face.

His failure to conquer the girl's fortress seems to have drained him. He leans against a tree and pulls her to lie down with her head on his lap so that he can caress her hair, which may have dirt tangled in it. He remains like that until the illusive dawn. He cannot remember when he fell asleep and for how long. He opens his eyes. Hanna is gone.

The scribe on his right shoulder writes:

He has been relentlessly pursuing his new search since the second morning after his return. Now, he sighs with relief. At noon, he puts down Hanna's dirt-covered bag and sits on the floor next to the window in Reyhaneh's room. The summer clouds are the color of festering, smog-tainted snow.

"The damn thing was buried behind Shahu's hut. Even a jinni would not have thought of it."

He does not have the courage to open the bag.

"Do you want me to open it for you?"

Reyha, undaunted by the dirt spreading on the floor, shakes the mud-crusted slider and pulls on it to open the zipper. It will not open. The fabric of the bag has frayed. Reyha tears it open.

On his right:

Reyha rips open the plastic bag. A Colt 38, an extra magazine, a bundle of fliers from the Kurdistan branch of the People's Fedai Guerrillas Organization. Three glass car fuses. The white cyanide powder inside them looks like scabs on a wound. A bundle of fifty-toman bills and a newspaper clipping in a plastic cover. Keyhan newspaper, the photograph of a few Kurdish terrorists, spies, saboteurs linked to governments hostile toward the Islamic Republic. There is only one girl among them. Hanna. Hanna Mianroody. The paper has yellowed. . . . And nothing else.

Reyha's eyes are brimming with tears.

"She left the newspaper cutting for me," he says. "Otherwise, she would never have done something this reckless. Now I know her name. And I have her picture. . . . Wherever she is, even if she has crawled under a rock, I will find her."

Reyhaneh sounds melancholy and skeptical.

"Many of them were executed. . . . "

"No! Never! Don't even say it. Look at her eyes in this picture. This is not a girl who would be easily caught. I will find her."

He holds the ring that is now loose on the fourth finger of his right hand up to Reyhaneh's eyes.

"But how? Where will you start?"

"I will start with the prisons. If she is not in prison, I will go back to Kurdistan. . . . "

"I guess you aren't going to sit still and live your life."

He sees Abu-Yahya carving a memento on the eucalyptus tree. With his fingernail, it seems.

"Will you come out with me today?"

"Where to?"

"First, take me to Uncle Arjang's house. I want to get something from him."

"What?"

Reyha pours some tea.

"What?" she repeats.

"Arak . . . don't worry, I will accept your sin for going with me. Tonight, I want to celebrate, get drunk. . . . Will you drink with me?"

"Don't be stupid! Of course I will not."

"You'll like it. I'm sure. . . . Let's get drunk together. It'll be fun."

Reyhaneh yields her eyes to his and bites her lower lip.

Amir, staring at Hanna's picture, says, "Until now, much of me has been nothing but what others remember of me."

It seems this time the sadness in his voice is not streaked with deception.

"I have been nothing but a suit of armor. . . . Once upon a time, there was a man who had armor so strong that anyone who saw it would know that no sword could pierce it. His armor was of a color for which there is no name. It shone, but more mysteriously than tempered steel. It was untouchable. It was of a substance that only he knew. Because of that armor, he never carried a weapon. People disliked him. He behaved in a way that seemed condescending. He ignored them and their stories that, for instance, he had tempered his armor seven times, soaked it in Zoroaster's spring, in the blood of a whale that killed itself, with the skin of a two-headed cobra, in the blood of a seven-hundred-year-old turtle, and then in the sap of a five-thousand-year-old cypress tree, and in the end, tempered it again and either shed tears on it or pissed on it. . . . It was obvious that even a dragon's teeth could not pierce his proud armor. . . . After years and years, a hater dared stab him in the side with a dagger and his blood gushed out, and everyone realized that he had woven this armor from his own skin. . . . "

He hears a cotton boll pop open.

"Reyha, did you weave your own armor, too?"

Reyhaneh is staring at him. It is unclear whether with sadness, confusion, admiration, or. . . . But she is silent.

"Take me to Meysam's house tomorrow."

"What do you want with him?"

"I want to grab him and force him to come and ask for your hand."

"The world is not as simple as you think, Dādāshi! . . . You have come back crazier than you were before."

It is not clear whether it is a smirk or an innocent smile on Amir's lips.

"News of the miseries you have lived through has spread among the Yamini clan."

"That is exactly why I am sure I can handle him. He will agree. I mean I want him to come and ask Agha Haji and our beloved Mother for permission to do my sister."

He gulps down his tea. With his mouth burning, he looks out the window at the Alfa Romeo.

"Don't worry," he says confidently. "I will not start a ruckus. It occurred to me on the way down the mountain. I will talk to him man to man, explain to him that I have paid for what happened to Khazar and will go on paying. I will tell him that it was Khazar who threw me out of her life with a kick in the ass. And I was punished for it—an arm fucked away and a head messed up for the rest of my life. I will say, Hey! Meysam, you louse! I will pay for what happened even more than you expect. If you are really the man you claim to be, then why don't you keep your man's word and propose to the girl who has been sitting waiting for you . . . pure and untouched. . . . "

"I do not want you to do any such thing."

"Then, when he comes over. . . . Does he still look as dorky as he did back then? The stubble on his chin smelling of mutton soup, shirt hanging over his pants. . . . "

"You poor thing, you haven't seen him! Now he dresses in the latest Islamic Paris fashion."

"Does he even know you have been waiting for him all this time?"

"He knows, he doesn't know . . . I don't know. How would I know?"

"I will drag him over here and make him fall at your feet."

It seems Reyhaneh is not the docile, submissive girl she used to be.

"You don't need to drag him here. Just prove to him that Khazar was the one who left you, that her suicide had nothing to do with you."

She points to his empty sleeve and his head.

"Make him understand that you killed yourself, too, and live worse off than the dead."

"I will rub his nose in the dirt if he doesn't come."

It is not clear whether it is a smirk or a welcoming smile on Reyhaneh's lips.

"Perhaps he will come."

EPILOGUE

The scribe on Reyhaneh's right shoulder writes:

From the full-length window in her room, Reyhaneh looks out at the rainless garden. It occurs to her. . . .

> «I don't know if it is good or bad that the second floor is always the second floor.»

She sees her confidante the cuckoo bird take wing toward the sea-green treetops. She still does not like to look at the Alfa Romeo. And she cannot tell whether she misses the sound of the rain in the house's old gutters.

She thinks, I did not tell Amir and I am not going to tell him. I waited all these years for that recreant Meysam to come and propose to me and he will come with a big, boastful head, as though a prince from the *One Thousand and One Nights*. He will lean back in his chair in the living room, waiting for me to hold the tea tray in front of him, thinking that I am so happy, so ecstatic. . . . But I think I have waited all these years so that I can hold the tea tray in front of him, look him straight in his stupid eyes . . . and say, *No*!

And perhaps the tea glass full of steaming hot tea will slide off the tray and fall on his lap.

The scribe on Reyhaneh's left shoulder writes:

It has been a long time since the gravel in the driveway lost the sound of Agha Haji's car driving away. Reyhaneh hears dishes being washed downstairs, and she sighs and thinks, Waiting was not the right thing to do. I must find a way to go and find the one I have spent all these years creating in the corner of my mind . . . perhaps sometime, some day, I have passed him on the street and not known, perhaps I have walked past the window of his house and not known, perhaps I have bought medicine at the pharmacy right after him and not known . . . but I will know him the moment I see him. I have seen his face in my mind. . . .

ABOUT THE AUTHOR

SHAHRIAR MANDANIPOUR (Mondanipour), one of the most accomplished writers of contemporary Iranian literature, has held fellowships at Brown University, Harvard University, Boston College, and at the Wissenschaftskolleg in Berlin. Mandanipour is the author of nine volumes of fiction, one nonfiction book, and more than 100 essays in literary theory, literature and art criticism, creative writing, censorship, and social commentary. From 1999 until 2007, he was Editor-in-Chief of *Asr-e Panjshanbeh* (*Thursday Evening*), a monthly literary journal that after nine years of publishing was banned. Some of his short stories and essays have been published in anthologies such as *Strange Times, My Dear: The PEN Anthology of Contemporary Iranian Literature* and *Sohrab's Wars: Counter Discourses of Contemporary Persian Fiction: A Collection of Short Stories and a Film Script;* and in journals such as *The Kenyon Review, The Literary Review*, and *Virginia Quarterly Review*. Short works have been published in France, Germany, Denmark, and in languages such as Arabic, Turkish, and Kurdish. Mandanipour's first novel to appear in English, *Censoring an Iranian Love Story*, translated by Sara Khalili and published by Knopf in 2009, was very well received (*Los Angeles Times, Guardian, New York Times*, etc.). *Censoring an Iranian Love Story* was named by the New Yorker as one of the reviewers' favorites of 2009, by the *Cornell Daily Sun* as Best Book of the Year for 2009, and by NPR as one of the best debut novels of the year; it was awarded (Greek ed.) the Athens Prize for Literature for 2011. The novel has been translated and published in twelve other languages and in fourteen countries throughout the world. Currently, he teaches creative writing, as a visiting Professor of the Practice at Tufts University.

ABOUT THE TRANSLATOR

SARA KHALILI is an editor and translator of contemporary Iranian literature. Her translations include *Censoring an Iranian Love Story*, by Shahriar Mandanipour; *The Pomegranate Lady and Her Sons*, by Goli Taraghi; *The Book of Fate*, by Parinoush Saniee; and *Rituals of Restlessness*, by Yaghoub Yadali. She has also translated several volumes of poetry by Forough Farrokhzad, Simin Behbahani, Siavash Kasraii, and Fereydoon Moshiri. Her short story translations have appeared in *The Kenyon Review*, *The Virginia Quarterly Review*, *EPOCH*, *Granta*, Words Without Borders, *The Literary Review*, PEN America, *Witness*, and *Consequence*.

RESTLESS BOOKS is an independent, nonprofit publisher devoted to championing essential voices from unexpected places and vantages, whose stories speak to us across linguistic and cultural borders. We seek extraordinary international literature that feeds our restlessness: our curiosity about the world, passion for other cultures and languages, and eagerness to explore beyond the confines of the familiar. Our books—fiction, narrative nonfiction, journalism, memoirs, travel writing, and young people's literature—offer readers an expanded understanding of a changing world.

Visit us at www.restlessbooks.com.